The Oathbound Devil

The Soul Mirror Duet, Volume 2

S.J. Brown

Published by S.J. Brown, 2026.

This is a work of fiction. Similarities to real people, places, or events are entirely coincidental.

THE OATHBOUND DEVIL

First edition. April 21, 2026.

ISBN: 979-8-9998532-6-4

Written by S.J. Brown.

Cover Art by S.J. Brown.

Edited by Cyndi Sandusky.

Trigger Warnings

Your mental health is important. Please read the below if you need to, skip if you don't. This book is quite a bit darker than *The Pactbound Angel.*

Sexually explicit scenes, violence, PTSD flashbacks, malignant narcissism, on-page depiction of a psychotic break, emotional abuse (not by main characters), traumatic death, grief, domination/submission scene, parent/child alienation, references to off-page domestic abuse, references to off-page torture, and references to off-page child abuse.

Table of Contents

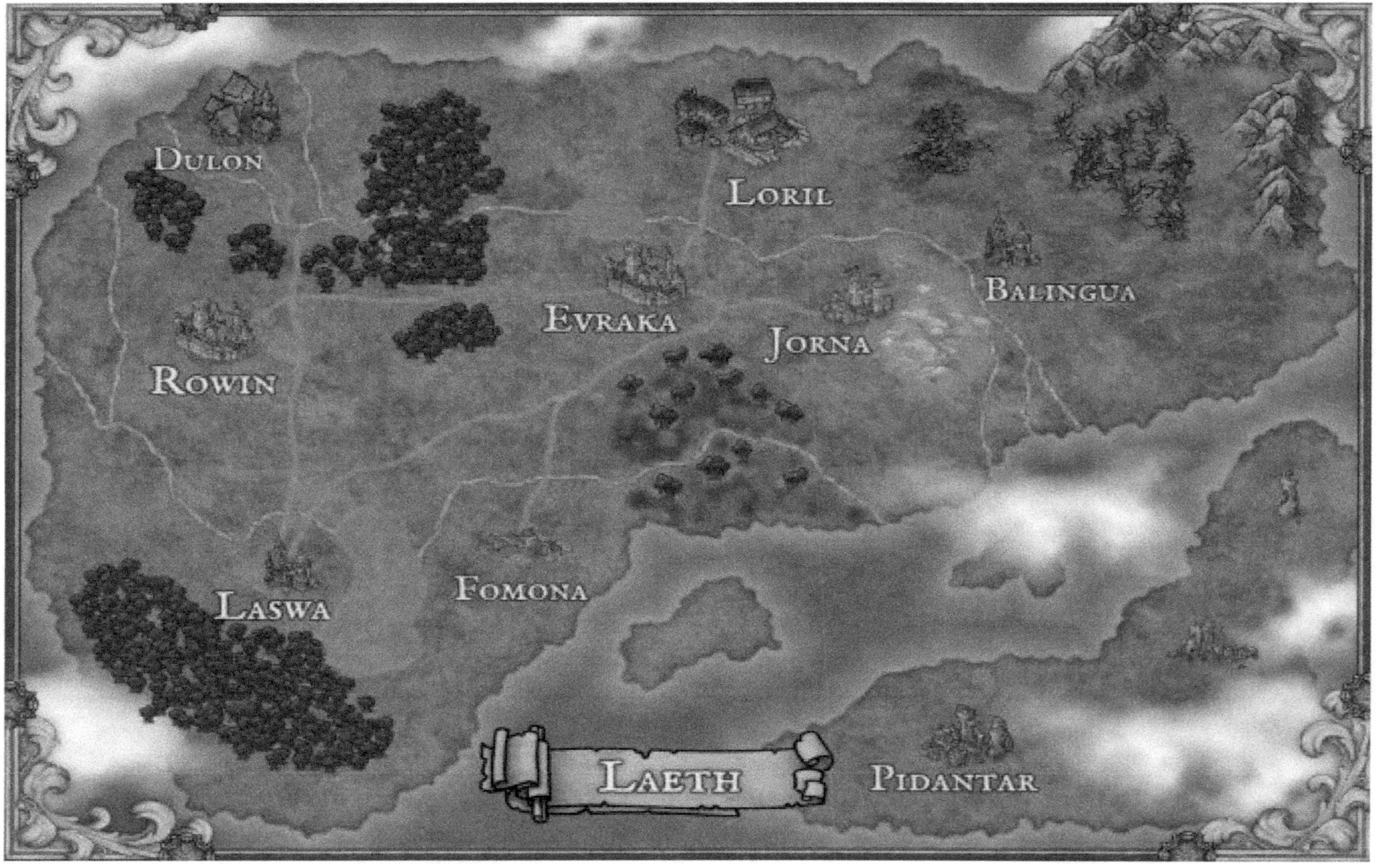

Dulon
Loril
Balingua
Evraka
Jorna
Rowin
Fomona
Laswa
Laeth
Pidantar

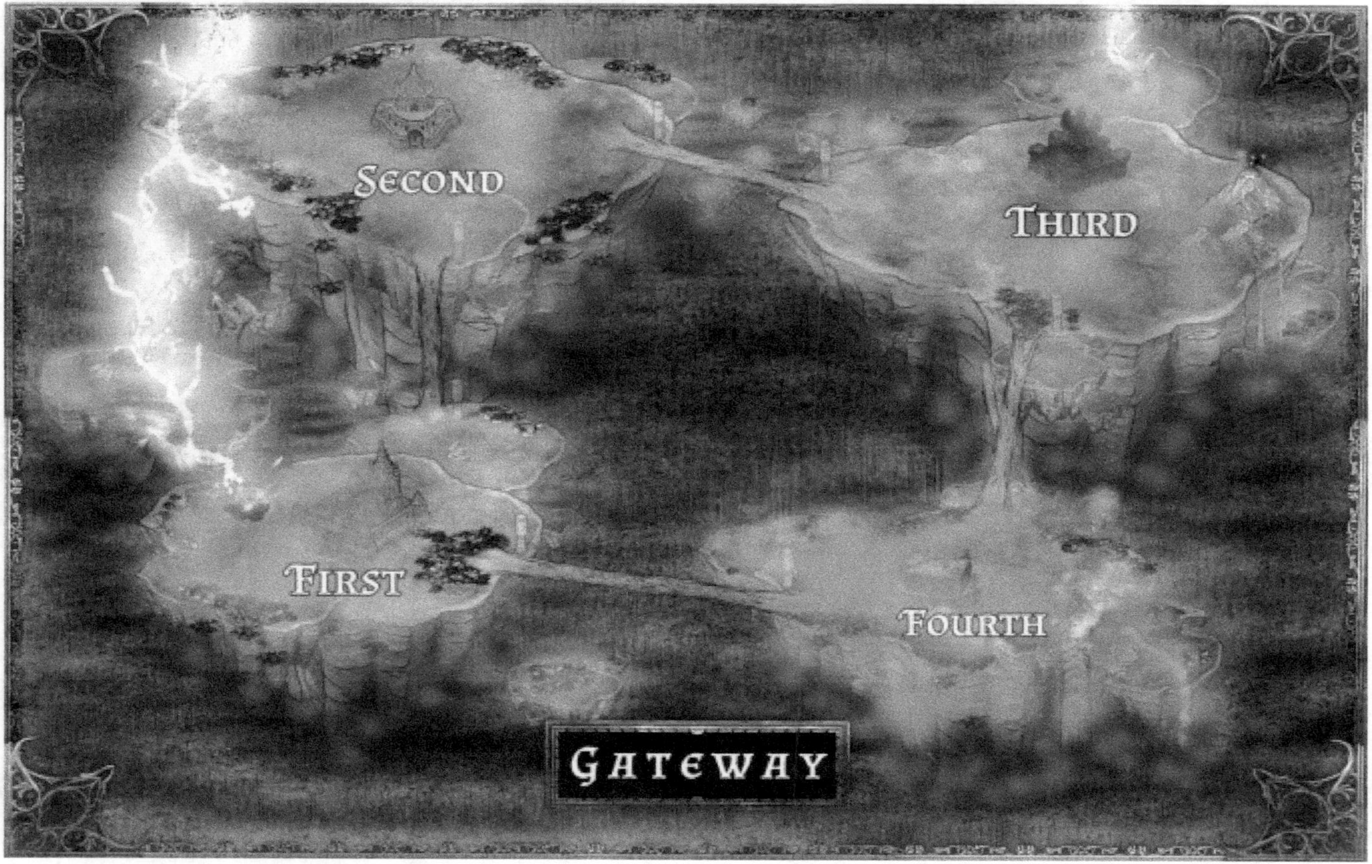

Second

Third

First

Fourth

Gateway

This book is dedicated to my wonderfully strong and spirited mother.

• • • •

I don't care if you've seen Lady Frankenstein.
I don't care if you've given birth to four children.
I don't care if you lived through the '60s.

• • • •

You're not reading this.

The Pactbound Angel Recap

(The underlined bits are especially important.)

Inigo Montoya: Let me explain.
[pause]
Inigo Montoya: No, there is too much. Let me sum up.
-The Princess Bride (dir. Rob Reiner, 1987)

TL; DR

Nathalia is a protector. Ramiren is a pactmaker. They and their friends accept a quest to kill hags in the Feylands. Nathalia and Ramiren make a "teach me how to please my future husband" pact, believing feelings wouldn't get involved.

Spoiler alert: feelings get involved.

After killing all the hags, Nathalia gets engaged to a fey prince, but she gets cold feet and runs to Ramiren. He takes her away but the ability he used to get them out of danger marked them for an arch-devil named Vrakus. Seeing Ramiren in danger, Nathalia takes her oath to protect him.

Full Recap

Resa Kett and Maxlian Swordhand fought a powerful druid who wanted to use a set of relics called the Twin Spheres. The druid disappeared to lick her wounds and plan anew.

A decade later, when Lady Nathalia Swordhand was nine years old, she and her younger sister Raewyn encountered a mischief hag at a carnival they weren't supposed to go to. The hag cursed the two girls by taking Nathalia's creativity and scarring her sister's face.

Nathalia grew into a protector, a bodyguard devoted to another person, wanting nothing more than to find a husband and begin her service. Her creativity gone, leaving a hole in her heart, she figured she might as well try to make the most of her life. Taking her adventuring parents into account, who met on the road, she started off, becoming a caravan guard.

Years go by before she encounters Raewyn on the road. Raewyn talked Nathalia into going back to the carnival. There they met Ramiren, a secretive pactmaker, for whom Nathalia immediately developed an attraction. Spotting another mischief hag in the crowd, they followed and came across a newly-cursed and surly Georgina with her automaton M.A.L.C.O.L.M. Intent on helping Georgina, and maybe themselves, Nathalia and Raewyn entered the singing contest to get close to the carnival's elusive headmaster to warn him the mischief hags were there.

It didn't work, but someone was eavesdropping.

That someone introduced herself as the druid Leraska. She told them details about the mischief hags, where they were known to be, how many there were, and that the abilities the hags stole were stored in magic vials. Agreeing to go into the Feylands to recover what was taken, Nathalia, Ramiren, Raewyn, Georgina, and M.A.L.C.O.L.M. go to the nearest city to rest after teleporting to the Feylands.

That night, Nathalia went to Ramiren's room and proposed a secret pact. "Teach me how to please my future husband, and I'll give you the luck stone I carry." He agreed, and they started immediately. Nathalia got her first taste and immediately wanted more.

_Nathalia purchased supplies for the road and learned more information about the Feylands and how it and Laeth mirror each other. "What affects Laeth affects the Feylands: buildings, cities founded, everything."

They traveled to the first mischief hag, clearing traps and riddles. After a short battle, the mischief hag was destroyed. Going into her cupboard to recover the vials, Nathalia found Ramiren's name on one. Shocked, Nathalia began to question the trust she had in him, as he did not tell anyone he too had something stolen: the ability to whistle.

Onto to the second mischief hag, Nathalia slowly came to terms with not needing to know everything about Ramiren, especially with his reassurance that his secrets would not harm her. "His secrets are his own." Their lessons continued, and they became closer, blurring the line between instruction and affection.

King Rofar of Tanta, learning the group was going to confront the second mischief hag, requested the group search for his daughter's vial, promising riches or favors should they succeed. They agreed to find it and break the vial. A visiting earl from Wistran, Lord Dalson, indicated the third mischief hag in his realm needed to be put down. Ramiren blackmailed the earl into helping the group get into the castle when the time came.

The second mischief hag invaded their camp one night, and Nathalia received a whispered warning from Ramiren. She arrived just in time to run the hag off and save Ramiren.

The group encountered the second mischief hag in her cave, but she was clever and evaded the group while throwing bottles of acid and other caustic fluids at them. Georgina, however, was prompted to see if her vial was in the hag's cupboard to aid in the battle. She did so, and the second mischief hag was defeated with a timely crossbow bolt from Georgina.

Making for the third mischief hag, almost at their goal, they stopped by Leraska's grove and informed her of what had happened, but Leraska already knew. Nathalia spotted a small blue orb in a hedge grove, which Leraska indicated was for scrying.

They came across a capra fey who sold fantastical animals but the animals were in rough shape and very abused. Ramiren traded the favor he got from the king for two animals, but the group tricked him into releasing all of his animals into their care. They took the animals back to Leraska's grove for safekeeping.

Arriving in the unwelcoming city of Carpatha, Wistran's capital, the group found the third mischief hag's influence everywhere. After defeating the third hag, with Nathalia killing her in a fit of rage at all she has had to endure, Raewyn and Nathalia broke their vials and got back their abilities.

Prince Jaylin, Wistran's crown prince, ran in to witness the aftermath and was seemingly spellbound by Nathalia's beauty, giving his intentions immediately.

After a meeting with the Wistran king, the prince escorted the group to their inn, as the mischief hag had henchmen, and they encountered a group of thugs. Without thinking, Nathalia thanked Jaylin for his help and became obligated to him. The prince asked her to come to lunch the next day to discuss something important, where the prince proposed to Nathalia.

No one else was happy about this. Raewyn tried to talk sense into Nathalia, but it backfired. The lessons with Nathalia and Ramiren continued, as Nathalia couldn't grasp the idea that she was about to lose Ramiren.

Nathalia was invited to the castle to meet the queen the next day, who told Nathalia to move into the royal residence and leave all possessions behind as they would provide everything she needed. Ramiren disagreed, shocked, and this triggered a panic attack in Nathalia. Ramiren calmed her and informed Nathalia everyone left to go back home.

After a week, the night before the royal wedding, Ramiren showed up at Nathalia's chamber door. They agreed to one last lesson, which made Nathalia question everything. What her father told her about safeguarding her virtue, what was it all for, why was this necessary.

Nathalia and Ramiren made a new pact, without a virginity stipulation, and they finally made love.

The next day, as Nathalia stood beside the prince, her inner voice started screaming at her. Then she heard Ramiren's voice, begging her not to go through with it. She stopped the wedding ceremony .

The prince objected, trying to force the marriage. Nathalia ran for it, barely escaping through the closing doors. She stole a horse and made it back to the inn where Ramiren was staying. He whistled them away from danger, with the guards rapidly closing in.

Prince Jaylin searched for them, but Nathalia and Ramiren avoided him by trekking through the woods to Leraska's grove. They were sent back to Laeth by Leraska, the druid giving a cryptic final farewell.

Feeling safe for the first time in a while, Ramiren told Nathalia he'd like for them to go their separate ways. Nathalia questioned this, heartbroken, but Ramiren spotted a sigil on Nathalia's neck. The same sigil that was now on Ramiren's neck too.

As it turned out, the ability Ramiren used to get them away from the guards and out of danger had a downside. He would be hunted by the arch-devil Vrakus. Nathalia believed, because she benefitted from the ability too, she was now hunted as well.

Nathalia, knowing Ramiren needed protection more than ever, came to terms with him having always been her protector's charge and took her vows to him.

The epilogue showed the prince and Leraska conversing, where Jaylin called Leraska 'mother'. Leraska told the prince that they'd get the Twin Spheres back. With a new plan.

Prologue

The high-pitched whistle rang in my ears, even as Eronis, the gray-skinned devil who'd brought me here, released my arm. I swayed, dizziness turning my stomach as I looked around, an involuntary grimace tugging at my features.

Gateway's four main islands, floating above an endless void, were even more dismal than I'd heard them described. Scorching, dust-filled air rippled the red sky until it resembled a living flame. A smoky, sulfur-tinged fog hung above my head, courtesy of the distressing number of active volcanoes here.

In the distance, above the island called First District, I spotted winged devils dipping and soaring through the greenish-gray clouds. An indistinct dark shape fell from one of the flying fiends. When the shape began to flail and scream as it plummeted into the void below, the tiny hairs on the back of my neck rose.

Poor bastard.

I turned away from the grisly sight toward the obsidian structure before me. The enormous black-stone castle sat with its iron gates open, though I suspected that was less as a welcome and more to do with its broken hinges not allowing the gate to close.

The grinding of sand and moving stone echoed in a dull roar, occasionally broken by the crack of thunder following a bolt of red lightning. Underneath it all, the soft whirl from the Dark Drop itself whispered like a far-off waterfall. Aside from that doomed mortal, I noted a distinct lack of mocking laughter and terrified screams. *The tales of this place must've been exaggerated.*

"Where is he?" I asked the scowling devil still at my side, arms crossed as he waited for me to move.

The devil smirked, waving a hand toward the castle. "I'd bet in there." His arm forcefully brushed my shoulder as he moved past me, almost knocking me over.

I peered at his retreating back, adjusted my jacket, and walked forward; the heels of my boots cracked against the cobblestones of the courtyard, then the black rock of the castle's interior. The surrounding volcanic glass did little to cool the air within, but it at least stopped the sting of blowing dust.

Taking out the square of parchment to study the provided directions, I turned left and right when needed in the dimly lit hallways toward my eventual destination.

The soft chatter of the room's occupants reached me as I moved through the double-door threshold, allowing me a few precious seconds of warning. I stopped short when my eyes fell on two men whom I didn't immediately recognize standing next to a small table.

Though both were roughly the same height as me, their similarities ended there. Where I took after our father, my brother took after our mother. The junior man's soft brown eyes met mine, and he gave a toothy grin. "Brother. Congratulations." He broke from our father's side to stride toward me, arms wide for a welcoming hug.

I returned the smile easily and the embrace with reflexive apprehension. "Ravik."

It had been a full decade since I'd seen my father and, aside from a few rare glimpses due our nigh-simultaneous training at the Citadel, the same could be said for my older brother.

Ravik, with his reddish-blond hair tied back into a small plait at the nape of his neck, had gone from lanky teenager to grown man. His soft, boyish features had morphed into sharp edges and a square jaw covered in stubble. He appeared human, except for his elongated canines. Those were thanks to our father, who cleared his throat pointedly to get our attention.

Both of us turned to him as he stepped closer, slowly putting one foot in front of the other. The deep rumble of his voice echoed in the cavernous room. "Ramiren. It's been too long."

My smile, easy with my brother, turned hesitant with my father. His skin color had changed from a perpetual olive tan to brick red. His black horns, once like mine, had doubled in size, and his eyes now glowed faintly.

"Far, far too long, son. Running off with your mother, then to the Citadel for pactmaker training. I feel like I've barely been able to see you."

He placed a black-clawed hand on my shoulder and gave a small squeeze as my interest piqued. I'd asked my mother countless times for the details regarding what happened to make her leave with me in the middle of the night, but she'd never told me.

Pushing my father for the story seemed an equally futile endeavor, but it likely had something to do with his ascension as an arch-devil, which occurred shortly after. Even now, the wish for answers needled me.

Patience. Asking him at this time would be ill-advised.

I'm not going to ask, Dredon. Calm down.

My fussy pact vizier, and constant companion since I completed my training, stood ready to offer advice, whether regarding the fairness of a pact or to tell me something I already knew. His presence in my mind was new, and he had yet to figure out that my inner thoughts wouldn't necessarily become outer actions.

My father's hand dropped from my shoulder, and he turned his red eyes back to the table. "Shall we begin, then? I'm eager for you to see your graduation gift." He scratched his black beard with one dark claw as he headed back toward the small table, upon which rested a beige scroll. He picked it up, unrolling it to look it over. "It took us a little while to get the wording right, but I think you'll appreciate its uniqueness."

I stepped forward to take the offered scroll, both apprehensive and curious about what he had come up with for me. It crackled as I held it up to read, its texture smooth in my hands. Ravik followed and looked over my shoulder as I scanned it.

"Actual calfskin vellum? You spoil me, Papa."

My father grinned in reply, with a sheepish shrug. "It's a momentous occasion. I wanted it to be special."

I squinted at the neat Infernal print laid out in red ink, indicating the terms were indissoluble and to be kept secret. My squinting barely helped, though I did notice a large empty section at the bottom. Presumably space for addendums, if requested.

How did you make it through your training with bad eyes?

The writing was never this small.

After you leave, go to Tirvinir. The gnomes there have ways to help with inadequate vision.

Then I will rely on your help here. What does it say?

It's a melody. A riddle.

••••

Purse your lips and whistle shrill,
Out of danger, no foe to kill.
But my mark on your neck be laid,
Brought to me, your presence in trade.

••••

If another be whistled along,
A pact required for magic strong.
This I give to you, my son.
A devil's whistle for training done.

••••

So it's a way to escape a threat? He's giving me a conditional devil's whistle?

But you will be tracked and brought here after your escape in trade for the privilege. It allows you to bring another with you, though. So two out of harm's way.

Is it a fair trade?

Calculating. It does not list how long your presence is requested. Require clarification.

Without looking up from the vellum, I asked, "Papa, how long am I to stay here? Should the devil's whistle be used to evade danger, that is."

A soft chuckle came in answer. His hands waved in the air, as though considering the question. "Oh, let's say a week per whistle use, so nothing too egregious, but I appreciate you asking the question. You'll make a fine pactmaker, son."

The rise of pride and warmth in my chest snuffed out the apprehension from earlier. *I hope so, Papa.* "And the passenger, should I have one? Will they also be marked and brought to Gateway with me?"

The corners of Vrakus's eyes crinkled with his smile. "The ability to carry a passenger with you is merely a bonus. I have no interest in any random clients you might need to whisk away, and the pact that is required is only needed to link you magically to your passenger. Honestly, it was quite fussy to work out the logistics. And so you understand, an existing pact isn't sufficient, I'm afraid."

Additional Infernal writing appeared in the empty space at the bottom as my brother moved his index finger through the air. Dredon checked and confirmed the addendum's wording.

My eyes squinted again at the writing. Something about this felt off. The words *marked* and *hunted* echoed in my mind. "Hunted? Why wouldn't the devil's whistle just bring me straight here? It'd be more efficient."

My father smiled genially. "Apologies, son. You know there aren't many words in Infernal for finding someone. Forgive the harsh language. The intent is for you to get your affairs in order before coming here. I'm sure you'll be quite busy, so I don't want an unfortunate or threatening event to derail any business you had at that moment."

Anything more?

Require clarification. The passenger will need a pact for the whistle to work?

"The additional passenger whistled out of danger with me would require a pact to come with me?"

My father nodded. "Correct. You will need to be linked magically to the other person for it to work. After all, what would stop your enemy from pouncing on you just as you whistle? The pact is necessary only until you're both out of harm's way. After that, you can dissolve it, if needed." My father nodded to Ravik, who again waved his finger in the air. The new addendum flared on the parchment. "Any other questions?"

I don't like this.

Nor do I, but why?

It feels too simple. He must gain something from this that we don't see.

He wouldn't harm me. He's my father.

With a small pause, he replied, ***Then why did your mother run?***

If we were truly at risk, she would have taken both Ravik and me. Do you see anything amiss?

No.

Then let us be done with it.

I stepped around my father toward the table, where a dipped quill sat. Papa pointed a claw at a small line for my signature. A few scratches of the inked quill affixed my name to the parchment.

Ramiren Orasti

Taking the quill from my hand, my father added his name on a line under mine.

Vrakus Orasti

My brother stepped forward at my father's nod and tapped the vellum with his index and middle fingers. A duplicate parchment, addendums, signatures, and all, appeared next to it.

My father stepped back with a light clap of his hands. "Wonderful. Give your la'kora my love, Ramiren." He grinned, looking quite pleased, and turned to Ravik. "Pass him the copy and send him back home. We're done here."

Though I wasn't sorry to leave this place, my father's cold dismissal stung. Ravik stepped forward with a grimace, likely seeing the hurt on my face. "It was good to see you, brother. Give our mother my love too."

Before I could reply, he placed the parchment copy into my hands and tapped once on my forehead with the same two fingers he'd just used.

The instantaneous transport shocked my system. The sudden temperature difference, from stifling heat to fresh but cold air, sank into my skin. Shivering, I opened my eyes to see the Dulonian cottage my mother and I had shared in Laeth before my pactmaker training started three years ago. She'd moved five times since, citing the need to see new places.

No, my father wouldn't harm me.

Chapter One
Homecoming

Forty Years Later...

The fragrance of oranges followed Nathalia, and her grin lit her entire face like a wash of sunshine the moment we stepped into the villa's open foyer. The butler, a gaunt human fellow, bowed, then closed the large front door behind us before departing, his shoes making sharp clicks on the floor.

Large windows on either side bathed the foyer in midday light, which bounced off the crystal chandelier above and illuminated the twin staircases leading to the second level. The air smelled of fresh greenery and flowers, courtesy of the colorful arrangements brimming from vases placed upon every available surface.

The marble flooring had been replaced, and the wood of the banisters and heavy furniture gleamed as though a darker stain had been applied, then polished to a shine.

Five years since I'd been here, and only a few subtle changes were evident. Portraits had been removed to make way for oil-painted landscapes, but the same large family painting, depicting Lord Maxlian and Lady Resa sitting and surrounded by six children of various ages, still took center stage on the left wall.

So, renovations of this sort would cost—

Stop it, Dre. I'm not working.

Gods above, I'm* bored, *and seeing as you've not stopped working in forty years, it's a difficult habit to break.

I've taken appropriate rest.

Liar.

Nathalia looked back at me over her shoulder, and her happy expression made my chest pinch painfully at the same time as a pleasant warmth pooled in my gut. *Have I ever seen her this happy?*

Multiple times, Ren. Especially when you two are fu—

Rhetorical question.

Nathalia shook her head, her eyes darting around the foyer. "Still looks the s—"

"Natty!" came a feminine cry from a side hallway.

I moved to the side automatically as Lady Resa rushed through the open foyer toward us, laughing, her arms spread wide. Nathalia mirrored her, stepping forward to wrap her mother in a warm hug.

I pivoted to give them some privacy and barely stopped myself from stumbling into an enormous ficus. Rubbing a smooth leaf between my thumb and forefinger, I averted my eyes, but my ears still caught everything.

Lady Resa's voice became muffled. "We just got your note yesterday. You barely beat the messeng— Oh, you really *weren't* joking about bringing him."

Nathalia chuckled as I pried my attention away from the large plant to see Lady Resa look me up and down, then cast a sly grin at her daughter. "Ramiren. It's good to see you again."

A genuine smile came unbidden as I bowed. "And you, Lady Resa. I hope your family is well."

"Max is in the training yard with our youngest. Aside from a few aches and pains from trying to keep up with a young woman at his age, he's probably all right. The rest are growing like weeds between cobblestones." Lady Resa kissed her daughter on the cheek. "Go get yourself and your guest settled, then come back down. Supper is in an hour. Theoretically, anyway. Kaleb insisted on cooking again."

The matriarch shot me a wink before turning to head farther into the villa, leaving me and Nathalia alone.

Nathalia inclined her head toward the stairway on the right and began walking that way, and I followed. "Mother didn't specify a room for you, so you can take one of the family bedrooms."

"I recall you have a sizable family." Catching sight of the family portrait, I struggled to find accurate but not insulting words. "Holidays must be...interesting."

Nathalia's eyes glittered with amusement. "You mean chaotic? Yes. Complete and total disarray, as my mother prefers." At the top of the stairs, she turned right down a wide, carpeted hallway that ended in an open window. The warm breeze caught the sheer curtain, bringing with it the scents of the expansive gardens beyond. Four closed doors, two on each side, each painted in a different bright color, made up the hallway's most defining features.

Nathalia motioned toward the yellow door nearest the window. "This one is yours. The red one is Raewyn's. Big surprise there. The purple one is Kaleb's. I'm not sure if you met him five years ago. He would've been thirteen at the time. Tilla and the twins, Bryn and Bryl, are in the opposite hallway. Mine is there."

She pointed toward the light blue door on the opposite wall, marred by a series of horizontal faded lines. I stepped closer and quickly realized the lines were height markers, going back over twenty years, based upon the date next to each dash. I looked around to see every door had similar marks on them, except for the yellow one.

"How old are the twins and Tilla?" I asked, turning to her.

Nathalia thought for a moment, apparently doing calculations in her head. "The twins are fifteen now. They're at the Sorcera Academy, hopefully not setting too many things on fire. Tilla is twelve. She must be the one harassing my father in the training yard."

I gave a low whistle, then grinned crookedly. "A formidable wife and three formidable daughters? Though I don't know your brothers' capabilities, your father is practically outnumbered."

Nathalia snort-laughed before gesturing toward his room. "I'm afraid we don't have the in-room plumbing that the Feylands have. It's the one thing I'll miss from Castle Carpatha. Our bathhouse is downstairs. I'll show you after you get settled." She opened her door, and a strange crinkling sound from within her room made me look inside.

The breeze from the open window caught and rustled dozens, perhaps hundreds, of yellowed scraps of parchment tacked to the light blue walls. Scrawled writing obviously done by a child's hand covered each piece.

Though I would need to move closer to actually read the writing on them, it wasn't difficult to figure out what they were.

I looked at Nathalia with a raised eyebrow. The hauntingly wistful look on her face combined with the scent of sea air. Yearning. Instinctively I lowered my voice, like one does in a sacred temple, to not disturb the moment. "Your childhood songs and stories?"

She blinked and nodded slowly, then walked a few steps into the room. "Yes, but I don't know why they're hanging up again. I took them down shortly after—"

"*I* put them up," said a familiar voice behind me.

Fuck. Here we go.

Nathalia straightened and spun to face the speaker. "Raewyn."

"Didn't expect you to visit so soon." Her eyes darted to me when I turned to face the priestess, then back to Nathalia with a question in them.

I moved so Nathalia could explain our presence here at her family home without my hovering. Inhaling deeply, I noted the coppery aura of anxiety hanging like a heavy cloud around them both, though more so from Nathalia than Raewyn.

I should give them some privacy. "I'll go."

Nathalia placed a hand on my arm to keep me there. Her fingers gave a brief, gentle squeeze, a silent plea that might as well have put lead shoes on my feet.

She said to Raewyn, "I didn't get married."

Raewyn hummed. "I gathered that. And why not?"

"As it turns out, Jaylin was a..." Nathalia frowned, as though searching for the right word. She dropped her hand from my arm. The instant chill following its removal, as happened every time she stopped touching me, still continued to surprise me.

Raewyn said what Nathalia would not. "A prick?"

Nathalia looked down at the intricate rug under her feet, toeing a woven filigree line on it. She muttered under her breath, "You could say that."

"I *did* say that, but would *you* say that?"

Nathalia huffed. As though rising to the challenge evident in her sister's demeanor, she lifted her chin. "Considering the last interaction I had with him involved me throwing a middle finger in his face and telling him to go fuck himself? Yes, I would."

A delighted smile split Raewyn's face. "Rude gestures at royalty? Cursing? A shiny spine? Well done, Nat." Raewyn's anxiety disappeared, the coppery tang in the air replaced by the warm musk of amusement. "Or should I congratulate Ramiren?"

Me?

Raising my hands in protest, I said, "I assure you, I was *not* present for this. I had nothing to do with it."

Dredon's voice chimed in my head. ***You liar. You begged her.***

The heavy shame burned in my gut as I remembered sitting alone at the dismal Black Unicorn Inn, tightly clutching a smoky necklace between my numb fingers and praying to a cold empty room for her to not go through with it. *Not intentionally. I still don't understand how she heard me.*

"Oh, I doubt that, Ramiren." Raewyn's grin somehow got wider. "I think you had a lot to do with it."

But she heard it, all the same. She said so, even if you never admitted to doing it. It gained you nothing of true value and cost you greatly.

On that, I disagree entirely. Figuring pragmatic logic would finally grant me some gods-damned peace from my vizier's opinions, I countered. *It gained me a protector.*

We both know how well you can take care of yourself, Ren.

"He wasn't there, Raewyn. It was my own decision to refuse my vows."

Raewyn's eyes narrowed at Nathalia.

Just like that worthless necklace. I told you not to accept i—

This is your last warning to be quiet.

Which one is your la'kora now, Ren? The necklace or h—

We're done.

I held the intention in my mind and, behind my back, snapped my fingers to temporarily silence Dredon.

Meanwhile, the ladies' conversation continued. I took the opportunity to study their interaction. Their words didn't line up with their emotions, and it became obvious both were trying to hide their true feelings from the other.

They never could hide them from me.

My nose remained unfooled by Raewyn's flighty behavior, as some seemed to be, even her eldest sibling. I caught the emotions hidden beneath her teasing quips. Her scent and her demeanor always remained at odds. Childishness and immaturity were to Raewyn as a sword and shield were to Nathalia. The Minuen priestess felt too much and too deeply.

Raewyn showing her real self, her real emotions, remained a true rarity I'd witnessed only a few times, most notably during their fight after Jaylin's proposal.

The scent of their whirlwind emotions had pummeled me and added to my own inner turmoil about the whole affair, causing a splitting headache.

I realized I'd missed something when Raewyn said, "Sure. That makes sense," then turned to me. "So, Ramiren. Glad to see you as well. What brings you to our doorstep?"

Having anticipated this question but unfortunately having no satisfactory answer, I simply smiled, as I always did when I needed to feel in control. Of myself. Of the situation. "Traveling with your sister. We have things to discuss with your parents."

Raewyn's eyes widened, and she gasped as her hands flew to her mouth, her exclamation slightly muffled but high-pitched with excitement. "Minue's tits! Are you two—"

Nathalia and I responded simultaneously, "No."

The red-haired priestess's hands dropped as her face scrunched like a petulant child being denied candy. "Aw! Why did you have to phrase it like that, then?"

I was amused, despite my feelings on *that* particular matter. "Apologies, Raewyn. It wasn't my intention to give you a false impression, I assure you."

"Well? What do you need to talk to Mom and Dad about? Ooh! Are you going to send assassins after Jaylin?" Her small hands clapped with anticipation as her eyes bounced between us, not sure who would answer her.

Once more, we answered simultaneously, "No."

She scowled. "Attacking Wistran?"

Again. "No."

She grimaced and dropped her hands to her sides dejectedly. "Fey-flavored bonfire?"

My mouth opened to answer, but nothing came out. Nathalia picked up the slack, a look of befuddled confusion twisting her lovely features. "What is it with you and *flavored* bonfires?"

Raewyn shrugged, grinning wolfishly. "I just like evocative language. I thought you'd appreciate it, Lady Writer." The priestess slid over to Nathalia and wrapped her arms around her sister's waist.

Nathalia's arms went wide as her worried golden eyes met mine. She didn't need to voice her thoughts. Even if it hadn't been a much-discussed topic on the purposefully ambling road we'd taken to get here, I'd still know.

And even if I couldn't detect the scent of her emotions, Nathalia had always been easy for me to read.

Nathalia cleared her throat. "Raewyn, I'm—"

"Forgiven."

Nathalia sagged, like her marionette strings had been cut, and her arms went around her sister's shoulders in a warm embrace.

This time, I smiled just because.

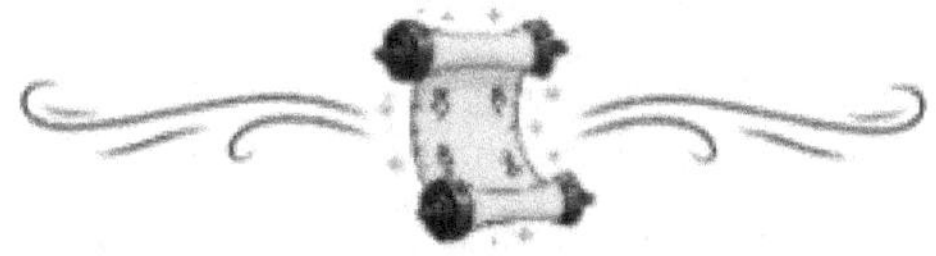

Two sets of eyes stared at me from across the table. The warm brown of Lady Resa's reminded me of my mother's eyes, filled with affection and concern.

The other set, molten gold and filled with suspicion, reminded me of my Citadel instructors.

Maxlian Swordhand, Lord Protector and High General of Camlynn, turned to his daughter. "Your account confirms Raewyn's. She told the same story, just with a bit more embellishment. But there is one outstanding question you've yet to answer. You almost married the crown prince of Wistran and didn't tell us?"

Nathalia winced. "His mother told me she informed you of the wedding but that she'd received no reply." She looked down into her lap, twisting her fingers around each other under the table. "I thought you didn't want to come."

"Natty, love." Her mother's husky voice stayed stuck somewhere between admonishment and sadness. Her eyes flicked to mine for a brief moment before landing again on her daughter. "We wouldn't miss your wedding for the world. I hope you know that."

Nathalia lifted her head and gave a small nod. That simple gesture, combined with the gloom rolling off her like a reeking fog, sent sharp, prickling needles into my chest. I almost lifted my hand to take hers in comfort, but while Nathalia might appreciate the gesture, I didn't want to add to her burdens with the questions that would inevitably follow.

May I talk now?

Depends. Are you going to say anything useful?

I think it's useful.

What is it, then?

I calculate a 74% chance of Lord Maxlian attempting to run you through if you touch his eldest daughter in front of him. Based upon voice and body language, he loves her very much **and** ***has a temper.***

I closed my eyes so no one could misinterpret my annoyed eye roll as Nathalia and her parents continued their discussion.

Well aware, Dre. Thank you.

However, I calculate a 93% chance of Lady Resa stopping him. She is your ally here. If it comes to blows, perhaps that would be the opportune time to tell them about Lady Nathalia's protector oath with you. I'm still not entirely sure why neither of you mentioned it.

Before I could respond, Lord Maxlian stood from his chair, his massive white-feathered wings stretching the entire length of the large family's formal dining room table before folding back again. An easily interpreted intimidation tactic, if I'd ever seen one. "Well, if you're hunted by this Vrakus, then you're safe. Devils can't enter Rowin. The city is warded."

A fact Nathalia had shared with me several weeks ago, and which I'd noted upon first arriving. The walls encircling the city possessed a green, swirling glow when observed through my glasses. The obvious advantage of being surrounded by family, allies, and a powerful protective ward overrode my hesitance. Unfortunately, it left one glaring problem.

I didn't want to stay in Rowin for the rest of my long life. Since birth, I'd been pushed and pulled along at another's insistence. To be forced to remain seemed somehow worse, even for *her* sake.

That fact didn't feel good. In fact, I felt like a selfish bastard, but I would bear it with a genuine smile if I had to. The alternative remained the worse option.

Lady Resa and I stood, yet Nathalia stayed seated. She spoke up in a concerned but confident tone. "Father?"

"Hm?"

Nathalia pursed her lips, as though loath to speak. She shook her head, then said, "We can't hide here forever."

I was unsurprised at her use of "we," even here. Since my initial blinding panic at her sudden involvement with my father, I had come to terms with the fact we were once again united in a common goal.

Only this time, our bond was rooted far deeper than the warm comfort her companionship had always provided, the confusingly intense affection I'd slowly developed for her, and beyond that, the unexpected but undeniable chemistry that always had me at half-mast in her presence.

She'd said her oath and bound herself to me as a protector. When Nathalia had knelt at my feet on the soggy ground, I'd understood what her words were promising for the next two centuries that would make up our probable lifespan. However, just because I understood didn't mean I'd come to terms with what she'd sacrificed on my account. She'd sworn to me instead of her husband, like she'd always intended to do.

Truth be told, it fucked me up a little. Though grateful beyond words and profoundly moved, the guilt ate at me, because I *knew* I didn't deserve her devotion.

Frankly, with what I'd been keeping from her, I didn't deserve her at all. Deep shame held my tongue as surely as a scold's bridle. Every time I thought I finally summoned the courage to tell her, to withstand the inevitable look of rage and betrayal in her eyes, my words failed me yet again. The longer I held out, the more difficult it became.

Lord Maxlian chewed on his cheek, thinking, then he finally looked at me. "Please give us the room. I need to speak with Ramiren for a moment."

Nathalia stood hesitantly and shuffled out, with Lady Resa hooking her arm around Nathalia's as Nathalia looked back at me uneasily. Once they'd gone, I turned to Lord Maxlian.

Gutting in 5...4...

Be quiet.

The angel in front of me smiled wanly as he crossed his arms over his broad chest. "Now that that's over, are you going to tell my firstborn daughter that Vrakus, the Arch-Devil of Gateway's Third District, is your father?"

My heart and stomach both shot into my throat like poisoned arrows as my chest constricted. I couldn't even manage a smile.

3...2...

Shut the fuck up, Dre!

I saw no point in hiding or prevaricating here. His eyes held no patience, and the scent of barely contained irritation, cloying and sickly sweet, infused the tension-filled air. "Yes. Eventually. How did you know, and for how long?"

He ignored the first question but answered the second. "I've known for decades."

That would explain his coldness during our negotiations five years ago. I tried to keep my voice calm and free from accusation, but the tightness in my throat couldn't be helped. "Why didn't you say anything in our previous dealings? You could have refused my service when your original pactmaker had to be recalled to the Citadel. He performed an eidetic transfer to me of all your discussions and decisions, and still you stayed silent. It's unheard of for an angel to knowingly associate with an arch-devil's child."

He shrugged as if I'd asked him whether he preferred white or cream-colored dinner napkins. "As it turned out, it had no bearing on our pact."

I raised an eyebrow in disbelief. "And you expected it to?"

He ignored that question too. "You were watched, I assure you. We make it a habit of keeping track of the Lorindar's generals, and they'd never appointed an arch-devil with a *family*. Vrakus managed to not only have a wife but also two sons named Ravik and Ramiren. Both broodlings, as their father had once been. Third District's seat of power sat vacant for centuries, and your father ascended before I relinquished my status with the Tarindar and retired from their command."

Lord Maxlian came around the side of the table slowly and stopped next to me. His hard tone softened. "I'm sorry, I don't know your mother's name. Very little could be found out about her, and the Tarindar don't interfere with mortal lives, only the balance that must be maintained."

I cleared my throat and did my best to present an unbothered figure, but inside a wave of grief, only slightly blunted after all these years, passed through me. I slid my hands into my pockets so Lord Maxlian couldn't see them curling into tight fists. "Her name was Ana."

He frowned. "Was?"

With a curt nod, I cleared my throat. "She died. About eight years ago. Old age."

"Human, then?"

I gave another nod. "Yes."

Lord Maxlian stepped away, running his hand along the polished surface of the dining room table. "My condolences. Those of us with a longer-lived heritage have to come to terms with the frailty of shorter human lives in our own way. Long life is often synonymous with heartache."

I smelled a hint of acrid, pungent smoke in the air. Fear. It didn't take me long to suss out why, given Lord Maxlian's own situation with his wife.

May I talk yet?

Not now, Dre.

It's important.

I don't care.

Aloud, I said, "Everything the eternal remembers, even the most ephemeral thing, becomes eternal too, if only in memory."

Lord Maxlian stopped and slowly turned to look at me. "That sounds like a quote."

Considering the author penned the sentence while lying on my bed, clothed only in loose silver hair, I'd surprised myself by remembering it at all. But her teasing smile and the feel of her soft skin, rather than her nudity, were what I remembered best. The corners of my mouth twitched up at the memory as I answered him. "It is."

The angel let out a long sigh. "By whom? One of those overly romantic philosophers, I suspect?"

My smile turned into a brief grin as I shook my head. "Close. Your eldest daughter."

Chapter Two
A Simple Wager

The next morning at breakfast, I poked at the eggs on my plate with a silver fork, pretending to eat. The chatter of the Swordhand family surrounded me, though half its members were absent.

Raewyn and Lady Resa had early business, and the twins were away. Tilla, a small sprite of a girl with silver hair in a long braid and mischievous brown eyes, occupied her father's attention by rambling about the value of knives versus swords.

Cutlery scraped across plates. Birds sang outside, perched in the many fruit trees just beyond the open doors leading into Lady Resa's gardens. Morning light filtered into the dining room, accompanied by a warm, fragrant breeze. The sounds were hazy and diminished further as my thoughts wandered.

Staring down at my food, I suspected it'd taste like ash. The truth about my past barreled toward my immediate future, looking to intercept me at the worst possible time. I could no longer ignore it. Secrets always demanded a price, my payment now past due. As I was reminded of something Nathalia once said about secrets being assassins, the corners of my mouth lifted slightly. *They kill when you least expect it.*

Fear and a hollow ache made my eyes stray to my left. Nathalia passed a platter of bacon to her brother Kaleb.

"So, Nat, now that you're rested and less grumpy, I can finally ask. It's been a month since you left the Feylands. Where have you been?" Kaleb's gaze flicked to me, as though silently insinuating I had something to do with the delay.

You did.

Fuck off.

Nathalia wrinkled her nose at her brother. "Maybe you should pay more attention to your cooking. Your eggs are runny."

Kaleb frowned down at her plate, where almost all the eggs she'd placed there had been eaten. "That's how you're supposed to cook them."

She shook her head. "That's the problem. They're *not* cooked."

He groused, "You ate an awful lot for having complaints."

Immediately, Nathalia replied, "That's because I love you and don't want to hurt your feelings."

Kaleb's jaw dropped dramatically. "Bullsh—"

Lord Maxlian grumbled, pausing the fork on the way to his mouth, "No cursing at breakfast."

Kaleb pointed an accusing finger toward his eldest sister, whose profile appeared stoic, but the tension in her shoulders and spine was obvious. "You've never cared about hurting my feelings."

Nathalia rolled her eyes and waved her hand dismissively, going back to eating her breakfast. "Lies." She took a bite of the crispy potatoes she'd piled onto her plate and chewed tauntingly.

I will give it to you, though. She is quite clever, as it looks like she's distracting her brother from asking questions. Unfortunately, she's also naive.

She's become much more savvy.

Still too naive to question the real reason you suggested going to the Citadel. Shame the library was lacking in information.

She trusts me.

Naively.

Before I could respond with a sharp rebuke to Dredon, Lady Resa walked in, wearing training leathers and an excited expression, carrying a long, messily wrapped, and vaguely kite-shaped package in one hand. In mid-argument with Kaleb, Nathalia snapped her head toward her mother as she approached and held out the package.

Her mother gave a crooked grin, shaking the mystery item in her hand as if begging Nathalia to take it from her. "I can't wait. You know how I am with gifts."

Nathalia took it after a short hesitation. "Thank you. What is it?" Lady Resa, not answering, practically vibrated as my protector removed the yards of jute string holding the cloth wrapping and slowly unveiled the object underneath. A sword with a leather-wrapped grip and a red jewel set into the pommel.

Nathalia blinked and stood, sliding the cloth off completely. The additional room on the grip would allow for two hands to be used instead of one, but otherwise it appeared nearly identical to her standard longsword. Looking at it through my glasses, I noticed a slight glow radiating from it.

Quite the treasure. Shame you didn't get* that *for your underpaid lessons.

Not responding, I decided to do something far more worthwhile, like study the beautiful blush coloring Nathalia's cheeks and that gods-damned bite into her full lower lip that never failed to twist my insides into knots.

***Hm. Seems like you're ready for yet another* lesson.**

I subtly adjusted myself under the table, fiercely grateful that all the attention remained on my protector. *Not something I can help, Dre.*

Nathalia looked up at Lady Resa. "Mother..." She gazed back down at the sword, running her fingertips over the pommel and hilt. Awe spread across her face, the emotion perfuming the air with the scent of cherries.

You've never had a problem before. A multitude of skilled men* and *women have graced your bed, but* she *turns you bowlegged?

Your point?

Who said I had one? I just find it hilarious.

"A proper weapon for a proper lady. The edge is keen and will cut through just about anything, besides perhaps solid diamond. I told you those swords the Horyn Academy issues aren't *real* longswords. Any weapon that can't be wielded by two hands is useless. The fact they give you that toothpick as a standard weapon boggles my mind." Lady Resa rolled her head back to look at her approaching husband, his hands behind his back. "Why do they do that, anyway?"

"Mostly because they're easier to make. For a protector, fighting is both offense and defense." He smiled down at his wife, stark affection practically glowing from his golden eyes. "Not everyone can have your...passion for aggressive negotiations, love. Some say a protector without a shield is no protector at all. Speaking of..." Lord Maxlian took out the object hidden behind his wings—a bright steel shield with a golden four-pointed star engraved into the face. "I decided not to wrap this. I saw little point in it."

Nathalia leaned the sword her mother had given her against the lacquered table and took the gift from her father. Her eyes glittered with delight, turning the shield this way and that to catch the light before hugging it to her chest. "Thank you." She glanced down at the shield, then back up to meet her father's soft gaze. "This looks like your shield."

"That's because it *is* my shield."

Nathalia's eyebrows rose as her eyes widened. "Wait. You're giving me your *personal shield*?"

"It's time." He shrugged, as though the gift meant nothing. Nathalia, however, looked like he had given her the moon. The clear emotion on her face underlined the light lemony scent of gratitude. I wanted to reach out to her, give her hand a gentle squeeze, a friendly way to tell her she'd earned it. But I didn't particularly feel like losing my head in a violent manner, so I kept my hands to myself. As a result, my palms began to itch with the need to touch.

She cleared her throat. "So. What does it do?"

Lord Maxlian raised an eyebrow in question. "Do?"

"Yes. Mother said the sword has a keen edge. Does this shield have some sort of special ability?"

Lord Maxlian grunted, as though he finally understood what she meant. His next words came out matter-of-fact while he remained completely straight-faced. "Well, it has this really handy feature of blocking incoming attacks..."

Nathalia's expression went from happy to unimpressed in less than a breath. "Father!"

He tilted his head as he inspected the shield. "And if you shine it up nicely, it can serve as a mirror..."

Nathalia huffed in exasperation. "That's not what I—"

He narrowed his eyes and tilted his head back as another idea occurred to him. "I suppose, if you're *really* desperate, it can be used as a serving platter."

"*Father!* I mean, what *magical properties* does it possess?"

His thoughtful expression cleared, instantly replaced by a teasing grin. "Oh. It's blessed, but aside from that, it's just a pretty shield, sweetheart." He leaned in with a gentle hand on her soft hair, kissing Nathalia's forehead in a small peck of affection.

The itch in my palms became distracting. I rubbed them on my thighs in a futile effort to reduce the irritating sensation, but it helped little.

"Come on, you. Get changed and into training armor. I need to reacquaint you with proper combat. Expect mud and blood, daughter." Lady Resa traipsed off, the smell of oranges trailing behind her as she practically skipped out of the room.

Nathalia chortled and picked up her new sword in her other hand.

Kaleb began to follow his mother out of the dining room, stopping only to look Nathalia in the eye. "I hope she knocks you on your ass so hard you can't sit for a *week*."

In a petulant voice that could've come from Raewyn, Nathalia responded as he turned to leave. "They were runny."

He yelled over his shoulder in response just before he exited the room, "They were *perfect*."

She looked at me, her eyes twinkling in amusement, as though her pseudo-argument with her brother had lit her up from the inside. It reminded me of how my brother and I used to rib each other long ago, and a sharp pang stabbed my chest.

"Will you watch?" she asked me. "My mother is quite vicious. It's a sight to behold."

Refusing to let my inner turmoil show, I gave her my customary smile. "I'd be honored to see the famed Lady Resa Swordhand in action."

She laughed silently and left the room, leaving Lord Maxlian and me alone.

Yet again.

Lord Maxlian spoke first, "Do you recall our pact a few years ago, Ramiren?"

I met his hard stare, his point clear. "I do, sir."

The first pactmaker assigned to deal with Lord Maxlian and Queen Uldanna of Camlynn had given me his memories via eidetic transfer. They included an angry monarch, a stoic angel, and a box with a necklace, the bauble bespelled to immediately leech a deadly poison into the one who put it on, though it had not yet reached its intended target.

He responded in a low voice after a slight pause. "Then you know exactly how far I will go to protect my daughter, and it is obvious you *still* have not told her who actually hunts you."

I inhaled and exhaled slowly before answering. "I am well aware."

"Good. I know it's a difficult conversation to have. After sleeping on it, I've decided I'll give you until the end of the week to tell her, or I will."

I meandered toward the training yard, nearly running into a table as my thoughts wandered.

Five days. I had five days to figure out how to unload fifty years of heartache, abuse, and fear. *A full story that I've never written down and only two others know.*

I didn't know where to begin.

Taking a seat on a long bench an arm's width from Kaleb, my gaze stayed on Lady Resa as she stretched and warmed up her muscles by swinging her two-headed axe in one hand, then the other. The training yard boasted small puddles from the storm that'd hit last night, drying slowly at the behest of the warm, partially cloudy day. It smelled earthy and clean, with a few pungent notes, like a well-maintained farm.

Bundles of straw and a few strawmen impaled on posts lined the partially fenced perimeter. Beyond the fence, a mixture of tidy thatched outbuildings and a few smaller barns enclosed the area. The large, wide-open yard had been designed with roughhousing in mind.

I hadn't had the chance to see this or much else of their estate the last time I'd visited, mostly keeping to Lord Maxlian's study for the paperwork.

I certainly hadn't been personally introduced to the pact's catalyst. Nathalia had been sent back to Horyn Academy to complete her training immediately after the nearly catastrophic incident.

I heard a deep mutter and turned my head to look at its source. Kaleb sat slouched forward, slowly breaking bits of straw in his hands and flicking them away as he watched his mother prepare.

The wet straw scent hovering in the area mixed with the smell of fresh mud, though I couldn't tell if it emanated from the yard or Kaleb. With mud being the scent of melancholy, perhaps it was both. He sighed and said, either to me or to himself, "She's too much like Dad. By design."

Though his eyes were on the lady of the house, his statement obviously referred to another. I couldn't help myself. Though I knew Nathalia very well—what she considered important, things she loved and hated, what brought her joy—my interest in her bled into craving the ordinary details too. The mundane tidbits that filled out her life, especially prior to us meeting, were just as real. Just as wanted.

When he didn't elaborate further, I prompted, "Nathalia?"

He slowly nodded, then tapped the remainder of the straw in his hands against his fingers. "Firstborn. She trained them on how to parent, really, just like they trained her to fight. My dad said he'd never even held a baby before she was born. It's no wonder he molded her after him. He didn't know any better."

Wondering where he was going with this, my lips stayed sealed. I'd learned people cannot bear silence, often filling it without thought, leading to the divulging of secrets to an audience not meant to hear them.

That's because I beat it into your head for years.

You're being extra bratty today, Dre.

I'm eager to work, and you're taking a vacation.

You told me I haven't taken appropriate rest.

You've rested for a month. I would think you'd be fine by now, but you still grump at me like an old man scolding a child.

I have to protect her from him, Dre. This place is warded. I'll not risk her until we figure out our next move.

She's *supposed to protect* you, *Ren, not the other way around.*

Apparently the silence had become too much for Kaleb, because he finally spoke again, "Let's just say my father can be...critical."

Though I barely knew the boy, I felt a twinge of guilt. I agreed with Dre that Nathalia had teased her brother to cover for me. Before Nathalia, the uncomfortable emotion would've been ignored.

But now?

I let out a measured sigh. "Your culinary skills are very good, especially for someone your age. Your sister likely didn't mean what she said."

He turned to me with a frown. "How do you know that?"

Trying to keep my voice nonchalant, I responded, "She didn't like your question about why it took a month to get home."

He froze for a moment, then a quizzical twinkle lit his eyes. He dropped the rest of the straw to sit straighter. "Oh, is that so?"

I nodded slowly. "You see... The delay was my fault."

With a head tilt, he smirked but didn't respond.

A beat of silence. Then another. Another.

A flicker of anxiety bloomed in my gut just before I realized his ploy, staying silent so I'd be the one to divulge information. Just as I had done to him.

Ooooh! I like this one. A fast learner.

That finally got me to smile. "I took your sister to see something. A place very important to me."

"And where's that?"

I cleared my throat, knowing exactly what my confession would mean. "The Citadel." At his confusion, the same confusion on Nathalia's face when I told her where we were going, I elaborated, "Where pactmakers are trained."

His eyes went wide. When he opened his mouth, his voice squeaked in that awkward way of teenage boys. "*Excuse me*?"

Either the gods had a good sense of humor or merely a good sense of timing, because Nathalia chose that moment to step into the yard, wearing fitted buckskin. Unlike her thick chain armor, the leather hugged the generous curves she'd earned from both intense training and a healthy appetite. I remained grateful for both as my gaze followed the concave line of her back, tapering inward at her waist above her perfectly round ass.

She approached her mother, carrying her newly gifted sword and shield. "Ready?"

Lady Resa frowned, pointing with her axe. "Get that shield out of my training yard, young lady. It has no place here."

Despite Lady Resa's harsh tone, Nathalia laughed and carefully propped the shield against a strawman. She straightened and faced her mother, still amused, which made Lady Resa scowl. "You did that on purpose, Natty."

"Guilty. Shall we spar or—OH SHIT!" Nathalia barely managed to get the sword out of the scabbard before blocking her mother's downward swing. Tossing the scabbard aside and gripping the sword with both hands, Nathalia swept her mother's axe to the side in order to adjust her stance.

"Rude, Mother."

"Fighting should never be polite." As if to emphasize her point, Lady Resa pivoted, punching with the steel point topping her axe, which Nathalia dodged easily. They both stepped back, circling each other.

Though their gazes and body language read as aggressive, the unmistakable scent of wholesome pride, blueberries mixed with cream, filled the air from Lady Resa.

Kaleb leaned over and whispered, "Wager?"

I shot him a crooked grin. "A gold on your sister."

Kaleb licked his lip before responding. "Pastries for life on my mother."

Good wager! Take it! Takeittakeittakeit.

I watched mother and daughter clash, sparks coming off their weapons when one attacked and the other parried. The half-dried mud under their moving feet began to soften and splatter, leaving their legs caked after only a few passes.

Though unfamiliar with Lady Resa's style of fighting, I'd become familiar with Nathalia's. She'd easily adjusted to account for the two-handed weapon she now wielded, as though she had trained with it before and simply needed to reawaken her muscle memory. Both were quick. Both were competent.

And both were holding back. This sparring session existed as nothing more than a precursor to the main event, where I suspected things would get very interesting.

I hummed, shaking my head. "That hardly seems a fair wager, Kaleb. I'm sure your pastries are worth far more."

Idiot!

With a casual shrug, Kaleb grinned. "Maybe, but I'm also confident."

"In your mother's abilities?"

He shook his head, his eyes watching the fight closely. "No, in her *competitiveness*. She's never lost against Nat."

Seeing the light of determination in Nathalia's eyes, even from a distance, I had a feeling today would be different. "One hundred gold, then, and I'll call it."

His eyebrows went to his hairline. "Your funeral."

I agree, you moron.

The two women stepped away from each other, neither out of breath. Lady Resa flipped her auburn braid over her shoulder and settled into a balanced fighting stance. "Ready?"

Nathalia did the same, one foot wiggling and squelching in the mud as her knees bent. Her own stance set, she smiled. "Horyn bless your blade, Mother."

"Bari bless yours, daughter."

The air thickened with the sudden scent of sunlight on freshly cut grass. Resolve.

I grinned as Kaleb muttered under his breath, "Here we go."

There was no chance to respond, because my tongue became stuck to the roof of my mouth. I watched, transfixed, as Lady Resa and Lady Nathalia's blades collided in a mesmerizing blur. Their footwork perfectly matched their strikes, staying balanced and giving nothing away regarding intention.

I had a hard time, even with my glasses, following their deft movements. They were two warriors with reflexes honed in both training and real combat.

Now neither held back, and it left me without air in my lungs.

Perhaps your pact with her wasn't for naught. One-on-one, she could beat you, Ren, and that's saying something.

I couldn't disagree. While Lady Resa's movements shrieked with brutality and fervor, Nathalia's sang with grace and the patience to wait her mother out.

Without warning, a feral scream echoed across the expansive yard as Nathalia swung down in a wide diagonal stroke, just like her mother had done in her opening volley. But when Lady Resa lifted her axe to block, Nathalia's blade sheared her mother's weapon straight through. The cut was so smooth, it took a full breath for the severed half of the axe's head to fall into the churned mud at their feet.

While Lady Resa's eyes bugged, looking at her broken axe, Nathalia lifted her sword without missing a beat. "Yield?"

It took a moment for Lady Resa to respond, not moving except for her labored breathing. "Yield."

Nathalia lowered her sword slowly as Lady Resa lowered what remained of her axe. The two women stared, panting from exertion, until both simultaneously squealed in excitement. Their weapons fell to the ground as they met in a fierce embrace.

My cheeks hurt from smiling as I applauded and watched them jump up and down in each other's arms, laughing with glee.

Happiness remained by far my favorite scent, and I breathed in the fragrance of oranges coming off them in waves.

"Are you fucking kidding me?" Kaleb whispered as his head lowered into his hands.

I stood from my seat on the hard bench, still clapping my hands, and spoke to Kaleb without looking his way. "My favorite pastries are fruit-based. I'm particularly fond of cherry, apple, and cranberry-orange."

Chapter Three
Symphonic Lights

Nathalia found me in the gardens, her warm demeanor a welcome sight. Her attention wandered from one thing to the next—the trees, the flowers, and finally the cobblestone paths meandering about the space. "My mother's work. She's always had a penchant for growing things. It's probably why she had six children."

Though Lady Resa's reputation as a fierce combatant was well earned, as I'd witnessed earlier that morning, it didn't surprise me that her primary love was building and nurturing rather than using and destroying. *If only more parents were like that.*

"When we met five years ago, I didn't get to know her very well. My attention was elsewhere. Even knowing his famed fairness, I was focused on your father's reaction to me and making sure I didn't invite suspicion. Not everyone, especially angels, react to broodlings well. Doubly so for one often mistaken for a full devil. Any...misunderstanding could quickly become very dangerous." I paused. "In the end, it went fine, though I had a feeling he found my concerns amusing."

Her smile widened as she stepped closer, putting her hands behind her back. "My parents are far too well traveled to judge a book by its cover. One of my mother's best friends is a swamp hag named Jenny. Always treated my mother as the daughter she never had. Which was good, because my mother never knew her own mother. Or father, for that matter. She was quite literally raised by wolves and born a half-orc rather than the human she appears to be now."

Interesting. "I'd heard the rumors, but I always had the good sense to not repeat them, so I never knew the truth of that story. Is her heritage obscured by some kind of illusion magic while in public? While my attention has been on you, I'm confident I'd have noticed...tusks."

A soft laugh escaped her. "No. She's fully human now. For doing some great service. Let's just say she's been granted divine intervention. The story goes that her half-orcish nature impeded her clear thinking in battle, and she wished to rid herself of her mindless bloodlust. So she asked the gods to change her, and they obliged."

With a one-shouldered shrug, she added, "At least, that's the story she tells. Who knows how true it is?"

My smile turned wan. "I understand feelings about the nature associated with a person's heritage all too well. While I don't think I'd change my blood or remove its effects on me now, there was a time, as a younger man, when I might well have requested something similar."

Her head bowed as she toed the edge of a cobblestone with her shoe. "I can't say I understand, as I've been privileged to have a bloodline that is lauded." She paused, then her eyes brightened as she lifted her chin. "I came out here to ask you something. Are you available tonight?"

Distracted by the shine in her gaze, my mind stuttered at the sudden change of subject, and I took a moment to think of a reply.

"I am. You look as though you have a plan in mind."

Delight spread across her face. "At sunset, meet me in the foyer. I have a surprise for you. And, um..." After she ran her gaze up and down my body, she added with an impish glint in her eyes, "Wear your best, please."

The last of the sun's rays disappeared below the horizon, leaving the villa in a mixture of twilight and golden flame from ensorceled sconces. My boots tip-tapped on the marble steps as I descended, adjusting the collar of the black jacket with red trim she liked so much.

Nathalia waited off to the side, her attention focused on a small landscape painting. She stood with her back to me, and I stopped to admire the drape of red silk overlaid with black lace that pooled at her feet and hugged every curve from shoulders to thighs.

As she turned, my eyes scanned upward. Now visible, the low neckline thickened my tongue, rendering me unable to speak. Smiling as brightly and broadly as possible to hide my stolen speech, I stepped closer and held out a hand for her to take.

I pulled her into the light to see her more clearly and stall for time until I regained control over my vocal cords. The golden light glinted off the red-jeweled choker resting just above the hollow of her throat as though winking at me.

Mockingly.

Nathalia took pity on me as she reached out to touch the lapel of my jacket, where a pinned spray of wildflowers once rested. It'd been my ticket to a random carnival, and it had changed my life. "My favorite jacket." She looked down at herself. "You're a vision, but I didn't intend to match you."

I'd never been a possessive man, but then I'd also never had a reason to be. Everyone had agency and was free to make their own choices. However, the satisfaction stuttering my heart's normally steady rhythm indicated the besieged organ disagreed. It reveled in the idea of others seeing our similar colors and naturally assuming she was taken.

By me.

She continued, "I can change if i—"

"No. No, that's not necessary." I hated interrupting her—everyone did it—but that idea needed to be removed from her mind entirely. "You look stunning. Please don't change."

She looped her arm around my elbow, moving her velvet reticule from one hand to the other, and ushered me to the front door. "As I'm sure you can probably guess, I'm taking you out."

"I gathered."

We stepped out into the warm evening, and I saw a small, plain carriage sporting a footman and a driver. The footman opened the door and helped Nathalia inside, and I followed, sitting across from her.

The unadorned exterior contrasted with the lush and comfortable interior. The half-closed curtains made of sheer crimson silk provided privacy while allowing us to see outside.

The footman closed the door, and the carriage jostled as he resumed his place at the back. Two sharp thumps on the roof, and the driver moved the carriage forward and onto the streets of Rowin.

We sank into the plush seats, our knees brushing every so often with the rhythmic sway of the carriage. Leaning back against the padded rest, I took a deep breath and closed my eyes.

Silence. A sweet fragrance drifted toward me that never failed to make my mouth water. Subtle at first, but quickly getting stronger.

No doubt the carriage had been cleaned, but the scent of vanilla they'd used to freshen the space now mixed with the delicious smell of honey.

My second favorite aroma, indicating only one thing, triggered a dull ache in my balls as my blood started to abandon its current route and migrate south. My fingers brushed through my beard to hide a wince when my trousers became uncomfortable.

Fuuuuuck.

I heard devious laughter in my head, followed by Dre's voice. ***There's no way you're going to survive this evening.***

Is my attraction to her that funny to you?

The laughter got louder. ***Oh? Attraction? Is that what we're calling it?***

What would you call it?

Denial.

Thankfully, Nathalia's soft voice cut in before Dredon could continue with his stupidity. "The first place we're going is a restaurant. It's known for privacy, so we can discuss events freely."

I nodded slowly. "Or, for just one evening, we can ignore them."

"Pretend?" A wolfish expression crossed her face. "Did you bring my shawl?"

Her mouth distracted me, full lips curled with mischief. So caught up in imagining what her capable mouth could do, I missed the reference. "Shawl?"

"Mmm. You know. The water nymph's shawl that you still haven't returned to me."

Leveling her with a stare, I peeked over the rims of my glasses. "Technically, it's *my* shawl."

She sniffed indignantly, pulling the curtains aside to look out. Her grin softened. "We had a deal. Are you backing out after I completed my end of the bargain?"

"But you didn't."

Her eyes narrowed in challenge. "I assure you, I did everything you asked. And now you have my oath. My sword and shield. My friendship." She tilted her head as her brow lowered. "My bed. What more do you want from me?"

Everything.

The intense and sudden thought startled me so much, I wondered if Dredon had said it. But no, it'd been my inner voice, not his. *Why did I think that?*

That one simple word rebounded inside my skull like a sling's lead bullet, and instead of dissipating, it only got louder, refusing to abate. I expected to hear a mocking jibe from Dredon, but he remained dead silent.

Realizing I too had been silent and given no answer to her question, I shook my head, partially to clear it and partially to answer her, my eyes staying on her. "Nothing. I'm teasing you. Your shawl is in the room. You'll have it by the end of the evening." My smile turned crooked. "One way or another."

The honey aura deepened into a distractingly rich dessert I fully intended to savor. *Later.*

I adjusted the position of my leg to give my now aching cock a bit of room.

If I make it that long.

Dredon's singsong voice replied, ***Doubtful.***

The intense quiet was the first thing I noticed at the fine restaurant when we arrived. Through the tall crystal windows, I could see people chatting. Food being eaten. But when we stepped through the glass doors, no noise came from the clinking of plates or private conversations. For a moment I wondered if I'd gone deaf, but the host greeted us with a bow and loud but genial "good evening." When Nathalia gave her name, his bow deepened.

We were led to a two-person table near the large window overlooking an uncrowded lit fountain surrounded by lush ferns and crimson flowers, and full formal place settings awaited us as the host waved Nathalia forward. I moved to push in her chair, but the host beat me to it. His smile looked more smug than friendly on a face growing more and more punchable by the second.

"Your waiter should be here shortly." He pointed to a small rune at the center of the table. "If you so choose, you may activate your privacy ward by tapping it thrice. Enjoy." His eyes flicked down Nathalia's body as she sat, and an involuntary low rumble vibrated in my chest.

I cleared my throat to cover it and gave the wide-eyed host a smile that I hoped he took as more sinister than sincere. "Pardon. Scratchy throat."

The host recovered quickly, straightening so fast his back cracked. "Then I do hope our wine selection will soothe you. A good evening to you both." He bowed again, this time not even looking at Nathalia, and departed in haste.

Attraction is such a dull word. Meaningless, really. It implies nothing more than a pull toward something. Or someone. You, my friend, are more than pulled. You're being practically territorial. Perhaps you should rub your scent glands on her too.

It took me a few long seconds to respond. *I'm not an animal, and he was being disrespectful.*

Could've fooled me, kitten. He's allowed to look.

That I couldn't dispute. I had no right to stop others from admiring her, even with blatant interest, and also no way to stop the tempest slowly brewing inside me. Once the storm cloud finally burst, I had zero idea what would happen, and that honestly frightened me.

No, I was not nurtured to be a possessive man, but by nature, my father bestowed upon me the potential for rapacity, especially when it came to a beautiful woman I had all-consuming but frustratingly undefinable feelings about.

My heart and soul insisted that I cherish and respect her.

My body and mind demanded that I claim and defile her.

Essentially, I was duly and completely fucked.

Nathalia took one hand off the embossed vellum listing available wines, gently tapping the rune at the table's center three times. In the next breath, the clicking of hard-leather shoes on marble floors, the chatter of busy waitstaff, and even the soft rush of the fountain's water beyond the window faded away.

When she finally spoke, I still heard her voice clearly. "It's different from what we've been used to on the road. I wanted to treat you."

My thoughts flitted from one thing to another. *No one has ever done this for me before. You're a marvel. Your presence is the treat.*

Unfortunately, the only thing my tongue managed was a mild thanks. Admitting anything else felt far too pushy.

Based upon the clench in her jaw and fidgety fingers, she seemed nervous. I inhaled to get a better idea, but I only smelled traces of honey and stronger hints of blood. Anxiety.

When she'd come back from meeting with the Queen of Wistran to organize the nuptials, the scent of blood was so overpowering I thought she'd been harmed. She had been, just not physically.

A waiter came by to take our drink requests—white wine both—and returned, putting two crystal glasses on the table. He walked away again without taking our meal request. My face must've shown my confusion, because Nathalia laughed softly. "I hope you don't mind, but I wanted the chef to choose what we should have. I assure you, she's quite good."

A grin split my face, even as I did my best to ignore the blood-scented air. "A chef-curated menu? You continue to spoil me."

She swirled her wineglass around on the linen tablecloth before picking it up and taking a drink, likely to prepare herself for whatever she wanted to tell me and my reaction. After clearing her throat, she started, "Ramiren..." Fiddling with her glass again, she cleared her throat and took another drink.

I inhaled again to get a hint of her emotions, and my breath stalled. Acrid smoke. Fear.

Did Lord Maxlian tell her about my father?

With no idea what to expect, a tingling sensation began simultaneously in my fingertips and toes, then rapidly shot toward my chest. My head spun. My eyes homed in on her every movement, every minute twitch in her expression. All in the time it took for her to set her glass down.

It was a foreign feeling, being this fixated, and I didn't know what it meant.

"We can't stay in Rowin forever, so we have to figure out where to go from here. And when."

I exhaled harshly, finally able to breathe. "That's it?"

Nathalia blinked, her lips parting in astonishment. "What?"

Gods-damn it.

Smooth.

With clenched fists and jaw, I closed my eyes tightly for a moment. "Sorry... I mean, is that what's been bothering you?"

My protector's lips pursed, her mouth closing so fast her teeth clicked. "How do you know something has been bothering me?"

I couldn't tell her I could smell her emotions. Not yet, anyway. *Gods, I don't even know how to broach that topic.* "You forget, you're like a book to me, but I can only see the synopsis, not the details, not the full story. Never be afraid to tell me your thoughts, Nathalia. No matter what."

Under the pad of my thumb, I felt a soft bump. I looked down, wondering what I was touching, and noticed that not only had my hand reached across the table without me realizing it, but my wayward thumb was caressing her knuckles.

Without taking my eyes off our hands, I said softly, "But you're partially right. *I* cannot stay here forever, but perhaps you could?" With the irate look she gave me in response, I held up my free hand with a slight grin to defuse the tension. "Mercy, my dear." My thumb continued to caress her knuckles in slow circles. "Difficult habit to break."

The smell of smoke receded, replaced with a complicated mix of vanilla, caramel, and dark chocolate. I still hadn't figured out what it meant, because I'd never smelled that particular redolence in six decades of life. Just since meeting Nathalia.

She smiled down at our joined hands. "What's a difficult habit to break?"

"Being alone."

Two hours later, happily sated from one of the best meals of my life, we walked into the expansive lobby of our second destination. A single massive chandelier rimmed in gold and green cord hovered far above our heads and lit the room brightly. Dark-green velvet hung in front of the floor-to-ceiling windows that lined the lobby. The marble beneath our feet was pure white and veined with gold.

The prized piece, however, was the ceiling itself. A mural of a green dragon in flight, rendered in exquisite detail, spanned the entire width, from the doors we'd just entered to the open doors we'd eventually need to walk through to take our seats.

The distant cacophony of a full orchestra tuning its instruments filtered from those open doors that led into the concert hall. Many of Camlynn's nobility were in attendance, a few I'd even dealt with in previous years. I caught a few women and more than a few men looking our way, all dressed and coiffed within an inch of their lives.

A casual glance at those milling about in the open area and standing at the small polished wooden bar off to the right, waiting for the performance to begin, told me something I'd already known.

The woman on my arm had no equal, and they were all wasting their time.

"Lady Nathalia?"

Both my protector and I turned at the masculine voice. A sandy-haired human man, smartly dressed and looking astonished, stepped toward us. As though I were invisible, he gawked at my lovely companion, blinking. "I had no idea you were in Rowin. You look like an angel newly arrived from the Pearl Gardens." He took her free hand and kissed the back.

Those fake compliments never work. Trust me, I've tried.

Nathalia smiled, but I could tell there was strain in it. "Lieutenant Lan—"

"Captain now, Lady Nathalia." His back was stick-straight, one hand grasping the open front of his black coat that partially hid a green waistcoat underneath. His broad face glowed with pride. "Queen Uldanna commissioned me herself."

Nathalia's eyebrows rose, though it felt more performative than genuinely impressed. "Oh. Well done, Captain Landa." She smiled at me, the first genuine gesture she'd made since he approached us. "This is Ramiren, my escort."

Captain Landa finally shifted his eyes away from her to me, and his gray eyes darkened like a thunderhead about to unleash rain. His jaw tightened. "Lady Nathalia, may I speak with you, please? Privately?"

My instinct was to tell him no, but the question was not posed to me. It was her call entirely. When she acquiesced with a simple nod, she removed her arm from around mine, and it felt like she'd removed my heart from my chest.

I gave my customary smile to hide my emotions. "I'll get drinks, unless you don't want one?"

She chuckled softly. "Thank you. You know what I like."

That you do.

I made sure to have my back turned before shaking my head. I was not in the mood.

As I approached the bar, my gaze kept straying to her and the overdressed interruption, nearly bumping into more than a few scoffing patrons. I ordered two glasses of Evrakan white. The man behind the gleaming counter nodded, and I leaned against the bar to observe Nathalia and Captain What's-His-Name.

Though there were no outright threatening gestures from either party, and I couldn't smell their emotions from this distance, their body language told me all I needed to know. While hers was angry, his was overbearing. Even possessive. When he raised a hand to grip her upper arm, my vision tunneled. Annoyance was replaced with rage within the span of a heartbeat.

Get your fucking hands off her.

She swiveled her head in my direction to look at me, mouth hanging open in astonishment.

As though she'd heard me.

My anger lowered to a simmer, distracted. This was the third time it had happened, and I still had no idea how. It wasn't a thrown whisper. That required intent. A push of magic. *This* was seemingly random, happening only under extreme emotional distress, something that was uncontrollable. Even the books in the Citadel libraries couldn't provide an explanation.

A dim voice behind me murmured, but I couldn't focus on the words. As the handsy captain leaned in to whisper in her ear, I slapped two gold coins onto the wood without looking and took a step in Nathalia's direction.

Her eyes widened, either from what he'd said to her or my movements. She flicked her eyes toward the door, silently pleading with me to leave.

"**Trust...m...ple...**," whispered a halting voice I'd never heard in my head before, but one I'd recognize anywhere. I stopped mid-stride, and my fingernails dug into my palms.

Oh, how fun! She can do it too?

I was stuck, caught between helping her and trusting her, as she'd asked. Elated that she apparently also had this confusing ability, outraged because it only seemed to happen due to danger. I was trapped between a rock and a hard place and had to make a decision. Now.

With every ounce of self-control I had, I made my choice and turned toward the doors leading outside. Moving through the crowd and stepping into the night air, I heard a loud masculine groan followed by a communal gasp behind me. Before I could see what had happened, Nathalia squeezed through the door, and her hand captured mine to pull me toward the line of waiting carriages. When she snickered, the tension in my back and shoulders lessened. "Time to go, Ramiren."

After finding and entering our carriage and giving instructions to the driver to head home, I looked at her flushed and amused face. The carriage jostled as it joined the other conveyances on the street. "Is everything all right? More importantly, are *you* all right?"

She met my eyes and grinned like the cat that ate the canary. "Oh, perfectly fine. *Captain* Landa is an old sparring partner who didn't take too kindly to your presence, that's all." She shrugged one shoulder, almost casually. "Apparently he still doesn't like being kicked in the balls."

I barked a laugh. "Subtle."

She chuckled ruefully, playing with the thin curtain beside her, rolling the fabric between her fingers. "I try."

After looking out the window, she sighed. "Shame. The orchestra plays enchanted instruments where you can actually see the music. It appears above them, like the northern lights off the Tirvinir coast, far from the factory smoke." Shaking her head, she crossed her arms and finally looked at me. "One more thing that ridiculous asshole ruined."

The smell of fresh mud suffused the small interior of the carriage, and her melancholy became mine. I wanted to offer her something to make up for the interruption of the enjoyable evening she had planned for us. I was extremely tired of people trying to take from her instead of giving.

"If you'd like, that part of the night need not be lost. That's an enchantment I can manage, and I still remember how to play. My pan flute might not be the equal of a full symphony, but I'm willing to make the attempt."

I had a hard time pinpointing exactly what I felt toward my beautiful protector, but I put what I could admit to feeling into my smile, a full one and wholly genuine. My silent prayer to Jessina bade she see it, just to make her a little happier. "A private concert, as a small and humble thank you for this night."

When she returned my smile, even though hers was slight, my chest warmed with a sharp stab straight through my heart. "I'd like that very much."

I'd talk to her about her newfound mental whisper later. At that moment, we both needed something that didn't involve words.

Uncaring if the curtains were private enough, I curled a hand under her silky hair to grip the back of her neck and pulled her close for a kiss. My jaw clenched at the sensation of her soft lips on mine, and I instinctively bit down. Nathalia inhaled so sharply, it sounded like a hiss. Breaking the kiss to apologize, I took in the look on her face. That, along with the honey-scented cloud around us, stopped my words from forming.

She didn't look to be in pain. Her irises were dilated as she stared at my mouth. Testing the waters, I tongued one of my canines. Her cheeks colored, and I knew.

"You enjoyed the sting," I said, framing it as a statement of fact and not a question.

It took her a few seconds to respond. "I did." Her lips pursed as her eyes strayed to mine. "Maybe you can do it again sometime? Somewhere else?"

Months ago, this woman wouldn't have asked for anything. It was a small step, but a good one. "Just so you're aware and fully understand what you're requesting, for devils and broodlings, a bite isn't a nibble. It's an instinct. We're possessive bastards by nature, and we mark what we deem ours. Do you understand?"

Nathalia nodded. "I understand. I'm ready to leave now."

With one hand still around her neck, I snapped my fingers with the other.

Chapter Four
All Bells

"Bruised. Mushy. Bruised *and* mushy." Kaleb muttered while looking through the bushel of yellowish-green apples in front of him. He frowned and added one perfect specimen to his basket, bringing the grand total of chosen fruit to two.

"For fuck's sake, Kaleb. The apples don't have to be perfect," Raewyn muttered, holding one up that displayed a slight discoloration. "See? This is perfectly fi—"

"It's *not*, and *yes, they do*." Nathalia's younger brother plucked the fruit from Raewyn's hand and put it back on the pile. He sniffed. "I don't work with poor ingredients."

"It's just *him*, Kaleb." The Minuen priestess jerked her thumb in my direction. "He won't care!"

"I have a reputation to uphold. I'm not going to ruin it because *you're* impatient." He added a third perfect apple to his basket.

Nathalia and I shared an amused look. But where I grinned, she rolled her lips between her teeth to mask hers. Though we'd been at this market for a good hour, at least, it was a lovely autumn day spent next to a beautiful woman. The sun was shining. A myriad of scents filled the air, hints of happiness and cinnamon and brewed wheat beer.

And I had entertainment.

"Wh—" Raewyn's eyebrows went to her hairline as her eyes bugged. Her voice took on a squeaky tone, equal parts outraged and astonished. "*A reputation to uphold*? Did you *really* just say that with a straight face?"

When he didn't reply, she crossed her arms and tapped her slippered toe in a rapid staccato. "I'm not impatient. *You're* just being weird. Weird and fussy."

When Kaleb ignored her again, she sighed and picked up as many apples as she could, then dumped them into her brother's basket. His sputter of umbrage told everyone within earshot what he thought of his sister's assistance.

Kaleb's eyes held murderous intent as he began to pick through the unwanted fruit. "Damn it, woman!"

Raewyn's chin lifted imperiously. "Don't *woman* me, young man. I changed your diapers and saw your tiny little baby—"

"How much for the apples, sir?" Nathalia interrupted, looking at the stall vendor, who had been watching our group with crossed arms and a smirk.

Kaleb put two back hurriedly and looked for more. "Gods bless it, no! I'm not getting these. They're foul and probably poisoned."

The vendor craned his neck over the boxes of fruit and vegetables he'd set out and peered into Kaleb's basket, pointedly ignoring the boy's flaming face and less-than-stellar review of his produce. "Eight apples? Eight coppers."

She slipped a silver into his meaty hand, which he snapped up with a grin. When he tried to give Nathalia her change, she waved him off. Turning again to Kaleb, the vendor said, "I got some nice blackberries too. I wouldn't recommend choosing each single one, though. Go grab a parchment cone of them, and we'll call it even."

Kaleb sighed, shoulders rising and falling, then moved over to the blackberries like he was trudging to his execution. Raewyn followed close behind, obviously intent on continuing her unsolicited advice regarding produce.

"He's being especially dramatic today," Nathalia murmured to me.

My grin turned crooked as I looked around at the bustling market set up in the open city park. There wasn't a single inch of space wasted. Carved tables and colorfully painted wagons laden with trinkets, spices, food, whittled figurines, and bolts of cloth were set up next to threadbare blankets bearing similar items.

Beyond the market tables, in an open, grassy square, children flew fluttering green kites in the shape of small dragons with the help of their parents. The echoing voices of barkers selling wares called out over the murmur of fellow shoppers. "I think he's still mad about our wager."

"You think so? I'm not sure I agree. He doesn't mind losing. What he minds is disappointing people. He just doesn't realize no one has higher standards for him than he does for himself." She stepped toward her siblings, now arguing over berries, hooking her fingers into the crook of my elbow to guide me along.

"Sounds like someone else I know." Without thinking, I placed my hand on hers. Her skin usually felt cool compared to mine, due to my heritage, but when I touched her, she felt noticeably warm. I frowned, giving her hand a squeeze. "Are you feeling all right?"

She smiled, fanning herself with her free hand. "I am. It's just a warm day."

"Let's get you something to drink, then." I peered around and saw a small hand cart several stalls down, burdened by a large glass dispenser that contained a pale liquid. Slices of lemon floated on its surface. "Lemonade?"

"Please. Thank you."

She removed her hand as I stepped away. Halfway to my destination, the long, low bong of an enormous bell sounded in the distance. The chatter of market patrons and vendors ceased immediately as every single person turned their head in the bell's direction. Then the peals and dings of countless other bells, both large and small, created a jarring, discordant clamor throughout the city of Rowin, from the far-off castle district to the market district I stood in.

There were a few around me who cried out and began scurrying, but most made an orderly, if hurried, exit from the park. I turned to find Nathalia rushing toward me, Raewyn and Kaleb close behind. "We need to go home."

I followed her, figuring she could explain on the way. "What do the bells mean?"

She scowled, her brow furrowed in confusion. "All Bells either means a royal birth or imminent danger." Nathalia led us down a narrow street, away from those dashing around. "And no one was celebrating."

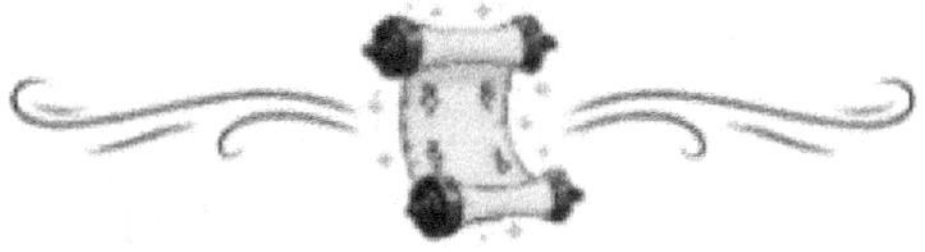

We arrived at the villa just as Lord Maxlian was leaving, dressed in full regalia and looking just as confused as we felt. The first hour of waiting involved tea and throwing around theories on what was happening. Devils? Bad weather? Magical mishap?

The second hour brought stronger drinks and increasingly dramatic suggestions. Some waited for news more patiently than others. Tilla left the room, saying she needed to sharpen her knives in case of violence. I didn't question the twelve-year-old girl's enthusiasm, especially after Kaleb smirked in response.

To no one's surprise, Raewyn attempted to wear a path in the sitting room's thick rug by pacing back and forth. Lady Resa tried to cajole her into sitting down, grousing that she was making everyone seasick.

In the middle of the third hour, Lord Maxlian stalked into the room where we'd been huddled around a blazing hearth. Without preamble, he said in a gruff voice, "Wistran is marching on Rowin. Scouts say the fey army is fully armed, including siege towers to gain entry without damage to the city walls, and appears prepared for battle."

Raewyn finally sat down between Kaleb and Nathalia, covering her mouth with both hands, as I leaned back in my chair. The room was silent until I spoke. "The fey kingdom of Wistran has come to Laeth and is preparing to attack a sovereign nation it has, correct me if I'm wrong, an alliance with?"

Lord Maxlian nodded as he shrugged, appearing baffled. "Allies since the Siege of Rowin, two decades past."

Nathalia scoffed in disbelief, looking from me to her mother, then to her father. "What? Why? When?"

"Might as well get the *how* and *where* in there too," Raewyn muttered behind the fingertips resting on her lips. When Kaleb slapped the back of his hand across her arm, she hissed, clutching her bicep. "Ow! *Asshole*!"

Lady Resa slipped a hand around Lord Maxlian's waist as she passed him a tumbler of amber liquor. He took it and pulled her closer with his arm around her shoulders. "Their army is half a day away at a double-march pace. They must have had gods know how many mages portaling them straight into Camlynn if they're already this close to our capital. I'm sure we'll find out *why* when they get here. But we can guess." His eyes, golden and angry, settled on Nathalia.

Before I'd met her, Nathalia might've shrunk back from that look, even if he was angry at the situation and not her. Now she raised her chin and met his stare. "Perhaps, but everyone is responsible for their own actions. Right, Father?"

And their own inaction. How's that still-relevant life story coming?

There are more important things going on right now.

How very convenient.

Lord Maxlian kissed the top of Lady Resa's head and released her gently. "We're to convene in the queen's throne room within the hour." He winced and turned his gaze on Nathalia again. "Given the nature of what happened in the Feylands, it might be best if you come with me to tell Queen Uldanna your account. You too, Ramiren. You were there for part of it. And Raew—"

Raewyn held her hands up. "Nope. Pass."

Nathalia groaned and put her head into her hands. Her fingers gripped her hair, as though pulling at it would make the situation disappear entirely. With a slight shake of her head, she muttered, "Fuck."

Camlynn's throne room, like Castle Carpatha's, was a wide-open space made of stone and silvery quartz. Colorful statues posed gracefully along the walls, and a dark-green runner embroidered with a dragon's head led from the double doors to the dais, where a woman stood, waiting with obvious impatience.

The venerable Queen Uldanna descended the three stairs, the steel tip of her old cane making echoing *tap-tap-tap* sounds.

The monarch slowly paced back and forth in front of our party of four. We had lined up near the base of the throne room's dais, and the Queen of Camlynn had taken the opportunity to observe us more closely. "The Assembly and I have managed to agree on a basic plan, Tarindar be praised. We've recalled almost four hundred soldiers from the harvest fields, and the grain from nearby silos is on its way as we speak. However, I'm quite confused as to why this is happening at all. Rumor says this is a personal vendetta brought about by a spoiled girl's broken promise to a sulking boy, so pray explain what happened, Lady Nathalia."

Nathalia gave her account of the events in the Feylands as though providing a report to a commanding officer. She left nothing out, save our pact.

Though the human queen was nearing eighty-five years, she still moved with grace and spoke with a clear voice. "So let me get this straight. You, a subject under my authority, received a proposal of marriage from the crown prince of Wistran, proceeded to not gain my permission for this union or even send word to me of it occurring, changed your mind, left him at Valiset's altar in front of his entire kingdom, and have sought refuge within my borders. And now there's an army arriving at my doorstep. Do I have that right?"

Though she hadn't looked at or addressed the person she was chiding, we all knew who needed to answer. The overly simplistic summary of events caused my teeth to grind painfully.

Beside me, Nathalia stood with her hands clasped behind her, back straight and chin lifted. "Yes, Your Majesty. That is correct."

Perhaps not as naive as I thought.

You've never admitted to being wrong before.

Rare events demand commentary. Even now, Nathalia isn't falling to pieces, and you're not plotting the Queen of Camlynn's grisly demise. Miracles do happen.

Queen Uldanna continued to make ungracious insinuations, ignoring context and nuance. The monarch walked right to the edge of suggesting Nathalia had orchestrated the attack but didn't step over into flagrant accusation. Still, Nathalia stood without moving a muscle.

"What do you say, High General? How shall we fix the exasperating problem your daughter has caused?" The queen bared her teeth in a serpentine smile at my protector. "*Yet again*?"

At this, Nathalia winced with a subtle twitch of her eyes.

The queen's insistence on bringing up past mistakes, especially one caught before any harm could befall the elderly monarch and with appropriate reparations given for the offense, outright disgusted me. Not throttling the Queen of Camlynn, let alone hiding my disdain, was an exhausting exercise in self-control.

With a false smile, I pressed my palms to my thighs to keep them in check and prayed for this meeting to end quickly as a heavy pressure began to build in my skull.

Or maybe you* are *plotting her grisly demise.

She's being ridiculous.

If you were gifted a poisoned necklace by a naive and manipulated girl, you'd be surly too.

She was compensated with Lord Maxlian's service to the crown. Monarchs shouldn't hold grudges.

People are never perfect. You know that better than most.

Lord Maxlian looked at his daughter, then back to his queen. "It's possible that an attack or siege could be avoided. Diplomacy can still prevail. A talk, perhaps, can settle tempers. If nothing else, it will stall the start of the conflict and allow us to find out what they're after, as well as the size of their army and if they have siege weapons other than those towers."

Queen Uldanna smiled like she'd been waiting for the opportunity he had just presented. "An excellent idea, High General, and who better to handle the negotiations than my general, his charge—the girl who started this mess—and the pactmaker who already knows our particular history?" She grinned ferally at the angel as the pressure in my head built, pounding with a relentless rhythm at my temples. "If the negotiations fail, she can simply present a special necklace to—"

The pressure in my head burst.

"*Enough!*"

My interruption reverberated in the vast chamber, bouncing off the quartz floors and high ceilings. This room was made for acoustics, for words to carry loudly enough for anyone within its walls to hear clearly.

And mine most certainly did.

The queen slid in front of me and tilted her head, appearing more curious at my outburst than angry. "You have something to add, pactmaker?"

I quietly exhaled to give myself a moment to respond. "Rehashing past mistakes will do little to confront the danger now before us, Your Majesty. We are at your service and will help to quell this aggressive action."

"Mm. See that you do. Because if what they're seeking is Lady Nathalia to return and do as she promised, I will not hesitate to hand her over to spare my realm another war."

Blistering hot panic slid into my gut like a freshly forged knife. With the overwhelming metallic fragrance of blood in the air, I was not the only one here feeling it.

Lady Resa smiled at her queen, but it was not a nice smile. "We assure you, that will not happen, Your Majesty."

Queen Uldanna stared unblinkingly back at the formidable woman, not the least intimidated. "See that it doesn't. Now leave. All of you."

Chapter Five
(Almost) Homophones

One by one, we shuffled through the villa's front door, feeling as though the impending war had already started with a bloody and vicious first battle. Exhaustion curled Nathalia's shoulders inward, while Lady Resa's were pulled back with tension.

Raewyn called out from the same sitting room we had all gathered in an hour prior as Tilla ran into the foyer to greet us. Lady Resa opened her arms to the young girl, embracing her tightly.

Tilla looked at everyone with a frown. "What happened? You all look like you had Kaleb's minced-meat pie."

Kaleb stepped to his mother's side, glaring down at his younger sister, "Shut it, Til. It wasn't *that* bad," he mumbled.

As Lord Maxlian and Nathalia headed toward the sitting room, Lady Resa gave her youngest daughter a strained smile, brushing messy silver hair out of the girl's face. "We'll talk at supper, hm? Go get cleaned up. You look like a feral child."

With a grin that said she took the comment as complimentary, Tilla ran up the steps, feet slapping on marble, and disappeared from view.

Without another word, we followed the high general and his eldest. A cold teapot sat next to half-full cups in a range of sizes containing various liquids on the low table situated between the two sofas. Lord Maxlian leaned against the side of the stone hearth, careful not to singe his feathers, while Nathalia and I settled on the unoccupied sofa across from Raewyn.

"So," Lord Maxlian started slowly. "That could have gone better."

Raewyn sank into her sofa's back with her arms crossed. "What happened? And don't give me that 'we'll talk at supper' nonsense."

Lady Resa shook her head as she headed for the door. "That lazy she-cow said if we can't find a way to negotiate with the Wistran army, they'll hand Nathalia over, should they wish it." She huffed and threw up her hands before stalking out.

Both Raewyn's and Kaleb's jaws dropped simultaneously. He yelled, "What?" as she exclaimed, "Over my dead body!"

Lord Maxlian nodded, then looked at Nathalia. "You know that will never happen. We won't let it."

Nathalia sighed, then gave a breathy, rueful laugh. "Let? Come now, Father. Just because you don't *let* something happen doesn't mean it *won't* happen. Your permission is not what determines whether I'm handed over like livestock."

Lord Maxlian shook his head and fixed his eyes on the floor, grumbling, "That's not what I meant, Nat."

"I know. I know. But if Queen Uldanna says I go, then I go, whether I want to or not. She's not above dragging me out of my home and throwing me at their feet. Dark Drop, that'd probably make her happy." Nathalia scratched at the sleeve of her gown. She had been doing it during the carriage ride to the castle district, while we were waiting for an audience, and as we rode back in silence. Already, the sleeve had begun to fray.

Nathalia flopped back into the sofa's cushions, rubbing a hand down her face as Raewyn chirped, "You know, I get it. It sucks. You safeguarded your virtue, as Dad said, and look where it got you. You didn't get a husband; you got a *stalker*, Nat."

My palms began to itch maddeningly, and Dredon's tone carried a note of warning. ***Ren...***

I don't fucking care.

Consequences be damned, I placed a hand on Nathalia's and squeezed. "None of this is your fault."

There was a sharp inhale from Lord Maxlian, but his subsequent response was one filled with confusion, not violence. "Wait. As I said?"

Nathalia raised her head to meet his eyes, equally confused. "Safeguard your virtue? She's right. That's what you always told me." She frowned, muttering loudly, "Not that I appreciated my *virtue* as being a subject of debate."

Lord Maxlian's head slowly tilted with utter bewilderment, as though Nathalia was speaking in some obscure language. "I'm sorry. Virtue?" He peered over at Raewyn, seeking clarity in her brown eyes, until understanding dawned on his face. He turned back to his eldest. "Oh. You mean verrtu."

"Right, that's what I said. Virtue."

"*Verrtu.*"

Nathalia, befuddled, stared at her father. "Virtue." She slowly stood, eyes staying on him. "Vir-tue."

Oh.

Oh no.

Oh shit.

A chill of awareness that a great misunderstanding had occurred, multiplied, and then taken on a life of its own, skittered up and down my spine like a cluster of tiny spiders. I stood quietly to move off to the side, away from Nathalia and her father. Raewyn did the same, standing behind me as though to use me as a meat shield if needed.

The air was perfumed with the woodsy scent of wariness mixed with the smell of blood.

Dredon chimed in, sounding practically delighted. ***Oh dear. And here I am without roasted hazelnuts to snack on for the show.***

This isn't funny, Dre.

Agree to disagree.

As though subconsciously detecting immediate danger and likely feminine rage, a unique sense no doubt developed over years of sharing the same house with several indomitable women, the lord protector said hesitantly, "*Verrtu*, Nat. The phrase I said was 'safeguard your *verrtu*.'"

Nathalia stood stiff as a board, and the temperature in the room dropped. With careful steps, she rounded the drink-laden low table situated between the sofas and came closer to Lord Maxlian. Her hands fisted. White knuckles. Tight jaw. Hard eyes. "Vir. Tue."

Lady Nathalia's father shook his head twice, still blithely unaware of what chaos he had wrought. "*Verrtu.*"

Nathalia strode up to him, forcing Lord Maxlian to take a step back. With the cold light of realization bringing fire but no warmth to her face, my protector pressed her attack. "Safeguard. My. Virtue. You always told me to *safeguard my virtue.*"

Lord Maxlian reached for her, wrapping his large hands around Nathalia's biceps while he leaned down to look at her eye-to-eye. Confusion was slowly giving way to sadness as he shook his head. "No. Nathalia, I said, 'safeguard your *verrtu*.' You know, your essence. What makes you, you." He lifted a hand to tap a finger on the center of her chest, as though underlining the point.

But the only point Nathalia appeared to understand was that the word she'd heard since she could hold a shield had been something else entirely. With a venomous smile, Nathalia said in clipped speech, "And just what kind of fucking bullshit language is *verrtu*?"

Lord Maxlian's eyebrows shot up at either her tone or her cursing, but he answered her calmly just the same. "It's Celestial, but a rather obscure term, admittedly. And Raewyn tended to interrupt your studies by teaching you Celestial swear words, so maybe you missed it if it was mentioned? Why the language of the angels can say 'cocksucker,' I'll never know." He playfully chided Raewyn as he looked at the priestess over Nathalia's shoulder.

I, on the other hand, smelled the air and took a step back.

Nathalia spit out a hiss, "*Father*!"

Seemingly unconcerned with the fury and even-odds bloodbath in Nathalia's eyes, Lord Maxlian looked back at her. "Hm? Oh yes. You weren't bad at it by any means, but you did have an easier time reading Celestial rather than understanding it when it was spoken. It's a fussy language to speak and hear."

Nathalia's expression cooled in a blink. She nodded slowly and whispered, "Oh. I see."

I took another step back, standing beside Raewyn, who appeared as delighted as Dredon sounded. Kaleb stayed seated and watched with keen interest, as though he too was being entertained.

Without warning, her hand struck like a waiting asp, slapping her father's arm. Hard. Though I was half expecting it, I still winced.

I'm really mourning the lack of hazelnuts right now.

Lord Maxlian recoiled, glancing down at where she'd hit him. "Ow! What was that for?"

She slapped him even harder in response.

This time, he flinched. "Ow, damn it! *What*?" He tried to reach for her again, but even he was stalled by the look in Nathalia's eyes.

Nathalia proceeded to punctuate each word with another hard slap. "I. *Thought.* You. Said. *Virtue.* Chastity. Celibacy... Horyn's. *Cock!*" She practically vibrated with rage, the scent of decaying vegetation thick and heavy. "Fucking...*innocence and purity*, you gods-damned *naro-ni*."

Raewyn grinned happily and muttered just loud enough for me to hear, "See, I *knew* that word would come in handy someday."

Lord Maxlian sputtered, rubbing his arm absently. "I-I thought you'd like it! You know. A flowery Celestial word for heart. Sort of. It's poeticalized." He smiled nervously. "And since when have you cursed so much? Did those caravan guards teach you spicy words? Your mother will be thrilled."

Raewyn spoke low, as though she didn't want to intrude on the scene. "Oh, I'm *definitely* thrilled. Nathalia cursing like a sailor and realizing she can fuck whomever she wants, while my father is getting his comeuppance? This is my favorite day."

I managed to keep my attention on the drama happening before me, rather than turning to glower at Raewyn. But only just. *She most certainly will* not *be fucking whome—*

My thought was interrupted by a loud, masculine exclamation of pain preceded by another loud slap.

Nathalia hissed and raised her hand again, preparing another strike. "*Poetic*, Father. The word you're looking for is *poetic*!" When the inevitable strike came, Lord Maxlian didn't even twitch.

I suspected his arm had long gone numb from the barrage.

As Nathalia began to pace with an irritated growl in her throat, curled fingers clutching her hair in stark disbelief, I anticipated an explosion, a sapper's bomb awaiting its devastating detonation. What happened next, however, came not with a bang, but with a harsh whisper that was somehow the loudest thing I'd ever heard. "I was a virgin for over twenty-seven *years*, for fuck's sake!"

Oh no.

Dredon cackled. ***Oh yes!***

We all watched in silence as Nathalia stomped out of the room. I prayed to Jessina for mercy. For their hearing to have failed them at a key moment. For the dormant luck stone around my neck to suddenly develop magic and grant me a reprieve. But after a beat, Raewyn confirmed without a doubt that I had never been lucky. "Whoa. Wait. Wait. Wait. What does she mean *was*? That's past tense."

Lord Maxlian, Raewyn, and Kaleb simultaneously turned their eyes toward me, all speechless, as the room filled with the overwhelming scent of wood lacquer. Shock.

Fuck

Raewyn yelled, "Dad! Dad, stop!" as Kaleb ran out of the room calling for his mother.

This is a very violent family. He could have at least let you take your glasses off first.

With a groan, I fell back against the wall behind me and slid down on my ass as I clutched my nose in both hands. Based upon the copious amount of blood and stabbing pain, there was a better than even chance it was broken. My aforementioned glasses had flown off to Jessina knew where, so when Lord Maxlian moved to loom over me like a bad dream, all I saw was an oddly shaped blur.

But that also probably had something to do with the fact that my eyes were watering like I'd sat too close to a wet-wood campfire.

"Explain!" Lord Maxlian barked.

My head throbbed in time with my rapid pulse. Trying to talk made the pain increase exponentially, but I managed to wheeze out a few nasal-sounding words. "True. It's true."

Nathalia's father crouched down to get closer to me, making his blurred form a little more visible. Though he looked furious, I felt far more resigned than intimidated. This was the cost of secrets, and debts were paid in tears. "And just how long have you been *involved* with my daughter?"

I raised an eyebrow and immediately regretted the decision, learning the hard way about facial muscles being connected to the nose. With a grunt, I lowered my hands to face him directly. "That, Lord Maxlian, is none of your business."

The angel's golden eyes burned molten as he leaned in. With a soft whisper that belied his barely controlled temper, he replied, "Would you like to repeat that, Ramiren?"

Taking out and unfolding a silk handkerchief I'd no doubt have to burn later, I dabbed at my nose. "My exact words were 'That, Lord Maxlian, is none of your business.'"

Great. Now tell him you love his daughter so I can fill out my Drama Score Card.

Lord Maxlian snarled and pulled his closed fist back to deliver another punishing blow. I didn't flinch; I just mentally hoped he didn't strike the same place twice. His bloodied fist shot out just as a blue haze formed between us like the curtain dropping on a performance. His knuckles met it with a low, hollow ding, and he hissed, recoiling.

Gawking at the conjured shield that blocked him from me, Lord Maxlian stood and stumbled back with a curse, "What the f—"

Nathalia screamed in a savage roar from across the room, "Keep your fucking hands off my charge!"

Drained both physically and mentally, my eyelids shut as my head fell back against the wall behind me with a dull *thunk*. I couldn't see the look on her father's face, but I damn well heard his sputtering choke. "I beg your pardon?"

Rapid, heavy footsteps came toward me, presumably Nathalia storming closer to us. "You heard me, Father. Get away from him right now."

"Your...your charge? *Your charge?* Did I hear you right? This-this-this... His fa—" Lord Maxlian stuttered, sputtering. "He's a-a-a..."

Nathalia's calm answer was a line in the sand that would yield for none, not even a beloved and respected hero. "A good man, Father. He's a *good man*. If you attempt to harm him again, I will defend him, and you know to what degree. This is your only warning."

With my eyes still shut, I couldn't see anyone's body language or facial expressions. With my nose still broken, I couldn't smell emotions. I relied on my ears, but there was a heavy pause where no one said a word.

After a few seconds, I heard soft footsteps and small, gentle hands on either side of my face that definitely weren't Nathalia's. I cracked my eyes open to see Raewyn murmuring prayers to Minue, Nathalia behind her, facing away from me with a rigidly straight spine.

The pain in my face and skull gradually lessened, then disappeared entirely as Raewyn's prayers were answered. The combined smells of blood, fresh mud, cut grass, and acrid smoke hit me at once and churned my stomach before I had the wherewithal to breathe through my mouth.

I thanked her as she helped me stand, finding Lord Maxlian and Lady Nathalia staring at each other in a silent deadlock. His furious eyes screamed with impotent rage as they moved from her to me. He scoffed bitterly. "Be grateful I promised, Ramiren. You don't deserve her."

I know.

He turned heel and departed, a few broken white feathers floating to the floor.

We all watched him leave before Nathalia looked over her shoulder at me. Her sorrowful eyes whispered apologies and regret. "Are you all right?"

I gave a small nod and moved to throw the ruined handkerchief into the hearth. "I am, thank you." My gaze swept the room, and I spotted my glasses underneath a plush chair. I shifted the fabric of my trousers' legs as I crouched down to grab them.

"So," Raewyn drawled. "When are you two getting married?"

My throat closed. I couldn't have responded, even if I wanted to, so I busied myself with inspecting my glasses for damage. They repaired themselves via the enchantment put into them, but the two ladies with me didn't know that.

Thankfully, Nathalia did reply. "We're not getting married, Raewyn."

"But your plans." Raewyn screwed her face with a tilted head as though what her sister had said wasn't logical at all.

And I understood why, because it *wasn't* logical.

Nathalia shook her head and shrugged casually. "Plans change, Raewyn."

Raewyn snorted. "Uh. Yeah. Sure. *Yours* don't, though. You've been talking about your charge being your husband for, what, over a decade now?"

Though Nathalia had assured me she had no expectations toward me, cold guilt flooded my veins instead of warm blood. It reached my heart in one beat, causing the organ to ache even worse than my nose had minutes before.

Intellectually, I knew it wasn't my fault. At least, not entirely. Many things, including unintended circumstances and long-game schemes, had come together to put us in this position. We were doing the best we could with what we had.

Still, the guilt lingered as I pushed my glasses up onto my healed nose.

I could never give her the life she had longed for because pactmakers did not marry.

Nathalia responded in a tone that would brook no argument. "Yes, well. My plans did."

Raewyn picked up a leftover glass of red wine and downed the rest of the liquid as Kaleb rejoined us, Lady Resa trailing behind.

The matriarch of the Swordhand family looked me up and down and grinned brightly. When she rushed at me, I instinctively checked to see if she had an axe in hand before the woman swept me up in a tight hug.

Normally, I despised hugs. A childhood and early adulthood spent being suspicious of pickpockets and wary of knives in the dark made me paranoid about close, unguarded proximity to another. Before, I'd only accept an embrace from my mother. Then Dredon and Nathalia. People I trusted, or had trusted, with my life.

Even lovers would need to be unclothed completely before I'd get too close. Based upon the inexplicable but undeniable contentment I'd felt immediately upon meeting her, that Dredon had confirmed was not any kind of charm or compulsion magic, Nathalia had been the only exception.

But this? This felt...nice. "I knew I had a good feeling about you," Lady Resa whispered into my ear before letting me go.

At least you weren't gutted.

Where have you been?

It's bad form to talk at the theater.

Chapter Six
The Ghost of Proposals Past

There was a great deal of concern when we rode to the marquis tent set up right outside Rowin's gates. Not just due to the nature of our meeting or the fact that all parties had to arrive unarmed, but because we were beyond the wards protecting the city, and by extension Nathalia and me, from devils.

The fact that the ward had been provided by the same realm now armed and armored and standing ready to besiege at a moment's notice was not lost on me. However, I saw no need to worry.

There'd be no reason for them to remove the barrier, as any marauding devils who realized the ward was down would wreck the city and their own due to the mirrored nature of Laeth and the Feylands.

In a straight line, equal distance between them, stood five siege towers, or belfries as they were apparently called, all tall enough to allow enemy soldiers past the thick, tall walls of Camlynn's capital city. Fey of various types and sizes were arranged in neat files twenty deep and ten across. I quickly counted the number of...boxes? Units?

Twenty-five units of enemy soldiers.

A large but simple calculation. Let's see. That's twenty mult—

"Five thousand troops," Nathalia whispered, looking over the same field that I was.

Oh, all right. Well, if you don't take her, then I will. There's nothing more attractive than a woman doing math.

You too, Dre?

I murmured to her, "You did that in your head?"

My service ends after a century, and I'm almost halfway through. Think she'd wait for me?

I knew. I *knew* my bastard pact vizier was trying to goad me.

And, frankly, it worked, because my hackles rose like I was an angry tomcat guarding its mate. But she wasn't my mate, and I had to remind myself *yet again* that I had no right to be jealous.

As a reply, Dre's dark chuckle held a hint of mockery.

Nathalia smiled sheepishly at me, as though not realizing she'd been overheard. "I have a good head for numbers."

"You have a good head for many things, my dear," I whispered in response and tried to distract myself by keeping watch.

With my eyes sweeping the area for both the threat of fey violence and the magical signatures indicating a devil under my father's command was inbound via whistle, we dismounted and handed the horses' reins off to waiting pages.

The same four who had been called before the Camlite queen the day before—me, Nathalia, and her parents—stepped through the tent's open flaps, Lady Resa and Lord Maxlian ahead of me. Nathalia, as always, took up the rear. She was arguably the most important piece of this chess game, but she still didn't like leaving my back unguarded, a habit I had noticed and appreciated when traveling the Feylands with her and three others.

It had been a very long time since I didn't have to worry about being caught unaware, all thanks to her. Her vigilance made me as fiercely protective of her as she was of me, hence why I continued scanning the tent's interior for anything that could harm her.

It may not have been my job, but it *was* my privilege.

A shadow darkened the tent's other opening on the far end as Prince Jaylin of Wistran walked through and stopped short upon spotting our party. His eyes snapped to the woman half hidden by my body, and I instinctively shifted in front of her to intercept his gaze. With a smile, I bowed slightly. "Prince Jaylin, it has been a while. I hope you're well."

With a snap of my fingers, my pact ledger appeared in a puff of purple smoke. I opted not to have it make a dramatic entrance with a bird's call, a flash of flame, or the smell of sulfur, though I was tempted to see Prince Jaylin spooked by magical theatrics.

The prince's eyes narrowed as his father, King Torin, shuffled forward beside his son. He was bent over a staff, and his golden hair had long since turned gray and wispy. His stooped posture and the cloudy film covering his irises were as I remembered from our introduction to him just over a month ago. Behind me, Lady Resa gasped softly.

"King Torin, peace and blessings upon you." Lord Maxlian bowed, his expression stony. "You have...changed since we last saw you nigh thirty years ago."

"Eh? Oh. Have I?" The king looked at his son for confirmation, which Prince Jaylin did not deign to give. The king squinted at us. "Who are you? Where are my glasses?" He began patting at his robes with liver-spotted hands.

We all introduced ourselves, though Lady Resa did so looking far more pale than her olive skin should have been capable of.

The king was still looking through his pockets when Prince Jaylin turned his full attention to us and spoke curtly, "Now that these blasted niceties are out of the way, let's talk about compensation for the pain and suffering Lady Nathalia has caused, not only to the fey realm of Wistran, but also to me."

I smelled acrid smoke billowing from Prince Jaylin and smiled, realizing what it meant, but I kept that information to myself.

Lord Maxlian raised an eyebrow. "Pain and suffering? Isn't that a tad dramatic, Highness?"

Prince Jaylin had the audacity to give an unconcerned shrug. "Call it what you will, my lord. I granted her a place at my court and was publicly snubbed. It is a black mark on not only my name, but my family's as well. That demands recompense."

Thousands of years of fey culture, learning, and pride, only to produce that man. I would be embarrassed if I were fey instead of an elf.

Agreed.

Nathalia stepped around me. Her face held nothing but poorly disguised contempt. I couldn't blame her for being unable to keep it in check. The man before us was putting on the equivalent of a boy's temper tantrum, and it was most certainly a performance, based upon the fear rolling off him in waves. "What do you want, Prince Jaylin?"

"Ah, a good question, Lady Nathalia," he replied coolly. He eyed her up and down like he had the right to and smiled crookedly. "Perhaps you believe I want you returned? That you expect me to say *you*?" He clicked his tongue thrice in disapproval. "But that's not the case, I assure you. As far as I'm concerned, you're a spoiled commodity, and I mean that in *every* way possible. No, what I want is for you to suffer just as I have."

It took a few seconds for Dredon to start laughing through our link, as though he had been shocked into momentary silence. In fact, Dre was the only one in our party to have any kind of verbal response. Everyone else simply stared at him quietly.

When his words didn't have their intended effect, Jaylin scowled, shifting his weight back and forth on his feet.

There was another moment of silence before I waved a hand at him, urging him to elaborate as though coaxing a child to further develop their idea. "And how would you go about doing that?"

"By eliminating everyone in this city, down to the waifs, whores, and gutter rats."

Nathalia scoffed, then let out a small derisive laugh. "Your army couldn't even destroy one hag. What makes you think you could take Rowin, especially without damaging anything?"

I had my suspicions, unconfirmed as they were, that Prince Jaylin was not entirely innocent with regard to the attempted assault on the mischief hag who had taken up residence in Carpatha. With the many unanswered questions surrounding him, Leraska, and his mother, I kept a lookout for hints, indications about what was really going on with the unlikely trio.

I again peered at Prince Jaylin through my red-tinged glasses, finding the same bits of small magic glowing about his person, from his sword to the single ring on his left hand, that I'd seen upon first meeting him. The king still didn't possess even a single magical signature, and I tucked that bit of information away as well.

The two women who had accompanied Jaylin and his father, on the other hand, practically radiated magic. The strong aura surrounding Leraska, with her druidic abilities, made sense. The overly powerful illusion-based magic around Queen Milanda of Wistran's face and scattered about her person could have been from keeping her wrinkles hidden and her figure trim, as I initially believed, which was not an uncommon occurrence among vain royals.

I knew I was missing something. I just didn't know what, exactly.

You know, I wonder what Queen Milanda looks like with the illusions removed. She must have the jowl of an old hound with the strength of magic she uses.

Prince Jaylin chuckled softly in response to Nathalia's question regarding his army's capabilities. "Your army is out of position, and you're at the cusp of the harvest season. An important time for winter stores, which will be needed to withstand a siege. Your ripe fields will burn as we keep the city choked and cut off." With a mocking grin that spoke volumes about how clever he thought he was, he continued, "Why do you think we waited so long?"

But the disgusting smell of acrid smoke belied his words.

Then a nagging thought, prompted by Dre's musings, popped into my mind and latched on like a dog with a bone.

Perhaps Queen Milanda was disguising more than just a few wrinkles. Perhaps her true appearance? Her full *appearance?*

The pieces on my mental chess board moved, rendering such sudden and startling clarity that my heart went into my throat.

Oh, shit.

Oh, shit is right.

Lord Maxlian opened his mouth to reply angrily when I cleared my throat. He obviously hadn't forgotten our tussle from the previous day, given the glower on his face as he looked at me, but I hoped he also knew me well enough to realize I wouldn't cut in without cause.

When he nodded for me to go ahead, I faced Prince Jaylin. "Our deepest apologies, Highness, but I believe any negotiations should be discussed with Her Majesty, Queen Milanda, also in attendance. Should we expect her presence soon?"

A twitch at the corner of Prince Jaylin's right eye, barely perceptible, gave me more information than he had probably intended. "Regretfully, my mother is indisposed and will not be joining us. My father and I are perfectly capable of handling the surrender of Rowin."

"Mmm. I see. I see. Shame she had something more important to do than be present for the cessation of hostilities between allied realms. With her unfortunate absence, I'm afraid we cannot continue here. Good day, Highnesses."

Prince Jaylin stepped forward, nearly stumbling into his father. "Your own queen isn't even here. No royals are present on your side, only their general." He lifted his chin in Lord Maxlian's direction. "Why can your queen be absent, but not ours?"

Since my placid smile seemed to perpetually anger him, I kept it on. "Simple, Highness. Our queen is not an aggrieved claimant. Yours, however, is. It was her family you feel was insulted by Lady Nathalia's smart run from the altar, not Queen Uldanna's. To address all issues, all affected individuals must be present for mediation. What's to stop Queen Milanda from coming to us later, demanding additional tribute not accounted for in this dialogue? It would be a hanging thread that Queen Uldanna will not accept."

Prince Jaylin's annoyed frown grew deeper the longer I talked. When I was finished, he hissed. "Her *smart* run? We have an army outside Rowin's walls, ready to strike. Do you really think it's wise to say something like that to me?"

With a feral grin, I replied, "Apologies, Highness. Smart also means 'quick.' She did run quite swiftly from you, yes? Now please inform the gate guards once your mother shows her *enchanting* face, and we can continue discussing the peaceful end to this conflict."

I turned to leave, intentionally giving Prince Jaylin my back, and as I expected, the royal prick railed at us between gritted teeth, "Surrender! That is your *only viable option*." Though entirely invisible to the naked eye, the smoke smell of fear was damn near choking.

I went to dismiss my pact ledger when Lady Resa's hand on my arm stopped me. Addressing King Torin, she asked, "What is the current condition of the Twin Sphere that was entrusted to your realm, Your Majesty?"

Before Prince Jaylin could silence him or remove him from the tent, King Torin answered in confusion, "What? Twin Sphere? I don't recall a Twin Sphere." Lord Maxlian and Lady Resa shared a silent exchange, and the acrid smoke scent in the tent somehow doubled.

The king rambled as Prince Jaylin quickly herded him out, "I recall twins once, *big-breasted* girls who giggled. Their tits looked like spheres..."

Lady Resa looked at my pact ledger, then me. "You got that down, right?"

We went straight to Castle Rowin to report to Queen Uldanna what had transpired at the initial meeting. The streets were eerily empty, aside from messengers scurrying about, drunks entering taverns that couldn't afford to close, and patrols of Camlite foot soldiers ensuring that if any Wistran aggressors set foot inside the walls, they would soon regret their decision.

We met the queen in her throne room, as before, standing in front of the dais, as before. The queen sat upon the surprisingly simple chair, made comfortable with soft cushions. "Report, High General."

Lord Maxlian stood at attention. After sending a look at Nathalia, he began. "Five thousand soldiers confirmed. Prince Jaylin and King Torin were in attendance for the negotiations, but Queen Milanda was not, so talks have stalled."

Queen Uldanna waved over an approaching attendant in livery who carried a filled glass on a silver tray. She took the glass and waved the man away, and he promptly bowed and departed. "Stalled, you say?"

Lord Maxlian gave a single nod. "Yes, Your Majesty."

The queen huffed, then took a sip. "And what of your irresponsible daughter's situation? Did they indicate this matter could be put to rest by her surrender?"

Lady Resa answered, shifting her weight from one foot to the other. "No. The prince told us he didn't want her. He demanded Camlynn's surrender."

The queen tapped her cane hard on the quartz, chips flying and divots joining the many already gouged in the flooring at her feet. "Demanded, did he?" The queen narrowed her eyes in thought. "Troops and towers at my gate. A scorned prince willing to lay siege to an allied realm but who doesn't want the woman who broke his heart, even to punish." She frowned deeply. "After you left, I attempted communications with Queen Milanda. She and I have a friendly history, and I'd hoped she'd have a way to rein in her wayward pup. But she didn't answer me." She tapped her cane again and stood. "Something stinks, and it's not the other throne I sit on daily."

Lady Resa glanced at me and stepped forward. "Something happened during the negotiations, Your Majesty. I asked King Torin about the Twin Sphere in his realm's care." She met my eyes again and nodded, indicating for me to show and tell. "He claimed no knowledge or memory of it."

Queen Uldanna turned so fast that the liquor in her glass sloshed out. She stared at Lady Resa. "I beg your gods-damned pardon?"

I conjured my pact ledger, willing it to show the previous record. "It's true, Your Majesty. I have the transcript here. It's at the bottom."

Queen Uldanna moved with surprising swiftness to see our evidence. Scanning the full record, her face went from vaguely annoyed to pink with anger. With an outraged whisper, she muttered, "That daft, bloody bastard." With a nod to me to dispel the ledger, she looked at us. "Anything else? I want everything brought to light. Leave nothing out."

With the full understanding of what exactly I was about to relay, my reply was confident and unwavering, "Yes. I have reason to suspect that Queen Milanda and Leraska, the druid who assisted us and set us on the path of the mischief hags, are the same person."

Nathalia, Lady Resa, and Lord Maxlian snapped their heads to me. Nathalia's lips parted in wordless shock.

I continued, "Queen Milanda has very strong illusion magic about her person. I initially believed this to be merely cosmetic, but now I believe she's actually disguising her true appearance. I don't yet know why. When I observed Prince Jaylin and Leraska interacting prior to our escape from the Feylands, their familiarity with each other seemed beyond acquaintance or even friendship. She touched him freely, more than would have been proper for a royal and his subject. He leaned on her for comfort when he was angry. There's something there."

The queen mused, lifting her glass to her downturned mouth, "Maybe they're lovers?"

With a shake of my head, I answered her. "Doubtful. This seemed more familial than romantic. No kisses except for upon his brow or her cheek. Their hand placements and body language were appropriate for a mother and son conversing."

The queen grimaced, changing her grip on her cane in a fidget. "Most strange. Anything more?"

Nathalia whispered, "Yes. I have a question." She looked at her parents. "What are these Twin Spheres I keep hearing about?"

Lord Maxlian and Lady Resa looked to their queen, who appeared annoyed by the question but nodded in resignation. "Might as well tell them. Gods above, we'll all need whiskey for this conversation."

We were all settled into a comfortable and private sitting room with a tumbler of the promised whiskey when Lady Resa began.

"It started almost a year before you were born, Nat. We'd heard a powerful fey druid known as K'sar had begun a campaign of destruction throughout Laeth. Her movements seemed random at first. She bounced around from place to place, stayed a few days, burned homes, murdered many, overgrew the surrounding flora until the area was choked and unlivable, then left. One of the rare survivors of her attacks reported she had questioned people about a set of relics called the Twin Spheres."

Lady Resa took a sip and put her whiskey down. "As K'sar hunted for this set, we did as well, not even fully understanding what they did until Kesseth found the place where they had been crafted. There were pages of schematics, magical formulas that took many scholars to understand. When we realized what the Twin Spheres did, we doubled our efforts."

My knowledge of the elf Kesseth was fragmented and more based on legend than fact. An ancient mage more interested in books than people, he'd provided his services to Lady Resa and Lord Maxlian before retiring to parts unknown.

She sighed, flicking her eyes at Lord Maxlian in an indication for him to take over. He lifted his wife's hand and kissed her knuckles. "The Twin Spheres were made long ago by vindictive fey druids, full of venom and spite that their beloved forests could be destroyed at a moment's notice by a Laethi builder. I'm sure you know that the Feylands mirror Laeth?"

Nathalia and I nodded as Queen Uldanna refilled her glass.

"There is a reason for that. Laeth was, at one time, fracturing. Dying. No one knew how or why. Earthquakes, violent storms, and decay rattled Laeth until Worin of the Lorindar finally figured it out. Laeth is a living land. It has a soul, you see, much like a person does, and the God of Destruction realized that soul was slowly deteriorating, fading to nothing." Lord Maxlian downed his glass and held it out for Queen Uldanna to refill it, which she did with an unladylike snort.

"A balance exists between the two pantheons, beyond their opposing domains. The Tarindar create souls, and the Lorindar possess what is called a soul mirror." Lord Maxlian rubbed a hand over his mouth, as though considering his next words. "Should a soul begin to deteriorate, for whatever reason, the Lorindar can hold that mirror up and create a companion soul. The companion soul acts as a healing anchor, a comfort, to the original, to bring it back from the brink of annihilation. That's why what happens to Laeth affects the Feylands, but not the reverse. The Feylands were created from Laeth. What affects the original affects the companion."

For some reason, an overwhelming, foreboding chill ran up my spine, but I chalked that up to the new information and heavy subject matter. The impression on my mental painting's surface continued to become clearer, and I focused on figuring out how everything fit together. There had to be a logic to it, a rational and quantifiable reason that events spanning eons were linked.

Nathalia asked, "And the Twin Spheres?"

Queen Uldanna muttered into her glass, "Would flip the anchor so Laeth would be affected by the Feylands and not the other way around. At least, that's what one sphere does."

I prompted her by asking the next obvious question. "And the other?"

Lord Maxlian replied, "Nature would reign supreme. The cleared fields that grow our food, tidy villages filled with lively and welcoming folk, and progressive cities that allow for culture, art, and civilization to flourish would be overrun with vegetation and wild animals."

I slouched in my chair, my fingers tapping my jaw in thought. "If Wistran had one sphere, who has the other?"

Queen Uldanna cackled. "Camlynn does, and only three people know where it is."

Lady Resa leaned forward, elbows resting on her thighs as she weaved her fingers together. "We defeated K'sar and split the Twin Spheres up—one in Wistran and one in Camlynn—to greatly lessen the chance they'd be used. We tried destroying them, but we were unable. Even Kesseth couldn't figure it out."

Nathalia plucked at her sleeve as she addressed her parents. "Can you describe what the spheres look like?"

"They're round," Queen Uldanna murmured.

Ha-ha. Funny. Rude, but funny.

Lord Maxlian shot a look at his queen, who smirked and shrugged petulantly before she elaborated. "They're each about the size of a grapefruit. Perfect spheres that glow golden when the two relics are together, signaling activation, blue when apart."

"Wait..." Nathalia's stunned face lifted to look at the queen. "Blue?" When Queen Uldanna confirmed with a nod, Nathalia covered her face with a tortured groan. "Oh gods... Oh fuck..."

At her distressed tone, I shot up in my chair and craned my head to see her lowered face. In a soft voice, I asked, "What's wrong?"

For me, it's the depressing lack of hazelnuts.

Lowering her hands, her face pale as moonlight, she replied while looking at everyone in turn, "In Leraska's grove, there's a hedge maze. At the center, I saw a glowing blue orb, roughly the size of a child's toy ball." Her eyes lifted to me, horror-struck. "Leraska has the Wistran relic, and that's why she's here. To claim the second. This isn't an attack; it's a diversion."

The painting became clearer still, sketched lines filling in with color until the blurry and incomplete picture took shape. I ran a hand through my wind-tangled hair and tugged on it. "Leraska indicated to us that she'd had something stolen from her. We initially believed it was an ability the hags took and stored, but there was no vial with her name on it. What if the thing stolen was the Twin Spheres? What if Leraska *and* Queen Milanda *and* K'sar are one and the same?"

Chapter Seven
When Art Imitates Life

After sending a message to Raewyn to watch over Kaleb and Tilla, we got to work. The long night was spent in discussion, heads bent over scattered parchment copies of the agreement between the fey realm of Wistran and the Laethi realm of Camlynn.

When Lord Maxlian asked if Queen Uldanna planned to move the Twin Sphere in her possession, she replied in the negative, insisting it was safe enough.

The queen offered the four of us apartments in the guest wing, as it was well past moonrise by the time our stiff necks and strained eyes demanded we stop to rest. A firm strategy to stop this poised conflict would need to wait until sunrise.

My room stayed comfortably warm, the flickering fire in the large and ornate fireplace against the far wall casting countless shifting shadows on the floor in front of the hearth. A waist-high stack of dried wood in an iron basket had been provided to keep the fire going.

A carved cherrywood desk sat between the tall windows that let in the silvery light of a three-quarter moon. The bed felt cloudlike and soft beneath me, the sheets silky. Yet my head lay heavy on the downy pillow, and I couldn't fall asleep.

I watched the shadow of the window's grilles slide across the floor as minutes blurred and blended together. I had no idea what time it was when there was a soft knock at my door, followed by Nathalia's voice. "Are you awake?"

I suppose she can't sleep either.

I know what's going to happen, and I'm not staying to watch.

Good work today, Dre.

See you later, procrastinator.

I realized I hadn't answered her when she spoke again through the door, "Ramiren?"

"Oh. Um. Yes. Sorry. I'm awake. Please, come in."

Moonlight caught the pale green door as it opened and almost immediately closed with a slight *click*. Though the fire and the windows provided little light, I could see her clearly in the dim room. Her dove-gray shirt, the stretched collar hanging off one shoulder, reached to her mid-thighs. Long, bed-mussed hair flowed in tangled waves to the tops of her breasts. She hugged herself as though cold, stepping forward.

She was lovely at the worst of times, sleep-hazed at dawn or even dirty from travel. In fact, I found it extremely endearing when this fastidious woman became filthy.

But this was the best of times. When she stepped into the light streaming in through the windows, her hair turned molten, refracting the light like tiny prisms. Even the unremarkable ashen shirt she'd worn to bed had turned into something captivating as the pale fabric turned sheer, showing shadowy curves I wanted to run my hands over.

She flopped onto her back at the foot of the bed with a soft huff, staring at the ceiling. The current of air from the movement pushed her clean scent toward me, as well as the sweet smell of honey.

Dre was right to leave.

I fussed with my pillows so I could lean back against the headboard. "You can't sleep either, hm?"

"Not at all."

With a nudge of my foot from under the covers, I smiled and patted the bed to my right. "Come here."

She rolled to her hands and knees to crawl over me, and a throb shot through my cock and balls simultaneously. I froze, trying to tame my groan before sliding down to lie next to her. We turned to face each other, and she stole a pillow and grinned at me. "Just like your tent in Tanta," she whispered.

My reply was at a normal volume, "Except you don't have to whisper here. I doubt Raewyn can hear us—"

Nathalia choked, putting her fingertips against my mouth to silence me. She whispered harshly, "Shh! My family isn't that far away."

I grinned mischievously against her fingers, then snapped my mouth open to capture the tip of one in my mouth. Careful of my canines, I let my teeth gently catch her index finger. She squeaked but didn't pull back.

Closing my lips over it, I gave the lucky tip two sucks before letting it go. "There's a place we can go and be as loud as we'd like. Do you consent?"

With her nod, I snapped my fingers. The transition to my pact room was as comfortable and familiar as slipping on a pair of old boots, and I had done it hundreds of times before. Sometimes it was nothing more than a simple room with just a table and chairs. That took but a moment to make.

Comfortable and complex rooms, such as for the pact between Nathalia and me, were far more difficult to construct, even with Dredon's assistance. But some deep part of me had felt it was important to get this *particular* pact room right, and I was consciously ignorant as to why.

I realized there was something powerful and almost reverential about this place, though I had barely changed it since our first lesson here, even if it took a mere thought to change details. It had been purposefully made to mimic the Forever Inn's room where we made our initial agreement, and it held more than a few good memories for me.

We were now standing before each other. Honey perfumed the air as she finally saw I had been sleeping nude. Her eyes ate me up, and I became lightheaded from the rapid movement of blood going south. Reaching toward me, she brushed her cool fingers along the outside of my hips and slid them with a teasing pace to wrap around my swollen shaft.

I inhaled sharply from the burst of ecstasy flooding my veins and thrust myself forward into her hand involuntarily, closing the distance between us.

She gave me a crooked grin and began to pump her hand up and down as she turned her attention to the room for her customary inspection of our surroundings.

Ignoring me.

Gods-damned maddening woman.

She was the picture of nonchalance as my knees nearly gave out from her perfect grip and slightly rough palms. A pulsating throb, beginning in my balls and shooting to the tip in time with my increasing pulse, made me hiss a breath through my teeth. The pleasure of her touch, combined with her casual attitude, was a private game she seemed to enjoy playing.

I leaned in, my harsh breathing stirring her hair as I murmured near the shell of her ear, "Careful, angel. Tease me at your own risk." I glided my hand up her arm, under the sleeve of the sleep shirt she wore, and felt goose bumps forming. "Or are you doing it on purpose?"

The painting behind her has to go.

She smirked without even deigning to look at me. "I haven't decided yet." Nathalia peered behind her, finding the erotic painting that had been Dre's idea gone and the wall now bare. "Wait, there's a painting miss— OH!"

Nathalia released my cock, and her arms wrapped around my neck as I hooked my fingers under her thighs to lift her. She was no delicate flower, but she might as well have been with how light she felt in my hands.

Her soft thighs wrapped around my waist, and she hooked her ankles together without prompting as I walked her to the bare wall and pressed her back against it. Her dilated eyes widened as she realized what I had in mind with her body caged.

Her full breasts pushed against my chest, and her bare pussy butted up against my hard cock. I bit my lip to keep from moaning. She didn't keep her own moan in check as the back of her head thudded against the wall.

She looked at me with half-lidded eyes. "C-Can you do this? Hold me up?"

I rolled my hips to massage her clit with the underside of my cock, skin slipping against skin easily with how wet she was. My tongue ached to taste her, to take my time, but there was a needy animal in my head screaming at me to take and corrupt. It was impossible to ignore. "Easily. Now hush. The only words I want to hear out of you now are 'please,' 'more,' and 'harder.'"

I lifted her a tad higher as I angled myself to her entrance. The compulsion to sink into her lush body rode me hard, but I refused to relent to the whims of instinct.

With one arm under her and my body keeping her aloft, my free hand reached between us. I rolled the pad of my thumb over her clit in a slow circle, just as she liked, and a sweet peach blush ran from her neck down her chest. Her hips lifted to get closer to my touch, and I leaned in to run my canines over the side of her neck. I sighed, flicking my tongue along her pulse. "Greedy girl." Drawing her lower lip between my teeth, I bit down with a quick, hard nibble that made her inhale, and my tongue invaded to swipe over hers hungrily.

I almost snapped when she bit my lip in return, and her long, low groan was music to my ears as I slowly entered her. It never failed to take my breath and deny my lungs any air. Though she was soaked, I had to go easy. At least initially.

Her arms and legs constricted, and her short nails managed to find purchase in my shoulders. Their sharp bite went straight to my cock, and I slipped in a bit more.

She broke our kiss to groan out, "More." Her hips wiggled impatiently, and I sank an inch more. When I continued my slow plunge, her groan turned into a soft whine.

Her pussy pulsed, and a streak of lightning lit up my spine. Pushing in another slow inch, I grinned and nipped her shoulder. "Patience."

She opened her golden eyes, beautifully lust-drunk, and I saw calculation there. Without warning, her arms and legs partially released me. Instinctively, I tried to catch her with both hands and by pressing her into the wall with my body. That action made the last few remaining inches of my cock slam into her, and I had to clench my jaw to keep from shouting at the sudden rush of pleasure now boiling my blood. My fingers bit into her thighs, and I was beyond caring if marks were left.

The animal in my head *purred*.

Nathalia shrieked and then shuddered as her pussy clenched around me. With my hips fully flush with hers, I felt her everywhere. On my cock. Under my skin. In the marrow of my bones.

It took a few fast breaths to regain the frayed threads of control I still had left, and a low rumble vibrated out of my chest. "That...was naughty."

The smug defiance in her hazy eyes made those frail threads snap completely.

My rasping exhale fanned over her hair as I gritted out, "Fine. Maybe you *do* need the brat fucked out of you." I pulled out to the tip and drove back into her, and she choked on a satisfied whine. I did it again, swiveling my hips, and her arms and legs tightened even more.

My face pressed into her neck, teasing the skin with my teeth and tongue as I plunged into her again and again. She lifted her face and whimpered 'more' and 'please' as close to my ear as she could. A familiar tingling sensation started at the base of my spine, and I was lost to her cries and sobs.

I could feel my canines elongating, and the rabid beast howling at me to bite her nearly drowned out her scream as she came.

Not without her permission.

I did, however, mourn my current inability to devour her tangy and decadent essence. Her taste was most delicious when she came.

The enraged creature, defied yet again, snarled, but I ignored it as my vision whitened with starbursts. Every muscle in my body tensed, and my hips stuttered in their rhythm as my ecstasy peaked. With a wheezing cry, I emptied myself inside her still-pulsating pussy, as though it was coaxing everything I had out of me.

I eased her feet to the floor while we tried to catch our breath. My forehead found hers as my racing heart calmed. Eventually, her voice broke the long silence. "I don't think it worked. I still feel bratty."

A soft laugh bubbled out of me as I wrapped my arms around her waist. "I can help with that in a bit. I want you too spent to have an attitude."

She nuzzled the base of my throat with her nose. "Yes. One of your many talents." She hummed and kissed my collarbone. That simple act made me semi-hard again.

Gods above, this woman.

I chucked her under her chin and smiled gently. "And yours are apparently sword fighting, mathematics, and exasperating my cock."

She tilted her head back and closed her eyes in contentment. The look of naked bliss on her face made me want to capture the moment somehow. I feared my memory would be insufficient to hold the vision before me for the rest of my long life, if the worst should happen.

Maybe this would be a good time to start again.

My lips brushed her cheek as I whispered, "Do you want to know what else I have a talent for?"

"Mm? What's that?"

I pointed at the floor with what I hoped was a serious look on my face. "Stay right here."

Going to the side room that was filled with bookshelves and chairs, I opened a small table chest. Plucking the item I wanted from it, I returned to find her just as I'd left her with a perplexed look on her face.

Stepping closer, I met her eyes. Lifting my right hand, which held a stick of charcoal, I stared down at it as though wary it would bite. “I haven’t done this in a very long time. I wanted to, for you, but I never tried.”

“Charcoal? You want to draw me?” Nathalia appeared delighted as she glanced at the dark gray stick in my hand, then frowned with a tilt of her head. “But why haven’t you?”

With complete seriousness, I replied, “Because I was afraid I couldn’t do it right.”

An amused smirk curled her lips, and she crossed her arms. “Right? Like you’d make my nose too big?”

I chuckled sheepishly, running my fingertips from her soft cheekbone to her jaw. “No, because I only do charcoal drawings. Black and some shade of beige, based on the parchment used. Just black and beige. Colorless. But you? You’re all color. Peach skin. The tiny freckles on the bridge of your nose, especially after the Tanta Desert. An alluring apricot color when you blush.”

My eyes had mapped her lovely features countless times. The lines, angles, and planes that made up her sweet face were already a work of art, and I’d never thought my meager abilities would be enough.

I shook my head, sighing ruefully. “The real problem is your eye color. It doesn’t matter if I just use charcoal. There are no paints, pencils, or wax crayons that could capture the colors. Yes, plural. Gold leaf is closest, but that’s just gold. You have brown, green, and silver too. Even blue, but that only happens when you’ve been crying.” My lips thinned. “But not everything can be perfect, just a few rare things.”

I moved my hand from her face to tap the center of her chest, and she seemed confused as she looked down. “Are you referring to my breasts?”

With a toothy grin, I said, “Your heart, angel. But, yes, your breasts too.” I kept my tone teasing, even if my words were serious. “Now hold still. And for the love of fuck, don’t distract me. This is going to be difficult enough as it is.”

With a long exhale to settle myself, I lifted my left hand and pressed the palm to the wall beside her head to partially cage her against the wall again. On the opposite side, I brought the charcoal to the bare wall, and, for the first time in eight years, I submitted to the ebb and flow of creation.

It started as wispy lines to guide the final piece. I soon realized that I was barely looking at my subject's face. I didn't need to. Though we had known each other for less than three months, a brief time in my already long life, my hands had charted her almost to the point of memorization. And what few inches remained of her that my hands hadn't touched, my eyes had.

Blessedly, she stayed completely still. I could feel her gaze on me like a tender caress, but she didn't move.

The faint outlines I'd made became bolder with each confident pass. Soon, her wide-set eyes appeared, followed by her nose that was ever-so-slightly crooked from past brawls. Her lips came next, pouty things that were red and swollen from my attention on them earlier.

Her hair was last. It was wonderfully wild, even more so than before, and I didn't attempt to make it neat. Fuck neat. She looked ravished, and I wanted to commemorate it.

When it was done, I lowered my hand, and the charcoal dropped to the floor with a *plink*.

All right, are you done yet? I—oh shit! You drew?

Yes. And yes.

I stepped back so she could turn around. Almost fearfully, she rotated to look at what I had rendered. After a long moment of anxiously awaiting her reaction, my heart attempting to break out from beneath my ribs, the smell of oranges diffused around us in a fragrant cloud. Without looking at me, she whispered, "This is what I look like to you?"

My heart finally granted me mercy and burst in a colorful spray of warmth and light. I gazed at the portrait I had created and shook my head with certainty. "No," I said huskily. "There's an unfortunately large divide that separates the limits of my ability and you, angel. I can try, but I'll never capture it."

She frowned at me over her shoulder. "Capture...it?"

I leaned in to kiss the top of her head, trying to think of a response.

Don't do it. Don't you do it. You'll ruin it.

My lips twitched against her soft hair as I thought of the perfect one. "You know, *your verrtu*."

Nathalia rolled her eyes.

Dredon muttered, ***You're hopeless.***

When I woke the next morning, it was to the sound of vague but panicked chatter outside my room. Silvery moonlight had been replaced by the pale glow of dawn, indicating only a few short hours had passed. Blurry-eyed with too little sleep, I stared at the door in confusion.

What the—

The three loud bangs and Nathalia's muffled yelling through my door awakened me fully. "Ramiren, wake up! Wistran didn't wait."

Chapter Eight
A Haunting Awareness

Something is wrong.

Maybe because we're in a city under siege? Or because you got roughly two hours of sleep after railing your—

What? No. Something else.

I couldn't put my finger on why my apprehension had spiked. The feeling rode me like a fading nightmare, leaving cold dread in its wake. Three siege towers stood tall against the walls of Rowin, ingress points where the Wistran army concentrated its assault. Two towers lay in ruins, one covered in burning oil after a Minuen priestess's well-placed bolt of fire and the other brought down by uneven ground.

The city was holding its own, even with its diminished defenses. Nathalia informed me it was far easier to defend a fortified place than to attack it, especially when the aggressor doesn't want to destroy buildings. I could that see with my own eyes; she was right.

Still, the dread persisted.

Lord Maxlian, as High General of Camlynn, had left to issue orders to lieutenants and marshal the soldiers and city guards still in Rowin. He'd been muttering as he left about the cowardice of an enemy attacking as harvest season approached, with most Camlite soldiers having already returned home to provide needed hands on family farms.

Lady Resa wanted to assist with the fighting, but her husband insisted she stay by his side. Their argument was uncomfortably heated until Lady Resa eventually, but grudgingly, relented when Queen Uldanna ordered them to remain together, with the reasoning that if Lady Resa died, her protector would have to follow.

Losing the realm's general, she'd pragmatically mentioned, was something we could ill afford.

We'd been instructed to refrain from participating in the initial attack. Nathalia was far too distinctive and tempting a target for the opposition, and it would be a blow to morale if the attacking force managed to capture or kill a coveted quarry.

Nathalia was equally as surly as her mother had been, but there was no resistance from her regarding the order to keep clear.

We were walking briskly back to the villa so that Nathalia could fully arm herself, should she be needed. Carriages had been forbidden on the streets once the fighting commenced, and our own horses were back in the villa's stables. The mounts we had borrowed the previous day to meet the Wistran king and prince were regrettably unavailable.

After our time in the Feylands, I'd become quite tired of walking, even with my comfortable boots, but there was nothing to be done about it.

Little conversation passed between us, and my gaze kept flicking toward the distant clash of weapons hitting weapons, screams of pain or rage, and the roar of commands given by stalwart leaders to their soldiers. I couldn't see the battle at all. The tops of inns and other buildings along the avenues we traveled blocked the view entirely, only showing occasional slivers of the solid city walls when we crossed Rowin's main thoroughfare.

The dread continued. I couldn't shake it from my mind. *What am I missing?*

You're right. There's something wrong.

I hate that you can confirm that.

Knowing and being unable to see is the worst sort of torture.

I couldn't argue against Dre's point. He was entirely right. This was a torment I'd have to figure out eventually, or I'd go mad.

We came through the villa's front door and were immediately accosted by Raewyn, Tilla, and Kaleb as they demanded to know what was happening.

Raewyn and Tilla doggedly followed Nathalia into her room to get my protector's account of the past day, while Kaleb went to his room.

I searched for my Extended Pouch, finding it under the bed for some reason. Surmising it must have fallen off the nightstand and gotten kicked, I reached under the bed's frame to grab it. I heard the bedroom door open and close. Figuring it was Nathalia, I called out, "Be right there. My pouch must've fallen."

In my position, I could only see boots, bigger than the ones Nathalia wore, as whoever it was moved to stand beside my crouched form.

Who i—

Kaleb's voice was monotonal. "So. You're fucking my sister, hmm?"

I jolted, and my head collided hard with the wooden frame of the bed.

Ha-Ha.

Cursing with a hiss, I rubbed at my scalp with one hand as I dragged my pouch out from under the bed with the other. Righting myself, I straightened to look up at Kaleb. He wasn't angry, a fact confirmed by the miasma of burned toast surrounding him. It was the scent of disappointment, and though a part of me understood the emotion, it still rankled.

"That's none of your business, Kaleb." I stood and looked through my pouch, mostly to have something to do other than look at his face, which no doubt held an expression that would lead to yet another altercation with a member of Nathalia's family.

My nose still smarted from the phantom pain caused by Lord Maxlian's fist. I didn't want to become intimately familiar with how well Lord Maxlian had trained his son in devastating right hooks.

Your shame has, time and again, made you into a coward.

I'm not ashamed. I just don't have time for this.

Did your mother make Denial your middle name? Sure seems that way.

Kaleb's clipped tone set my teeth on edge. "You're right. It's not really my business, but that's my sister you're sleeping with. My sister who protects you and expects nothing from you. She might be more of a fighter than I am, and I have no doubt you could beat me down if I went after you. I just hope you understand that, if you hurt her, it wouldn't stop me from trying. Again and again. I like you, Ramiren, but I only have to win once."

I finally lifted my eyes to look at the young man before me. He was good-natured, smart, and good-looking in a way that would break hearts left and right in a few short years. His tall and lanky frame, the same height as mine, bore the promise of solid strength to come. He was still at that age just before manhood filled out his body, so it wasn't the physical threat he presented that caused me to pause.

No. It was the fire in his golden eyes, so much like his sister's, that made me actually take a moment to consider what he'd said. He'd looked me right in the eye and warned me, not about being with Nathalia as his father had done, but about hurting his eldest sibling. He clearly understood, based on the set of his square jaw and the rigid set of his thin shoulders, that I could retaliate at any time for his words.

I liked Kaleb, and I enjoyed his company, but this showing had earned him my respect.

With a resolved sigh, I inclined my head in acknowledgment. "Understood. Please know that I'd rather eat my own heart than hurt her."

With a scowl, he countered, "So you love her, but you won't commit to her?"

Gods above, I love this kid.

Be quiet!

My mind instantly rebelled against his statement, and I shook my head, rubbing the back of my neck. "I didn't say that, and it's not that simple." When I turned to step around him, he moved into my path to stop me from leaving.

"Oh, I think it *is* that simple."

With a frustrated groan, I hung my head forward. "Kaleb..."

"What? What is it, Ramiren? Why can't you?"

My hand went to my forehead to rub at the throbbing headache now plaguing me, either from this conversation or the head injury I'd suffered a moment before. It was impossible to tell which was more aggravating. "It's not a simple thing, all right? There are many reasons, and one of them I can do absolutely nothing about. *Pactmakers don't marry.*"

With a head tilt that made him look even more like his sister, he raised a skeptical eyebrow. "Don't or *can't*?"

I shrugged with as much nonchalance as I could muster to disguise the fact that there was a rolling boil of anger and, for some reason, fear in my gut. "It's the same, regardless. The only thing pactmakers love more than making pacts is continuing the traditions of the profession. We go where the wind takes us, and that leaves little room for a family. Trust me, it's easier this way. For everyone involved."

"Easier for everyone, or just *you*?" He didn't try to physically stop me again as I moved to the door, but he did have one loud, parting remark. "That's bullshit, Ramiren!"

I jerked the doorknob in my hand and walked out as quickly as I could.

Perhaps it is bullshit, but it's the truth.

A haunting, prickling awareness made goose bumps erupt over my skin as I stalked down the hallway toward the foyer stairway. The combined scents of fear, anxiety, and anger caused my heart to skip a beat. My steps slowed as I attempted to pinpoint the exact cause, but I couldn't until I came to the top of the stairs and looked down.

Oh, shit. Oh, fuck. How?

Run!

I couldn't. I couldn't leave Nathalia, who stood with her two sisters already facing the five large devils blocking the front door in a half-moon formation.

And Nathalia couldn't leave at all.

Whistle her out?

No. She'd never leave her family.

I remembered the gray-skinned devil in the center of their curved line, and as his dark, gleaming eyes found me, it seemed he remembered me as well.

"Ramiren. It's been a while," he said in Infernal and greeted me with a bow.

"Eronis," I replied coolly as I began to descend the stairs.

He grinned widely, showing sharp, crooked teeth perpetually stained red.

Though none of the devils had moved to grab Nathalia, or her two sisters standing behind her, they were eyeing all three like starved men about to dine on a banquet.

Raewyn had placed a spitting-mad Tilla behind her, and her hand was clutching the Minuen symbol around her neck as though readying prayers. All three looked nervous, not only at the devils looming over them, but because they likely couldn't understand Infernal.

"Get out, or I'll gut you!" Tilla screamed, knives raised as she tried to get past her priestess sister.

Nathalia's shield was up, her new longsword in her hand as she swiveled her head to each devil, watching either for sudden movements or an attack that would kill everyone here except me. Even marked, if Nathalia perished in the ensuing fight, I doubt my father would be upset at only having me brought to him.

Knowing Nathalia wasn't the intended target for the second tracking mark produced from my devil's whistle muddled everything.

But that did give me an idea of a way to potentially get Nathalia out of this. "This woman was not meant to receive the mark. You may anger my father if you bring back the wrong one."

Eronis barked a short, mocking laugh. "A good try. I go by who is marked. Nothing more, and nothing less."

My feet ambled down another few steps, stalling the inevitable. "Rowin is warded. How did you get here?"

Eronis sucked on his teeth as though trying to extract the blood soaked into them. "Yes. Well. About that... It seems you've made some enemies who had a say in whether those wards remained intact. What's that old mortal saying? The enemy of my enemy is my associate, and all that?"

"Something like that." There was no Infernal word for friend. A fact I would've found funny under different circumstances.

I closed my eyes in stark realization of what that nagging feeling must have been.

The few glimpses of the wall I'd seen on the way here showed no green glow, and it was my fault I hadn't noticed it. *Leraska removed her wards. She must have cut a deal with them to take us off the board.*

This one likes to hear himself talk, so keep him talking. Get more details.

Descending a few more steps, I asked, "How'd you know we'd be here? Wards prevent tracking."

A few devils smirked, looking at each other as though their cleverness was something to be celebrated. Eronis replied, "Oh, a bit of chance combined with a bit of knowledge. This is her property." He pointed at Nathalia, and the almost overwhelming urge to break the offending finger off and shove it down his throat nearly cost me information. "We saw an opportunity and took it. We were told to take two others." He shrugged dramatically. "Not that we had time to search a city for angels and middle-aged women, but a very obliging half-elf in a comfortable tent outside the gates confirmed you were here too."

I stalled on the last step, hoping my face read as curious rather than furious. "And who would that be?"

"Fuck me, I don't remember *mortal names*. It's bad enough I have to remember *yours*. Dodsen? Dudley?" He waved his hand. "It doesn't matter. Now, are you going to come quietly or loudly?" He put his palms together, as though begging like a child. "We *crave* loudly."

Not Leraska, but Lord Dalson, the earl who tried and failed to smuggle us into the Wistran castle. It has to be.

That slimy motherf—

Nathalia bared her teeth in a challenging smile. "Let's move out to the street, hm? My mother wouldn't be thrilled about devil's blood ruining her floor."

My gaze and the gazes of the five devils present rested on Nathalia, all of us likely wondering the same thing.

Shit, can she understand Infernal?

As though it didn't matter in the slightest, or perhaps because he didn't want to address a lowly mortal woman, Eronis looked back at me. "So? What shall it be, Vrakus-spawn? Quiet or loud?"

My rapier was stowed in my pouch, so it would take me precious seconds to fish it out. Nathalia was capable and ready, as were Raewyn and even Tilla. But that wouldn't be enough. Not even close.

We were outnumbered and off keel. They would be torn to pieces.

It pained me to say the words, but I said them in Common as I descended the last step, "Stand down, Nathalia."

The consummate warrior, she never took her eyes off the devils before her, though her body language told me she'd heard my order.

Moving to her side, I placed a hand on her armored shoulder. "I said stand down. I'm sorry, but we have to go with them. Everyone in this house dies if we don't."

Raewyn pleaded, "Nat, don't."

Tilla echoed her sister. "Fight, Natty! We can take 'em!"

When Nathalia finally looked at me, the look in my eyes must have told her how serious I was. Her lips bunched and hardened, as though willing herself to stand firm against the tumult of emotions no doubt playing havoc within her.

I leaned in and whispered, "Please trust me."

After a few tense seconds of indecision, Nathalia lowered her sword and shield.

Behind me, the sound of feet quickly descending the stairs, followed by a confused and panicked, "What in Paqua's name is going on here?" told me Kaleb had finally found us.

Nathalia looked over my shoulder, and her eyes widened. "Kaleb, don't!"

Kaleb passed me in a rush, pushing air filled with the scent of decaying vegetation toward me. I lunged for him, but my hands came up empty. Before Kaleb could bring his fist up to deliver a blow, the devil to Eronis's right lashed out with a claw.

All three of his sisters screamed as Kaleb stumbled back, clutching his chest.

He fell to his back on the marble floor, showing the torn shirt and deep gouges in his flesh that were welling with far too much blood.

Eronis snatched Nathalia around her middle when she moved to attack, and the devil who'd hurt Kaleb grabbed me.

Before I could say a single word, all five devils whistled.

Chapter Nine
Blood in the Water

The heat of Gateway coated my skin like a heavy blanket the moment we arrived. Crimson lightning lit the sky, and the rumble of far-off volcanoes and moving landmasses crashing into one another was near deafening, broken only by the distant screams of those ill-fated enough to end up here.

The rocky ground was uneven, and I pitched forward slightly, though the devil still holding my arm kept me from tumbling. My mouth filled with saliva when my stomach rebelled in a nauseated roll. Though I wanted to close my eyes to relieve the tunnel vision, I didn't.

There was someone else with me who had no business being in this grotesque place, and I didn't want to lose sight of her.

Nathalia gave a shuddering cough into her free hand then a groan. She wheezed out, "Gods above. You...*Kaleb*." When she coughed harder, it might as well have shaken my own chest.

"No gods above, kiuro-spawn. Just below." Eronis grinned down at my protector as he let her go, dumping her at his feet. I moved to catch her, but the devil at my side jerked me back.

Eronis chuckled and spoke down to her in broken Common. "It good place, yes?" Her forehead was already slick with sweat, and her hair stuck to the sides of her reddened face.

I twisted and managed to shake off the one holding me, leveling Eronis with a glare. Pointing at his face, I gritted out, "Don't touch her again, Eronis."

The devil tried to restrain me again as Eronis went to pick up Nathalia, and I took the opportunity. My rage at the situation, at what my past actions had led to, at Nathalia being manhandled, I channeled all of it into my clenched fist. I took a step toward Eronis.

He was much taller than me but well within reach as he bent down. With a roar, I smashed my fist into his jaw, and the ensuing crunch filled me with an intense craving for another. He recoiled with a howl, and I advanced for another blow.

But by the time I'd taken another step, Eronis had recovered enough to lash out with his own fist. It kissed my cheekbone, and my head snapped to the side as my glasses flew off my face. I stumbled back but barely registered the pain.

Nathalia shot up to her feet and slashed at him with the sword still clutched in her hand, grunting with the effort. But the oppressive heat had made her sluggish and unsteady, and he moved out of the way easily.

Eronis's chuckle turned into a sharp laugh, but he didn't move to grab her again. "Fire. Devil like fire. Vrakus have fun." He ripped her sword away by grasping the blade and twisting. The sword's keen edge bit into his hand, and his black blood began to drip in a steady stream from his fingertips to the gravel below.

"I said don't touch h—"

Another devil went for her shield, but the second his claws touched the metal, they smoked and melted like a cheap candle. The devil recoiled and let out an animalistic scream. Gaping at his now blunted hands, he hissed in Common, "Bitch!"

A mocking laugh erupted from me. Lord Maxlian had mentioned his shield had been blessed. I'd never actually seen what a blessed item did to a devil, and I couldn't deny the satisfaction thrumming through me as the devil whimpered.

Stooping down to pick up my dropped glasses, throwing the devil off when he tried to snatch me yet again, I smirked. "Careful, Eronis," I said in Common, so I could be sure Nathalia understood. "You wouldn't want her shield to touch your pretty face now, would you?"

Eronis scowled, but he kept a careful distance from the blessed metal. "Waste time. Move. Go." He motioned a hand to the iron gates in front of us that were, even after all these years, still unable to be closed.

The devils herded us through, though the declawed devil clutched his hands to his broad chest like a precious babe. He glanced at the sickly pink-skinned devil beside him, his wolf-like head giving him the appearance of an ugly shaved dog, and murmured in Infernal. "They will come back, right?"

The pink devil answered with a shake of his head, "No. You're fucked."

It was the only comfort we would likely receive here.

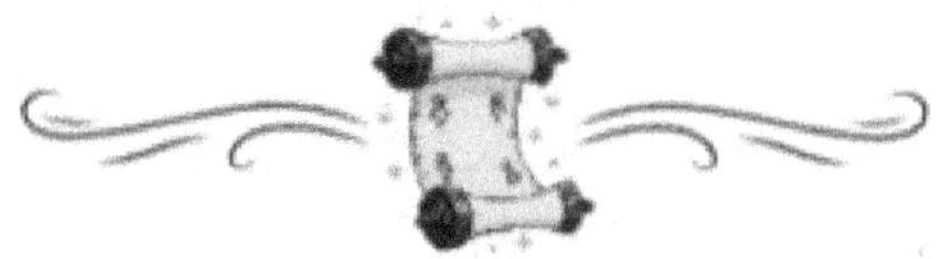

This place sure could use some color. Your father has abysmal taste. Get it? Abysmal?

Though Dredon's tone was light and amused, I detected an undercurrent of concern. I also knew that his concern was not for my sake, but for *her*.

Though Dre's initial reaction to Nathalia's oath to me had appeared to be one of distaste, I'd begun to understand it wasn't that at all. He liked her, and he, like Raewyn, hid what he was really feeling.

And right now, I'd place a wager on that feeling being abject terror.

I couldn't blame him, because I felt the same as we entered my father's throne room.

The perimeter of the hall was lined with Vrakus's various sycophants, at least three rows deep. Devils who served at my father's whim stood at attention like eager soldiers, just as he preferred. He fancied himself their king, not merely their general, and they did nothing to quash that delusion.

Vrakus, watching us enter with an exaggerated bored expression, sat back on his obnoxious gold throne, the inset red jewels barely twinkling in the dim blue-white firelight flickering from scones set into the glossy black walls.

No one here needed the illumination, except for Nathalia. He merely liked the effect.

We were pushed to the center, flanked by our captors, as a mocking murmur began to spread among the crowd gathered to witness my father's apparent triumph.

Only he didn't look triumphant. Under his disinterested gaze blazed indignation and anger, and I knew why.

He'd wanted my mother but got Nathalia instead.

Nathalia, back straight and chin lifted, wavered on her feet as she met my father's eyes. "You must be this Vrakus I've heard so much about."

Father grinned, throwing his hands wide as though to present himself for her inspection. He answered in perfect, albeit accented, Common. "And? Do I measure up to your standards?"

I recognized it for the poorly disguised trap it was. No doubt a common tactic he took with every wretched person brought here. They either cowered in fear, which gave him joy, or took the opportunity to insult him out of either pride or bravado, giving him an excuse to inflict maximum agony for the disrespect. Nothing my father did was ever his fault.

Nathalia ran her hand down her face and sighed as she wiped the gathered sweat off onto her thigh. With a soft huff, she replied, "You certainly leave an impression."

Her response brought a smile to my face.

Prevarication. A good tactic.

My father laughed, and the devils around us followed in kind, as though they'd awaited his permission. "Clever child. And my home? Do you like it?"

She glanced around warily. "A little warm for my taste." As if to underline her statement, she fanned the back of her neck with her ponytail.

Again, my father laughed. And again, the devils joined in.

His eyes finally settled on me. "Hello, Ramiren. It's been a while."

I closed my eyes, knowing this was the moment I destroyed the woman beside me. My secrets were about to be repaid, but with her tears, not mine. With a deep breath, resigned to my fate, I cursed Past Ramiren's inability to admit my actual relationship to the monster now before us. "Hello, Father."

Nathalia whispered, "What?"

I didn't want to look her in the eyes and see the betrayal there. But I needed to. I owed it to her to suffer with her.

When I turned, instead of betrayal, I saw confusion. Then realization crossed her features as my words sank in. A myriad of emotions followed, playing out on her face in quick succession. The air was too thick with smoke and sulfur to smell them, but I didn't need to. Her face was readable as an honest clerk's ledger.

Her lower lip wobbled, and she bit it to keep it still. The shame was too much to bear as agony rippled through my chest, radiating into limbs now heavy and torpid from the naked condemnation and anguish in her eyes. Droplets of moisture ran down her face, and I wasn't sure if it was sweat or tears.

A heavy heart clogged my throat. Before I could respond, my father did. His smooth voice held a chiding tone, "Why Ramiren, I'm shocked. You didn't tell her who I was?"

I knew my father was delighted by this, but I didn't care. I didn't even care about how blurry my vision was, except that it became harder to see her. I spoke to her, and only to her, "I'm sorry. I'm so very sorry."

Not bothering to wait for my confirmation, Vrakus continued as he stood from his throne and walked down the few steps from his dais. "Quite the predicament we find ourselves in, son." He called out as he continued to approach us. "Ravik!"

My attention left Nathalia to see the crowd to my right parting, and Ravik stepped into view, looking mournful. He nodded to me, murmuring, "Brother," and went to stand behind our father as the arch-devil stopped in front of Nathalia and me.

Under her breath, Nathalia muttered, "A brother too?" She barely managed to stifle a whimper, the noise coming out as a soft grunt instead.

Vrakus inspected Nathalia from head to toe like she was a piece of artwork, tutting at the shield still strapped to her arm. "Why wasn't her shield removed?"

Eronis, still standing behind us, answered in halting Common, as there was no word in the Infernal tongue for such a thing. "Blessed."

"Ah," Vrakus chuckled and looked at me. "Remove it."

Every inch of me snarled in rebellion at taking Nathalia's shield from her, the one thing present that had never let her down. I hissed, "No."

"No?" He faced me fully, eyebrows raised in surprise. "Did you just say *no* to me?"

I was about to tell my father he could bend forward and suck his own cock when Nathalia said with cold steel in her voice, "It's all right, Ramiren. Take it." She presented her shield arm to me with her face turned away.

I shook my head vehemently, "No, I—"

"*Take it!*" she shrieked in grief and anger, the sound like a clap of thunder that bounced around the vast chamber. With a harsh exhale, she rolled her lips between her teeth to keep them from trembling.

My quaking hands moved of their own accord, and I began to unbuckle the leather straps from her forearm. Her shield lurched crooked with the first strap removed. With the second, I caught it before it fell to the floor.

"Ravik," Vrakus prompted, and my brother stepped forward to relieve me of it. When the exchange was done, the arch-devil smiled broadly. "Very good. Now, since secrets are coming out right and left, I'll let you in on one of my own. My alchemists have been busy. They've perfected a recipe that will be quite useful to my devils, but some of the ingredients are difficult to come by. Virgin's blood, for one." He turned a feral grin on Nathalia. "I don't suppose you're one, are you?"

Nathalia sent a chilly look my way. "Sadly, no."

I winced. Paqua's flaming sword sent straight through my gut would have hurt less.

There was little doubt that Vrakus understood what her response meant. "Ah, a shame. Ramiren does like to ruin my fun. It's no matter, as there are a few others, but the most difficult to acquire is angel's hair. The sword, Eronis."

When the gray-skinned devil passed me and placed Nathalia's sword into his grip, my knees nearly gave out.

Fuck! No!

Before I could make a mindless attempt to take it from him, Eronis wrapped an arm around my shoulders to hold me against his chest as Nathalia watched my father walk behind her, stone-faced and rigid. She made no move to get away from him, either not understanding or not caring about what he intended to do. Or, perhaps, knowing there was nowhere to go.

I thrashed. I kicked. I clawed. And it was no use. Even with my strength, Eronis was stronger still. All I had left was my voice, and if begging meant she'd be free, then I'd beg. "Let her go, gods-damn it! *Please!*"

Fast as a snake, Vrakus's free hand lashed out to seize Nathalia's ponytail. He jerked her head back, and she gasped in a sob. She reached behind her head to clutch my father's hand as her eyes closed, causing welled tears to finally break and fall down her temples.

The snarls and laughter of the devils observing barely registered as blind horror turned me feral, but even through the frenzy, and the bloody gouges I left in his arm, Eronis held fast.

Vrakus's amused smile widened as he watched me struggle. Craning his head down, he said, "Ask nicely, and I might not take it, young lady."

She bared her gritted teeth, seething, and ground out, "*Fuck you.*"

"Pity." Vrakus tutted. "The recipe needs twice the amount from a celestial, but you know the saying. Beggars. Choosers." He yanked as he brought the sword's edge down, and her hair gave way like butter against a hot knife, leaving a blunt stub at the back of her head.

He released her with a push, and she caught herself in one step. Nathalia slowly lifted a hand to the back of her hair, probing at what remained of her once long, silvery tresses. Removing the leather thong to run her shaking fingers through the choppy, chin-length hair that she had been left with, she sniffed and spun, her closed fist making a loud *crack* as she slammed it hard into my father's cheek.

Everything went numb. There were a few things Vrakus would tolerate. Someone, especially an angel-born, humiliating him in front of his court was not one of them.

Ravik, eyes gone wide, nearly dropped the shield he still held. The entire room held its breath as Vrakus brought his face back to center to glare at my stubborn and fierce protector. "Take her to the room I prepared for my wife." He turned back to his throne.

Two devils came forward to drag her away, and Nathalia screamed as she kicked and spit threats and promises of pain. Her unhinged reaction caused even the monstrously strong devils trouble, but she was losing ground quickly. Vrakus's smile returned. Desperation turned to a frantic search for something, *anything*, that would stop this. Help her. Get her out of here. Safe.

A week! She only has to last a week! Tell her!

Just as she was being dragged over the threshold of a cased opening leading into darkness, I cried out to her, "Nathalia, listen to me! The whistle pact said we are bound here for a week by Laethi time. A week only! Survive, and you'll go home! I promise you!"

Vrakus stopped short and turned with a heavy sigh. "Stop," he commanded as he held up a hand to the two devils taking Nathalia away from me. "Ah, yes. That cursed amendment you had me add."

He closed his eyes as if trying to remember the exact phrasing. "*Those carrying the Arch-Devil Vrakus's mark will be free to leave Gateway upon the passing of seven full days and nights by Laethi time,* I believe it said." His dark eyes, sparkling with happiness, flicked Nathalia's way as he approached her.

"Thank you for reminding me, son. I'd nearly forgotten. You *did* tell her of the pact, didn't you? I felt your betrayal. What a wicked boy you are. I do believe that means your consequence for a broken pact is in order."

"But not from *you*." My struggle against Eronis's iron arm nearly dislocated my shoulder, but I was beyond caring. Beyond angry. "Fate determines the consequence, you bastard, not you!"

"Oh." Vrakus looked back at Ravik, who at least had the decency to appear ashamed. "Normally that's true, but the pact indicated I had the authority to provide the consequence."

My shoulder finally gave way, and the sudden sharp pop of stabbing pain fueled my words. "*You filthy, fucking liar!* I've read that pact a hundred times. There was *nothing!*"

His clawed hand raised as he tapped mockingly on his chin. "Hm. Then I suppose that means you never bothered to look at the *back* of it?"

My entire body stilled as my heart stopped beating. I tried to get my lips to move, to say something and deny what he was claiming. But I couldn't. The best I could manage was a slight parting of my lips from my wheezing breath.

Smirking, he said with a hint of delight, "It's at the bottom. I had a trapped sprite with the cutest, *tiniest* little pen write the addendum before Ravik imbued the vellum to be binding."

I wanted to deny it. I sought any indication that he was lying. A twitch or even a change in his voice, but I couldn't see one.

Dre. Help. Help me.

For several drawn-out seconds I didn't hear anything, until he finally confirmed my fear. ***He's not lying. That kind of addendum shouldn't be possible anymore.***

Vrakus drew up to Nathalia's side and rested one claw on the red sigil upon her neck, making Nathalia close her eyes and twist her mouth in revulsion. I held my breath as Vrakus concentrated with a deep frown. *Jessina. Please.*

My prayer went unanswered, either because the Arbiter of the Gods couldn't hear me in this place, or because She was unable to intervene. The mark slowly disappeared, my optimism with it.

"There!" Vrakus crowed with a clap of his hands. "All gone off that pretty neck of yours. Isn't that better, young lady?"

The small spark of hope I'd given her left her eyes like a snuffed candle.

My knees finally gave out, and Eronis let me drop to the floor.

"I can let *you* go, Ramiren. After all, I did once before. Remember? When your mother decided to take you and abandon me? Abandoned us and all that we could have meant. That mark was meant for her, not this girl. I'm a little disgusted she's even here and what that means. A *celestial,* Ramiren? Really?" He shrugged. "But one mustn't look a gift horse in the mouth. So she'll be your mother's proxy."

A thousand knives stabbed me, but I wasn't lucky enough to bleed out. "What do you mean *proxy*?"

"Since your mother somehow continues to evade me, I must make do. For every offense she gave me, I will visit it upon your new la'kora ten-fold." As he took the four steps back up to his throne, he ordered over his shoulder, "Take her to her new accommodations."

Nathalia screamed as she disappeared into the darkness.

Chapter Ten
The Price of Secrets

"You need to have that set, brother, or it won't heal right."

I lifted my face from my hands to peer up at Ravik, and he recoiled as though suddenly confronting a rabid animal. The past hour must've shown on my face, based on his reaction. My rage and heartache had achieved nothing except a dislocated shoulder, and it brought joy to those who witnessed one of the worst moments of my life.

I slowly turned my head to my injured shoulder, as though indifferently inspecting a colorful rock or an odd bug. Interesting, but ultimately of little consequence. The joint did indeed look misaligned. "That's probably true."

Ravik's lips thinned in worry, but I was unsure exactly why. There were too many reasons to worry and not enough actions to remedy them.

My eyes lifted to see where I had been taken after Nathalia was taken from me. A blank spot existed in my mind, and there were no memories between her removal and when I'd been tossed into this room.

Shock. Probably shock.

My new quarters were comfortable but very cluttered with pieces gathered from Laeth and the Feylands both, as though Vrakus wanted me to be both claustrophobic and overwhelmed with affectionate gifts.

His boons always came with barbs.

Ravik tried to engage me again. "Our father sa—"

"He's not my father, Ravik." I wanted my tone to be one of finality, to say once and for all that Vrakus had no claim on me, but it instead came out as broken.

Ravik knelt in front of me, bringing us to eye level. "He is, Ramiren. A tragedy, yes, but it's the truth. You can't choose who made you."

I sneered but did not reply, opting instead to stare at the floor.

"Here, let me help you." As his hands reached for my hurt arm, I instinctively flinched. He'd had a hand in what happened. As far as I was concerned, he'd hurt Nathalia just as much as Vrakus had, and I wasn't known to forgive easily.

Do you think she will forgive me, Dre?

I don't know, Ren. All I know is that you need to at least try to earn her forgiveness.

"Ramiren, I need to set your shoulder, or it'll cause worse problems for you."

I need to talk to her first. To ex—

Stop.

What?

You don't need to talk. You need to* do. *You earn her forgiveness by acting, by getting her out of here.

Ravik reached for me again. Vaguely aware of the lifting and twisting and pulling, I responded to Dredon instead. Sluggishly, ideas started taking shape. *Vrakus will never let her go, and I can't whistle us out of danger again because that'll just start the whole process over. So...I need to find an ally who will help me.*

My awareness came to the present just as Ravik set my shoulder with a loud *pop*, and I grunted at the slice of red-hot pain that rapidly cooled to an intense soreness. I muttered a thanks to him, then sighed. *Best to just come out with it.* "Ravik, we need to get out of here."

His brown eyes held sympathy in them, but fear too. Unsure which would win, I continued, "He'll hurt her, and she's done nothing wrong. She's good and kind and—"

Ravik raised a hand to stop me. "You don't need to justify it to me, brother." He looked behind him to make sure no one else was there before turning back, whispering even though we were alone. "I'm working on how to get you out, but I need time."

"Time is precious, Ravik. I don't—" I swallowed down the lump poised in my throat. "I don't know what he has planned for her. Do you?"

The shift in his expression answered my question, and I reached out to grasp his arms. "You do, don't you? Tell me."

"Ramiren, I—"

"*Please.*"

He gently extracted himself from my fingers that had begun to dig into him harder than I intended. "You know damn well he forbade me from telling you." An audible exhale later, he spoke again. "So don't *torture* yourself with questions I can't answer, Ramiren. He's a *cold* bastard, as you *well* know, and this is a *dark place* to be kept."

I listened to his words but paid more attention to how he was saying them, chills rolling up my spine in cascading waves with each hint.

Torture. Cold. Well. Dark place.

I gave a slow nod, "I understand, brother. Please do what you can. As quickly as you can. She's strong, but..." I trailed off, not needing to describe what Vrakus was capable of. I didn't want to put that out for the Lorindar to hear as they floated around in the Dark Drop below, waiting for mortals to fall in and spend an eternity wondering when they would be devoured. The malevolent gods that devils served had little else to do besides consume souls and listen.

It was bad enough that Ravik and I had discussed plans, but the Lorindar were well known to be capricious and bored. They might allow us to succeed just to watch the ensuing chaos.

"I will. I promise."

After Ravik left, I attempted to head out in a blind search for where my protector had been taken, but a shimmering veil pushed me forcefully back into the room when I tried to cross the door's threshold.

Too troubled to rest and too exhausted to do anything useful, I collapsed into bed shortly after. Hovering somewhere between sleep and consciousness, my mind flitted hazily from one thought to the next. Besides the knowledge that Nathalia was in extreme danger, not knowing just how extreme was the worst part.

Devils were not gentle hosts to their mortal guests, especially ones where an arch-devil had taken a special interest in their welfare.

I had begun to doze off when a crackling, splintered voice entered my head. Waiting, convinced I'd dreamed it in my semi-coherent state, I heard only silence. But when the voice came again, my eyes shot open as I jolted up in bed, fully awake and aware of who the broken voice belonged to.

Nathalia?

Shoul...der...all r...t?

My head dropped to my shaking hands. My eyes stung as an intense and indescribable feeling choked and burned my throat.

I didn't know how to respond, or if I even could. I wasn't currently being threatened, but she obviously was. I tried to throw a whisper, but whatever veil covered the door and blocked my exit also prevented me from whispering.

Dre, how do I do this?

A hypothesis. Your inner voice increases in volume, so to speak, when in a heightened emotional state, pushing it into the air. Try that.

Thank you, Dre.

Who...Dre?

Elation met confusion, but I ignored one to concentrate on the other. I didn't understand how I was talking to her. The push of intent and words felt the same as if I were purposefully talking with Dredon, but just as with Dre, sometimes particularly strong thoughts and feelings were conveyed as well.

Dredon. You met him at the Citadel, remember? My pact vizier who helps me with my work.

Oh...I s...

I waited for more, but there was nothing. Even if she were to rant and scream at me, I wanted her to keep talking. Aside from tidbits of information from Ravik, who had promised to visit me daily to provide a coded status of her condition, this remained the only way I'd know if she were still alive.

Nathalia, are you well?

Not...answer...question. Always...avoid...questions...

Her voice gradually began to come through clearer, and I wondered if that had more to do with the sharpness in her tone than whatever magic was fueling this ability. If that was the case, I was so very thankful for it. I deserved it, anyway.

Apologies. It's a hard habit to break.

Try.

That had come through loud and clear with a forcefulness that bordered on aggression. I deserved that, too.

My shoulder is fine. I pushed past my fear of her answer to my next question. I had to know, and I wanted her to understand where my concerns were. On her, where they should have always been. *Are you all right?*

Been...better.

What's happening? Where are you?

Hole...rock...dar...fly...can't...

Though her speech remained stuttered, she'd partially confirmed what Ravik had told me. She was in a hole or well, probably warded like mine to prevent escape. I filed that information away for later.

It's a little difficult to understand you. Whatever this ability is, it's a little unstable. Can you hear me?

You...uns...too.

Despite the wobbly chatter, it brought a smile to my face. Her fractured voice was a comfort, and I prayed mine was one for her as well.

I'll get you out of here, Nathalia. I promise you. I'll throw myself into the Drop if that means you leave here safe and sound. You're going home, I swear it. You'll find someone worthy of you and live a full life and die old and content.

...forget...Ramir...you die...I do...

I had forgotten. She'd told me what happened to a protector if their charge perished. The unfairness brought tears to my eyes.

I'm not worth throwing yourself on your sword. I'm so sorry, Nathalia. For everything.

There was a long pause before she replied, **Pact...broken...How still...in play?**

Though she was coming through a little clearer, it still took me a second to understand what she'd meant.

A pact can only be terminated completely if it's dissolved. Broken just means the offending party is punished.

Why didn't...dissolve...pact with...father? For...whistle?

It was done in red ink, meaning it's indissoluble. The pact stands until either my father dies or I do.

...ever seen...consequen...of... broken pact...determined by...other person?

Personally, no. I know that's how it used to be, long before I became a pactmaker.

Why did…change?

Only vague ideas are known. Abuse of the system, somehow. I've asked ancient elves what they knew, but they refused to answer. Original books didn't survive that long, and I don't believe anyone copied them down. So logic says it was a bad time.

What…la'kora…?

I sat still as a mill pond. I wasn't entirely sure if I could move, anyway. My instincts, the deep, protective part of my brain that did what it could to keep me from harm and vulnerability, demanded I dodge the question. To keep the secret. But where had secrets gotten me? *It's a phrase in Infernal. It means "greatest treasure." It was an endearment I used for my mother when she was still alive.*

…Vrakus think…I…la'kora?

He doesn't think. He knows.

Silence replied to me, and I didn't push. What I'd just said was a heavy thing, and I wanted to give her time to process it.

I tried drifting off to sleep again, blanketed by the warmth and comfort our short conversation had given me. While I had promised her I'd get her out, I also promised myself I'd never take her for granted again.

But sleep eluded me, because there was a thought that had been needling my mind ever since our strange conversation had started.

Surely she'd been distracted, so how did she know I'd hurt my shoulder?

Chapter Eleven
Day One

I felt disoriented when I finally got up. Through the dark-tinted window, I could see the Orb in the red sky above District Four. It provided extreme warmth, like the Laethi sun, though in far more abundance, but it stayed aloft and didn't move except for one specific reason, so I had no idea how much time had passed. Devils instinctively knew the time and date in the mortal realms, so they had no need for a visible indicator.

I poked around my room that, upon getting a closer look at it, resembled a storage room more than a bedroom. There were chests filled with stiff, rumpled clothing various years out of date and bookshelves with diaries and some half-finished works on Laethi flora and fauna. Pouches of rock-hard rations, herbs long dried and turned to powder, and a large, rickety basket holding patinated copper coins.

There was nothing valuable or even nice to look at. Everything was junk. Mundane, in every sense of the word.

The more I looked, the more I understood what this room was for. It *was* a storage room, but for a very specific purpose. This was the room where they kept the things they'd taken from people condemned to descend into the Drop until consumed by the Lorindar, first as a person, then as a soul.

Even if a mortal imprisoned here tried to relieve their torment by suicide, their souls were still dragged down. Devils didn't have to push people in while still alive; they just enjoyed the terror it produced.

This was a room of trophies, commemorating destroyed lives, and it seemed like that's exactly what Vrakus saw me as. A trophy to win.

But whatever he'd intended to do to Nathalia was the greater evil, and I couldn't let that happen.

Eventually, my brother returned with some food and water for me. The constant rotten-egg miasma in the air killed my appetite, but I managed to at least gulp down a fetid cup of water. The lavatory he took me to, while under heavy guard, was little more than a small hole in the floor leading outside.

No words were spoken between us until we returned to the room.

"How are you?" he asked as we sat down in two rickety chairs.

I leaned forward with a frown, squinting. "Is that a serious question, Ravik?"

He let out a soft exhale and slouched in his chair. "Of course it's a serious question. I can't do much, but is it a crime to show concern for your well-being?"

I scowled at his attitude and, if I was honest, his lack of understanding about the precarious position we were in. "And *I'm* far more concerned about the woman who came with me, brother."

The prick shrugged. Actually fucking *shrugged*. "I've already been to check on her." He lifted a corner of his mouth and shook his head. "She's not a wilting flower, that's for sure."

When he didn't elaborate with more detail, I nearly ground my teeth to dust. "*And?*"

Ravik looked up as he tongued his cheek, then wobbled his head back and forth while considering his words. "She's...persevering."

My left eye twitched in irritation. "What *else,* Ravik? Is she unharmed? Has that narcissistic *tyrant* touched her? Is she being fed? Given water?" My volume had increased with each question until I was practically yelling, but I didn't bother to temper it. I probably couldn't have if I'd tried.

Ravik dropped his head forward and rubbed his fingertips into his temples. "Look, Ramiren. There is a finite amount of information I can give you. You two aren't the only prisoners here."

With an indignant scoff at his insinuation, my back hit the back of my chair. "Prisoner? You're his favorite; you can leave any time you want."

He dropped his hands into his lap and leveled me with a glare. "He has doomed me into lifelong compliance, Ramiren. He gives orders, and I carry them out. Do you understand what I'm saying?"

A scornful laugh burst out of me. "What? You don't know how to refuse him? Even Nathalia, who was born when we were *already* grown men, understands how to say no."

With an exasperated roll of his eyes, Ravik replied, "No, brother. Vrakus..." He exhaled a pained sigh then muttered, "He fucking *breathed* on me."

Every part of me lit up in awareness, and goosebumps skittered across my skin. *There's no way I heard him right.* "What?"

With a nod, he confirmed I'd heard right. "He used Incubi's Breath on me. Just like he threatened to do to our mother."

Though she'd finally told me the truth many years ago, being reminded of the last catalyst behind the downfall of our family reopened the jagged wound her story had caused. It'd been a watershed moment and affected the trajectory of my entire life, though I'd initially believed he had been bluffing and didn't actually have that ability. Not many devils did, even arch-devils. My next question came out choked. "When?"

Ravik kept his eyes on mine as his expression went stony. "When he realized that you and she were gone, he woke me up from a dead sleep and exhaled until I choked. Then he kept at it until I lost consciousness. When I woke up again, my ability to ever say no to him was stolen from me."

I was eleven when we left, which meant he was... "Gods above, you were a *kid*, barely—"

"Thirteen. I was thirteen." He huffed in dry amusement. "I guess it *is* an unlucky number."

An abrupt thrum of panic seized my heart, causing it to stutter. "Nathalia. He's not planning to—"

He held up his hand to stop me from going further. "No. At least, not that I'm aware of."

The confirmation was a small mercy, but it did little to provide relief. Even if she didn't become Vrakus's thrall, she was still in a life-threatening *and* soul-threatening situation. My fingers tugged at my hair. "I need to get her out of here, Ravik."

"I'm working on it."

I chewed on my lip, feeling useless. I had to do *something*. "Just...tell me what I can do. I can't just sit here, Ravik."

"Father i—" At my glare, Ravik corrected himself with his hands held up in surrender. "Sorry, *Vrakus* is going to request to talk to you tomorrow. Perhaps you can convince him."

A guttural groan escaped me. "Slim chance of that happening." My lips thinned, but I nodded once. "But I'll try."

He raised an eyebrow, and it wasn't readily apparent if the gesture was questioning or teasing. "For her?"

I'd practically said as much, but agreeing with him somehow felt more like an uncomfortable confession than a simple confirmation. Especially in this place. "For her *sake*. And because what he's doing is petty and wrong. Nathalia has done nothing to him besides exist."

He snorted. "Well, that makes sense. *He's* petty and wrong, but as I said, I'll do what I can. It might take me a few days, but I swear I'll think of something." He smiled, then looked curiously around the room, though I was sure he'd been here many times before. "At least one of us should be free of him. And I'm the eldest. It should be my burden."

I was grateful to have an ally, at least, but there was something that didn't make sense. "So Vrakus was expecting that I'd have to use the whistle to save our mother? Was that his plan?"

He nodded once. "He had a few irons in the fire to get her here, and you were one avenue out of many. He also sent out scouts to find her and paid mercenaries to either hold her until devils could take her to Gateway or nudge her into dangerous situations, so you'd be forced to use it, but they never had the chance. Something about her moving to parts unknown before they could act, and they'd have to start the search over again."

He ran a hand down his face and scratched at his beard. "Fuck, two of the mercenaries who reported failure got brought here and dropped. Then word got around, and no one would accept the bounty anymore, knowing they might end up the same way. Every plan failed. Your whistle was the last remaining piece he had."

She'd always told me and Ravik she'd been born on the road, so she'd die on the road. My mother had never wanted to stay long in one place, even before Vrakus's change. It remained unclear if she'd moved so often because of the threat Vrakus posed or due to her perpetual wanderlust. Likely both. "And he's been holding a grudge against her this whole time?"

"It started years ago when the Orb was over Third for a little while. He was seeing things in the shadows. Paranoid. Angry. If he'd ever bothered to talk to the other arch-devils, they wouldn't hesitate to gloat about it being normal for a disgraced arch-devil." He grinned with glee, as though the thought of the Lorindar's anger toward Vrakus and the frustration it no doubt caused brought at least a little joy. "Eventually the Orb moved over another district, but the grudge has been beyond hateful ever since. Like it was somehow her fault the Lorindar had taken their displeasure out on him."

I hummed thoughtfully. "Well, he'll never get the chance now. Small comfort, I suppose."

With a frown, he gave me his full attention. "Why not?"

I closed my eyes in regret. *Fuck. I'd never had the chance to tell him.* "Our mother died, Ravik. Eight years ago."

"Oh. Right. She was human." He huffed a grunt, as though what I'd said had confirmed something. "Huh."

My eyes opened, and I looked at him with a furrowed brow. "What?"

He puffed out his cheeks and let the air inside go. With a scratch to the back of his neck, he replied, "Well. I mean, I'd have to verify, but the Orb settled over our district about eight years ago."

Ravik chuckled at another example of Vrakus's misery. "He never *could* figure out why the Lorindar had moved it. They must've known he'd failed to satisfy his revenge and punished him. It was so hot that everyone had to move to the bowels of the castle when our devils started to lose consciousness from the heat. Gods below, I had to go to the Citadel until the Orb moved again, or I would've died."

His face fell without warning as a thought occurred to him. "You know, I don't even remember what she looked like. I remember what she *smelled* like, though."

I smiled slightly at the memory of her potted plants, their bounty perpetually hanging in our covered wagon's rafters. "Herbs. She always smelled like dried herbs." My eyes took inventory of his features. "You look a lot like her, actually. Same hair and eye color." I smirked with a teasing head tilt. "Your jaw and nose are a little bigger, though."

He didn't look amused, and he whispered his question. "Was it peaceful?"

A few quick nods of my head answered him. "Want to know what the last thing she said was?"

"Yes. Please."

My mother possessed a sweet voice, one I'd heard often in front of adoring crowds before we disappeared. She'd never performed again and kept to herself, but her voice was always ready to soothe or entertain, even if it was for me alone. It echoed in my head like a welcome phantom. "She sang a lullaby. Do you recall 'The Dreams We Remember'?"

He hid the bittersweet memory of the song she'd sung when we awoke from bad dreams with a forced chuckle. "Gods below, that old song?"

"Her music was her life, and now it's our loss."

Ravik smiled sadly with a shake of his head. "He never played the fiddle again. He actually tried once, but his new claws broke the strings. He threw it into the Drop, used the bow to beat prisoners, and never mentioned it again."

A loud silence stilled the noxious air until I broke it. "I'm sorry, Ravik. You shouldn't have had to deal with him all these years."

He waved a hand dismissively and adjusted himself in his chair. "Don't be. In a way, it was my choice."

Um. What? "What do you mean?"

He threaded his fingers together on his stomach and crossed his extended legs at the ankles. "Do you really believe she would've just left me? Our mother tried to get me to go with you two that night, but I refused. She pretended like we were going out for sticky buns to get us out the door quietly, but it was late, so I wasn't hungry. I asked her to bring me back one for the morning and went to bed."

"And then he—"

With a slow nod, he shrugged like it didn't matter. "Next thing I knew, I was choking."

I stayed silent.

"She took who she could. I don't blame her for not telling me. I worshipped the ground he walked on, so I wouldn't have believed her. Fuck, I probably would've gone off to tell him. She took a huge risk to even try." He sighed, closing his eyes. "I wish I'd had your sweet tooth."

Awake?

I laid down on the bed on the off-chance anything she told me would make my legs give out. I projected my voice inside my head to her. *I'm awake.*

Treated...ight?

Better than I deserve, if I'm being honest.

Perhap...but I still wa...ou unhar...d.

Like I said, better than I deserve. From everyone, especially you. Are you all right?

I'm well.

I couldn't tell if she was making a pun or being serious. *Is that a joke?*

Yes. I don...much el...do.

I'm serious, Nathalia. Is it cold there?

You...ould find it...ncomforta...I'm...ine, actua...

My brother had said the place they were keeping Nathalia was cold, but cold to a broodling and cold to a celestial were two very different things.

I didn't want to ask this next question. I didn't want to go from furious to outright feral when I saw Vrakus the next day, when I needed to keep a calm head if I wanted Nathalia freed, but part of me had to know. *Has he hurt you?*

A thick wall of silence separated us until she replied. **Yes.**

My nails bit into my palms until the skin broke. I remembered Ravik mentioning Vrakus used his bow to beat his prisoners. I wasn't sure if I hoped he used that or his fists. What would hurt less?

How badly? What has he done?

Jus...fists, tha...all. Nothi...more.

I was positive this woman would be the death of me. *Oh. Just fists. So that's perfectly fine.*

You an...I both kno...could...far worse, Ramir...

I *did* know. If he had been willing to use his Breath on his wife and son at the beginning of his horrific transformation from broodling to arch-devil, he was capable of committing more atrocious sins than the beating of a celestial woman after having been an arch-devil for four decades.

Can you heal yourself? Like you did with Georgina?

...tried to...that but...Tarindar a...silent do...here. I can't hear

Just stay alive, Nathalia. I contemplated telling her this next part, not knowing if my father could hear this exchange, but I had to give her something, anything. *I'm working on a plan to get us out.*

When she didn't say anything for a minute, I prompted her. *Nathalia?*

I'm sorry. Yo...brother...here wi...food. I'll...alk soon.

I whispered into the void, "Thank you, brother."

Chapter Twelve
Day Two

I'd stayed up most of the previous night, pacing around my room like a caged animal and trying to think of things I could say to make my father let her go, most of them dismissed as soon as they manifested. I contemplated lying to Vrakus about where my mother was living, but there was a better than even chance he'd not only see through the lie but take his anger at being deceived out on Nathalia.

I always came back to the same thought.

I'd long suspected my father wanted to give me the veneer of choice. He had to know I'd eventually see the addendum, penned in that invisible but somehow binding ink that would have my brother disgraced if not outright removed from the Registrar of Pactmakers at the Citadel if they found out about it.

No. Neither. He was breathed on, unable to not comply with Vrakus's demands.

In that situation, integrity and resistance were as impossible as going back in time to correct your mistakes. To give information or confess secrets that might not have made a difference in the eventual outcome. But it certainly would have prepared us better for this inevitability.

Secrets and lies were no more than fear masquerading as protection. I realized too late that I didn't need secrets and lies to protect me anymore; I had Nathalia.

When you're used to doing things alone, relying only on yourself, leaning on another can feel like surrender.

I requested Vrakus's copy of our pact, which was brought to me a short time later. I scanned the back of the calfskin vellum I had admired all those years ago, and sure enough, in a tiny scrawl that was no bigger than my thumbnail, were the words indicating Vrakus was free to provide the consequences should the pact be broken, foregoing Fate's privilege to decide on the punishment.

And even with my glasses, I still had to squint and hold the vellum not two inches from my eyes to read it.

"Fate's power to give the consequences for breaking this pact and for breach of contract is hereby bestowed upon Vrakus, Arch-Devil of Third District. May his reign be— Blah, blah, blah," I muttered, rubbing my sore eyes from the strain.

I'd never seen it before. I'd been over every square inch of the front side that held the actual pact's details, but not the back. For Vrakus to force my brother to destroy his integrity in such a way was not the worst thing he'd ever done, but it was at the top of the list.

I turned the vellum over to the front, the red ink still as crisp and small as it had been all those years ago. My eyes scanned it again, though I'd memorized it long ago, and rested on the invisible addendum I hadn't been able to see until I'd had my glasses made. It was the addendum that would have damned my mother if I'd been forced to use the whistle to save myself.

Ramiren's La'kora shall too be marked,
And likewise, for her, Third's devils embarked.
No longer can she hide from me,
My vengeance I'll take, perpetually.

I understood why he'd had to phrase it in that manner. She could have changed her name, so he couldn't say "Ana Orasti." He couldn't say "Ramiren's mother," because there was no word in Infernal for mother. Devils were made, not born.

It was a small mercy that pacts were null and void, their cosmic thaumaturgy shattered, if more than one language was used in the document itself. Unfortunately for Vrakus, the magic in the invisible ink he'd used would not allow any language but Infernal.

I understood why, but now that nonspecific wording had backfired on Vrakus. He probably thought he'd been clever by phrasing it in such a way, but the end result was neither what he'd expected nor desired. That phrase had marked another, and she would pay until the end of her days if Vrakus had any say in the matter.

So I paced around my prison, trying to think of a way to escape. To rely solely on my brother to get us out, especially knowing he could be ordered to simply put a knife through her heart at any given moment, would be foolish.

I went over what Nathalia had told me in our strange telepathy. Vrakus hadn't breathed on her. Ravik would've told me, and I'm sure Nathalia would have noted caustic red smoke being pushed into her lungs. He'd beaten her, yes, and for that he would pay, but my priority was her freedom and not revenge for every bruise Vrakus had battered into her skin.

That would come later, but it would come. After Nathalia was home and out of his reach.

With every heartbeat, resolve and resignation mixed heavier in my blood, pushed into every vein and artery until I was filled with them.

I knew what I had to do. And if it meant her freedom, it would be the easiest deal I'd ever made.

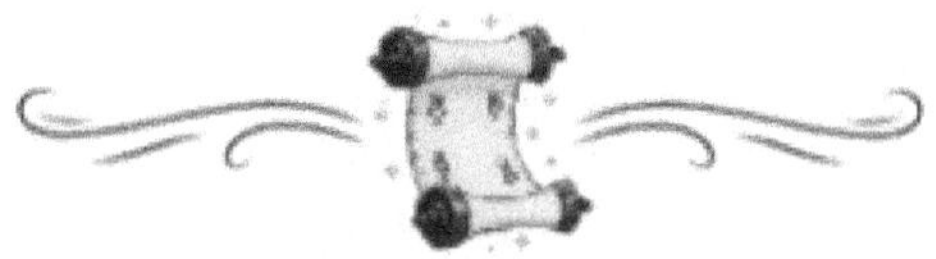

I greeted the arch-devil before me with a clipped nod. "Vrakus."

He hummed in disapproval, "Not 'Father'? You greeted me so wonderfully before, why stop now?"

For fuck's sake. "I'm calling you by your given name, yes? That should suit for this."

"Shame. You used to call me Papa. Do you remember? You were a good boy, as biddable as a lamb. You used to follow your mother around like a sweet little puppy when she tended her plants, holding cut herbs in one little fist and dead stems in the other. But then it was Father when you arrived here two days ago, and now it's simply *Vrakus*. I did nothing to deserve such coldness, son. Ultimately, it was your mistake that brought her here." His smile was serpentine, and his words did what they were supposed to do. They pierced my skin and left their venom.

Nathalia. Think of Nathalia. Don't get distracted.

I won't.

"That's what I've come to talk to you about, and how you can start to fix what you broke."

He retorted condescendingly, "As I recall, it was *you* who broke it."

"Regardless of the technicalities, *Vrakus*, I'm willing to negotiate."

He barked a laugh. "Isn't the time for pact negotiation and addendums long past? It's signed and carried out, after all."

"I think you'll want to hear what I have to say."

Ravik stepped to my side, and inclined his head toward me. "Hear him out, Father. It might cure your present boredom, in any case."

A prickle of annoyance tickled my palms, and I dug in my nails to relieve the sensation. I knew he was playing a part. I knew it down to my bones, but I still hated it.

Vrakus leaned his head back with a dramatic sigh. "Fine. Let's hear your proposal, Ramiren. I have an appointment, and she grows impatient."

My left eye twitched.

Don't.

Fucking fuck. I know.

Dredon, having been quiet most of my time here, knew when he was needed, and I was grateful for both his previous silence and his currently calming advice. Even if it wasn't necessarily needed. I'd take all allies now.

I began. "You and I both know that you don't want her here. Nathalia's not the one you wanted. You're hurting someone simply because she's available to be hurt. So my proposal is this: Release her back to her home, never to trouble her again, and I'll stay here with you and Ravik."

"Oh, you'll stay with me, hm?"

I didn't flinch, even as I knew exactly what I was agreeing to.

"Yes."

He tilted his head to the side, observing me like an interesting specimen. "You'll willingly take her place? An angel's get?"

"Yes, without hesitation or addendum. Do what you will, just let her leave here hale and whole."

"Minus her lovely silver locks, of course. Those I cannot give back. They're already being used by the alchemists."

I answered him through gritted teeth. "Yes, without her hair."

"I've been informed her hair made a batch that resulted in nearly a hundred vials. Remarkable. She had a beautiful, thick mane. Soft, silky, and well maintained. I must ask what concoctions she used to make it so nice." He ran a red hand through his own inky-black hair, so much like mine. "I could use the recommendations."

He is exhausting. Truly. Are you certain your mother didn't have one night of passion with another broodling? That unhinged automaton had more of a heart than this monster.

I let Vrakus mutter about potions while I responded to Dre. *Fairly certain.*

A shame.

Vrakus clicked his forked tongue, bringing me out of my thoughts. He spoke as he meandered about. "Now, Ramiren, as to your proposal. It would be quite difficult for me to send her back. A deal is a deal. You understand. But if you agreed to lead my scouts to your mother? Well, that's something I would consider. She should be, what, nearing her nineties now? Surely her bleeding heart would be willing to take your new la'kora's place? Though I'm not certain how she'd take the knowledge that her pretty pedestal has been usurped. Might kill her outright. Humans are so very frail at that age."

Oh gods, he doesn't know. Your brother didn't tell him. Can we use that?

If he lets Nathalia go first, yes. It doesn't work otherwise.

I glanced at Ravik, and his eyes confirmed it. He hadn't yet informed Vrakus that our mother had died. I would have to do it, and I had no idea how he would take it.

I cleared my throat. "I would be willing to lead your scouts to her, but-"

Ravik interrupted me, "But, alas, she has passed."

My chest tightened, and a lump made of frustration and anger burned in my throat. My fingers curled as I imagined throttling my brother. He hadn't been compelled. That was all him. *You godless fucking bastard.*

Vrakus stilled and stared at Ravik with hard eyes. "What did you say?"

I hate it, Ren, but he might've just saved Nathalia's life. I don't think it's possible to lie to him.

"She died eight years ago. Her soul passed peacefully on to Celestia."

Vrakus sent a meaningful glance my way, and based upon what my brother had told me regarding events roughly eight years ago, it seemed logical that the arch-devil was connecting the dots.

"So I was punished for failing to bring her here. That's why we got the Orb over us," Vrakus spoke to Ravik, but it was more like he was musing to himself than giving his thoughts to another. When Vrakus's eyes again turned to rest on me, they were cold and brittle. "I'll consider your proposal. Now, if you'll excuse me." He moved to stalk out of the throne room, toward the same hallway that Nathalia had disappeared through, and my throat closed.

My feet followed of their own accord, grabbing at his arm to turn him around. To see reason. "Gods-damn it! Stop and fucking *listen*! You need to let her go!"

He shook me off and went immediately for my jacket, clutching handfuls in his claws and ripping the fabric as he pushed me into the nearest wall. My feet left the floor as he lifted me to eye level. I glared at him as he glared at me. "No, *you* need to listen, *pup*! *I* decide what happens here, not *you*. And *I* will be the one to decide her fate, not *you*." He dropped me to the floor without warning, and I stumbled.

"I said I'd *think* about it, Ramiren. That's the best you'll get today." Vrakus untangled his claws from my ripped shirt and shredded jacket, the cloth rubbing against the cuts he had rent in my skin. "Now, I h— What the fuck is this?"

I looked down as he plucked up the luck stone Nathalia had given me as payment. The plainly embellished smoky gem, the mundane and wholly unremarkable jewel that had changed the course of my life. "Where the fuck did you get this? Are you trying to taunt me, boy?" Vrakus shook the necklace in his hands. "*Answer me!*"

A desperate need to get it out of his hands, to at least keep something of Nathalia safe, made me grasp his hands in mine. His sharp claws bit into my fingers, but I continued to fight for it. "I don't fucking know what you're talking about. I got that from Nathalia. It has nothing to do with you, now *give it back*!"

But instead of letting it go, he broke the chain and shook me off. When I went for it, he pushed me against the wall again with an iron hand. I slapped and punched at his forearm, but he held firm.

Vrakus rubbed the gem and smirked. "It has everything to do with me." When he dangled the necklace in front of his face, it swung back and forth from my jostling attempts to free myself and the necklace from his grip. "This was the gem that made me into what I am today, but I lost it when my change happened. Funny how Fate likes to fuck with us."

The fight left me. With a glance at the necklace, my glasses confirmed its lifeless aura, indicating there still was no magic imbued within it. I wheezed my reply, more from my shock than the crushing palm keeping me against the glossy wall. "What?"

"This little thing? It was thrown to us as payment for our music. Ana didn't want it. Metals gave her hives, so I took it. I intended to sell it for coin, but I couldn't part with it. It felt *special*, somehow. Every city and village we went to, I asked about it. To figure out why this bit of junk called to me." Vrakus swung the necklace back and forth like a hypnotist's pendulum. He continued with a rueful laugh. "Eventually, in Evraka, I found a mage who told me it held an arch-devil's essence inside. Trapped, like an insect in amber. He told me to never put it on."

He finally smiled broadly, pride and obsession twisting his face into a macabre mask. "This ordinary bit of jewelry gave me the power to make kings quake and priests pray. It gave me everything, and your mother lacked the vision to understand. Thank you for returning it to me." He finally let me go and threw a command to Ravik over his shoulder as he again moved toward the darkened threshold. "Put him back."

When Ravik gently took my arm, it might as well have been a vise squeezing my chest. I shook him off and tried to follow the arch-devil again, praying that some semblance of the broodling who had raised me was still in there somewhere. "She doesn't deserve this! *Please!*" Ravik grabbed my arm again, harder this time, and hauled me back to his side.

Just before being swallowed by the darkness of the doorway, Vrakus faced me again. "Neither did I, Ramiren, but we don't always get what we deserve, do we?"

He left, taking my last hope with me.

Nathalia was silent for the rest of the day.

Chapter Thirteen
Day Three

My eyes flitted around to peer at the multicolored lights floating above my head, the bubble-like spheres glowing with both illumination and the hint of magic that made them shine in reds, blues, greens, and yellows.

Feylights were a rare thing outside of the Feylands. No heat radiated from them, but they were quite beautiful and never needed the upkeep or replacement that standard torches required. They also had the added benefit of harmlessness, necessary with so many children running around with reckless abandon.

Coming to places like this allowed me an undisturbed opportunity to watch people. I observed their unguarded smiles when among friends, how they laughed at the jokes their companions told. Their body language spoke of deep affection and the closeness that manifested from secrets shared and gently understood.

The happiness in their eyes, brought about by treats and even magically manipulated games, warmed me. I loved places like this, because they always smelled like oranges.

A soft tap on my right shoulder made me turn. The apparent source was a petite woman wearing the crimson robes of a Minuen priestess, arms crossed and smirking. Her carved porcelain mask covered half her face, but I could tell she was a lovely creature, if a bit dusty from travel. Her auburn hair was artfully curled, her curved mouth the same color as her robes. The fragrance of amusement and mischief floated toward me, and I smiled down at her. "Yes?"

The robed priestess giggled. "Hello, sir. M— Whoa!"

Out of the corner of my eye, a flash of silver sprang into view in the form of a ponytail and steel chain armor. I couldn't see her face, as it was turned away from me, but she was far taller than the red-haired girl she was dragging away. On her back rested a shield with the four-pointed star emblem of a protector. I assumed she was the priestess's protector doing her duty, preventing the girl from going up to strange men.

The newcomer, with a nervous laugh that echoed her nervous scent, called out over the din of the carnival, "Sorry! My sister is very drunk! Minuen priestesses, right? Never met a drink they didn't like!"

The priestess screeched, pointing at her protector's torso. "Wait, Nat! You've got dirt on you!"

The protector immediately released her arm, looking down to search for the dirt that almost certainly wasn't there. She sounded alarmed as she replied, "Wait. What? Where?"

The second her arm was released, the priestess slunk back to me with light steps that spoke of many nights tiptoeing into and out of places. It was still roughly an hour before I had to meet my extraordinarily anxious client for the wine trade agreement, so I watched the scene play out as an unbidden grin parted my lips.

The girl was nearly to my side when she let out a triumphant cackle, giving away her intentions, and the sudden distance between them, to her...sister?

I looked back down at the priestess, her brown eyes twinkling, as she spoke quickly, knowing she had limited time to offer her proposition. "My sister is badly in need of sexual company for the evening. Perhaps it'll improve her mood. Would you be so kind as to provide it?"

My eyebrows rose in abject surprise. For her sister, then, and not her?

The protector had scurried to her sister's side, but she stopped dead with a low groan at hearing her sister's words. Her hands rested on the priestess's arm, but her head was still down. This time in apparent defeat.

I inhaled the earthy smell of mushrooms and loamy dirt, indicating deep embarrassment. The protector choked out, "Oh, gods..." Her face fell into her hand, still obscured.

I felt strangely annoyed at the suspense. I'd yet to see what she looked like, and I found myself very much wanting to. The silver-haired woman squeaked out a few words, as though having trouble speaking. "She...she's drunk. So, so drunk."

The priestess's grin was teasing as she peered at her. "Nat, if you need help getting started, I can show you how."

The protector practically sank into the ground, and the situation finally broke me. I couldn't help myself. I laughed. Giving the protector a moment to gather herself, I looked back to the impish girl. "I cannot say I would be able to provide that kind of company, but I can at least introduce myself. I'm Ramiren, and you are?"

The priestess opened her mouth to reply, but the protector's scent suddenly changed from mushrooms to wood lacquer. Shock. "You're Ramiren. The *Ramiren? I've heard of you. I just can't remember how."*

My eyes finally fell on her face, and the sounds of laughter, excited children, carnie barkers, and general chatter faded to nothing. Everything except her face became an indistinct haze, and I mapped it like a cartographer discovering a new and beautiful land.

Her golden eyes were dimmed with confusion, and I feared what they'd do to me when alight with happiness or even passion. Small strands of hair had escaped her ponytail to frame her oval face. Her cheeks' color, still visible from her previous embarrassment, was that of a perfectly ripe apricot. Her parted lips were full, the bottom one indented by her teeth in chagrinned uncertainty.

Her sister was lovely, but the celestial now in front of me was the most beautiful woman I'd ever seen.

Get it together**, Dredon muttered at me. **She's just a woman.

I ignored his dismissive statement as utter nonsense.

No, Dre. This is an angel.

I straightened and tried to present my best smile. "You have? Good things, I hope."

Please only good things. Please only good things.

Her molten eyes ran over my face like a caress, and it took everything I had to stay still and keep my gods-damned hands to myself. I wanted to learn everything I could about her and share everything in turn, but I noticed my shoulders, usually bunched tight, had released their typical tension. My body was relaxed and at ease, as though I'd just exited a long, hot bath.

It was unnerving.

The soft feelings, ironically, made me suspicious. She held no magic that I could see, aside from the pouch at her side. I knew what it was, as I too had one. Was there something inside I needed to inspect? Had an item she carried bewitched me? Was she *a witch?*

I had to find out. Whatever this was, I needed to know.

*Dredon mused, **Stay close to her and gather information?***

Just as I was about to agree to the suggestion, the protector's face distorted slightly, wavering like the air above a flame. The unnaturalness of it sent a cold shiver down my spine. The feylights above our heads dimmed, their light turning her lovely face dull and gray.

Nathalia's mouth curled into a rictus grin as she stepped closer, and a sharp pain seized my stomach. My eyes dropped to find the grip of her sword in her hand—when had she drawn it?—and the blade sunk hilt deep in my gut.

The feylights dimmed further.

She was close enough that I could hear her whisper. "You are a devil, and devils deserve no mercy."

I was shaken awake by a firm hand on my shoulder, and my blurry, sleep-filled eyes spent precious seconds trying to focus on my visitor while my hands clutched my stomach, the phantom pain there still throbbing. When I saw a large man with brown eyes and reddish-blond hair, I relaxed. "Ravik." I sat up briskly rubbing my damp face. "Fuck, I don't know how I fell asleep."

He moved back to allow me some room. "You were crying and muttering, so it probably wasn't a good dream. I brought you some water and food. You really should eat something, and I'll take you to the lavatory afterward."

"It was a good dream." With a frown, I continued, "Until it wasn't." I attempted to choke down the stale food he'd provided me. He was right. I was getting weaker from not eating, but the sulfur in the air made it a difficult task.

"Any news?" I asked between reluctant bites.

"No. He hasn't made up his mind yet. I'm sorry."

I dropped the bread onto my tray and leaned back in the chair to level him with a glare.

He held up his hands. "I'm trying, Ramiren. I really am. I said I'd get you out, and I will. Don't worry. I have a few ideas up my sleeve. She'll be fine in the meantime. I promise that too. Truly."

I stared, waiting. When he didn't say anything, my scowl deepened. "And? What are these ideas? Remember, I haven't exactly forgiven you for telling him about our mother."

He scratched the back of his neck. "Well, I was thinking a confrontation of some sort might be needed. He's gathering his lieutenants soon. Perhaps a distraction?"

I nodded like I was in total agreement, but inside I fumed. Impatience had become my worst sin. Helplessness was a terrible thing, and it broke me apart piece by piece. I was on the verge of crumbling. It was nothing compared to her predicament, but it was still torture.

I needed to change the subject. "Ravik, you handled the pact for the whistle, and a pact always requires a payment to the pactmaker. What were you given for it?"

"Ah. He, uh, he named me his heir."

"A powerful, immortal arch-devil with likely no intention of ever stepping down named you his *heir* in payment for trying to kidnap and torture your mother? Why did you acce— Oh, he ordered you to."

He gave a humorless smile. "Correct."

My fingers went to the bridge of my nose, where I rubbed at the mounting headache. An unbidden smirk twitched my lips. "Ridiculous."

The silence that followed was comfortable. As promised, he took me to the lavatory and brought me back to my room. Before leaving, he asked, "Do you remember when we were little and our parents refused to tell us when we were born? They always celebrated our birthdays on different days to surprise us?"

I frowned, unsure where he was going with this. "I do."

Ravik's eyes became unfocused, looking off to the side, and he smiled bitterly. "Bastard still won't tell me the real date. Did our mother ever tell you yours?"

"No," I replied, then shrugged one shoulder. "But then again, I never asked."

He left, leaving me confused regarding where that thought had come from. I headed back to the bed and dropped onto the hard mattress, leaning my aching head into my hands.

Nathalia?

Here. I...here, Ramiren.

How are you? You're coming in more clearly.

You are too. I'm...right. You?

I'm all right. I'm so sorry, Nathalia. I understand if you never forgive me. I'm sorry I failed you. I'm sorry I kept things from you. When we make it out of here, I'll never keep secrets from you again. I swear it. On my life, Nathalia. Never again.

I'm n...mad, Ramiren. Just...hurt. I underst...I do. Shame...stroys us. It'll b...all right.

I wished I could believe her, but my hopes rested on a broodling who had spent half a century under Vrakus's thumb. I didn't know what to expect or exactly what he was planning.

My head already bent forward, I laced my fingers together and prayed. Not to Jessina, who couldn't intervene, but to Horyn. Nathalia's god.

Please help her.

Chapter Fourteen
Day Four

I'm going mad.

I'd heard nothing from Ravik, and Nathalia remained silent. I knew, *I knew* she was still alive, but for some reason, she wasn't answering me.

Perhaps she finally became sick of you.

Dre. Kindly fuck off. You're not helping.

Apologies, Ramiren. You're right. It was poor timing on my part. The other alternatives are either she's unconscious or d—

No. She's not dead.

How do you know?

I just do. *There's something else going on. Maybe Vrakus or the Lorindar blocked whatever type of communication this is. Maybe she—*

Ravik burst into my room, out of breath, urgency written all over his face. "It's time. We need to go. Now."

I sprang up from my unmade bed and followed without another word, elation and relief replacing the red blood in my veins. It sustained me now, pushing into my limbs and lungs with each beat of my heart and giving me life.

We ran, making left and right turns in dizzying succession. I had no idea where we were going, but Ravik clearly did, so I trusted him to guide me. I knew *who* we were heading to, and that was enough.

When we came to a wide doorway, I prepared myself for what I would see. But as we passed the threshold's veil, Ravik's hand on my arm so I could go through as well, I found myself in a storeroom. Stopping short, my eyes looked at the mortal weapons hanging on walls and resting on shelves, armor new and old heaped into a disjointed pile along the far wall.

"Ravik, what is this?" I whispered, unsure if anyone could hear me.

"We're getting your and Nathalia's things before you leave." He opened a fortified chest next to a mannequin stand displaying a set of dwarven splint plates and began taking out the contents one by one. Nathalia's pouch was on top of her blessed shield, then her sword. My pouch was next, followed by Nathalia's chain armor.

He passed me the pouches and picked up the armor and shield in one hand and the sword in the other. "Your rapier's in your pouch. Let's go."

When Ravik walked out again, I decided to risk it, albeit still whispering. "Guessing Vrakus is otherwise occupied right now?"

He replied, muttering to keep his voice from echoing off the obsidian stone on either side of us, "He's meeting with his lieutenants right now in the throne room. That's why you don't see anyone. This is our best chance."

Wait. Something is...

"Won't you be missed?"

He rolled his eyes. "I told Vrakus I must've eaten some spoiled food." He shook his head, chuckling in soft exhales. "I was quite descriptive, and he remembered enough about being mortal that he demanded I leave immediately."

Ew.

Another few turns and a dark room came into view. The chill from it filled me with dread, and I knew this had to be it. Intellectually, I understood Nathalia could handle colder conditions than I, but this seemed far from comfortable, even for her.

We stepped in, and my eyes adjusted immediately. The only light within came from the small brazier in the corner—burning with the blue-white flame Vrakus preferred. It was a plain room, chiseled out of the obsidian stone the castle was made from. The only notable features were a large hole in the center, roughly five feet in diameter, and several stone tables, upon which sat various blades, chains, and forceps of different sizes.

And all of them gleamed from the brazier's light like they were still wet.

I felt hot and cold at once, merging into numbness. I wanted to punch something. Kill something. My fists tightened in preparation to do so when my brother knelt next to the hole and whispered, "Nathalia?"

A dry croak replied, the hollow echo indicating the depth of the pit. "Here."

Ravik pointed at a winch on the wall next to the door. "Pull that, and prepare yourself, brother."

Placing the pouches down, I did the first. But as Nathalia rose from the hole, I realized I hadn't adequately done the second.

Her short, choppy hair was streaked with dried blood and matted to her scalp, no longer the sheen of silver I was used to. I saw the nails from her fingertips had been removed as she reached out for Ravik to help her up, and she limped off the metal grate she'd been lying on to stand on the solid floor.

When she looked at me, her golden eyes were stark against the lividness of her skin. Incisions, burns, and bruises marred her face. She smiled, her pale lips cracking from the effort.

Gods knew what other atrocities were hidden beneath her soiled and torn clothing.

I rushed to embrace her, but Ravik pushed me back with a firm hand on my chest. When I turned to him, irrationally ready to turn my fury onto any available target, he shook his head quickly. "Not now. We don't have much time." He patted himself and, finding what he was looking for, dug a hand into his left pocket. Pulling out a silver vial, he handed it to Nathalia. "Here, drink."

She lifted her shaky hand and drank without hesitation, and I had to consciously stop myself from doing anything that might disturb her or make her drop the vial.

I sniffed, my eyes stinging. Blinking them clear, I watched as her wounds healed before my eyes. The dried blood didn't go away, but her dimmed eyes came back to life as her ghostly pale skin became peachy once again.

She stretched, joints popping, and sighed in relief. "All right. I can take them now." Her voice sounded steady, and I wondered what was in the vial. Ravik handed her the sword and shield, but she refused the armor. As she belted her sword about her waist, she pointed her chin at the two pouches I'd placed on the floor. "It'll take too long to don. Put it in my pouch, please."

I stood, staring, while Ravik threaded the chain armor through the opening. "Nathalia," I whispered, still trying to catch my breath. "Why didn't you tell me?"

She tightened the shield's straps on her forearm and, with an edge to her voice, she replied, "Do you really think you have a right to ask me that question, Ramiren?" When she raised her eyes, the same sharpness shone within them that I'd heard in her question, and my hands became fists again.

"No," I grunted. "I don't."

Ravik stood, holding a pouch in each hand, and approached us. He gave Nathalia a once-over and asked, "Are you ready?"

What I expected from her was a "yes," or even a nod.

But I didn't expect her to say, "You held up your end. I'll hold up mine."

A panicked shriek exploded within my skull. Every muscle in my body tensed, as though a great threat fast approached. My head snapped to look at her, eyes widening. *I heard her wrong. I must've heard her wrong.* "What?"

You didn't, Ren.

The two pouches, mine and Nathalia's, hit my stomach, and I instinctively moved to catch them before they fell. "What is th—"

"Sorry, brother." Ravik tapped his index and middle fingers to my forehead. The transport was instantaneous, just as it had been forty years ago.

I found myself in the bright foyer of Nathalia's villa. The rapid temperature change made me shiver, and the pouches thrust into my hands dropped with dull thuds to the marble floor at my feet. Wordlessly, I looked around the empty room, let out a sob as my knees gave out, and emptied my lungs with a feral scream.

• • • •

Chapter Fifteen
Whispered Prayers

I heard murmurs. Soft, distant voices whispering indistinct words. A clatter to my left drew my attention, and on the stone floor lay a familiar double-headed axe. I wondered how it got there as the gentle brush of calloused fingertips placed on either side of my face turned my head. When my vision focused and I saw soft brown eyes, I lashed out with my fist, expecting them to belong to my deceitful brother. But instead of hitting a square jaw, it met the palm of a catching hand.

"Hey. Hey. Ramiren, it's me," Lady Resa's voice floated through my head, and I looked again as her face came into focus.

"I... Fuck, I'm sorry," I croaked. She let my fist go, the only thing holding me up, and I fell against her. My forehead hit her shoulder, and her arms enveloped me. "I'm so sorry." Sulfur still clung to my nostrils, so even this close, I couldn't smell what she was feeling.

The tip-tapping of several sets of shoes amplified, closing in. A gasp and a choke preceded Lord Maxlian asking in a hard voice, "Where is she?"

"Max...give him a second," Lady Resa whispered as her embrace tightened further.

"A second? Devils in my house, an ongoing siege, my daughter gone, my son almost killed, and now *he's* back, but Nathalia isn't? A second might be valuable, Reese." The stomping clops of hard heels getting louder caused me to turn as Lord Maxlian knelt beside me. His golden eyes burned like embers. I could tell he was trying to restrain himself.

I wished he wouldn't.

"She must've made some kind of deal with my brother. He sent me back, but she said she was going to do something. I don't...oh gods." Like a sudden bright light in my eyes after coming from a dark room, I winced as I realized just what she was going to do.

"What?" Lady Resa whispered. "What is it?"

I looked at Nathalia's mother, then Nathalia's father, wondering how I was going to tell them that not only was their daughter going to die, but she'd spend the rest of eternity falling. Forever.

I knew I had to, though, so I did. Avoiding hurtful truths because of fear was what started this.

"I think she made a deal with my brother, Ravik, to confront Vrakus. I think she's going to fight him."

Lord Maxlian's face fell, the life sucked out of him in an instant as he understood what I said. He dropped forward to his hands, palms on the floor, as he struggled to hold himself up.

"She's going after an arch-devil?" he murmured.

My throat felt like it'd collapsed in on itself, so I confirmed his fears with a nod.

His reply came in the form of instant rage as he launched himself at me, feathered wings spread wide like the avenging angel he was, bent on destroying the fiend that had destroyed his daughter. Me.

I was jerked from Lady Resa's embrace, pushed to my back as Lord Maxlian's hands went around my throat and squeezed with surprising strength. I didn't even try to fight him.

"Max! Max, stop!" Lady Resa wrapped her arms around his shoulders and pulled, but she couldn't dislodge him. "Stop! Stop it!" Her boots slipped with a lack of traction against the smooth floor as she tried desperately to get her husband off me, but he didn't budge.

My lungs and face burned from the lack of air and blood flow to my brain, but I simply lay there, staring up at the hate-filled eyes of my protector's father. Darkness began to dot my vision, and I willed it to take me under.

"Max! Gods-damn it! You kill him, Nathalia is dead for sure! *Get off him right now!*"

Lord Maxlian hissed, leaning down to put his face an inch from mine. He whispered so only I could hear. "*Ta dana ou.*"

I didn't know what he said, but the context was clear. Angels shouldn't be capable of hate, but there's a first time for everything.

When he released my neck, unwelcome air filled my lungs again as a spasming cough racked me. Raewyn ran to my side to help me sit up. "Are you all right?"

My voice was cracked and hoarse when I replied, "Unfortunately."

"Tell us what happened, Ramiren. Please," Lady Resa implored. She kept her hands on her husband, both to keep him off me and to comfort him. "Start at the beginning."

I sighed, coughed again, and rested my forehead on my raised knees. "The beginning. Sure." When my coughing continued, as I rubbed my throat, prayers fell from Raewyn's lips to help repair what her father had done to me.

I felt guilty at the relief, but I nodded my thanks to her. "I already told you Vrakus tricked me into a deal for the devil's whistle, allowing me to get out of danger. But there was a hidden addendum attached. It was meant to mark my mother. However, she's been dead for years. Instead, it marked Nathalia."

I cleared my throat before continuing. "When Leraska dropped the ward from around this city, it allowed the devils to collect us. They brought us to Gateway and separated us. I tried to get her out. I swear to the Tarindar, I did. I offered to stay with him in exchange for letting her go, but he wouldn't agree to it. My brother made other arrangements. I believe he made a deal with Nathalia to get *me* out, so long as she confronted Vrakus herself. He sent me back here before I realized the plan was to attack him."

Raewyn gripped my arm in both of her small hands to get my attention. "Can she, though? Fight him? Beat him?"

When no one answered her, Raewyn stood, looking at everyone gathered in the foyer. "*Well?* Can she?"

Lord Maxlian replied, his tone hard. "She can try, yes. It's winning that's the problem."

"No. Unacceptable." Raewyn crossed her arms and paced, looking defiant and ready to burst. "That's my *sister*. That's Nathalia *fucking* Swordhand, and she does *not* accept failure. So I'm going to ask *again*. Can. She. Fight. Him?"

Again there was silence, but now was the time for harsh truth, not keeping things hidden. So I gave it to her. "I don't know, but it's very unlikely. She has the sword you gave her, Lady Resa, and the shield you gave her, Lord

Maxlian." I looked at each of them in turn as I spoke, then closed my eyes. "But Vrakus is an arch-devil. Immortal and very strong, even without the hundreds of soldiers around him."

Raewyn turned to her father just as a strange crackling sensation started in my skull, like static in the air just before a lightning strike. The arguments around me dimmed to nothingness as I tried to concentrate on it.

Nathalia? Angel, is that you?

I knew it was her, and I inwardly cursed myself. I hadn't possessed the presence of mind to make an attempt to talk to her like this. It was such a new thing, to be able to do it. There'd been too much going on, too many distractions, I hadn't even thought to try.

Nathalia?

The crackling cleared just enough for me to hear seven precious words.

I love you. My life for yours.

Someone near me said my name. I didn't know who, and I didn't care.

The pressure in my head competed with the pressure in my chest. *Nathalia? Is th... Fuck! Please don't, angel. Please, please stop. I'm begging you. Just turn back. I can fix everything. There's still time. Please just fucking stop!*

There was no reply. Without warning, a void opened where my heart beat like a hummingbird's wings, fast and easily broken.

What... What's going on? Nathalia? Nathalia! Answer me!

That voice. The same voice from the pact room, speaking in a foreign tongue, responded, *Cordani tro dasha.*

My mouth moved, but it felt like someone else was speaking for me. Like the breath used wasn't actually mine. "No. No, no, no. She's— No." I shot to my feet. I couldn't keep still; I had to move. My jittery hands gripped my hair as I paced. Walk, spin, walk, spin.

Dizzy. It was too bright.

I couldn't see anything but light. More voices, some in my head and some outside of it, murmured.

Babbled.

Incoherent.

Like a brook. A babbling brook. Babble, babble, babble. Laughter. Distinctive. Soft, a giggle.

Then louder.

Maniacal.
My face felt
cold and
wet.

Then darkness devoured me.

The next time I opened my eyes, I was in the guest bedroom I'd been given under the Swordhands' roof, lying on the soft bed, a woven blanket tucked around me.

I lay there, unable and unwilling to move. I couldn't tell if the feeble light invading from the outside was from a sunrise or a sunset. Either way, it'd been at least a few hours since I'd presumably passed out. I twitched my stiff fingers. I swallowed bile. I blinked my blurry eyes. I inhaled misery and exhaled agony. By all accounts, I still lived, but I felt dead and long buried, just waiting to finally turn to dust.

Ren.

I didn't have the energy to answer him, even in my mind. It only made him more annoyingly insistent.

Gods-damn it. Ren!

Fucking gods, Dre. What?

You're not alone.

I barked a humorless, empty laugh.

Aren't I? She's not here. He said a confrontation was needed. He was talking about her. I'm here, and she's not. Poof. Ephemeral. The word triggered a memory, part of a phrase that Nathalia had written not long ago, and a new tidal wave of sorrow battered me. I dug the heels of my hands into my eyes, trying to stand against the flood pulling me under. *It's all right. She's all right. Just unconscious, maybe.*

You—

No. Tears started to slip from the corners of my eyes and slide down my temples. *She's not dead. Injured, maybe. That's all. Just hurt. She took some hits, but she's strong. So fucking strong.*

I know you're mourning, but—

Nothing. But nothing, Dre. I can't—

Ren! You're not alone* in the room*!

Dredon had never screamed in my head before. Never once. The internal volume made me jolt slightly off the bed, and the blanket tangled in my legs. *What?*

"Hello, brother. I was waiting for you to wake up."

With those words, I scrambled off the bed, ripping the blanket from around me. I turned this way and that, looking for his familiar reddish-blond hair and bullshit-colored eyes. My vision was blurry from my lack of eyewear, so I couldn't see him, but I knew beyond a shadow of a doubt he was here.

I was grateful he *was* here, honestly. Because now I had a target, a deserving recipient for the inferno building inside of me. "Come out, Ravik," I said, low and rumbling, to the room.

Out of a dark corner of the room, where the tepid sun's rays didn't quite reach, Ravik slowly and carefully stepped closer, a large bruise darkening his left eye. With his hands raised in front of him, he looked as though he was approaching a wild animal.

He was.

"Ramiren, I can exp—"

Though I didn't have feathered wings to give me a push, I didn't need them. Finding a reservoir of strength that came from the anger only despair can forge, I threw myself at my traitor brother, my claw-like fingers aiming for his throat.

Chapter Sixteen
The Passing of Memories

My ass hit the upholstered chair, bouncing once, as I glared up at my older brother. I wiped the blood from my once-again broken nose with the back of my hand, embracing the lesser sting this one caused. I considered seeking Raewyn out, but answers needed to come first. "Where the *fuck* is she, Ravik? Is she even alive?"

Ravik gently palpated the red marks, vaguely finger-shaped, at his throat as he sat down in the chair next to mine. He pulled his hand back with a wince and let out an exhausted sigh that I had zero sympathy for. With a hoarse voice, he began. "Look. Ramiren. I don't know what to tell you—"

I pointed an accusing finger at his battered face. "You do. You can tell me right *the fuck* now *where* she is, *how* she is, and *why* I shouldn't kill you, Ravik. Explain to me why I shouldn't cut out your heart and eat it while you *fucking watch*."

He narrowed his eyes in disbelief. "Honestly? Because you *can't*." Dre's voice carried a tone of warning. ***Ren.***

What?

Listen to him.

Fuck, Dre. You too?

Please.

I scoffed indignantly, shaking my head. My hand waved in the air lazily. "Fine, you ridiculous piece of shit. Talk."

Ravik leaned forward, elbows on thighs, and rested the side of his kissing palms against his mouth like he was engaging in a profane prayer. "There are some parts I can tell you, Ramiren, but there are other parts I'm incapable of describing. I have to show you. And you need to understand the context before you see what happened."

I massaged my throbbing left eye with my wrist. "Show me?"

"Eidetic transfer."

I chuckled ruefully then tongued a sharp canine. "You want to show me your memories? You want me to actually watch her and Vrakus fight when you won't even tell me if she's alive or dead? I asked about her status, but you wouldn't tell me. Overly dramatic. That's exactly what Vrakus would do. You're psychotic, Ravik. Truly."

He briskly scrubbed his face with his hands, his black claws scratching at his blond beard. Black claws I hadn't taken note of until now. I fetched my glasses from the table by the bed and stared at them, then him, through my glasses. A black miasma coalesced in his chest. Just like Vrakus.

Everything clicked, including the fact that I couldn't smell his emotions.

My next words came out as a harsh exhale. "Your claws...she..."

"Yes. Now, again, do you want me to show you?"

A part of me abhorred the idea of possibly watching her final moments, of seeing her eyes go lifeless and the light in them dim and fail.

But a larger part of me wanted to see her last miracle. "Show me."

Ravik took my hand in a steel grip, and the world fell away.

It took me a moment to get my bearings, as it always did with an eidetic transfer. However, I didn't expect the first thing I'd see was Nathalia's fist flying into my face. There was no pain. Eidetic transfer doesn't provide thoughts or feelings, only what can be observed. Intended as a way for pactmakers to quickly and efficiently pass on accurate information, it served a greater purpose now.

Still, I reflexively winced, watching the world spin precariously when her punch slammed into Ravik's face. The vision righted as Ravik steadied himself. He was on the floor, and I realized she must have knocked him on his ass. I felt the punch, dulled as it was. Thankfully, the eidetic transfer didn't pass along pain.

Nathalia approached, eyes blazing, and bent down to get in my...Ravik's...line of sight. "You didn't even let me say *goodbye*." She straightened to kick his side while he was down.

I could hear a grunt, presumably from Ravik, before he replied as he rose to standing. "No time, Nathalia. We need to go. *Now.* I'm sorry, but it had to happen that way. Otherwise, your goodbye would have eaten up the window of time we have."

Nathalia drew her sword, muttering in a clipped tone, "Yes. Fine. Lead the way."

Ravik started walking, occasionally looking at Nathalia. She looked strong. Jaw set. Determined. Pride tinged with profound sorrow flared. If she was about to do what I believed, then—

Ravik said, "How do you feel?"

Her eyes stared straight ahead as she answered, "Can't complain." She glanced at Ravik. "How's your eye?"

"Sore."

"Good." She muttered under her breath as she turned the corner. "Fucker."

I smiled despite myself.

We passed through the hallways, each looking identical to the next. It was beginning to irritate me how often he looked Nathalia's way, flicking gazes that she didn't catch. It was probably just concern over whether or not his gambit would succeed, but it did give me one thing. Yes, she looked strong. Far stronger than she should.

My curiosity piqued, I whispered, "Ravik, what was in that vial? What did you give her?"

He replied in a low tone, concentrating on the transfer. "A chance."

The distant boom of a masculine voice, crowing and laughing, reached us as we neared our destination. Another corner turned, and on the other end of the long hallway, I could see blue-white light flickering in a cavernous room. Shadows from the countless devils present danced along the walls, and Vrakus's voice grew louder and distinct enough to hear.

"...Best time is near. The thousand vials stored and ready, one for each of you, will be the key. And thanks to the generous donation of our newest guest..." The rumble of soft laughter followed, punctuated by high-pitched cackles. "We're ahead of schedule. The Lorindar will watch, and we will act."

Nathalia and Ravik stopped just before the threshold. One last moment of peace and reprieve. He looked at her, and she met his gaze.

A small, sad smile curled her lips. "You know, I never really got it until now. The Tarindar and Lorindar balance each other. Horyn's protection is offset by Worin's destruction. Minue's love by Ephine's hate. Bari's life to Irris's death. Valiset's health and Atia's disease. Paqua's light against Garus's darkness. And the Tarindar's selflessness to the Lorindar's greed for more. Neither winning nor losing. They balance each other, because one cannot exist without the other to compare it."

She adjusted her shield's straps, lips thinned and brow furrowed in concentration. "Even this sword and shield are a balance, Ravik. Attack and defense. But many don't know that the reason the protector's sigil is a four-pointed star is because it resembles a sword. Two sides of a hilt, a pommel, and a sword's tip. Yes, it's tradition for each point of the star to mean an individual tenet, but the true reason is that sometimes the only way to protect someone is to destroy that which threatens them."

Her golden eyes simmered, poised on a precipice like the calm before the storm.

Never before had I been so humbled by another, even when Nathalia swore her oath to me. With the unyielding and sacred purpose only a protector can have, she was doing what she'd promised.

My light in the darkness, and my hope when there was none.

Ravik whispered to Nathalia, "Should Vrakus fall, the devils under his command will be wild and feral. Without a master for the span of a resting heartbeat. The passing of power is nearly instantaneous. It's tricky timing, but if you succeed, you'll make it home. Shall we, Protector Advocate?"

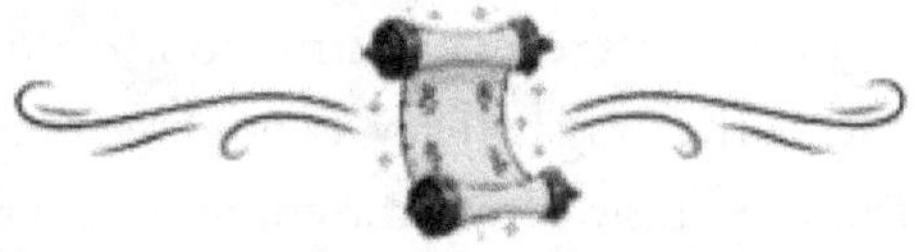

Nathalia answered with a single nod.

Ravik broke the transfer, and my mind slammed back into my body without warning. With the abrupt departure, my head felt two sizes too big.

I gripped my hair, reeling. "Ah, fuck! Ravik, what—"

Ravik leaned back heavily into his chair. "Ramiren, before we get to what happened next, I need to inform you of something."

Wariness tilted my head. "What is it?"

Giving a tight-lipped smile, he took a moment before responding. "Vrakus lied."

I sneered. "He did that a lot, so you'll have to be more specific."

"I was unable to tell you before now, as I was forbidden to, but..."

He pinched the bridge of his nose as if an internal battle raged inside of him. "He didn't remove her mark."

My mind blanked. "Wait... I beg your pardon?"

"He didn't remove the mark, Ramiren. He couldn't. He tried, but he couldn't. The marks were locked the second they appeared on your skin. Yes, there was an addendum that stated Vrakus could provide the consequences of a broken pact. That part is true. But apparently you can't take away a pact's benefits as a consequence. They have to be separate things, and with you adding the time limitation as an addendum, that those who bear Vrakus's mark go home after seven days and nights, that mark became both a liability *and* a benefit. He was cornered. So when he touched her neck, the pact thaumaturgy wouldn't let him remove it."

I stood and paced away so I wouldn't lash out at him again, but I didn't know where to look or what to do with my hands. "So we really only had to wait a week?"

Ravik nodded.

I paused and pushed down the injustice of the situation to keep calm. Then the jagged pieces finally clicked into place, and I glared at him. "He's about to say that. In your memory. Isn't he? That's why you stopped."

He stared into the hearth's dying fire to his immediate right, probably lit by the person or persons who'd brought me up here to rest. "Yes. He could have chosen anything as a consequence, but he wanted you to *choose* to stay. So he instead had to hide Nathalia's mark, so you'd offer to take her place."

For fuck's sake.

I threw my hands up. "Which I *did*, if you recall."

He nodded. "Yes, which you did. He wanted you to promise to stay in Gateway forever, so he needed to give you an incentive. To trade yourself for her, so she could go home."

Son of a bitch. "Then why the fuck didn't he take me up on the offer?"

He shrugged, as though the reasons for Vrakus's antics were obvious. "You know him. He still had three days to agree to the trade before his lie was exposed. He wanted to play with Nathalia a bit longer and watch you *squirm*."

When I said you're not alone earlier, I meant it in that way too. I'll be here through it all.

Thank you, Dredon.

I sat back down and extended my hand for Ravik to take again. "The next part. Show me."

Ravik placed his hand on mine, and the world fell away once more.

"... not them. They will try to steal them for their own devils, so double all guards around the alchemists and stockrooms. Anyone with wings, hooks, or more than two arms steps foot on Third, chop 'em and drop 'em. We have three days before I have to send the angel-spawn back and free up her attendants, so be ready. Understood?"

The murmur of assent mostly drowned out the sound of disgust from Nathalia, but I heard it.

"Your father is a child." She rolled her eyes and strode forward. "Excuse me. Thank you. Please move aside. Coming through." She only had to singe one or two devils with her shield before their shrieks alerted others closer to the front to move.

Vrakus continued his speech, turning as he spoke. "Now, with my—" He fell silent when he caught sight of us, looking from Ravik to Nathalia. "Sons. Speaking of which, hello, Ravik. I'm glad you're feeling better, and I see you brought a friend." He grinned, throwing his hands wide. "The protector appears to have brought some entertainment. Going to dance for us, young lady?"

She smiled and stepped forward. "I'm sure we'll both dance before long, Vrakus. Maybe you'll even sing."

Vrakus snorted in laughter, walking a few paces to the side. "Oh, I see why he likes you. Beauty and wit." He ran his gaze down her dirty frame with a once-over. "And, strangely, healed." Vrakus raised an eyebrow at Ravik in a side-eyed expression that promised a lengthy discussion later. "Quite impressive. How did that happen?"

Nathalia stopped barely ten feet from him. I wanted to reach out, to pull her back, but I was merely a helpless observer watching through the eyes of the active participant. "My angelic heritage. I can heal myself."

It was perhaps the most impressive lie Nathalia had ever told.

But when Vrakus smiled, both amused and unimpressed, I knew it wasn't enough.

"Angelic heritage, hm?" He blew out breath from his cheeks and clicked his tongue. "Ravik, since your stomach is feeling so much better, please get her out of my sight."

"Gladly, Father." Ravik moved forward to Nathalia as she looked back at him. Her guarded gaze looked wary and uncertain, as if she had no idea what to expect.

Fuck. *I* didn't even know what to expect.

"As ordered, out of sight." My brother reached out his hand to take her arm, but instead of grabbing her, he touched his index and middle fingers to her wrist.

Nathalia disappeared before my eyes, and the eyes of all assembled. Including Vrakus.

Ravik took a step back while Vrakus recoiled, stunned for no more than a moment before he hissed, "Boy, what ha—"

But his question was interrupted as Nathalia reappeared in front of him, the tip of her longsword disappearing into the center of Vrakus's chest. The blade sank deep, with a wet crunch of metal snapping and slicing bone. Blood, dark and thick, welled around the impaling steel and ran down the fuller as though it was collecting a prize.

Surprise combined with awe registered on the arch-devil's face as he stared at the glimmering red gem in her sword's pommel. It twinkled like a mocking star in the blue-white light.

Ravik had done nothing but turn her invisible to satisfy the command, but he'd given her an opening to attack.

If I wasn't so angry at him, I'd be impressed.

Vrakus snatched the blade with both hands to halt her progress, and pushed against her advance. He slowly gained ground, his grin widening as the sword began to exit his torso.

"Almost, young lady, but not quite." When he pushed hard, even with his fingers now slick from the blade cutting into his flesh, she stumbled back and immediately dropped into a fighting stance.

"Fine. I suppose I'll put her there myself. Devils, stay back." Vrakus took a step forward. Nathalia replied with a reposition, and so began the steady, rhythmic dance she'd promised.

Vrakus, claws black and extended, slashed out and barely missed a glance off her shield. He chuckled low and lashed out again, testing her guard and reflexes. Playing. Vrakus pivoted and walked around her. Golden eyes peeking just over the top of the blessed shield followed every movement of his feet, his steps, adjustments, and weight distribution.

Like with her mother less than a week ago, Nathalia's movements were sharp but efficient. She kept him at the distance she wanted, her longsword's reach against his shorter arm. But while Lady Resa had honed her savagery, Vrakus was all unrestrained brutality. She was, once again, waiting her opponent out, and maybe because of whatever was in that silvery vial she'd drunk, as Ravik had said, she had a chance.

The question was, what would it cost her?

Sparks flew when the steel of her keen-edged longsword collided with the arch-devil's claws time and again, tiny chips flaking off the black talons. When she lunged, he dodged in a blur. When he brought his claws down to rend, she sidestepped and counterattacked. Both were awaiting an opportune moment, when their opponent stepped a little too far or a weapon dipped a little too low.

Unfortunately, Vrakus's moment arrived first when Nathalia stepped to the side and slipped slightly, her leather boots squeaking and skidding on the dark liquid coating the floor.

The black and perfectly smooth obsidian had gone from stable to hazardous, courtesy of the blood drops from the arch-devil's hands. Reflexively I tried yelling to her, but I was tortured into merely watching as Vrakus brought down both hands.

Nathalia spun, overcorrecting in an attempt to force her shield to take at least one blow instead of her side or back. Vrakus's triumphant grin dimmed when he realized what was about to happen, his swipe having too much inertia to stop in time.

His left hand sliced across her flank, slicing deep and causing her to wobble. Though she grimaced, it spoke more of determination than pain. His right hand's claws met her shield and sheared four ragged marks through the blessed steel, tearing straight through the metal until the bent scraps flew off and clattered to the floor.

Only the shield's boss, with the top and bottom tips of the protector's star protruding in sharp points, remained strapped to her forearm. Nathalia never even spared a glance at her father's demolished shield. Her steps faltered as she adjusted her stance again, ready for another attack that never came.

A beat of silence, then a screech of agony and rage filled the room as Vrakus clutched his right wrist, where his arm now ended. His ruined appendage resembled more a melted candle than a limb, and the smell of melted flesh, sickly sweet and acrid, cut through even the ever-present sulfur.

Spittle and foul Infernal curses fell from his lips. Nathalia stepped to the side, lowering her demolished shield as she watched. Then what he'd actually done settled into his fractured mind, and he barked a maddened laugh. "What is a protector without her shield, then? What now, *la'kora*?"

Nathalia smiled and pushed her left foot back, changing her stance as her left hand lifted to join the right on her longsword's extended grip.

When she charged Vrakus, golden spectral wings emerged from her back, and a savage, feminine scream rang through the room. She arced into the air, high above Ravik's head, to gain leverage as she descended and closed in on her kill.

Every tiny hair on my body rose at the unbridled wildness in her expression as she bore down upon the Arch-Devil of Gateway's Third District.

Instinctively, Vrakus raised his unharmed left hand to catch her downward swing. The blade kissed his outstretched palm and continued its path, slicing, slicing, until it finally stalled in the middle of his meaty forearm.

I held my breath. My lungs wouldn't inflate anyway.

Without trying to dislodge her weapon, Nathalia dropped her left hand from her sword's grip. She pulled the arm back, then whipped it forward with another hoarse cry. With a sideways turn of her forearm to aim, the top star's point—the one she'd once told me stood for vigilance—which was sticking out of the broken shield sank into Vrakus's throat. She ripped it out immediately.

Though they were fighting in the center of the throne room, the thick torrent of blood, pulsing with every panicked beat of his heart, resembled the fountains of Ghau, nearly reaching the cloven hooves and three-toed feet of the fiendish spectators.

The arch-devil looked to his soldiers, eyes ordering them to defend him. To strike her down. But when he tried to give the order that would make them obey, no words emerged. He tried harder to talk, frustration and the threat of retribution in his expression, but his resulting gurgling held no command. Vrakus fell backward, no more hands available to clasp the hemorrhaging puncture wound.

When his body hit the floor, his melted neck gave way from the impact, and his head rolled across the slick floor and stopped a few feet away from his body. A dull gray cloud exited Vrakus's mouth on a last exhale and sped toward a new target.

Ravik.

Within a blink, the devils standing at placid attention became deranged animals. Whistle after whistle sounded in a discordant mix of tones and harmonies. I paid no attention, the noise like the distant buzzing of flies, as I stared at the victor, my protector. The woman who had defeated the ghost who had haunted me for most of my life.

Nathalia, out of breath, filthy, and exhausted, had never looked more beautiful as she turned my way, toward Ravik, and grinned with sweet relief. Hypnotized by the beautiful, radiant smile that beckoned me like a water nymph, I didn't even see it coming.

The smoky cloud was nearly to its destination when I heard Ravik scream and point. "Behind you!"

The cloud entered Ravik just as Nathalia turned, and Eronis's claws, seeking their vengeance for the old arch-devil's death, slashed upward. Her back was to me, and I saw only a great red mist materialize as her head was thrown back from the devil's attack. She toppled, hitting the floor hard.

Fuck! Gods-damn it! No!

I tore at my cage, at Ravik's mind, but he held on and continued the cursed narrative he'd insisted on showing me.

The moment the cloud entered Ravik's body, the new Arch-Devil of Gateway's Third District roared, "Stand down!"

Eronis backed away obediently as Ravik scrambled to her, immediately placing his steady hands on Nathalia's mangled neck. Fingers sank into the deep tears there in an attempt to stem the overwhelming red current. Unseeing terror filled Nathalia's eyes as blood filled and bubbled out of her mouth, spilling out the corners.

I knew this scene had already played out. What Fate had decreed here was already in the past.

I knew, and I yelled for him to help her anyway.

"*Fuck!* Aw, fuck. I— You! Fetch me an Angel's Tears vial! Now!" Ravik boomed the order at a short spiked devil, who ran off to fulfill his new master's request.

I could do nothing. Nothing but watch helplessly as her lips turned blue and her face once again became ashen, stark against the sanguine liquid.

"Fuck! Nathalia, it wasn't supposed to go this way. I wanted you out of here," Ravik rambled as he tried and failed to stop the precious flow of blood from her tattered neck. Blind faith kept telling me the vial would arrive in time, and she was just too injured to currently move. She was still in Third District, hurt but alive. That's why he needed me to see this. He needed to let me know what she'd gone through, but she was all right.

She was all right.

My protector's face relaxed and her fear faded, except for the gentle smile tugging at the corner of her mouth. When her eyes closed, panic and despair fought for supremacy within me. But as she furrowed her eyebrows in concentration, I went numb from head to toe.

Ravik sighed grimly, keeping his hand on her throat. "Pray if you need to, Nathalia."

She wasn't gone, and I knew she wasn't praying.

She was speaking her last words—her last promise and last confession.

To me.

Then her brow released its tension, like she'd merely drifted off to sleep, and her chest stilled.

"Na-Nathalia?" Ravik shook her gently as if to wake her, but my protector didn't reply to him.

Just as she hadn't replied to me.

Chapter Seventeen
In Her Silence

"I'm sorry, Ramiren. You have my sympathies."

When Ravik placed his hand on my shoulder, I slapped it away, skewering him with daggers from my eyes. I shot up, pointing a finger in his face. "You used her. You *used* her, you selfish fuck!"

He took a step back, scowling. "It was *her* choice, Ramiren. Her. Choice. She could have told me no. She could have spit in my face, but she jumped at the opportunity. I didn't have to convince her. I offered a way out, and she took it."

My eyebrows went to my hairline. A short laugh puffed out of me at his cheek. "Oh. Sure. Of course. Because being brutalized and kept in a freezing ditch to slowly die was a *better* alternative." I slowly shook my head at his ignorance, with no hope that he would actually get it. "You just stuck her in a bigger prison, Ravik."

Ravik took a few steps to the side and smirked, rolling his eyes. "Ironic. You lecturing me about keeping her imprisoned, when it was *her* oath to *you* that made her take the deal."

My teeth bared in seething frustration at his inability to grasp his part in her demise. "Fuck you, Ravik. I *know* I hold plenty of blame for this shit, but I didn't ask her to do that. She did it all on her own. But you? *You* gave a desperate, *tortured* woman an impossible choice. To do what you *never* could."

Ravik scoffed, throwing his hands up. "Precisely. I *couldn't* do it. Sure, he hadn't outright ordered me to never attack him, directly or indirectly. But if I'd tried? He'd simply order me to stand down. What part of Incubi's Breath do you not understand? This was the *only* way, and gods-damn it, I am *sorry* it ended this way."

"Then why didn't he just order *you* to stop her, hm? Order *any* devil under his command to stop her? Or breathe on her too, for that matter? He didn't use his most powerful weapon."

Ravik stopped to consider the question, frowning. He finally answered in an absent tone. "Incubi's breath takes a long time, several minutes at minimum. I got the impression he was both too angry and extremely bored."

Bored? He was fucking bored*?*

"And now you've ascended. A full-fledged arch-devil. King of Third District. Congratulations, Ravik, you turned out exactly like him. Throne, power, selfishness, and all. Bought with the life and now damned soul of the first woman I've ever lo—"

My jaw closed with a click of my teeth.

It had nearly escaped my lips, unconsciously and unbidden. I didn't need to evaluate the validity of it. The lightning-strike moment had arrived, and I was singed and electrified in its wake. Every anguished mote of my existence knew it to be true.

But I'd be damned along with her if he was the first person to hear it.

My arms crossed as I stared down at the intricate pattern on the carpet beneath my feet. I muttered, "What happened to Eronis?"

Gratefully, he went with my subject change. Amusement lightened his voice. "He went into the Drop. An alive, torpid shell falling for eternity until one of the Lorindar gets snacky. It was the least I could do." He sighed softly. "For her."

I didn't want to hear him be wistful when thinking of her. I didn't want him thinking about her at all. So I lifted my head and did my best to keep my voice soft but simmering. "Well, I hope you enjoy it, for however long you have. If I ever see you again, I'll find a way to kill you, and I promise I'll enjoy it. Now get the fuck out of my sight."

"Perhaps you shouldn't use that exact phrasing i—"

"Leave!"

Instead of doing as I'd demanded, he moved back to the shadow he'd materialized from. "I will, but I need to return these first."

"Return what?"

He stuck his hand into the dark corner and pulled out three items—a longsword with a red-jeweled pommel, a plain necklace with a smoky gem, and a large bundle wrapped in cloth.

"Before I came to your room, I placed her body in the villa's crypt. She's been...conserved. Her body won't decay, even once buried." He placed the items on the desk in the corner.

I didn't have the strength to thank him.

"Goodbye, brother." With his farewell, Ravik disappeared. Staring at the items he'd left, I clenched my hands in my hair, unsure if I wanted to look at what was under the cloth. Based upon the size, I could take an educated guess.

I blew out a breath then muttered, "Fine. Fuck it." Stalking over, I pulled the cloth aside and confirmed my suspicions.

The edges looked even more serrated than they had in the vision Ravik gave me. Vrakus's blood, long dried, stained the vigilance star's point and turned the gold to a muted brown.

My temper flared, hot as the Gateway Orb I hoped would hover over Third District until this world turned dead and barren.

I picked up the first delicate thing I could see—a porcelain statuette of nesting swans—and threw it as hard as I could against the wall.

Too heartsick to even speak aloud, I yelled in my head. *I should've told her, Dre. Why the fuck didn't I tell her?*

I didn't need to elaborate to Dredon what I was referring to. He knew and responded gently. ***You didn't know, Ren.***

I should've. Every indication was there, and I ignored them. I ignored every sign.

We can see the evidence of our true feelings, Ren, but that doesn't mean our perception of them is clear enough to interpret. Sometimes, comprehension only comes from hindsight.

Did you know, Dre?

I strongly suspected. Yes.

I couldn't blame him for staying silent. I would've either denied it outright or done nothing about it.

If you can't tell her, tell the universe. Be brave and say it, Ramiren. Even the Lorindar can grant mercy.

Or they'll punish her more.

Then go to a safe place where they can't hear you. Go to the pact room and say it.

It was the best I would ever get now. I would need to dismantle the room. I should've done it immediately upon learning of her death, but not yet. I needed to say goodbye first.

I picked up the necklace, the bit of unremarkable jewelry that had ruined my first family, then gave me a second one, and snapped my fingers. The yellow bedroom vanished, and another far more familiar bedroom took its place.

I looked around, as Nathalia used to do, and a wave of grief rolled through my body, making my eyes sting and throat feel swollen from something heavy stuck there. My lungs filled on a shaky breath. I knew I would need every puff of air in them to say what I had to.

The words came out shaky and broken, but I didn't care, because she wouldn't have cared. "Nathalia, it will be the greatest regret of my life that I never told you." I rolled my lips between my teeth. "I lo—"

A soft, resonant voice to my left interrupted me, "Cordani? D'ya lo?"

Startled, I whipped around to see a pearl-gray mist roughly three feet in diameter floating through a side doorway, sparks of light flitting about like indistinct, vapor-like fireflies. At its center, a small globe of light pulsed. "Cordani?" it asked again.

Too distracted by my mission, I hadn't noticed it. The air I'd filled my lungs with earlier, in preparation for speaking my heart for the first time in all my sixty-one years, fled in a wheeze.

Dredon and I both, simultaneously and with the same incredulity, whispered, "What the fuck?"

Chapter Eighteen
Devotion Unsaid

Clutching the broken necklace, I murmured, "Dre? Dre, what is this?"

I have no idea. I honestly have no idea.

"Who are you?" I frowned as I walked around it, trying to discern what I could. On all sides I could see, it appeared the same. I could detect no illusions, and its magical signatures were, in a word, odd. It gave off the strong aura that an immortal did, but that aura kept flickering like a sputtering lantern. "*What* are you?"

The light at its center wavered for a few seconds before increasing as it spoke in Common. "You are not speaking Gods-Tongue. Though I suppose you can't right now, with your vocal cords."

"I—No, I'm not. Again, I ask, what are you? The fact that you're a strange, puffy mist that apparently speaks Gods-Tongue and are here, in my pact room, makes me mighty curious. Keep in mind I've had the worst day of my life, so please indulge me."

Again, the cloud paused before speaking. "I understand, but you've never failed to speak Gods-Tongue before. I can't see your flesh, so it took me a moment." The hair on the back of my neck stood up at its phrasing, but I was on my last nerve, ready to tell whatever entity this was to fuck off, when it continued. "I am your cordani, and you are mine."

"Cord—" My brain stuttered. "Wait. You're the thing that put that word into my head? Into Nathalia's head? Explain how you got in here. *Now.*"

"What word, cordani?"

"*That* word. That *fucking* word, which I have no idea what it means and no way to understand it. I searched the Citadel library for 'cordani.' I used my ability to translate languages. Nothing."

The cloud chimed like a hundred tiny bells. *Was it laughing?* "You cannot use mortal magic to understand the language of the gods. And it has no script. There's no need for one."

"Mother fucking—" With an aggravated sigh, I placed my hands on my thighs as I leaned forward, head bent. My last thread of patience, frayed as it already was, disintegrated. "All right, that's it. That's fucking it. I'm done. I should've just dissolved this room like I was *supposed* to. Time to send you back to wherever you came from. So long, you voyeuristic fog bank."

I lifted my hand to snap my fingers, and the cloud responded. "Good. Thank you."

My hand froze, thumb and middle finger pressed together. With a deep frown borne of confusion, my head tilted. "Wait. Good?" I straightened, lowering my hand but not separating my fingers. "Am... Are you *trapped* here?"

"I believe so, as I cannot leave. Please do what you need to and let me go to Celestia in peace."

Celestia? So it's either an angel, a god, or a soul.

I've never seen or heard of an angel that looked like this, and based upon how rudely you've been talking to it, it's unlikely to be a god.

Then that leaves one option.

I stuffed the necklace into a pocket and lifted my free hand, holding it palm out. "I'm sorry. Wait a minute. Are you implying you're a *soul*? You're a *trapped soul*, is that right?"

The bright specks floating within it sped up for a second, swirling like a blizzard's snowfall. "That is correct. Now release me, please."

I shrugged, irritated. "Fine. I—"

Ren.

My instinct was to ignore him, I'd been so set on releasing it. But he might have some insight.

Yes?

I think that's Nathalia.

Pain in my chest at what he'd said, the stab burning a hole there, caused tears to well in my eyes. I huffed, threading my fingers into my hair. *That's not funny, Dre. That's not fucking funny.*

Am I laughing? This incompetence of yours is getting tiresome. Learn from your dumb mistakes and **listen.** ***Grief and shame have tilted you beyond reason.***

Harsh.

But necessary. Move past your emotions for a time. Ask it questions and confirm. It seems very coincidental that the pact room you made and

shared with her now suddenly holds a soul after she died. And you know what we always say about coincidences.

His words were a stinging slap, but a needed one. *Fine.* I cleared my throat thickly and began, "So, uh, what does 'cordani' translate to in Gods-Tongue?"

The soul responded, the globe at the cloud's center pulsing with each word. "The direct translation in mortal tongue is 'soul mirror.'"

I shifted, bringing my hand to my mouth, rubbing my lips. "Soul mirror," I repeated, trying to wrap my head around what this meant. "It's...it means '*soul mirror.*'"

"No."

I considered looking for something to throw.

Dredon hissed, ***Listen! We're missing something. Go back through that exchange.***

All right. All right. I took a deep breath in and let it out slowly. *I asked what it translates to, it said soul mirror, then I tried to confirm what it m— Aw, damn it. What's the first rule of language translation?*

Uh, context before vocabulary?

Exactly. I asked for the translation, then tried to confirm the word without context. Two different things.

"What does 'cordani' mean, then?"

Seconds, then minutes dragged on as it floated there silently. Doubt began to creep in until it finally replied. "It's the bond between the original and the companion."

A memory sparked. "You mean like Laeth and the Feylands?"

"Those lands have that bond too, yes."

Too.

I turned around. I didn't know where to look or what to do, so I plopped onto the bed. My back hit the velvet covers as a groaning sigh escaped me. "And you said I'm yours and you're mine. You— We're, what, each other's soul mirror? That's what...that's what you're saying?"

"Correct," the soul said, as if that single word didn't shatter my brain like cheap porcelain.

Oh.

Oh.

I removed my glasses, tossing them on the bed next to my right hip, and scrubbed my face with both hands. I had no idea how to process that information, and I most certainly wouldn't do it immediately.

"Now, release me from this place, cordani. Allow me to pass to Celestia."

A thought occurred to me, another fact I thought I knew made murky and uncertain, akin to a universal law being broken. "Fuck. Hold on. You died in Gateway. The Drop claims you if you die there. How are you here?"

"The home of the Lorindar, what you evocatively call the Dark Drop, tried but then rejected me, because, above all, the Lorindar are not *wasteful.* Now will you *please* let me go?"

It was my turn to not answer, as I was still busy trying to understand the implications of everything that'd happened in the past twenty-four hours.

In the past five minutes.

Dre, if she's not in the Dark Drop...

...that means...

...she can be brought back.

Hope and excitement bloomed, but I immediately squashed them into nothing more than cautious optimism. Fear, hope, denial, despair, and now hope again bobbed me up and down as though I were detritus in a rapid river instead of a person.

Managing my emotions would be the tricky part, perhaps even more than figuring out *how* to bring her back, but those emotions would be handled in increments, as needed. For now, I had to work out how to restore her to life and where to start.

I scowled, my fingertips now tapping my mouth. I whispered to myself, "But where?"

The soul's otherworldly voice intoned, "What do you mean?"

I murmured, more to myself than in an attempt to answer the soul. "I need to make a plan to bring you back to life."

Alarmingly, the cloud *hissed* like a cat. "But I don't want to. Let me go! I have fulfilled my purpose."

Rising up on my elbows to look at it, I decided to try another tactic. "From what I know of soul mi— Sorry, *cordani,* a soul sickens with deterioration, and a mirror is placed in front of it, making the second?"

The center light inside of it dimmed slightly. "Yes. That is correct."

I pondered out loud, hoping Nathalia's soul would confirm. "The original soul would have died without the companion soul, and the companion soul would not have existed without the original soul. Is that correct?"

"Yes, that is correct."

I frowned. "I see. How is this not more well known? Laeth and the Feylands are...bonded this way, but I've never heard of people bonded."

"A combination of rarity and one not finding out until after mortal death." The soul paused. "Usually, anyway."

"And Nathalia, as in mortal Nathalia, didn't know? That was your name, if you didn't know."

"Did *you* know before I told you?"

Well. Now we know her grumpy stubbornness goes soul deep.

I grinned crookedly, despite my stress. Warm affection settled under my skin, and for the first time that day, a modicum of happiness lit my own soul.

The soul's light pulsed slowly. "There are...hints, I believe, but mortals do not know for a fact."

I was considering what it said, especially the use of the word "hints," when the soul spoke again, softer this time. "Please release me. I have no more purpose here."

Consent and the right of another to govern their own autonomy and agency battled with my need to keep it here and bring Nathalia back. My mind told me to give it what it wanted, but my heart told me to refuse it. The two snarling beasts pounced and rolled, trying to gain the upper hand in a fierce battle of fur and fangs.

It's the soul's decision.

Perhaps.

On the other hand, I don't think it truly understands what it's saying, or that coming back might be an attainable outcome.

Perhaps.

Thank you, Dredon. Very helpful.

What do you want me to say? I can't make this choice for you, and it's entirely possible you'll be removed from the Registrar if the Citadel finds out.

That's the least of my worries right now.

Dredon laughed.

What?

I never thought I'd see the day, Ramiren. You choosing your heart over your head.

I—that's... Fuck.

He was right.

If I ignore its wishes, how am I any better than what Vrakus tried to do with my mother?

Vrakus wanted to control your mother, and he didn't care if she became a dead husk of herself.

And me?

I believe you want her alive, healthy, happy, and nothing more. Answer me this. If she were to awaken, thank you, and choose another to spend the rest of her life with, would you regret bringing her back?

I didn't even have to think about it. *No.*

There's your answer. You are not Vrakus, Ramiren. This choice is a gray one, I agree. Besides, ultimately, it is her choice.

What do you mean, "ultimately her choice"?

As I recall, from the limited available knowledge regarding resurrection magic, the soul has to be willing to return.

What, so this argument is all for nothing? I'm at a crossroads here, Dre.

Not for nothing, Ren. You would need to commit to even try to convince it. You would need to believe, down to your bones, that passing on would be the wrong call. That she should live, even if it's not by your side.

And the questions remain.

Do her soul's wishes take precedence over the desires of the person? Would Nathalia want to return?

I'd wager every memory I have of my mother's voice on it.

Then you have your answers.

One beast clamped its jaws down on the other's throat, and the other yielded. With a slow shake of my head, I responded aloud to the soul's request to be released. "No."

The soul's musical voice developed an edge sharper than even Nathalia's keen sword. "No? What do you mean *no*?"

"I mean no. I'm refusing your request, which is not something I take lightly. Frankly, this entire situation is abhorrent to me, but Nathalia died far too young." I slid my hand into my pocket, feeling for the necklace and rubbing my thumb on the smooth stone for luck. "Would you agree to a bargain? Give me three attempts. If, at the end of the three attempts, I still haven't convinced you to return, then I will dissolve the room and let you go."

The center light pulsed twice, then the entire cloud that made up Nathalia's soul moved for the first time since our discussion began. It hovered near the drawing of Nathalia I'd created on the wall, its light softly illuminating the portrait's features. The bright feylight-like globe faded to the weak glow of a dying candle. "Three attempts. For you, cordani. No more."

I gave a smile and snapped my fingers.

You worry too much, Ren. This'll be quite easy. I'm certain bringing your rapier was unnecessary.

He'll kill me, or at least try. Frankly, I'm surprised I'm still alive. Lady Resa probably tackled him to intervene.

Probably. I like her, but Kaleb is still my favorite. Something about him. He reminds me of you.

Me? Why?

He's sensitive. A bit naive, but with a good heart.

I've changed a lot.

Not as much as you think. You're still a gods-damned softie with a sweet tooth.

Muffled voices reached me before I stepped over the sitting room's threshold. I spotted Lady Resa and Kaleb in a heated discussion with a dirty and exhausted Lord Maxlian. I took that to mean the siege was still happening. He leaned against a heavy wooden desk, arms crossed and frowning deeply.

Oh. Whew. At least Kaleb lived.

On the couch, Raewyn sat on the sofa, lost in thought while staring into the fire and humming a familiar song I couldn't quite place.

They're not mourning. They don't know.

No.

Good luck.

Lord Maxlian, partially facing me, was the first to see me approach. He straightened as his arms tightened. I could see the clenched fists partially hidden by his plate armor, and his wings ruffled.

I stopped, holding up my hands in surrender. "Peace, please. I have good news and bad news. Which would you like to hear first?"

Kaleb and Lady Resa turned to me, and Raewyn sat up as though listening. Lady Resa shrugged, shaking her head, "Uh. Bad, I suppose? You always end on good news, so..."

"Wonderful. Lady Resa, please take hold of Lord Maxlian's wrist...great, thank you. Now. The bad news is...well, all right. Good news, then bad news, then good news. First, Nathalia defeated Vrakus. He's dead."

"She—" Lord Maxlian's eyes nearly popped out of his skull, his deep voice cracking like Kaleb's occasionally did. "She *what*?"

Here we go. "*But* she was attacked by an uncontrolled devil upon Vrakus's demise. She died. In Gateway."

The second of silence broke when Lord Maxlian roared, drowning out the reactions from everyone else present. "In Ga— You *fucking*—" He tried to come toward me, but Lady Resa tightened her grip. She slowed him down, but only barely, as he dragged her along.

When Lord Maxlian pulled his longsword from its sheath, Lady Resa yelled, her lip wobbling as she fought to hold back tears. "Good news, Ramiren! Now!"

To both comfort her and get out of harm's way, Kaleb scurried to Raewyn's side, who had started sobbing, and wrapped his arms around her.

My hand moved to my rapier's grip as I obliged Nathalia's mother. "I can get her back!"

"Bullshit!" Lord Maxlian screeched, his voice distorted from either strain or grief. When the angel attacked, I unsheathed my rapier and backhandedly tapped the side of his sword on his downward swing. The sword went wide, unbalancing him with my surprise parry. My rapier's tip flicked, adjusting to point directly toward his throat.

Lady Resa cried out, "Max! Max, stop!"

The high general's glistening eyes leveled me with a death stare before he threw his longsword down with a clatter of steel on marble. "Fine. Talk!"

I shot a grateful look to Lady Resa as my rapier's tip lowered, then continued. "Her soul isn't in the Dark Drop. It's...safe."

Raewyn wiped her teary eyes with her hands and spoke in a squeaky voice. "What? Safe? Wha— I don't understand. I thought—"

My index finger went into the air. "Yes. You die in Gateway, your soul gets pulled into the void. But she, uh...her soul is safe. I have it."

Raewyn narrowed her red eyes while Kaleb sniffled and whisper-yelled through the fingertips he'd pressed to his mouth. "I have so many questions!"

Lady Resa finally released her husband's wrist, scrunching her face as she rubbed it roughly. "So. I'm not even going to pretend to understand the hows and whys of what you just said, but you...you *have* her?"

When I nodded, Raewyn spoke softly. "I'll ask, then. *How* do you have her soul?"

My thumb rubbed the necklace in my pocket again as I answered her. "I can't actually tell you that. Not fully, anyway." I tried to think of a way to give an adequate response, enough that neither of her parents would murder me but where our pact, apparently still in effect, wouldn't be broken. "It's part of a pactmaker's abilities. After all, have you ever heard of a pactmaker having a protector? No. We work alone, by design." I tried to give my most confident smile, but it felt tight and wrong.

Lord Maxlian sputtered angrily, "Are you *kiddi—*"

Raewyn yelled brokenly to get his attention. "No! Dad. Leave it."

When Lord Maxlian spun to look suspiciously at the priestess, she shook her head, exhaustion shuttering her features.

"Fine," he replied in a tone that said it was anything but. "Fine. Is it possible to at least get her body?"

"I've been told it's in the crypt here."

Kaleb squinted. "Uh. It is? Who put her there?"

"The new Arch-Devil of Third District. My brother, Ravik."

Kaleb's head went into his hands as he muttered, "So, so many questions."

Chapter Nineteen
Anchor of Dread

I stared into the red-gold glow of the fire across the room, trying to distract myself by thinking of recent events so the priestess leaning over me could do what she needed to, but then Raewyn touched a tender area, and I jerked my head back. "Ow." My hand flew to my face without thinking, and she slapped it away.

Raewyn shot me an admonishing look but didn't verbally respond until her prayers ended with the customary benediction of "where love goes, beauty follows." I thanked her and took a deep, pain-free breath.

"I'm getting a bit tired of fixing this." She straightened and gave me a sad smile. "So who broke it this time?"

I scrunched and rolled my face to test my now-healed nose. "Ravik did. He came back without her, and I just...lost it."

She handed me a cloth and basin to clean up. "Did you get any good hits in?"

Accepting them with a nod, I put both on the small table next to me. "I throttled him, but with the transfer of power from Vrakus to him, he's quite a bit stronger than he used to be. Honestly, Nathalia got a better hit on him than I did."

After a sniffle that she tried to disguise as a weak snort, she asked derisively, "What'd he do? Rub dirt on her?" Raewyn picked up another cloth and moved to the copper kettle hanging over the sitting room's fire.

I managed a smile while ripples of sorrow cut my insides to ribbons. I inhaled to calm them. "She does...*did* hate being dirty, but no. He didn't let her say goodbye to me before he transported me here."

Like the surety of the changing seasons, I knew Raewyn would prod for more information. As she poured hot water from the kettle into the basin for me, she asked, "After you left? Did your brother show up with a shiner, then?"

Dipping my cloth in the water, I started to clean my face. "Yes. A nice one too." Knowing this would prompt even more questions, I prepared myself. "I saw it, Raewyn. I saw what she accomplished."

She straightened and frowned in confusion before placing the kettle on a trivet. "Saw? But you weren't there, right?"

A selfish part of me wanted to keep the details of what happened to myself, to hoard her final moments like a dragon with priceless gems, but I needed to learn to not keep secrets like I'd conditioned myself to. They hadn't directly led to Nathalia's death, but they'd played far too big a part. Besides, her heroism should be shared, especially with a person Nathalia loved.

"I wasn't, but I saw it. It's called eidetic transfer. A pactmaker ability that allows for one pactmaker to pass on what has been observed. It's meant to be used for negotiations, but..." I shrugged. "My br— Ravik is also a pactmaker. He was able to show me what happened."

Raewyn's eyes widened more and more the longer I talked. As I finished my explanation, she whispered, "Wow. That's...handy, I suppose."

The questions she had but was too afraid to ask might as well have been written in black ink all over her face. And with my nose repaired, I could smell the heavy scent of mud. I wanted to give her something in her grief, without a lie. "The one who killed her will suffer far more than she ever did."

With a bobbing nod, she replied quietly, folding the same cloth for the fifth time, "Thank you for telling me, Ramiren. That might be all I can handle hearing, to be honest, but knowing that much is a small blessing." She cleared her throat and finally set the cloth down to stare at me.

I frowned, looking down at my partially open black shirt to see if there were drops of blood. Seeing none visible, I met her gaze. "What?"

A smirk curled one side of her mouth. "I never got the chance to ask you. My sister didn't die a virgin, hm?"

I rolled my eyes as my hands went to my shirt ties to close it. When I didn't respond, she pushed again, "When, Ramiren?"

My continued silence only seemed to egg her on, because she stomped over and poked me in the chest. "*When*?"

My fingers dropped the shirt ties to rub where her sharp nail had scratched me, and I did my best not to show I was enjoying her irritation at my reticence. To see a small spark of life in her brown eyes was a lovely thing, and I wanted to keep it going for as long as possible, because I wanted to tell Nathalia about it if...no, *when* she returned. I faked a long, heaving sigh. "Raewyn—"

Her poking finger moved to point at my face. "Nope. Date, time, place, *and* positions. *Now.* Keep in mind, I'm not above feather torture."

Standing from my chair, I picked up my jacket, which was draped over the armrest, and maneuvered her away so I could put it back on. She tried to stand her ground, but I was far bigger than she was. "Are you asking me because you can't ask Nathalia?"

She looked me dead in the eye and replied, "I did ask her."

You know, I'm a little impressed. She has very few tells, and I almost didn't catch the lie.

Same. "Oh? And?"

Raewyn shrugged with perfect nonchalance. "I want to confirm what she said. That's all."

My answering unmoving smirk made her pout when she realized her ploy hadn't worked. "That's an ineffective trick, Raewyn. A word of advice in the form of the *second* oldest tip in the book. 'Don't try to bullshit a bullshitter.'"

She leveled me with a stare, her innocent facade dropping. "And what's the first? 'Don't use your teeth'?"

"No, that's the third." After fixing the cuffs of my jacket, I adjusted the front and collar. Lowering my hands, I smiled down at her. "The first is 'When people want to talk, let them. When they don't, wait.'"

Stepping out into the hallway, I looked up and stopped short with a squeak of my boots on the marble floor. "Fuck. This family has too many people in it."

"Oh, just wait until you meet the twins." Kaleb stood there, leaning back against the wall with his arms crossed, as though waiting for me. "Hey,

Ramiren." The air smelled like blood and fresh mud. I took a guess as to where that came from.

My hands went up in surrender. "Look, I just got my nose fixed. *Again.* Please don't break it for a third time. Raewyn is already very displeased."

He raised his eyebrows in surprise. "Why break your nose when I can just put aloe vera juice in your pastries?" A small grin that didn't reach his eyes lifted his lips. "They're ready, by the way."

I'm starting to believe I like him more than you.

Putting my hands down, I responded to both Dre and Kaleb. "Understood." I stepped a little closer to him, and he moved off the wall. "I'm glad to see you've recovered from the devil's attack, and I'm sorry for my part in your injury. What can I do for you, Kaleb?"

He inclined his head for me to walk with him, and I accommodated his request. We came to the hallway leading to the kitchen, and he said, "Something has been bugging me, and I wanted to talk to you about it."

Opening the swinging doors, we stepped through into a warm space, courtesy of the enormous cooking hearth. The walls were covered with neatly hanging copper pots and skillets, shelves filled with mixing bowls and other cooking vessels.

Two long preparation tables took up the center. The table closest to the hearth, with two plain wooden stools on one side, was cleared except for two plates, two napkins, and a black metal pan piled high with steaming turnovers. The second table was covered in bowls, bushels, and baskets overflowing with wilting produce. I spotted the bruised yellow apples, now half gone, that Raewyn had forced Kaleb to get at the market.

My eyes focused on that small bowl of fruit, feeling wistful, and the wave hit again. Shutting my eyes tightly, I took a deep, cleansing breath. Opening them again, I saw Kaleb staring at me with understanding in his gaze. "Me too," he said quietly. "Just sort of comes out of nowhere, doesn't it? Drags you down like an anchor." He motioned to one wooden stool while rounding the preparation table.

With a nod, I pulled the stool to the opposite side of the table from him and sat, my back to the fire. He placed a turnover on the plate and slid it over. I peered suspiciously at the potted plants set in a large wooden rack near the open window to my right.

He grinned genuinely this time. "No aloe vera. Promise."

When I picked up the turnover, the pastry made a satisfying crunch in my fingers. "What did you want to discuss?" I took a bite and hummed as the flavor of apples and cinnamon burst on my tongue. Covering my full mouth with my other hand, I murmured around the food, "This is excellent, Kaleb." His smile sent a pang to my heart.

"Thanks." He plated his own turnover then handed me a napkin. "As I said, there's something bugging me. About your story."

I shot him a questioning look as I took another bite.

Kaleb fidgeted with his turnover, as though debating whether or not to say whatever was on his mind. "Why did Nat get the mark at all? The devil's mark, I mean. In the foyer, when you came back, you said it was meant for your mother, but my sister got it. Why?"

"That's...a good question, Kaleb. One that I just realized no one in your family has asked me." I placed the pastry back down and wiped my hands on the napkin. "The original pact I had with Vrakus was, as I said, for a devil's whistle to get out of danger, but the intention of the clause was to mark my mother. The wording on the pact stated my la'kora would also be marked."

"La'kora? What does that mean?"

"It's Infernal. It means 'greatest treasure.'"

"You called your mother your greatest treasure?" His eyebrows rose in surprise. "That's an odd thing to call her. I mean, I love my mother, but..."

I smiled to myself. "That's the problem. Infernal doesn't have a word for 'mother.' Devils don't have mothers. Infernal also doesn't have a word for family, love, home, or comfort, but they have words for actions. For *things*, like treasure. Or, in Infernal, kora. 'Greatest treasure' becomes 'lak kora,' shortened to 'la'kora.' The Infernal phrase is tawdry, but my meaning behind it made it affectionate."

Kaleb broke off a bit of the turnover crust absently, lost in thought. "So what you're saying is that, in language, context means more than the definition."

In my head, Dredon sighed wistfully.

My smile widened, feeling oddly proud. "In language and in everything else, yes. You understand the context, you can understand just about anything."

We sat in silence, eating another turnover each. After Kaleb cleared our plates and napkins, he turned to me. "And was she? Your greatest treasure?"

The context and subject of his question were plain, even if his wording was vague. I cleared my throat, a feeble attempt to get past another sudden wave that made it difficult to speak. It didn't work, and my reply came out rough. "She'd still be alive if she wasn't."

Lady Resa's voice called from the hallway outside the kitchens, "Kaleb! *Kaleb*!"

Kaleb huffed and yelled back, "In here, Mom!"

Lady Resa came through the swinging doors, dressed in her fighting leathers and braids. Her eyes were puffy and red, and I didn't envy any Wistran soldiers who tried to breach the current siege. "Kaleb, I— Oh, sorry for interrupting. Kaleb, I need a favor."

"Sure, Mom." Kaleb nodded to me as I sat, still stunned at my newfound understanding. "Thanks for the talk, Ramiren." He followed his mother out of the kitchen while I continued to stare straight ahead.

"That's it!"

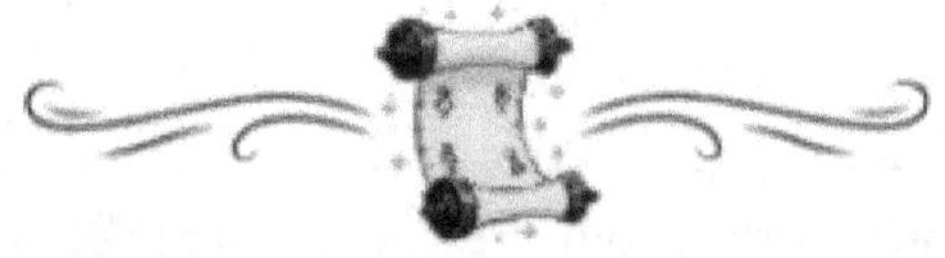

Bursting out of the kitchen, I started yelling. "Raewyn! Raewyn!" I ran down the brightly painted hallways, getting strange memory flashes of obsidian passages, as I searched for the priestess. I rubbed at my eyes, willing the visions of Vrakus's, and now my brother's, home in Gateway to go away. "Damn it! Raewyn! Where are you?"

Taking the stairs two at a time, thinking she was in her bedroom, I knocked on her door. "Raewyn? Are you in there?"

A wet sniffle down the hall caught my attention. Approaching the light blue door, I called a little softer, "Raewyn?"

"Here, Ramiren. I'm in here." Raewyn's voice replied from inside Nathalia's room.

With a deep breath, I opened the door to find Raewyn sitting on the neatly made bed in the twilight. No candles. No lanterns. Merely holding a dark box with a white tag tucked into the red ribbon wrapped around it.

My excitement at potentially finding a solution dimmed considerably when I saw her tear-streaked face. "I can talk with you later if you need a moment alone."

She sniffed again, rubbing her eyes with the sleeve of her robe. "No. It's fine." With a chuckle and another sniffle, she looked up at me. "Please don't tell me Kaleb broke your nose too? We can't keep meeting like this, Ramiren."

Closing the door behind me, I took a few steps forward, then stopped with a smile. "No. He wanted to talk. Even baked me some pastries."

"Hm, that's almost worse." Her tone was teasing but bittersweet. "What did you need?"

"I think I have an idea how to get Nathalia back." When she sat up, eyes wide, I continued, "Do you remember King Rofar of Tanta? The favors given for breaking his daughter's vial? Mine, I gave to the fey animal abuser, but the king still owes one to Nathalia. Perhaps he can help?"

Raewyn graced me with a watery smile and said nothing, merely nodding.

My guilt deepened, feeling as though I'd intruded for a silly reason, even if it certainly wasn't. "I'm sorry, Raewyn."

"No. No, it's all right," she whispered. "It's a good idea. In fact, I'd like to go with you, if that's okay with you?"

A surge of gratitude had me smiling broadly, even with the twin scents of pain and melancholy in the air around her. "I'd like that." Approaching one slow step at a time, I pointed at the box in her hands. "What's that?"

"Oh. Um." She rubbed her thumbs over the glossy wood, biting her lip. "I was looking through Nathalia's room. Just to be close to her, you know? Please don't tell her I snooped. But, uh, I found this on her desk. It has your name on it." She passed it to me.

I took it, then sat on the bed beside her. "What is it?"

A pained smirk crossed her face. "No idea. I didn't open it. Shocking, right?"

Setting the necklace-sized box down between us on the soft blue coverlet and feeling strangely nervous, I confirmed the tag bore my name, then slid the ribbon off. I removed the box's top, and Raewyn gasped. I made no sound at all.

Well. She was right. She does like to spoil people.

Inside was a set of birdpipes nestled in a bed of silk. The reeds were made of a beautiful dark wood inlaid with mother-of-pearl. On top of the instrument sat a strip of paper.

Holding it up, I read aloud, "For music is the breadth and soul of life, and within its tiny notes do we savor its wondrous variety. Love, Nathalia." I didn't vocalize the postscript, which indicated she was looking forward to a private concert.

My fingertips brushed the wooden reeds reverently. "She must've had this made. Before." I inhaled deeply, the tiniest sound of a sniff escaping. "Thank you for finding this, Raewyn."

I stood, taking the box and precious slip of writing in hand, stopping when Raewyn asked behind me, "Do you love my sister, Ramiren?"

My steps slowed, and my feet became leaden. I hoped my gossipy heart didn't give me away. I prayed to Jessina that Raewyn couldn't hear my pulse pick up as the vital organ ricocheted against my ribs. Smiling at her over my shoulder, I responded, "You know I can't answer that."

She looked out the window with a pensive expression on her face. The curtains were partially open, letting in a little light from the darkening sky and the streetlights below. "You know, the Church of Minue likes to wax poetic about what love is. It's actually a really simple thing. You try to imagine a world where your loved one is not in it, and you just *can't*."

"Good night, Raewyn."

I walked out of Nathalia's bedroom and didn't breathe properly until I'd closed the door behind me.

Chapter Twenty
No Hope for the Dawn

After escaping to the solitude of my room, I placed the box on my bed and stared down at it, wary that it might grow fangs and bite if I glanced away for even a moment. My fingers fidgeted absently with the tag and the note that had come with the gift. No doubt Nathalia would be upset she couldn't give it to me herself, but she needed to be alive to be so.

She'd once told me she liked to spoil her friends on special occasions, and I wondered what special occasion had prompted the obviously custom-made piece. Perhaps it was to make up for her lack of a material gift for my birthday.

"Shame. I was hoping for a pony," I whispered to the room with a slight grin. I knew down to my marrow that a wave of grief was coming with the memory. When it finally rolled over me, I snapped my fingers. I required inspiration, because telling her what she'd left behind and the resulting grief would be my tactic for this first attempt.

My boots touched down on a plush rug. Though the light in here was roughly at the same intensity as the guest bedroom's, my eyes still needed to adjust as I caught sight of the pact room's other occupant. Watching Nathalia's soul move about the perimeter of the room like mist in a soft breeze was again an uncomfortable shock.

I still didn't understand what strange circumstances had led to her being trapped here. It was entirely possible I'd never understand, a fact I needed to resign myself to.

Not everything comes with an available answer.

The center light pulsed with each word when she spoke. "You've returned. Have you come to release me?"

I produced a smile, coming closer to her with my fingers laced together in front of me. "Hm, I believe I was promised three attempts. I've come to collect the first."

"As you wish, cordani. Proceed."

What do you call a criminal ghost?

My steps faltered.

Huh? That's a soul, not a g—

Shady.

For fuck's sake, Dredon.

I had no idea why Dredon was telling me a terrible joke right as I prepared to start. Perhaps to make me laugh or even smile, to cheer me up a little. But the only thing it did was make me angry. I'd come prepared, heavy heart in hand, to show Nathalia's soul she was missed. That she needed to return, because there were people she loved and who loved her.

Who couldn't imagine a world without her in it.

Now I was off balance and unfocused. My concentration was gone. All from a silly punchline.

I'd talk with him about that later, but for now, I forced my smile to return in an attempt to resume control of the situation. "I want to start off by saying I've never negotiated with a soul before, so if I use the wrong terminology, I apologize."

When there was no reply or acknowledgment of what I'd said, I continued. "This discussion, and the next two if they are required, is an expression of affection for the person you belong to. I don't do this to torture or torment you, or even overstep, though it may seem that way. I'm merely someone who cares for Nathalia and is trying to restore her to life. Do you understand?"

The cloud moved slightly closer along the wall, and I realized it was stopping at each painting as though appreciating the art. The soul's inner light pulsed. "Yes, I understand." When it paused to look at one featuring a water nymph, dancing in the foamy surf with her powder-blue hair and white shawl flowing behind her in the breeze, another wave of grief slammed into me.

Visions of Nathalia, covered only in a transparent slip of pale fabric with her skin and hair tinged the soft blue that all water nymphs had, flitted through my mind. The sadness returned, focusing me like I needed it to, but then the visions shifted to another unbidden. Lips and skin that same soft blue, growing more and more cyan as seconds stretched on endlessly. Her golden eyes turned from passionate to panicked as blood began to—

I shook my head to clear the image from my mind. *Fuck. Too much.*

"What's wrong, cordani?"

Lifting my gaze and seeing the soul had come closer, nearly within reach, I smiled again. *I'm fucking devastated.* "I'm sad."

"Why?"

Thinking I could perhaps use this for the benefit of my mission, I responded, "Because I miss her. I witnessed her death, and it's painful to be reminded of it."

The tiny sparks within the cloud flurried. "Pain? I know what that is but not what it feels like."

"Sometimes emotional pain is so overwhelming, it manifests as physical agony." Buoyed by this line of discussion, I built on it. It would pain me a great deal less if Nathalia came back."

"Pain isn't something I'm meant to see. Pain comes from mortality. Pleasure too, as the Tarindar and Lorindar pantheons intended. A balance. Heartache and happiness together make a mortal life. Perhaps Nathalia's death will serve a purpose, just as her life did. Perhaps you would not become who you are meant to be without her gone."

My jaw dropped at the cold statement. I realized I was speaking to a being with absolutely no emotions. There had never been any scent of emotions from this soul. At all. Just clean air. It took me longer than it should have to realize why.

It held no capacity for love or hate, merely pragmatism and logic. Taken aback, every part of me denied its insinuation. "That's... No, I don't believe that at all."

"And why is that?"

Frustration at the question, that I would need to explain emotions to an emotionless thing, and that my strategy was obviously not working, brought an edge to my voice as I began to pace. "I won't become who I'm meant to be with her *death*. That's a heartless outlook." I scowled as my frustration began to give way to anger. I tried to tamp it down, but I couldn't stop the torrent. "I will become who I'm meant to with her *life*."

"You are no far seer, cordani. Only Fate knows what's in store, and Fate does not share its knowledge freely."

"I just..." Growling as I stuck my fingers under my glasses to rub my tired eyes, I felt my doubts about whether I could bring her back at all pummel me, but I had to fucking *try*. Righting my glasses on my nose, I continued my thought. "I know it to be true. I don't know *how*. I just do."

"Don't mistake feelings and opinions for fact. It's a trap many mortals fall into."

Is this a joke? Is this a horrible, sick joke?

Mine doesn't seem so bad now, does it?

Shut up, Dre. Shut the fuck up, or I will come to the Citadel and strangle you myself.

Pointedly ignoring Dredon's incoherent mumbling, I understood my battle against this being, who was most certainly *not* Nathalia, remained delicately tenuous, and I had no idea how to gain the upper hand.

Pointing at the cloud, I muttered, "Ironic, coming from something that is obviously incapable of feelings."

"Negativity is a mortal failing."

Mortal failing. A fucking failing. I rubbed my hand over my face, scratching my beard as I gave a rueful chuckle. "You know, it's funny. It's believed a person with no empathy for others, no love or softness in them, is soulless. People think the soul has all their goodness stored within it." I approached, crossing my arms. "But that's not true, is it?"

"We are the spark, the catalyst, and necessary for life, just as an angel's wings are necessary for flight."

As I puffed out a breath to regain control of myself, my thoughts shifted in a new direction. "Nathalia had a favor owed from the Tantan king. It's entirely possible he will be able to foment a way to bring Nathalia back to life."

"Perhaps so. The fey are able to restore life?"

With a small shrug, I replied, "So the songs and stories say. The magic they draw upon is formidable."

"But you still need me to acquiesce."

My teeth clenched, frustration building again. “A hiccup, nothing more. I’m still positive I can convince you. Nathalia’s mother and father miss her. Her siblings miss her. *I* miss her. I miss her beautiful voice, and you sound nothing like her. I miss her grumpy frown, but you look nothing like her.”

“No, I don’t imagine so. I have neither a face nor vocal cords.” It paused, its light slowly dimming, then brightening again. “Speaking of which, your voice has changed again. Why?”

Feeling very unappreciative of the soul’s perceptiveness, I gritted out, “I’m angry. For one unable to feel emotions, you’re certainly good at sensing them.”

“I can see, and I can hear. I noticed something had changed. It goes against my very nature to cause you suffering, even in your mortal form.”

But you are.

The thought cut my strings, and my shoulders fell. “I miss her. I wouldn’t be here if I didn’t.” Tonguing the sharp point of a canine, I decided to at least make one thing clear. “Last time, you had concerns about our agreement. Rest assured, I’ll not keep you trapped here forever. There’d be no reason to, even if my distaste for doing so weren’t in the way. *You* are not *her*. It’d be like trying to keep a vase’s leftover water because you loved the flowers it sustained.”

“Hmm.”

Fuck. What did I say? “What?”

“So that is why you try so hard.” It floated a bit closer. “As I said, the loss you have endured and may very well continue to endure is not intentional on my part. But my purpose, the reason I came to be Nathalia’s soul, has been fulfilled. I was created to keep your soul and my cordani from harm, and I have done so. Fate decreed your soul would’ve deteriorated had you stayed with your father, as he wanted, and I would not have been able to stop it a second time. Now you are safe.”

I recalled the discussion before the siege properly started, about Laeth and the Feylands. “So you...are the companion soul?”

“I am, yes.”

“Which makes me the original soul.” When the soul began to float toward the threshold of a side room, I frowned and tried to follow. “Where are you going?”

"Your first attempt is over."

Frustration flared again. "Like *fuck* it is. I'm not finished!"

"But you *are* finished, and you have failed by coming here to argue with emotions I cannot possibly understand. Think of another line of persuasion and try again later. For attempt one, we are done." The tone of finality, combined with the soul disappearing into another room, made me stop following it.

Despite my profound irritation, I could grudgingly admit it was right. My preparation *had* been sentimental and incomplete, despite feeling confident—arguably bordering on arrogant—and I would not make the same mistake again.

The problem was, if I couldn't use grief to sway it, what could I use?

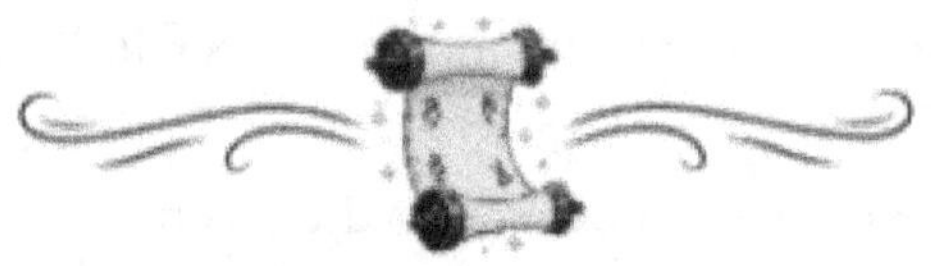

After I snapped myself out of the pact room, I flopped back onto the yellow bedspread in my guest room. Bone tired before I'd even truly begun, I couldn't remember ever being this beat down, literally and figuratively. Every muscle in my body, including my heart, ached with pain and exhaustion.

There was a brief moment where I considered the fierce need pushing me to have her returned. *Perhaps it's due to this cordani business?* As I'd told Nathalia's soul, I'd found nothing regarding "cordani" in the Citadel's library. The chance to research in that library, combined with the devil wards, much like Rowin once possessed, were the reasons we'd gone at all. The lack of information had been extraordinarily discouraging.

No, there was absolutely nothing. A fact that made sense now, upon receiving vague answers from a being I got the impression I wasn't even supposed to interact with.

Are you still upset with me?

At his question, the flare of anger returned, burning hot in my chest. Part of me wanted to be petulant and let him stew, but that would solve nothing. *Why did you do that, Dre? You sabotaged me. Now I only have two more attempts left.*

I'm sorry, Ramiren. Truly. I honestly thought it'd make you smile. Cheer you up a little, I suppose. You're so despondent, it's starting to affect me.

To say the least.

Though still irritated at his ill-timed joke, which wasn't even a good joke to begin with, I conceded my attempt would have failed anyway. I'd gone in with the wrong approach, using emotion to sway the emotionless.

If you want to make it up to me, help me process this. If she and I are bonded, do I feel this way because of the bond?

That'd be a good question to ask. I don't know any more than you do. I've never encountered this before. No one at the Citadel had any clue what you were talking about. Perhaps Lord Maxlian would?

I'd be more likely to receive a disembowelment than answers from him right now.

True. He's not your greatest admirer at the moment, but he'd likely be more amenable to a request for information if you had Nathalia, hale and whole, in tow.

If.

When. And for what it's worth, I don't think it's the cordani bond making you this way.

You don't?

No, at least not entirely.

Explain.

Just a feeling. That's all.

Much to Raewyn's chagrin, we readied ourselves to leave very early the next morning. I spotted Lord Maxlian heading out the door as Raewyn and I came down the stairs, and he shot me a glare that promised nothing I would enjoy.

He kissed Lady Resa goodbye and called out his wish for good luck to Raewyn with a wave, sparing me no words of encouragement or even another searing stare.

Though I knew he was leaving to aid against the latest push by Wistran to breach the walls, it was still startling to hear the sounds of distant yells when he opened the door to leave.

We reached the bottom of the staircase, and I moved toward Lady Resa, who was looking through the items in Nathalia's Extended Pouch. "I've been cut off from the outside world, and I'm afraid I'm completely ignorant. Any new developments with the Wistran siege?"

Lady Resa took a familiar but soiled green silk gown from the pouch and looked it over, scowling, as she replied. "Not much more than testing the waters. Max calls it 'probing the defenses.'"

Raewyn muttered, "That sounds dirty."

As though she hadn't heard her daughter, Lady Resa continued. "A few rumors here and there. Like shadowy men skulking about, but no one can confirm anything. Awakened ghosts in the castle, which, again, no one can confirm." She shrugged and handed Nathalia's pouch to Raewyn. "Hogwash and fear are bad bedfellows."

The priestess took it with a displeased frown, holding it aloft with her pinched fingers. She huffed a long-suffering sigh. "I swear to any god who will listen, if I have to walk again, you're going alone, Ramiren. And I am *not* joking."

I smiled at her. "But you *are* joking. You'd go if you had to crawl." Raewyn scowled, then forcefully pushed the pouch into my chest.

When I grunted at the impact, she grinned like her mother. "You get the bags. Nat's fancy pouch doesn't go with my robes." She threw her red silk cloak on, primly fixing the hood around her shoulders.

As she moved to fuss with her hair, I peered at Lady Resa. Her eyes were puffy and red-rimmed, but she gave me a small smile, which I returned. "Lady Resa, thank y—"

"Resa."

My eyebrows shot up, but by the look on her face, I didn't dare argue. "Resa, thank you for your hospitality."

She slid her arms around me, tightening them as she leaned into the hug and whispered, "Bring her home."

Returning the embrace with one of my own, I replied softly, "I promise."

The arms of a much smaller woman wrapped around us both, and Raewyn said, "We will."

Two sharp knocks at the door broke us apart.

"Ah, that should be the mages." Lady Resa surreptitiously wiped at her eyes and headed for the door, waving off the old butler, who turned on his heel to go back wherever he came from.

I'm starting to wonder if that butler is an automaton too.

When Resa opened the door, two people stood outside who couldn't look any more different from each other if they'd tried.

Everything about the lovely, delicate woman was short. Short stature, short blond hair, and based upon her hunched shoulders and lowered eyes, a short amount of confidence as well. She ran a shaky hand down the front of her immaculate green robes and stepped in first.

The man with her was tall, even taller than I was. His long brown hair was tied back with feathers and braids. Dressed in careworn trousers tucked into muddy boots, a ragged duster, and a half-tucked-in shirt, he grinned widely as he followed her inside.

"Ramiren, Raewyn. These are the mages, Idora Pascen and Tomin Wrosco. Idora will stay here with Nathalia, while Tomin will go with you two to Elancia. Once all is ready, Idora will bring Nathalia's...um." She cleared her throat thickly. "Bring her to you for restoration."

Tomin smiled what was probably his most charming smile at Raewyn, while Raewyn grinned at Idora.

Idora smiled at no one.

Raewyn awkwardly clapped her hands in front of her, and the breeze from it brought the tiniest waft of honey to my nose, making me breathe through my mouth. "Wonderful. Lovely to meet you both. Are we ready, then?"

Idora nodded at her then turned to Tomin. "Be safe, Tom." "Oh, I'll be just fine," he said, turning another grin to Raewyn.

"What's your name, sweetheart?"

Raewyn finally saw his teasing grin and looked him dead in the eye. Deadpan, she asked, "Do you know how to remove a man's tongue without him bleeding to death?"

Tomin blinked twice, glancing uneasily at his companion before turning back to Raewyn. "Um, no?"

"I do. Please keep that in mind."

The bravado left his face as fast as the blood did. He sent a wide-eyed look Idora's way, who rolled her lips between her teeth to hide a tiny but obvious smile.

Clipping the two pouches, mine and Nathalia's, to my belt, I cracked my neck. "Shall we?"

Chapter Twenty-One
To Beg the Monarch Fey

Infinitely grateful we didn't have to pass through the Tanta Desert again, or at least Raewyn was, we arrived outside the gates of Elancia. Weeks had passed since the general's death, and none of the mourning shrouds were still present, likely bleached by the sun and removed to indicate the mourning period had ended, only to be dyed again in preparation for the next noble's death.

The loud, crowded streets were a far cry from the silence that had blanketed the city previously. At a glance, one could tell who was a visitor and who was local based upon how heat-weary they appeared.

We passed by an inn where we'd once tried to get lodging, and the memories flooded in without warning. Nathalia, red-faced and annoyed, arguing with skeptical guards, faint freckles peeking through her sunburn. Letting it roll over me, I wondered if I'd be reminded of Nathalia everywhere I looked for the rest of my life. A prospect I relished if I succeeded, but if I failed?

You won't fail.

I'm afraid you're wrong.

I know, but someone has to be your optimistic toady.

As we dodged workers and shoppers on our way to Castle Tanta, Raewyn brushed sand and dust from her ruby silk cloak and robes, then ran her hands through her hair in a gesture that looked suspiciously like fidgeting. "So Georgina said something about there being a fancy workplace-thing here, right?"

It took me a moment to suss out what she referred to. "Workshop? Yes, that was what she asked for when we helped Princess Sornya. Why do you ask?"

She eyed a makeshift table covered in odd gadgets set up in front of a store. With feigned innocence, she chirped, "Oh, no reason."

From behind us, Tomin asked, "Hm, is she pretty?"

Raewyn wheeled around, pointing at his chest with a scowl. "Why are you still here? Don't you have somewhere else to be?"

He grinned with a rakish head tilt. "It's my job. So about this Georgina..."

Raewyn lifted her chin, eyeing the disheveled mage as though his line of questions were a challenge. "She's a very angry gnome who will use your nuts for M.A.L.C.O.L.M.'s bolts."

His grin disappeared, and his jaw went slack while he glanced at me with another question in his gaze. "I don't know what that means."

I cut in as we reached and immediately passed the first checkpoint without a fuss, realizing Raewyn had found her target dummy for this round of travel. "You two traveled back to Laeth together. How did that go?"

Raewyn waved a hand in my direction. "Oh. Fine."

I didn't see a twitch, scowl, sneer, or curse fly from her mouth, so I took a wild guess. "So you're on better terms now?"

Raewyn opened her mouth, then clicked it shut like she was confused by either my question or her response. "Yes. We're...friends, actually."

What in the world happened on the road to the Ivory Grove?

I prodded, "Friends, or...?"

A soft laugh escaped her when she realized what I was insinuating. She gently poked my arm. "Friends friends. It just felt strange to say it, that's all." She squinted in thought. "You know, normally I'd be all about going from screaming at each other to making each other scream, if you take my meaning. We're not like that, though. We met in the middle and compromised. Like *adults*." Raewyn screwed up her face like she'd swallowed a bitter pill.

Wonders never cease.

Ha-ha. I don't believe her.

"Really?"

I chuckled when she deadpanned, "I was pretty shocked myself." Tomin leaned in, putting his face between my and Raewyn's heads.

"Wait...do you like the company of both men and women, or only women?"

She sucked on her teeth and didn't even bother to shoot him an unimpressed glance. "You know, I get it now." She looked my way, making it clear who she was talking to. "I have enough self-awareness to understand this is how Nat must feel." Raewyn's face fell. "Or must've felt."

Tomin straightened and sidled up to Raewyn's side, apparently unable to handle being ignored. He spoke while looking around the city like a wide-eyed tourist. "I don't know what that means, either. Why would you know how a gnat feels? You're not *that* annoying."

She didn't respond until we'd passed the second checkpoint. "Not *a* gnat. *Nat*. Nathalia. My sister. You know, the one wh—" Raewyn stopped herself, puffing out a breath from her cheeks.

Tomin immediately sobered, muttering, "Oh. I see. Sorry."

Raewyn shook her head, eyes rolling so hard she showed more white than brown. "To answer your question, it's both, but women are far and away my preference."

The mage beside her open-mouth grinned at her like this information delighted him. "Oh. Like Idora."

Raewyn's head snapped to him, and she halted dead in her tracks. "I beg your pardon?"

He shot her yet another toothy grin, holding his hands wide. "Beg all you like, sweetheart."

She recovered, and for the first time Raewyn smiled at Tomin, looking proud and excited, though I smelled a sweet scent that was *definitely* not blueberries and cream. "I'm just surprised, that's all. You *finally* said something worth hearing." Then her smile dropped, face wiped clean, and she walked on.

"All right, if we have the same trouble with these idiot guards that Nat had, I'm setting something on fire," Raewyn muttered, her boot heels thudding as she stomped forward on the wooden drawbridge leading to the castle's gates.

Two guards, thankfully different from the stubborn ones we'd dealt with before, stood at attention on either side of the iron lattice door leading into the courtyard beyond, shoulders rolling back upon our approach. "Greetings," one called out cheerfully.

With a genuine smile, I replied, "Three to seek an audience with King Rofar, please."

The two guards looked at each other silently, then started giggling. "Oh, for fuck's sake," Raewyn groaned while I smelled blueberries and cream from the guards. *Why do they smell like pride?*

The guard to my right turned a happy smile my way. "Master Ramiren, I can't believe it's really you. And Lady Raewyn Swordhand! What an honor."

Raewyn looked at both guards then me. "Wait, what?"

A few rapid blinks later, my brain began to work again. I smiled, pushing my glasses back up my nose. "Apologies, gentlemen. You know about us?"

"Of course," the guard to my left exclaimed. "We saw you as you came back from killing the witch—"

"Hag," the other one corrected.

"Oh, right, the hag. You killed her and saved the princess's voice, yeah? The cook, Mrs. Dursley, wouldn't shut her yap about spotting you coming out of the meeting with the king. Said you looked like a fine specimen, whatever that means." The guard peeked around me at Raewyn. "And we heard from the laundry maids that you paid a huge stack of gold coins for a ruined napkin that got dropped in the madder dye vat."

My canines sank into my bottom lip to keep from smirking. Keeping my tone even and curious, I said to Raewyn, "Oh. So, that's where you got M.A.L.C.O.L.M.'s bow tie?"

Raewyn's jaw dropped, and her eyes flashed at me. "Hush, you." She turned back to the guards with a smile. "Any chance we can see King What's-His-Name?"

"Rofar," I murmured to her.

"Yes, sorry. Any chance we can see King Roofer?"

Fuck.

Ha-ha.

Tomin gaped at her. "Tell me you didn't just say what I think you said. Please."

Before Raewyn could respond, the guards giggled again. "Oh, that's good," the guard to my right said to the other. "King Roofer. I'm telling Mrs.

Dursley about that one."

A young fey wearing purple livery and a twitchy expression led us through a narrow hallway, made larger by the carved wood-frame mirrors lining the cream walls on either side. The illusion of infinite reflections was off-putting, but I thought that might be intentional.

The fey stopped in front of a white-washed door trimmed in gold and opened it to let us inside. The parlor's interior was simple, though considering how austere the throne room was, a place usually meant to intimidate and humble its visitors, I wasn't surprised.

There was no fireplace, but a series of small lit braziers set along the perimeter provided ample light and warmth. An enormous purple rug rested underneath six identical high-backed chairs, which were arranged in a circle with small drink tables between them.

King Rofar, reclining and comfortable, took up one chair. He motioned to the other seats wordlessly, and we sat next to each other across the circle from him. Tomin looked around the room while Raewyn fussed with her robes and cloak.

I inclined my head in respect. "King Rofar."

The king laced his fingers together on his lap as he rested an ankle on his other knee. "Ramiren. I'd send for drinks, but I get the impression this isn't a social call. What can I do for you?"

Taking a deep breath to prepare myself for the story, I began. "Well, I come with information and a request. A few days ago, Lady Nathalia Swordhand killed an arch-devil in Gateway."

The king's eyebrows rose, but he didn't comment. "Unfortunately, she was struck down by a wayward devil in the

aftermath. I recall she has a favor owed to her, by you. I'd like to see her returned to life with fey magic, if such a thing is possible."

The king mulled over my words for a long minute, then spoke. “Unfortunately, I see two problems, besides securing her consent to return, which I’ll assume you have, since you’re here?” The question in his eyes was more him making a point than an actual inquiry, and he didn’t press for an actual response.

“One: Though it’s possible to cleave soul to body once again, our magic cannot bring a soul back from the Dark Drop. The Lorindar will never surrender their ghastly food source. And two: I don’t allow favors belonging to someone to be used by another, even for that someone’s benefit.”

I had no way to predict if the king would know what this next part meant, and I simultaneously hoped he did and prayed he didn’t say it out loud. “For the first problem, she’s not in the Dark Drop. Her soul is currently milling about in a pact room.”

King Rofar stared at me without blinking until he finally said, “I’m sorry, she’s what? Why is her *soul* in a pact room?”

“Unfortunately, I can’t tell you.”

The king gave me a knowing look. “I see.” He shifted in his chair, moving his hands to the armrests. “However, I still don’t understand *why* her soul is in a pact room and not flying to the Aerie. Or Celestia, for you Laethi folk.”

I felt Raewyn’s eyes boring into my skull, but she said nothing. Thankfully.

I’d thought long and hard as to why Nathalia’s soul was floating among the erotic paintings and hanging silk scarves in our pact room, why she couldn’t leave, and why she seemed pleased at the prospect of my dissolving the room. I provided my best hypothesis. “For the Laethi, it’s Celestia, and I suspect it has something to do with the protocols we have in place to prevent that.”

King Rofar waved a hand for me to continue. “Such as?”

Though I’d been forbidden, as part of my pact with Nathalia, to disclose the fact there was a pact at all, I could at least infer there was one. The pact also contained verbiage that allowed for accidental discovery by another, and I leaned on that here. “We’re supposed to demolish a pact room if the person we have an agreement with dies. Immediately. It stands to reason that once a room is demolished, the soul goes to Celestia, and no one is the wiser regarding the soul having been there at all.”

The side of my head was burning from Raewyn's scorching stare combined with the strong smells of wood lacquer and decaying vegetation, but my eyes stayed on the king.

The king frowned in thought. "So it's a known problem?"

With a noncommittal shrug, I attempted to hide my fear about this being an acknowledged issue that was undisclosed to trainees, hidden with nothing more than a simple but firm protocol, like a bandage hiding a mortal wound.

And if that were the case, why weren't there at least rumors alluding to it happening? Surely I hadn't been the first to encounter this. "Perhaps it's known, at least to the Citadel's masters. It's certainly coincidental, but I can't say for sure. Unfortunately, I don't have weeks to comb through the archives at the Citadel or question taciturn professors on something I may or may not be privy to, not with a massive threat just outside Rowin's walls."

The king hummed. "Yes, I'd heard Wistran invaded its sister realm."

Looking down into my lap, I noticed my fingers twisting about themselves. Though I felt no anxiety, it seemed my body disagreed. Consciously relaxing my hands, I placed them palm down on my thighs. "It did. Rowin is currently under a stalemate siege, but who knows for how long the impasse will last, especially if our suspicions are confirmed and the druid K'sar is involved."

The king's shocked expression matched the pungent smell of wood lacquer that immediately doubled. "Lea K'sar? She's been gone for decades. You think she's returned?"

A bolt of lightning struck me. "Wait. Lea K'sar is her full name? Would you spell it, please?"

"Um. Hm. Let me think. It's been a long while." King Rofar scratched the back of his neck as his mouth moved silently, then he spoke out loud. "L-E-A K-S-A-R, I believe."

Well, that's not obvious at all.

I should've asked if there was a first name.

Raewyn snorted in laughter, covering her mouth with her hand at the same time. King Rofar narrowed his eyes at her. "Something amusing, young lady?"

Raewyn tongued the inside of her cheek and grinned. "I mean, in hindsight, it's funny."

Clearing my throat, throwing an admonishing look at Raewyn, I gave the king an answer. "We suspected K'sar has been hiding in plain sight this whole time, but we didn't know her full name. Always referred to her as K'sar when we spoke to Nathalia's parents about her. Her name confirms it as more than a mere coincidence. The druid Leraska's name is an anagram for Lea K'sar."

"I don't know this Leraska," King Rofar said. "Lea K'sar always preferred being called by her chosen last name, so most only knew her as that. I only know it because of luck. We found a half-burned journal supposedly belonging to her. It's a shortened Old Fey phrase used by her druid ancestors, who were ostracized for creating foul relics. It means 'Great Wilderness.'"

The king stood, and we three stood as well. He looked directly at me as he said, "If Nathalia's soul can somehow request her resurrection, then we'll return her to life. If not, another favor from me is needed, which I believe you chose as your boon after restoring my daughter's voice, yes?"

Raewyn muffled a squeak.

Shit.

Don't worry. I'm sure he'll take your explanation of what happened to his favor with absolute calm and not behead you for your insolence.

With a pained wince, I prepared for my execution. "I regret to inform you, King Rofar, but my favor was given away to a fey who either traded or still trades in fey animals. It bought the animals' freedom."

King Rofar didn't exactly look calm, but he also didn't look murderous. A silent beat passed before he replied. "You'd better go get it back then, hm?"

Chapter Twenty-Two
Coin or Keys

"Gods-damn it, Ramiren! Get back here *right now*!" Raewyn yelled as she followed in our wake. We exited through the front gates of the castle and crossed the drawbridge, her shorter legs pumping to catch up to us. Tomin and I weren't walking particularly fast, but her tone made me unconsciously quicken my pace.

My face must have shown my bubbling irritation, because those on the street either steered clear of the scene or slowed down to watch what appeared to be drama unfolding.

Beside me, Tomin peeked over his shoulder and turned forward immediately. "Oh, boy. You're in trouble now," he whispered to me. "Her face is almost purple."

I didn't doubt it. I also didn't doubt Raewyn would pester me until she had the particulars on the arrangement Nathalia and had I agreed to, down to every salacious detail. Unfortunately for her, not only could I not tell her, but I never would anyway.

She was so close now I could practically feel her breath on my neck, like a rampaging dragon in pursuit. "Ramiren! You have some ex—"

When I turned on my heel to face her, she collided with my chest with an "oof."

My voice stayed calm, despite my annoyance. "No, Raewyn. I will not be explaining anything."

She responded with a death stare and a threat. "Oh yes, you will. That's my sister, and if you don't tell me right n—"

I didn't plan to have a loud confrontation on the main avenue of Elancia in broad daylight with a crowd of onlookers gawking, but my plans of late hadn't survived first contact with the enemy. My irritation intensified and boiled into pure indignation. I leaned down until I was eye level with her. "Raewyn, I will tell you the same thing I told your sister. 'No' is a powerful word. It is a complete sentence, and it is *final.* I understand that you don't hear it often, but let me be crystal clear. You will get *zero* information from me. Do you know why?"

Pausing to wait for a reply, to see if she could figure it out on her own, I received nothing except silent rage.

"Because..." I leaned in and whispered, "It's none of your fucking business."

An outraged squeak left her lips, which were parted in shock, but I didn't give her a chance to respond. My back straightened, a placid smile slid into place, and I spoke with a light tone. "Now we need to learn where that animal-abusing fey is, which means we need someone with the ability to find people. Do any of you know how we should go about locating one?"

Raewyn crossed her arms, the picture of petulance, while Tomin spoke. "Well, we could pay a scryer. It's a big city. I'm sure they have a mage who can scry here."

The priestess scoffed, then muttered, "What, you can't do it?"

Tomin shook his head slowly. "Sorry, not my specialty. I'm pretty terrible at divination magic." His grin reappeared, and I got the impression he was trying to cheer her up. "Good with illusions, though. Watch this."

His hand danced through the air, index finger and thumb pointing out, and a shadow appeared and coalesced into an animal the size and shape of a large cat, dark and featureless. Its tail flicked and waved like a real cat's, leaving trails of wispy smoke. A woman nearby shrieked, while the little girl she tugged along beside her pointed and cried out excitedly, "Kitty!"

Raewyn didn't look cheered. She looked entirely unimpressed. "Put that away before you cause a riot."

Tomin's grin morphed into laughter. "Oh, if only I had a gold coin for every time I've heard that."

We talked to a few vendors and three innkeepers before getting information on a scryer in the city. Despite the vague directions provided, we found the right alleyway eventually, only getting turned around once.

The tiny cottage before us was homey and well kept, with little flower boxes lining the small square windows. The thatched roof was made with new reeds and fresh straw. After knocking on the heavy wooden door twice, a muffled but masculine "Enter" came from within. I obliged, followed by Tomin and a still-sulking Raewyn.

The brightly lit interior, courtesy of the uncovered windows, looked more like a museum collection than a functional home. Bookshelves filled with various tomes and strange objects, some glowing, lined every available bit of wall space, barely leaving room for the small bed in the corner to my left and a carved armchair near the fireplace on the opposite wall.

A hammered copper bowl with a clay pitcher inside it sat on a low stool near the fire and completed the rest of the minimal furniture. The air smelled like an old library, a distinctive combination of musty earthiness and vanilla.

The lone occupant, a large older human with a gray beard and round glasses, looked up from the book in his lap. "Can I help you?" His voice was rough from age, but his eyes were a soft blue.

It was his eyes, more than anything, that put me at ease. Kind and curious.

For some reason, I want to listen to him tell a bedtime story. Is that weird?

Though I didn't reply to Dredon, it did make me smile.

Moving to the side so Tomin and Raewyn could fully enter, I inclined my head. "Are you Rikk Bhaw?"

"I am," he replied, peering through his glasses at each of us in turn. "How can I help you?"

After I introduced us, Tomin spoke up. "We need to find someone. You're a scryer?"

"Oh!" The man placed a bit of thin fabric embroidered with lopsided faded flowers and the letters GB to mark his place in the book and stood with a groan. "Yes, I am. Who or what do you need to find?"

Raewyn responded bitterly, "A foul, goat-legged bastard who likes to abuse animals."

"Goat-legged? Oh, a capra fey? An ill-tempered lot, so I'm not surprised." Rikk took his glasses off to clean them on his open brown waistcoat. "Would you happen to have his name? True names or chosen names work, but true names make it easier." He slid his glasses back on his nose and bent down to pick up the pitcher and copper bowl next to his chair.

My two companions looked at me, and I shook my head. "No. Apologies, but I didn't care at the time to get his name."

"Hm, any defining characteristics?"

Raewyn scowled. "Uh. A lot of chest hair." Her scowl disappeared suddenly. "Oh! He had necklaces. A lot of them. Bones and teeth and such."

To my surprise, Rikk's face twisted in disgust. "That sounds like Corey the Capra. He comes to our market with his guards and sad caged animals, but he never sells any, for some reason."

"*Corey*? His name is *Corey*?" The priestess snorted derisively. "Ha!" She slapped a hand across Tomin's arm as if to emphasize how funny she found it, and just like that, her mood lifted.

Tomin rubbed his arm where she'd hit him and bit his bottom lip as the faint scent of honey filled the air. "Vicious."

I ignored the flirting and confirmed Rikk's thought. "That sounds like him. He said he only dealt in favors, not money. Speaking of which, would you agree to a hundred gold for this?" At his casual nod, I knew my assumption about the expected cost was correct. After counting out the coins, I handed them over.

"Well, let's see what we can see." He held the copper bowl in one hand and poured water from the pitcher with the other. Swirling the water like wine in a glass, he peered not into the water, but at the sides of the bowl where the water trickled along the hammered dents. Slowly, the bowl started to glow.

Intrigued, I watched as he made a thoughtful noise in his throat, swirling, swirling, then stopped to look up at us. "He's in Puldoni," he finally announced. "Not exactly sure where or for how long, but he's in the city right now."

Raewyn eyed the bowl in his hands, then Rikk himself. "How did you learn to do that?"

Rikk smiled genially at Raewyn like a proud grandfather. "Patience and a great deal of boredom, priestess." He took a step back to look at us all with the same expression. "Do you require anything else?"

"No, sir. Thank you for your help," Tomin said, extending a hand. "We'll get out of your beard."

Rikk set the bowl and pitcher down to shake Tomin's hand, chuckling. "Thank you. I was just getting to the good part in my book. I'll show you out."

Raewyn ambled to the door, looking around the small cottage. "You have so many. Which book is your favorite?"

The scryer opened the door for us. "The next one I read, priestess. Always."

There were far more rooms available this time around, and we had no trouble finding lodging. After a few glasses of mediocre wine and a long, unproductive discussion about possible plans to get my favor back, the only thing we agreed on was to transport to Puldoni a few hours after nightfall to look for Corey the Capra and decide on what to do.

Having no desire to be social, I went up to my assigned room to dodge lingering questions from Raewyn. Sitting on the floor, my back leaning against the rustic wood-framed bed, I mulled over recent events.

There had been no way to know that King Rofar's favor would play such an important part in my future, let alone Nathalia's. It had been given away on a whim, an easy bargain to buy the lives and safety of not only innocent but obviously intelligent animals. The cage remained one of the most evil inventions ever created, and I had acted on impulse.

I had no regrets about trading the favor away. It was the right call at the time, and as Nathalia's soul had said, I wasn't a far seer. Though the ability to gaze into the future would be mighty helpful, I would've refrained from utilizing it.

Like looking at the final page of a book, foresight was just another kind of cage, imprisoning a person in self-doubt and indecision about how they might bring about or change a vision. One must know the full story to understand the ending.

After all, if I'd known what Nathalia's end would be, I would've refused her protector's oath, refused the pact that brought us together, and refused the vial that returned my capacity to whistle at all.

If someone knew the future, they lived only in the future and ignored the present, to their detriment.

I exhaled as I leaned my head back onto the straw mattress to stare at the beige ceiling. Only two more chances left to convince Nathalia's soul to return, and I had no real idea how to proceed. It also wasn't lost on me that her soul was in a cage of my own making.

Fuck, I'm a hypocrite.

Would you like a suggestion?

You've been quiet.

Your thoughts are loud enough for both of us.

Fair point. What's your suggestion?

You can try logic. Nathalia's soul is a pragmatic creature who might not necessarily **want** ***to stay dead. It simply believes its purpose is over and done, right?***

That's what it said, yes.

So it needs a new purpose. A new reason to live. And before you say anything, I'm not telling you to confess your undying devotion and warm fuzzy feelings to it. It won't care. It needs purpose, not prose.

My mind quieted, and I understood what probably needed to happen. Unfortunately, it would take both attempts to do this right. If I was wrong, if I failed, then I'd be obligated to do something that would mean my end, regardless of whether or not I lived through it.

To succeed, I needed to ignore the possibility of failure, the fear of a million what-ifs, and the grief of having to let her go. A problem, because now that I'd lost her, all I felt regarding Nathalia was wild emotion begging to break free.

I'd been running on paralyzing fear and panic, and it swallowed what I should have told her long ago. My mind had been muddled by it ever since

Nathalia had accepted Jaylin's proposal, bordering on insanity for one reason after another.

She'd been there for me when I needed her, at every turn. Ever since the carnival, she'd been a light in the darkness. Right now, I needed to be a beacon for her to find her way home. Digging into the pouch at my side and removing the dark box, I opened it to reread the note nestled inside. Replacing the note, I tucked the box away.

What are you going to do?

I need a bit more information from it to be completely sure, but I have a feeling I need to give it more than just a purpose. A task of many large parts. How do you eat a dragon?

Is this a metaphorical question or a culinary one? Are you getting back at me for that ghost joke?

One bite at a time, Dre.

So...?

Metaphorical.

Thank you. In the meantime, I'm going to look into this 'pact rooms trap souls' business. Good luck.

I rubbed the stone of the broken necklace that was still in my pocket and snapped my fingers.

As I stood from the floor, Nathalia's soul floated through the doorway of a side room. "Hello again, cordani. Is this attempt number two?"

With a nod, I set my plan into motion. "How much do you remember of your mortal life?"

The soul hovered closer. "Vague things, more of an understanding about my mortal life than actual memories."

"What understanding do you have?"

"A sacred vow recited. This place. It seems familiar, but I couldn't tell you why. A life full of devotion and purpose."

"But you remember before? Before your mortal life?"

"Yes, I remember that."

My mind filled with questions, but this wasn't the time to poke Nathalia's soul for answers that had nothing to do with bringing her back. "You indicated once that you were the companion soul. Made specifically for me. To save me, and, in a way, to protect me."

"Yes, that is correct."

I jumped on the soul's positive response, seeking an opening as water seeks the path of least resistance. "I still need that."

"Perhaps. But I am not meant to return. My fated purpose is done." I concentrated on the wording it had used. "Not meant to return" wasn't "couldn't return."

You were right, Dre.

"That's your decision, and no one else's. If you wish to return, to allow Nathalia to live beside the one she was made for, you can." I bit my tongue hard, holding back the things I yearned to say, that I needed to confess, like an undeserving penitent who prayed for grace, but I couldn't.

They wouldn't work. Not for something that had no concept of affection, adoration, or passion, especially the agony of any of those being unrequited. It was a foreign concept to a soul that had never watched the one they love agree to love another, even if I hadn't entirely understood it at the time. I had to stay the course and give it reasons to come back that didn't involve emotion.

"What you are asking for is very difficult. For someone who is purpose-driven to live without a Fate-bestowed purpose."

"What if she were to bestow a purpose onto herself? Similar, but formed into something new. My dealings can be...dangerous. Often I'm able to head off danger with words and another's assumptions about me, but when I cannot, a shield is needed. Nathalia can be that shield."

"New? Was that not exactly what Nathalia did before?"

"Not precisely. Nathalia said her oath to me because of my father. At the time, we had no idea what he would do once he got his hands on me. Sadly, I was not the one truly in danger, but what *is* dangerous is some of the places I go to and those beings I negotiate with and for. Let Nathalia stand beside me and allow me to continue my work while guarding my back."

"Perhaps."

With a forward step, I pressed. "If it helps, I would show my thanks."

"Your thanks? What do you mean?"

"I'll show you soon enough." My words came out teasing, flirtatious even, and I hadn't meant for them to.

Smooth.

"If you're referring to sexual activity, cordani, I must warn you it will not sway me."

I grinned, despite myself, and dropped my head forward. "I wasn't, actually. You'll see soon enough. I need to do a bit of practicing first." The drawing I'd done of Nathalia caught the corner of my eye, and I approached it. A soft wisp of balmy air brushed my arm, and I looked down to see Nathalia's soul had floated to hover beside me.

My skin tingled with pleasant warmth where it touched me. I suppressed the urge to pull my fingertips through it. *With my luck, that'd be considered rude.* "I know what I'm asking of you. Of her. Nathalia lived for other people, selflessly so. That selflessness, combined with her protector training and the invisible wounds she's endured, manifested into constant self-doubt and a fear of failure. Despite those *mortal failings*, as you put it, she loved life."

I realized I was toeing the line and took a deep breath to push the emotions back down. When the storm inside me settled, I turned to face Nathalia's soul. "You were right. I can't see the future, but I also would never want to. I have no idea what Fate has in store for me, but I did know Nathalia. I *know* she would want to live."

Nathalia's soul didn't say anything for seconds that stretched on like winter nights. Finally, it asked, "This image. Was this Nathalia's form?"

My eyes began to sting, so I faced away from the portrait to look at her soul and gave a single nod.

"I see." It floated away, smoky tendrils stroking the air as it moved. "Your second attempt has failed, but you have given me things to consider."

I snapped my fingers, somehow feeling both hopeful and disappointed. In an instant, I returned to my barren room and pulled the box back out, ready to practice for the second part of my plan and my final attempt.

Chapter Twenty-Three
Whatever Desire, I'll Pay

Puldoni, Evraka's sister city and the trade hub of the Feylands, appeared to be celebrating yet another holiday for an unclear reason. Floating feylights hovered above the packed lanes and alleyways of the city, the soft glow illuminating the faces of those walking about as they watched acrobatic street performers, jugglers, and puppet plays on small stages lining the streets.

The distant clamor of deep drumbeats and reedy flutes and the distinctive tones of fiddles indicated more musically inclined performances were ahead. They provided background noise for the murmuring chatter of those around us.

With so many people around with heightened emotions, I made sure to breathe through my mouth.

I pointedly ignored the blade sign of the Forever Inn when we passed it.

"How are we supposed to find *Corey* in all this?" Raewyn wobbled forward on her tiptoes, jumping occasionally in an attempt to see over the crowd. By the petite priestess's grousing, it seemed she was unsuccessful.

Tomin bent down slightly, chuckling at her attempts. "Having trouble, sweetheart?"

Raewyn grumbled under her breath. I couldn't understand what she said due to the din, but Tomin must have, because his chuckling turned into barking laughter. "Here. I'll just do for you what I do for my brother's kids."

She hopped a few more times, absently replying to the mage, "What?"

"This." His hands gripped either side of her waist, and before she could squeak a protest, he'd lifted her and placed her neatly on his right shoulder.

"See? All better, sweetheart."

Raewyn teetered, causing her to wrap her arms around Tomin's head in a desperate maneuver to not fall to the dirty cobblestones below. "Pu-Put me down! *Put me down right now*!"

"Why? You can see now, right?"

"But—"

"And you don't have to walk."

"I— Oh, fuck. You're right." Raewyn straightened, still using one hand on top of his head to steady herself. "Very well. Walk on, steed."

Shuffling through the crowd was slow going, though with Raewyn on Tomin's shoulder, people seemed to naturally make room for one of the tallest figures in the area.

After a few minutes of discussion, with suggestions regarding going into inns, taverns, or even the market to look for him, Raewyn squealed, her free hand shooting forward and pointing straight ahead. "Minue's tits! Look!"

Tomin and I tried to spot what she saw, but her vantage point was now far better than ours. "What? What are we looking at?" Tomin asked. "I would recognize that pink hair anywhere." Raewyn cupped her hands around her mouth and yelled over the crowd's noise. "Georgina! Georgina! M.A.L.! Over here! Fuck!" Raewyn kicked Tomin's side like he was a horse. "*Move faster!*"

"Ow!" Tomin grunted but did walk in the direction and at the speed she'd demanded. I followed close behind, knowing that what was about to happen would be far more entertaining than what was currently being offered by the street performers.

Georgina must've finally noticed us, because she called out, "Rae! Raewyn, is that you?"

We closed the distance as the crowd parted between us and the gnome tinkerer. Georgina sat on M.A.L.C.O.L.M.'s shoulders, pink bow tie in place around his neck. She eyed Raewyn with an amused side-eye. "He doesn't look like an automaton."

"Oh, him?" Raewyn patted the top of Tomin's head. "No. This is Tomas—"

"Tomin. So you're the famous Georgina?"

Georgina grinned at him but said nothing.

"Sure. Yes, Tomin. Ramiren's around here somewh— Oh! There you are." Raewyn grinned wolfishly down at me, like I had magically appeared instead of having stood beside Tomin the entire time.

M.A.L.C.O.L.M. beeped softly. "Olleh! Woh era uoy?"

Dredon's laughter echoed in my head. ***I love that thing.***

My left eye twitched as Raewyn and Tomin stared. "Is that an automaton language?" Tomin asked, then laughed. "Is he speaking Automatic?"

"Auto— Ha! Good one." Georgina snickered at the mage. "No, sorry. I've gotten so used to it I don't even notice anymore. One of the other tinkerers played a prank on me. M.A.L.'s been speaking backward Common for a week now, and Prem, the prankster, won't tell me how to fix it until I get back to Tirvinir."

Beep. "Merp si a kcid."

"Though it is kind of growing on me. It's like a code." Georgina craned her head around. "Where's Nathalia?"

I anticipated the question, expected it even, but my chest pinched all the same. Raewyn's grin fell away immediately. The tinkerer looked at our faces and seemed to understand. "Oh, shit."

"Yeah." The priestess's smile returned, only dimmed and flat. "Long story. As in, 'we need a fully stocked tavern' kind of story, but we don't have much time for that. We're looking for that fey asshole who had the animals in cages. You remember?"

Georgina's face turned pink. "Yeah. I remember."

Raewyn continued, her eyes flicking to the automaton as an idea occurred to her. "He's in this city, and we need to get Ramiren's favor from him. I don't suppose M.A.L. can track him, can he?"

Impressed that she remembered he could track, I looked at the tinkerer for her answer, but she grimaced. "No. Not in this crowd or without a place to start. Where have you checked so far?"

Damn. My shoulders fell, but I tried to keep the disappointment from my voice. "We just arrived not too long ago. We haven't been able to search yet."

"Hm." Georgina tapped her tiny chin. "Maybe we should ask around? I'm sure someone in this town has seen him. He's pretty distinctive."

We spent the better part of the next hour going into establishments and asking resting performers if they knew of Corey, the capra fey animal dealer. Many knew *of* him, but it wasn't until we reached the night market that anyone could give us possible places he might be.

"Corey?" one vendor asked as he took a few copper coins from a patron buying two glazed buns from his cart. Still breathing through my mouth, I tasted rather than smelled the caramelized sugar wafting off the sweets.

When my stomach grumbled, I realized I hadn't eaten anything that day besides grapes in fermented form.

"Yes. *Corey*," Raewyn snorted, rubbing at her eyes with her fingers.

"I'm not entirely sure, but he always likes to brag about his winnings over at the gambling hall north of the city, The Mint."

"Gods above, thank you," I said, relief lifting the weight of hopelessness just a little from my chest. To soften the distraction our questions caused, I bought glazed buns for everyone just so I could have one. They were gone before we left the city.

As I sucked the icing from my fingers, a thought occurred to me. "Corey will most likely recognize us. I can alter our appearances a little, but creating even minor disguises for two people—"

"Three people, Ramiren," Georgina interrupted.

I shot her a grateful smile. "Thank you. Three people, will take a lot of my concentration. I won't be much use beyond that."

Tomin hiked Raewyn back up onto his shoulder. "Can we steal it? Is that the plan?"

"I wish we could," I replied. "You can't take favors, especially ones traded with a pact. It needs to be given willingly."

"Oh. Leave it to Georgina and me." Raewyn laced her fingers together and cracked her knuckles. "I think I know what we can do to get your favor back. You can put me down now, Tomin."

"No."

Raewyn scoffed and tapped the top of his head. "Down. Now."

"What did Ramiren say? 'No' is a powerful word?"

"Uh." Raising a finger to correct him, I cut in, "That's not what I m—"

Tomin blithely ignored me. "Rest while you can, sweetheart. Besides, I like your ass where it is."

"I'll set your hair on fire if you don't."

Tomin grinned at the ultimatum. "No you won't."

"Beauteous Minue, I beseech you for aid. Set fire t—"

Though I knew what Raewyn's prayers sounded like, Tomin did not. His grin disappeared like the glazed buns had, and he set her down on her feet then backed up a few paces. Holding his hands out in surrender, he stared at her wide-eyed. "All right! Shit, I'm sorry! You weren't joking."

Smug as a cat with cream, Raewyn sashayed toward the brightly lit building that could have only been The Mint.

Georgina, still perched on M.A.L.C.O.L.M.'s shoulders, smirked crookedly down at Tomin. "You haven't been around her long, have you?"

At Tomin's head shake, she gave a sharp laugh before telling the automaton to walk on after Raewyn. "She's many things, but she always keeps her promises."

I glanced back at a frozen Tomin, then moved up to M.A.L.'s side. "You and Raewyn were at each other's throats for most of our time in the Feylands. What happened?"

She glanced down at me and smiled. "It's amazing how amiable people can be when they're angrier at someone else and they need to vent."

The blaring noise from within the gambling hall, a mix of angry yells and happy cheers, told me my headache wouldn't improve anytime soon. "Time to focus," I said, placing my hand on The Mint's gold-painted front door. Glancing back at Georgina and Raewyn, I confirmed the magic still held.

Our most defining feature—our hair color—had to be adjusted to something a little less memorable. I'd altered my hair from black to blond, much to Raewyn and Georgina's extreme displeasure. Georgina's pigtails had been changed from pink to brown, while Raewyn's curls had gone from auburn to black. The magical strain of three disguises, relatively minor as they were, produced a stabbing pain just behind my left eye.

The bright feylights placed on every available surface that wasn't taken up by the crooked front sign—**Welcome to The Mint! We Make Money!**—or the gaudy gold trim also didn't help matters.

My companions' faces, highlighted by the obnoxious glow, showed varying levels of excitement. "Ready?" I asked Georgina and Raewyn.

"Yup! Ready!" Georgina chirped.

Beep. "Htaed ot Yeroc!"

Raewyn clapped her hands once. "Ready."

Tomin shrugged emphatically with a grin. "Sure. Htaed ot Yeroc. Why not?"

I pulled open the door, breathing through my mouth again, and walked through.

Though the place was even more riotously packed than the streets of Puldoni, we found Corey in under ten minutes thanks to the handful of elven mercenaries he kept close. The capra fey sat with his back tucked into the corner at a round poker table, appearing smug, with a large chip pile and most of the table's seats empty.

Handing Raewyn and Georgina each a heaping stack of gold coins, I told them good luck and watched, standing off to the side with Tomin and M.A.L.C.O.L.M., as the two women sauntered over to Corey's table.

Georgina toddled along, the same as ever, but Raewyn's body language shifted subtly. With just an infinitesimal tilt of her head, a slight sway of her hips, and the softening of her facial features, she'd changed far more than I could have manufactured through magic.

Beside me, Tomin murmured something I couldn't make out in the din of the open gambling hall. My gaze still on the poker table, I asked, "What?"

"Oh. Nothing," he replied with a sheepish tone, as though he didn't realize I'd heard him.

I grunted in acknowledgment and continued to watch as the priestess and the tinkerer caught Corey's attention. Raewyn turned a blinding, flirtatious smile on the capra fey. She said her line, and Corey laughed and gestured to the empty chairs. She and Georgina each took a seat, passing their gold to the goblin dealer.

My eyes stayed on Corey and his mercenaries to catch any hints of recognition, but all I saw was blind lust. Perfect.

Over the next half hour, hands were dealt and chips moved. Raewyn laughed when she lost, smiled shyly when she won, and played her part flawlessly. As planned, whenever Georgina won, she crowed happily. When she lost, her cards landed on the table with grumpy disdain. Her chip pile dwindled, leaving just enough to stay in the game.

Tomin and I refused pushy waitresses asking to take our drink orders. To ensure we weren't outed as non-paying customers and have the whole plan ruined by bouncers looking to fill a quota, I passed them a few silver coins to keep them happy and, most importantly, quiet. The throbbing behind my left eye became so unbearable I had to close my eyelids in an unsuccessful attempt to ease the pain.

Slowly, as time passed, Corey's face changed from pink to red to purple as his chip stack faded to nothing. Another hand found his many bone and ivory necklaces lying tossed onto the table as an ante, but those too were taken.

He leaned in, spittle flying, and yelled something while pointing at Raewyn's face.

"Do we step in?" Tomin asked into my ear, his gaze focused on the table. Or, more likely, on Raewyn.

With a slight shake of my head, I murmured, "No. She has this."

Raewyn calmly and casually replied to the angry capra fey, and he scowled while looking in a large sack at his side. My breath stalled and back straightened when I saw him take out a very familiar roll of parchment.

"That's it," I said, louder in my excitement than I would have preferred, but there was no way they could've heard me.

"Your favor?"

I nodded, sucking in a breath when I watched Corey put the parchment on the table to pay for the next hand.

Cards were dealt again, and my hand slipped into my pocket containing the broken, smoky-colored necklace. My thumb felt along the plain embellishments and its simple centerpiece, the ridges biting into the pad as I pressed down hard in my nervousness. I knew it had no magic.

There was no luck provided by the gem, but it didn't matter.

I rubbed the smooth cut facets and prayed.

Corey's expression went from angry to placid as he looked over his poker hand. I couldn't see Raewyn's or Georgina's faces, but their shoulders told a different story. Georgina's shoulders tensed as she scratched at her neck. Raewyn's muscles remained at ease, giving nothing away. I was grateful she didn't seem to have any obvious tells, but I wouldn't have minded a hint.

The capra fey transitioned from calm to ecstatic when he threw his hand down, laughing as Raewyn and Georgina leaned forward to see what he had. His laughter deepened as Georgina put her cards on the table.

But when Raewyn set hers down, his laughter sputtered and died. "Cheater!" he screamed loud enough for me to hear as Raewyn snatched up the parchment.

"Uh-oh." Tomin sighed. "All right. Time to go."

Corey reached for Raewyn's arm as she stood, but she managed to shake his hand off with a roll of her wrist. When the fey turned to his bored mercenaries, Tomin and I began to push our way through the crowd. I was almost to the table when an oblivious patron's elbow caught me in the temple, causing me to recoil and bring a hand to where he'd hit me.

Alarmingly, the headache disappeared.

"Oh, fuck. I think the disguises dropped," I muttered, nearly tripping as I rushed the rest of the way, only to find Raewyn and Georgina gone. Turning around, I searched for Raewyn's auburn hair and Georgina's pink pigtails, not thinking that I was known to him too.

"Hey! *Hey*! I know you! Guards! B— Aw, fuck it. Get him!"

Tomin grasped my shoulder to spin me back into the crowd. We drove forward, leaving grumbling gamblers behind. I stumbled through the gold-painted door, Tomin following.

"Did we lose them? Raewyn! Geor—"

"Over here, dummies!"

Peeking around the left corner of the gambling hall, I saw Georgina and Raewyn waving us over. We scrambled and made it out of sight as the door slammed open again, coupled with an angry capra fey yelling obscenities.

"You coming with?" Tomin asked Georgina.

She shrugged and replied, "Wouldn't mind the ride. Hold on, M.A.L."

"Everyone put a hand in." Tomin hunched over, sticking his left hand palm down in the center of our circle as his right hand danced in the air. "All right. Three...two...one."

"Les! Jham! There they a—"

The elven mercenary's voice was cut off as we bid The Mint goodbye.

Chapter Twenty-Four
The Terror of Failure

My oiled hands went into the warm water, the bar of soap slipping between my trembling fingers. Nathalia's gaze felt like a brand as she waited patiently for me to finish cleaning them, not knowing I didn't really need to. What I needed was a moment to breathe, to calm myself, so I didn't bungle our last night together and blurt out what I actually wanted.

As far as I was concerned, this *was a paltry consolation prize, but this night was for her, not me. I would never ask for something she had explicitly stated she was unwilling to give. Frankly, I'd be content just holding her until dawn if she'd allow it.*

That didn't make it any better. In fact, it made it worse.

This time tomorrow, she'd be in the arms of that pig of a prince, and I'd be nursing my sorrows in bad wine. Old Me would've laughed at Current Me, maybe with a hint of vicious mockery.

Old Me would've gotten a fist slammed into his smug face.

What I really wanted was to feel her. *There'd been hints of what her total surrender in my arms would be like. Small indications, really. Her thighs trembled when she was close. Imagining them wrapped around my waist caused everything from my chest to my knees to ache, then throb, in a perpetual cycle.*

She'd done it before, and I'd nearly painted her stomach with cum every time.

Her nails, short but sharp, tended to dig into my scalp when I sucked on her clit. The mental image of those nails sinking into my back while I sank into her was so vivid, both blissful and agonizing, that I considered capitulating to the screaming, needy beast in my head and outright begging her.

But I wouldn't, because she had explicitly said that it was off the table.

More than anything, though, were the noises she made. She'd never been a quiet, shy lover, and until my last breath, I'd remember and dream of the exact tone, pitch, and resonance of the moans my tongue and hands had managed to wring out of Lady Nathalia Swordhand, soon to be Princess-Consort Nathalia Loranaskan.

My hands shook harder as I rinsed the soap from them and dried them.

I took one step toward her and saw her beautifully flushed face, golden eyes full of anticipation. I realized I couldn't do this. Refusing would disappoint her. Fuck, it disappointed me, *but I couldn't pretend anymore that this wasn't destroying me.*

"I'm sorry. I don't think this is a good idea."

The anticipation in her eyes fled like startled birds, and guilt punched me in the gut. She fell back to sit on her legs, stricken, and asked, "What's wrong, Ramiren?"

Fuck. A reason. I need a reason. Something that won't hurt her feelings.

You're sick?

No, she'd heal me, or whatever it is celestials can do.

She's hideous, and you don't find her attractive?

A lie, and *a horrible thing to say, you bastard.*

Tell her you might accidentally go down the wrong path?

What?

Say you might slip from her anal region to her vaginal region accidentally. Better?

We'll talk about this later.

Maybe, but I'm leaving now. I'm too young to handle this.

You're over four hundred years old.

Exactly.

Seeing her patiently waiting, I said as calmly as possible, "I have excellent control, but there's too great a chance of me slipping and accidentally breaking the pact, bringing down consequences quite unfairly."

Nathalia tilted her head, eyes full of unease. "What do you mean slipping*?"*

My face tightened. I should have anticipated follow-up questions. "Entering one passage when I meant to enter another. It can sometimes happen, even with experienced lovers. I really shouldn't have suggested it."

She stared at me, her expression going from unease to anger as she scurried away.

Fuck! Fuck! Fuck!

She muttered something I couldn't quite make out. Probably a curse of some sort, based upon her expression.

My hand instinctively reached out for her, but then her face softened. Whatever she was thinking, I didn't want to interrupt it. So I waited. It might have been thirty seconds later, it might have been thirty minutes, when she finally spoke the words that tore my heart in two.

"I would like to dissolve the pact, Ramiren."

Shock, then abject devastation crushed my insides to dust. The magic holding our pact in place fled in a rush, and I knew we only had a few minutes before the room ceased to exist and we'd be pushed back to her bedroom in Castle Carpatha.

My world spun, and I didn't know which way was up or down. When it finally righted itself, I said the only thing I could. "Yes, I think that is wise. Tomorrow, you'll be wed and will no longer have a use for the pact. Tonight's lesson would have been helpful, but it's not strictly necessary." The lump in my throat refused to budge.

She raised her hand toward me, a simple gesture of friendship. In relief, I took it and threaded my fingers through hers. "I'm sorry. It was not my intention in the slightest to cause you pain. Quite the opposite. I am so very sorry, Nathalia."

"No, Ramiren. You don't understand. I would like to make a new *pact."*

What?

My eyes flew to hers. Did I hear her right? A new pact? "You're right. I don't understand. The hags are defeated. And after tomorrow, you'll have a husband. You'll no longer require my instruction."

She graced me with a sweet smile, and I wanted to run my thumb over her lips. "Even if the instruction is only for one night, I would like a new pact. And we would lose access to this place if we don't make one, I think. Would you like to?"

With no idea what to expect, I did the only logical thing. For her, I would've agreed to anything. "I would, yes. What are your terms?"

Her fingertips touched my mouth, kissing them, and it took everything in me to not kiss them back. Her gaze locked with mine. I saw affection there, but also resolve.

What are you thinking, angel?

"I want you to fuck me, Ramiren."

This isn't real. I'm dreaming. Hallucinating, perhaps. Those guards I managed to sneak past actually caught me, knocked me on my ass, and are torturing me as we speak. I'm disassociating with happy thoughts to preserve my sanity.

I managed to pinch my thigh with my free hand, hard, but the scene didn't change. Holy fuck, this is real. She's getting married tomorrow. Why would she do this? My jaw hinged open, and only one word came out. "Why?"

I'd asked a simple question. One word. The answer she gave me, however, was more akin to a song composed by the heart than a response composed of logic. For once, she was choosing to be selfish, and I couldn't be more gods-damned proud *of her.*

Fuck it.

I heard someone far away calling my name. It took me a moment to wake up enough to realize it was Dredon.

Yes? What?

Oh, good. You're awake. I wasn't sure if you'd died from exhaustion yet.

How long was I asleep?

Two hours. I'm so proud of you. You've managed to sleep about five hours in the past week. Most people go mad at this stage.

Him saying he was proud of me twisted around and collided with the last few thoughts of the dream I'd been having, and I rolled over on the sitting room sofa I'd collapsed onto shortly after Tomin transported us from The Mint to Castle Tanta in Elancia, stopping only to bid Georgina and her automaton a distracted farewell and dodge questions on whether or not Nathalia's soul wanted to return at all.

So I did what only a well-mannered and diplomatic pactmaker could do. I'd hidden in a random parlor and barricaded the door.

Did you need something?

Oh. Yes. Um, I need something because I* did *something.

Reversed the water pipes in the maester's bathrooms again?

No, though good callout. That was fun. No. I threatened Maester Vondo's life if he didn't tell me why there was a soul in your pact room.

All exhaustion left me as I sat up from the sofa. *You did what?*

Yes. He's not very happy right now, but it's his fault, really. I asked him, very politely, about souls and pact rooms and such. He ignored me. Just started walking away! You know how much I love being ignored...

Right.

So I, you know, tackled him and stuffed him into a utility closet and started to rip out pages from his book until he told me what I wanted to know.

When you say his book...

Yes, his book. **That** ***book. Needless to say, he folded like ol' Corey should have.***

Though I gave no fucks for Maester Vondo's hundred-year-long research project on the fundamental differences between verbal and written pacts, my palpitating heart understood the possible consequences for Dredon's actions.

What did he say?

Are you sitting down?

My heart palpitations got worse. *I am.*

Good. So, good news and bad news. The good news is, what happened to Nathalia is supposed to happen. Evidently, pactmakers used to be called soul keepers, specifically for important people and royalty. A binding agreement would bring the soul to a prepared space for it to be kept ready for resurrection if they were ever killed. There's a high chance of failure in resurrecting a soul from Celestia, even for the fey.

I'd expected something like that, but hearing it confirmed made me dizzy. *You're serious? So if—*

Yes. Completely serious, but I'm not done yet, because it somehow gets worse. Our predecessors were also a bit naughty. The soul keepers eventually noticed they held life, and by extension a nation's stability, in their hands and began to extort their clientele.

Is that the bad news?

Oh. No. So. Um. The bad news is also actually kind of good news. But also bad news.

My irritation at his babbling, something he was prone to do when nervous or excited, was countered only by my acknowledgment that there might not be any truly bad news. Aside from Maester Vondo causing problems.

You bring a soul from the pact room by using a soulstone. That worthless necklace you got from Nathalia for your super-sexy pact? That's a soulstone. But you're not supposed to have them. It's forbidden.

How can you tell? It's a plain, mundane necklace with no aura. Inert.

It's only mundane when it doesn't have a soul or essence within it. It held that arch-devil's essence, remember? That gem isn't quartz or glass; I think it's deibrium. Gods' Glass, which is always a dark gray color, according to Vondo.

It should have been obvious. Vrakus had already indicated it was capable of holding something of that nature, but I'd believed it was a one-time effect, leaving a useless trinket behind.

Deibrium?

Remember us being scoundrels? A bunch of shit happened that's not really relevant right now, our soulstones were removed, and we became pactmakers. The protocol to dissolve pact rooms was enacted after that "bunch of shit happened."

And you're saying Nathalia's necklace is a soulstone? When that—

Still not done yet. Gods above, you're squirrelly. Yes, that's what I'm saying. Anyway, here's the best part...

He trailed off, and I waited for him to continue. And waited. When the sofa's fabric under my hands ripped, I prodded Dredon. *What's the best part?*

There was no answer.

Dre?

Still no answer.

Dredon?

Fuck, sorry. Not being dramatic. I'm being chased. Well, not now. I'm hiding in that same utility closet I took Maester Vondo to. Would this be an example of irony or coincidence? I **always** ***get those two mixed up.***

Fucking gods, Dredon!

Right. So the best part is you don't need a fey to resurrect her. You can do it, assuming she agrees. You still need that part.

Of all the things Dredon could have told me, I'd hoped it'd be that Nathalia would return without the trauma of my father's fiendish hospitality. Or that she'd no longer be obligated by her protector's oath and could then take another oath to the man she chose to marry.

It certainly wasn't "you can bring her back yourself."

I—what? How?

He said you need to use the soulstone and call her back. I didn't have time to ask specifics, though, because the guards heard him yelling. But that's funny, right? You had the power the whole time.

No, Dredon. This isn't fucking funny.

I understand. You're tired and stressed, and that makes you a little pedestrian right now. However, this is good news. Now go talk her into coming back, become less pedestrian, and come save me. Please.

Thank you, Dre.

Awake and ready for the second part of my plan, and my last attempt, I snapped my fingers.

When I appeared in the pact room and turned, I choked on my tongue.

I expected a floating cloud with a center light to greet me, but a floating, partially transparent Nathalia, covered in the same shawl the water nymph wore in the painting across the room, did instead.

The same light that had been at the center of the cloud was now in the center of her chest, pulsing like a heartbeat.

My mouth opened, breath exited my lungs to say something, but my tongue remained in my throat. Instead of speaking to her, I gurgled at her.

Smooth.

I couldn't even yell at him for that as I stood there, making horrible sounds as she turned to me. "Nathalia" smiled brightly at me, and the similarities were uncanny. And they hurt. "You said this is what I looked like before, yes? How close am I?"

My instinct was to tell her to stop, to resume her actual form and not dress up as Nathalia, as the woman I loved, but that was wrong. Instead of demanding she go back to resembling a cloud, I took this as motivation. If she wanted to retain her connection to her mortal form, it should be encouraged.

I tapped my chest with my fist and cleared my throat. "You've changed," I grunted.

"Yes, cordani." She walked over, or rather, she *floated* over and pretended to use her legs and feet. It took everything I had to not recoil at the unnaturalness of it and stay completely still. It felt profane, as though a bad actress had taken Nathalia's form for a satire play. It was her soul, yes, but it wasn't *her*.

"When I was here before, I told you I would show my thanks to Nathalia, but I wasn't specific on how." I padded over to the bed, unhooking my Extended Pouch as I approached. Opening it to rifle through the contents, I removed the dark lacquered box containing Nathalia's note and the beautiful set of birdpipes she'd gotten for me but hadn't been able to give me. "Do you enjoy music?"

"Nathalia" showed her teeth as though trying to pantomime a smile but wasn't entirely sure how it was meant to look, making me suppress the urge to shudder. *I don't have to like it. I just need to stand it until it agrees.* "I do," it said. "We, you and I, would often pass the time with it. It's how I brought you back from deterioration."

The birdpipes nearly tumbled from my fingers. I furrowed my eyebrows. "Oh?"

"Nathalia" hovered closer. "When I came out of the mirror, your entire form was almost completely gone. The Lorindar barely got to you in time. You were so—" It cut off abruptly, though I couldn't tell why. It quickly recovered from whatever happened, no emotion showing on "Nathalia's" face at any point, and continued. "I did the first thing that came to mind. I pushed my form into yours and began to sing. And I kept singing. Every melody I could make up, until you were whole again."

"How does an emotionless being sing? Singing *is* emotion."

"I never said I was emotionless, cordani. I said negativity was a mortal failing, because it is. Things like happiness, love, and contentment are certainly within my ability to feel."

Oh.

You know what they say about assuming.

You assumed, too, Dre.

Yes, but everyone already knows I'm an ass.

"Not long ago, I offered Nathalia a private concert, so to speak. I never got a chance to play for her." I flipped the birdpipe set over in my hand, running my fingertips over the iridescent trim made of mother-of-pearl. "She either bought these or had them made for me, and I never got a chance to use them. She included a note with them, and what she wrote made me believe that perhaps you would enjoy it too. So may I?"

"Yes. Please do."

Taking a deep breath to calm my racing heart, I pushed out the worry, the shame, and the grief that had been battering me like hail since I'd watched Nathalia die, since I'd failed to tell her the truth, since I'd seen my father's sigil on her neck, and before, when I'd stood there as Jaylin took Nathalia aside to claim what he had no right to.

Putting everything aside, I pursed my lips over the reeds and began to play a song while concentrating on the subtle movement in the air. Between us, different-colored lights popped into existence and began to dance and sway, pulsing and moving to the music.

The conjured lights refracted off the sparks swirling within Nathalia's soul as she watched, creating the illusion of thousands of tiny embers floating within her. She seemed to catch on to the song that I played, because she began to sing along with it.

While mortal Nathalia's voice was beautiful, her soul's voice was unearthly and haunting as she perfectly harmonized with the birdpipes. The lights swirled into a synchronized whirlwind, mixing together as both the wind instrument and the voice created something new and sublime, but fleeting.

Ephemeral.

When the song ended and the lights dimmed, both I and Nathalia's soul remained silent, the echoes of the notes continuing to ring in my ears long after the vibrations in the air ceased.

"Nathalia" spoke first, its voice hushed. "Thank you."

My first smile of the evening curled the corners of my mouth. "You're welcome."

The soul stared at me a few seconds before asking, "Why?"

I set the birdpipes back in the box, giving myself time to figure out exactly what she was asking. When nothing came to mind, I asked, "Why what?"

"Why try so hard to have me return when I could await you in Celestia?"

I replied without hesitation, "Because I can't imagine a world without her in it."

It gave another smile, as though this answer pleased it, but a shiver still crawled up my spine at its aberrant grin. "You could have just said you loved her. Love is something I understand. She returned your love. I would have agreed."

Every muscle in my body seized, then released in rapid succession. So fast, I felt lightheaded.

Are you fucking k—

Leave before you pull defeat from the jaws of victory, you idiot.

I took a deep breath, trying to remain calm and not get my hopes up. "I should have. You're right. But I wanted her to be the first to hear it."

"Nathalia" paused to look around the room, then said the words I'd been waiting to hear. "Love is a righteous purpose. I agree to return."

Air rushed out as I exhaled a breathless thanks, then snapped my fingers and reappeared in the barricaded parlor. After a beat, the ecstatic roar that erupted from my lungs, as long and as loud as they would allow, echoed off the blank, dusty walls.

I paced back and forth, unable to contain my excitement.

A sharp, surprised laugh escaped as I raked my hands through my tangled hair. I'd done it. She agreed. Our—

"Wait, what the fuck am I doing?"

Swiping at my damp, beaming face, nearly knocking my glasses off, I began moving the piles of furniture barring the door.

It was time.

Chapter Twenty-Five
Through The Wind, The Sun, and The Rain

When I explained what had happened and the new information from Dredon, without mentioning the necklace, Raewyn shrieked with delight, then began to rattle off questions about his voice in my head. Tomin looked perplexed, murmuring something about my life being far too interesting.

Georgina's reaction, however, remained the most surprising, though she tried to cover up her teary eyes by explaining her extreme allergy to pollen.

As a group, we informed King Rofar what we had learned. Entering his small throne room was usually uncomfortable. With so much wood in the room, and by extension wood lacquer, I had trouble distinguishing whether anyone was shocked at the proceedings or if the castle staff was simply diligent regarding its upkeep.

The king sat on his simple throne, the smaller one beside him empty. He spoke with hesitation as he frowned down at the parchment in my hands. "I'm...not sure I understand. You no longer need our help because you can do this *yourself*?"

The smell of wood lacquer intensified, and I made an educated guess that it was from the king rather than his polished chair.

"That's what my pact vizier indicated, but I have my doubts. His instructions to accomplish this were very vague. The answer seems obvious, though." I didn't particularly want to ask this question, but now was the time for truths. "He said there's a high chance of failure for whatever ritual you and your people do to return someone. Is that true?"

King Rofar leaned back on his simple throne with a grimace. "Yes. That is true. It's far from guaranteed, as many things can go wrong. It's rare and not requested of the clergy often. A misspoken word or misplaced candle could literally be the difference between life and death. Fussy ritual, but calling a soul back is no small thing. Though I'm not sure the clergy have ever attempted to bring someone back from a pact room."

Calling a...?

I blurted out, "Your Majesty, you said 'calling a soul back.' May I at least speak with one of your priests or priestesses to discuss this? The reason I ask is because that's the wording my pact vizier used. Perhaps there are similarities between what they do and what I need to do?"

"That shouldn't be a problem." He crooked his fingers at a court clerk standing off to the side, who straightened to attention. "Bring High Priest Wohlin here," King Rofar said. With a bow, the clerk rushed out.

Raewyn hummed in thought beside me, crossed her arms, and blithely suggested, as if it were simple, "Maybe your clergy should practice more? Laethi clergy can't do it, but Feylands clergy can. Seems like you're wasting your capabilities, no?"

King Rofar chuckled ruefully at the priestess. "We respect Fate here, Lady Raewyn, though we do acknowledge there can be extenuating circumstances." His hands went wide in front of him in concession. "If, say, someone is taken far too soon, especially someone like Lady Nathalia, and what she managed to do."

He stood, hands pushing against the armrests as both he and the wood beneath him groaned. "The way I see it, you have one choice here, Ramiren."

I agreed, while Raewyn frowned. She looked at me. "I thought there were two choices?"

I replied to the Minuen priestess. "One, in reality. My way, with incomplete instructions, or the fey ritual, with the unknown probability of failure. In that order. If one doesn't work, we begin the other."

Raewyn responded quietly, "What if both fail, Ramiren?"

In the brief, quiet moments between planning, moving the necessary pieces, and frantic action to bring her back, I'd considered the what-if scenario of nothing working.

Though I'd survived sixty years without her, looking back, I realized it'd been a lonely existence, not unlike that of an automaton. Mechanical work occasionally interrupted by unfulfilling instances of leisure where I didn't even realize I was slowly bleeding out, drip by drip, just as if I was a mere soul again. Twice now, my deterioration had stopped and begun to reverse because of her.

Now, the idea of living even one year without her left me with stark understanding. It'd be a fugue life with the pitiful comfort of knowing I'd be reunited with a small portion of her upon my death. And when one lives to die, it happens sooner rather than later.

So I didn't have a real answer for her, just hedged reassurance while standing on the precipice of a bottomless void. "The best we can do is try."

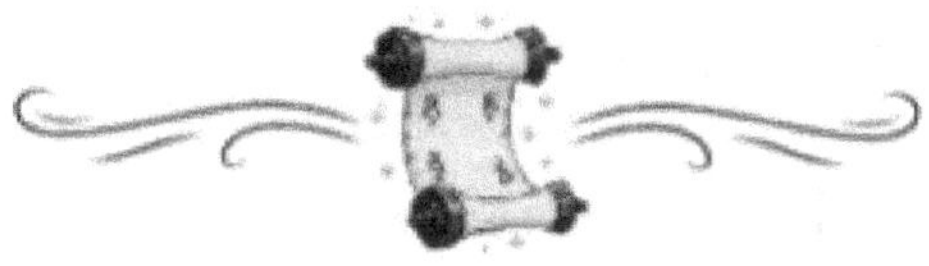

"Will you please explain to me the ritual of returning a soul to its body?" I asked the glowering fey priest in front of me. The sickly sweet smell surrounding him confirmed my suspicions about what he thought of this meeting. Wohlin glanced at his king as if waiting for permission to answer. At King Rofar's nod, he responded in a nasal voice that reminded me of Maester Vondo.

"Yes, well. It requires a ritual of exactly five priests and six priestesses, one for each deity. The first part, the Beautification, is the easiest and involves anointing the deceased's body. Their hair and entire body are cleansed and then consecrated with holy oils made from special herbs grown only in sacred groves. Cosmetics are sometimes used. Afterward, the body is clothed in pale silk embroidered in gold thread with each of the gods' sigils. Eleven lit candles, also bearing the gods' sigils, are placed equidistant around the body so it can be clearly seen. All eleven gods must unanimously agree the body of the deceased is an appropriate vessel."

Not too difficult, I suppose. "There was mention o—"

"The second part is the Adoration," the priest interrupted. "It is the beseeching of the Tarindar and the Lorindar for their mercy and aid. All eleven gods must unanimously agree to release the soul of the deceased from the Aerie, or Celestia as you call it, because it would be to the mortal world's benefit."

My head spun at the inane and exacting details, praying I wouldn't need to do this as well if the gods were looking for any reason to deny a soul's return. Noting I hadn't heard anything about a call, I prodded, "I s—"

Wohlin interrupted again, "The third part, the Calling, is the most important."

Finally.

"For fuck's sake. Do we need to sacrifice a blond virgin under the eleventh full moon, too?" Raewyn muttered beside me.

Raising my hand to quiet her gently, I nodded to the high priest. "Continue, please."

Wohlin, while looking disapprovingly at Raewyn's irreverence, did as I asked. "The Calling might seem simple, but it is perhaps the most difficult part."

Of course, it is.

"A mortal cannot see or speak to a soul directly, as only a soul can see and speak to another soul, but they must be guided back. Therefore, the soul of the priestess representing Jessina must leave her body and search for the soul of the deceased. Once the soul is found, the priestess calls out the deceased's true name. Should the soul agree to return, it will remember its true name and come at the Calling. It is Jessina's final approval on the ritual's perfection that must be obtained before the soul is funneled into the body."

I tried very hard to not let my elation show on my face or shake my voice when I said, "I have three questions, High Priest Wohlin."

Wohlin sighed tiredly. "Very well. Your first?"

"What if you know exactly where the soul is, and it's not in Celestia?"

Wohlin frowned as though not expecting my inquiry. "Then I suppose it will be a fast search."

"For my second question. What if you *can* see and speak to the soul directly?"

Wohlin rolled his eyes. "Then, in that hypothetical and illogical situation, the soul of the Jessinian priestess would not need to leave her body."

I took a deep breath and let it out slowly. "And for my third question. If a soul has different memories from the body, how would the Jessinian priestess remember the deceased's true name?"

I heard Raewyn's sharp exhale as Wohlin blinked and sputtered, "I'm sorry?"

"I'm guessing that this is the reason so many of these rituals fail, High Priest. Is that not the case?"

Wohlin's cheeks reddened. "It is, and hopefully you have some compelling explanation as to how you know that, *pactmaker*."

My smile pulled at my lips, going so wide I felt it crinkle the corners of my eyes. "I promise to tell you the story later, High Priest, but if one were to know the location and true name of the soul as well as be able to speak to and see it, how might one call the soul to return?"

The redness in Wohlin's cheeks spread to his forehead and neck like a peculiar rash. He faced his king, jaw hard and teeth grinding. "This is borderline heretical."

I pressed. "Even so, how?"

"It—" He shook his head quickly in exasperation. "I suppose you would guide the soul out of where it was, place your hand on the deceased, and call its true name to you, thereby funneling the soul into the body as the Jessinian priestess would. That part cannot be ignored, but..." He looked at the ceiling, though I was unsure if he was disgusted or praying for forgiveness. "If the soul does not need to be released from the afterlife, then it does not need the gods' permission. However—"

He stepped close and held up an index finger near my face. I didn't flinch, even when his finger shook and his tone turned gravelly. "If it is my king's command to enact this ritual, I will do it. *However*, the gods do not look kindly on *loopholes*."

"Your concerns are noted, High Priest." I turned to King Rofar. "Your Majesty, I believe I know what I need to do. I will attempt to bring her back my way while they either perform their ritual concurrently or after, should my attempt fail."

Wohlin narrowed his eyes. "Clearly, you have some sort of sorcery I'm not aware of. I would *humbly* suggest that both attempts be done concurrently. There are records of souls found but *unable* to find their body. If a soul is brought into the room, doing the rituals at the same time would double the possibility of her returning. Doing them one after the other means the soul has a chance to become lost and wander away."

Both the king and I agreed, and King Rofar patted my shoulder. "I admit, I'm curious, so I will make you a wager, Ramiren. If Nathalia's soul uses you to return, your favor is still available to you."

I wanted to tell him I didn't care. As long as she returned, it didn't matter who had been the one to bring her home.

But that'd be a lie, and there was nothing I wanted more than to be her reason.

Turning to Tomin, I said, "Please tell Idora to bring Nathalia. We're ready."

Leaning against the wall on the wooden bench, I cleaned my glasses for the fifth time. I wouldn't be needed until the third part of their ritual, and I suspected my pulled-at scalp and bouncing right leg's muscles would be sore by the time I was allowed in.

In the interim, I'd been left alone to think about what Dredon had said as the priests and priestesses prepared Nathalia's body for the first part. The Beautification.

We had been soul keepers before, housing the souls of those taken too soon, to ensure the stability of the realms. We'd been protectors, in a way, but more of economies, treaties, and lineages than of individuals.

Unfortunately, that sacred duty had been corrupted in the name of greed and power. I could only imagine what kind of "shit" Dredon had been alluding to.

I felt at odds with it all. On the one hand, I didn't believe they'd done enough to remove our ability to confine a person's soul. A simple process, no more than an emphasized instruction or footnote in a book, was the difference between a soul moving on and being trapped indefinitely.

On the other hand, I'd never been so grateful for a mistake.

Losing focus, I found my thoughts flitting from one to the next in a random pattern as my thumb rubbed the gem in my pocket. A few seconds of a pleasant memory, then a difficult conversation, the melody of a song, a trying battle, another good memory. Over and over until I felt a gentle hand on my shoulder. Startled, I looked up and saw Raewyn's tense smile. "They're ready for you now."

I wanted Dredon to wish me good luck, but he'd been silent since his last message from inside the utility closet. Without expecting a reply, I sent him one. *Thank you, Dre.*

Standing, I lifted my hand. "Lead the way," I said, and followed her in.

Raewyn took me through the wide temple doors, the inked quill symbol of Jessina embossed in the center, into a round stone room with enormous copper braziers dotted around that emanated warmth, ample light, and the heady scents of frankincense and myrrh. The curved pews had been set against the walls to make room for the people inside.

The ceiling held no ornamentation aside from a perfectly circular oculus, from which a stream of moonlight beamed down onto the center of the room.

Eleven clergy of all shapes, sizes, and colors stood facing the center. Not wanting to disturb what they were doing, Raewyn and I weaved our way around them to the middle of the room, where a rectangular altar made of blue crystal sat in the middle. That's where my steps slowed to a crawl.

On the altar lay Nathalia, seemingly in peaceful repose, her face as pale and glowing as the dress she wore, made even brighter by the silver radiance coming from directly above.

Eleven pillar candles with different sigils pressed into the wax with gold and silver wire encircled her, the tapers lit and swaying from a slight breeze. The smell of honey from the beeswax cut through the pervasive incense. No bandages were wrapped around her neck for her mortal injury. Her throat was bare and unblemished, just as I remembered her. My glasses fogged and my eyes burned as I came closer.

On the other side of the altar, High Priest Wohlin stood, peering down at her. A flare of intense protectiveness filled me, seeing so many surrounding her while she lay in such a vulnerable state. When he reached out to Nathalia's choppy hair, slicked back from the ritual oil they'd used, my hand acted of its own accord. My fingers snatched his wrist in a firm hold just before he could touch her butchered strands. "No," I gritted out.

Wohlin winced, then blinked a few times. “Oh. Apologies,” he muttered, bowing and stepping back without turning. An older fey woman with a frown frozen on her face took his place. She inclined her head to me and exaggerated lifting her right hand. I did the same, following her lead until our palms were placed side by side on Nathalia’s cold, unmoving chest.

I felt the bite of the necklace’s pendant on my palm as I pressed it to my protector’s cold skin. My stomach twisted and flipped, and I swallowed the bile that wanted to rise.

We held our hands in place as the ten remaining clergy around us started to chant, their tones low and murmuring, as the Jessinian priestess indicated she was ready. “Proceed, pactmaker.”

Filling my lungs with terror, I exhaled resolve as my thumb and middle finger connected. Just as I snapped my fingers, I felt something warm and soft brush my hand.

In an instant, the pact room came into view, and two souls with it. One belonged to Nathalia, her soul turning from the painting she was staring at, still in the effigy of her mortal form.

The other soul, in a misty cloud beside me, was presumably the Jessinian priestess. “Talia!” it called out, and my heart choked my throat.

No! That’s not her name!

“It’s time to go, *Nathalia*,” I said, emphasizing her real name.

Fuck, doing this at the same time was a mistake.

“Time to return?” “Nathalia” asked, hovering closer.

“Yes. You need to be guided out.” With that, I extended my hand to hold the broken necklace out, its smoky gem glinting every time the soul’s lights pulsed.

“Talia, lo’na!” the Jessinian priestess’s soul wailed, the sound bouncing off the pact room’s walls. “Ral tra to!”

I had no idea what she was saying, but “Nathalia” ignored her, her hand reaching out to me. A gossamer sliver, like a thin tentacle, extended from the priestess’s soul to “Nathalia.”

But “Nathalia” backed away before it could touch her and said, “Va da cordani.”

The priestess's soul immediately shrank away, giving "Nathalia" the opportunity to place her fingers on my palm, the feeling more like a balmy mist than a hand. *Thank Jessina.*

My relieved smile faded as Nathalia's soul came even closer, as though to wrap her other arm around me, a placid and unafraid expression on her face. "Wait," I gasped, but that didn't stop what was happening. The warmth resting in my hand traveled up my arm as the gem began to swallow Nathalia's soul.

"O-oh, fuck. What's— What am I doing wr—" I stuttered.

Am I hurting her? Killing her? Is this supposed to happen? Is this it?

The intense fear that I was doing something wrong nearly developed into blind panic.

I inhaled raggedly, clutching my chest, as though I were either gasping or trying to breathe her in. She sank into the jewel and disappeared. The fear faded, leaving the warm comfort akin to a loving embrace in its wake.

Now settled, it felt wonderful.

Extreme fullness combined with giddiness brought with it the scent of oranges. It took me a second to realize my own emotions were so strong I could, for the first time in my life, detect them.

Bring me home, cordani.

I stuck my hand into the Jessinian priestess's soul cloud, not pleased with her attempt but also not willing to trap her here, and snapped my fingers to return us all to the temple.

When the soft glow of candles and smell of incense hit me, the disorientation, along with the ecstatic headiness of her soul residing within my grasp, made me stagger on my feet. My fingers gripped the cloth of her dress, the gem sandwiched between the cloth and my hand. My hold on her was the only thing keeping me upright.

I have to do something. Something specific. Another part.

Silence battered my eardrums, as though every acolyte present held their breath with me, until I remembered. *Her name! Call her name!*

With a mental prayer to all eleven that this would be enough, the word left me in a rush.

"*Nathalia!*"

As the last syllable slipped past my lips, the fullness poured out of me like water leaving a pitcher. Even through my closed eyes, I could sense the lights in the room brightening. The blistering heat from the blazing candles singed my hair and roasted my face, enough to cause perspiration. The honeyed smell of melting beeswax candles and the flare of flames sizzling faded into the background as I concentrated on the warmth moving from my chest, down my arm, then to the hand resting on Nathalia's chest, until that too faded.

With the overwhelming sense of being wrung dry, I opened my eyes on a gasp and stumbled back two paces just as the candles, now mostly dissolved, snuffed out, tendrils of gray smoke floating upward. My lungs burned like I'd been running for hours as I stared down at Nathalia, searching for a breath or even a twitch to indicate it had worked.

Come on, angel.

I measured that moment in heartbeats. Two beats. Three. Until, finally, Nathalia's eyes opened with a deep breath that gave me permission to breathe too.

Sacred candles and fragile vials of holy oil crashed to the floor when I flew at her, empty arms demanding they get what they didn't deserve but needed anyway. My face pressed into the crook of her neck, nuzzling the now-present pulse, as I fought for air.

I felt Nathalia's touch, her hands gripping my bicep for the first time in what felt like decades. The warmth coming from her fingers scorched my skin like ten iron brands.

A voice husky from lack of use, more dulcet than any melody, croaked out, "Ramiren?"

Lifting my head, my hands went into her hair to support her head. *Take care of her. She'll be shaky and weak. She'll need gentleness. I need blankets. She's too cold.* Turning to order more fuel for the braziers and every blanket in the castle be brought, I saw that we were alone.

Everyone, even Raewyn, had left.

With no time to question it, my red eyes met her golden ones, beautifully alive but unfocused and haunted. "Ramiren?" she asked again. She lifted a hand to my cheek, swiping it across as though trying to brush something off. She looked, and I followed her line of sight to see droplets on her thumb.

Uncaring, I pressed my lips to hers over and over again, muttering words between desperate kisses. "I'm sorry. I'm so fucking sorry."

"Rami—"

"No. Please. Believe me. I never meant for *any* of this to happen." My fingers tangled in her short hair, slipping in the oil the fey clergy had used.

"Ramiren, I—"

"Nathalia, I won't ask for you to f—"

Her hand met my cheek in a stinging slap, and I startled. She hadn't hit me nearly hard enough for it to hurt, but it stunned me all the same.

Nathalia glared at me, her mouth a hard, thin line. "Don't interrupt me. It's *my* turn to talk."

My lips parted in shock, but I stayed silent. If she'd demanded my eternal silence, I would've done it. I would've agreed to anything at that moment.

She bared her teeth as she gritted out, "Good. *Thank you.* Now, that's out of the way, I *don't* forgive you. *You lied to me.* Kept secrets from me. I don't give a shit how ashamed or terrified you are. *Never again*, do you hear me? Never. Fucking. Again!"

She sniffed, blue flecks beginning to appear in her teary eyes. "No more, Ramiren. *I mean it.*"

All I could do was nod dumbly.

"Now you can spend a long time making it up to me. Sound fair?"

With a groan, I agreed. "Yes. Fair. All of it."

Nathalia settled into my arms with a sigh, blinking rapidly as her eyes cleared. She glanced around the room, puzzled. "Where are we? This isn't Gateway."

My thumbs stroked her jawline and under her ears. I licked my lips as I looked around with her. "Elancia, in the Feylands. I was using my favor to have you returned."

Her gaze returned to mine, then lowered as though thinking. "Like the song," she whispered, her voice cracking from either dryness or emotion.

"Song? What song, angel?"

Finally, the hint of a smile twitched her lips. "The song from the carnival. 'Seasons Change.' Do you remember?"

Bending down to kiss her again, I simpered against her mouth. "I remember the singer more than the lyrics."

"Just an odd coincidence," she mused. "What now? Where do we go from here?"

We simply start. "Well..." Knowing I'd devote years to paying for my mistakes, my secrets, I began this new era by disclosing my greatest one. "I love you."

She smiled. Even though it was a small smile, it still rivaled the sun rising, something her soul could never hope to replicate. "I love you too." The air filled with the fragrant mixture of vanilla, caramel, and dark chocolate, finally answering my question about what that combination of scents meant. It meant she was in love.

I'm sorry I didn't realize it sooner, angel.

Chapter Twenty-Six
Mistaken Reflections

Though I tried to insist she be carried to a comfortable room to rest, Nathalia wouldn't hear of it. The walk was slow going, her legs as shaky as a newborn fawn's but getting stronger with each step. I moved to the side to let her pass through the narrow doorway but stayed close enough to catch her if needed. High Priest Wohlin yelled my name from down the hall.

Oh, for fuck's sake.

Calling back to him, I hooked my thumb toward the door Nathalia had just gone through. "I have to tend to her."

Breathing heavily, he jogged at a snail's pace toward me. When he made it to me, he rested his shoulder against the wall, then held his hands out as though praying. "Just one moment, please. Two things, then I'll go. One, that was one of the most miraculous things I've ever seen in all my days. King Rofar indicated your favor from him is still intact and available."

"Oh." I craned my head through the doorway to check on Nathalia, who was standing off to the side of the bedroom staring at something. "Yes. Thank you. Now, if you—"

"Second, and maybe this is none of my business, but did I hear you mutter something about Prince Jaylin Loranaskan and his *eluva bond* before we left the temple?"

"I—" *Did I say that?*

"You were quite angry about it." Color rose in his cheeks as he smiled sheepishly. "It didn't seem the appropriate time to ask right then. It's just quite odd, given the circumstances. Perhaps it's a personal joke between you two?"

"No. No, that's something the prince told Nathalia about when he proposed to her. That they had something called an eluva bond." The look on his face confirmed the suspicions I'd carried but had been unable to verify. After Nathalia successfully fled her wedding to the bastard, I'd forgotten all about it. Or nearly forgotten.

Ah, fuck.

He fussed with his robe's sleeves awkwardly. "Oh. I see."

My tongue ran along my teeth as I peeked into the room again, this time to ensure she couldn't overhear. "It means 'asshole' doesn't it?"

"I—" He grunted. "Yes, I'm afraid it does."

I'd concentrated my magic on the word *eluva*, but it always translated to "asshole." I'd convinced myself I was saying it wrong. With no idea how to spell it, I'd asked a few Carpathan citizens about it, once Nathalia had moved into Castle Carpatha, as I waited for her to realize what her life would be like with him and leave. But every time I asked, people either didn't know what it meant, or they looked at me wide-eyed before scurrying off.

Shaking my head, I raised my eyes to the heavens, hoping any eavesdropping entity with a modicum of power would hear and bend Fate's ear to see my silent vow done.

Put him in my path, and I'll take care of the rest.

"Um." Wohlin bowed low. "With that, good evening, Pactmaker." He backed away and disappeared back down the hallway before I could reply.

My forehead lowered to the door jamb as I exhaled a slow, deep breath. The violence within me lowered to a simmer, enough for me to feel like I could walk into that room without throwing something satisfyingly breakable.

I passed the threshold of the dark bedroom, moonlight streaming in from the large bay window to my right. The silver rays landed on the curtained four-poster bed with a closed door on either side. In the far corner, Nathalia was looking at herself in a standing full-length mirror.

I crept to her, watching her frown as she gazed at her reflection. She picked at the dress she'd been clothed in, running her fingertips over the gold embroidery.

"It's funny," she said, throat still hoarse. "When I saw this in the mirror, I thought it was a wedding dress."

She needs water.

Glancing around, I saw a copper water pitcher dotted with drops of condensation standing on a corner table with two glasses set beside it. After unhooking the two nearly identical pouches from my belt and placing them on the table, I picked up a glass and poured her some. "What mirror?"

"The one at the carnival just before we found the mischief hag and Georgina. It showed me in this exact dress with my arms around a faceless man. I looked happy and thought it showed me at my wedding." The despondency in her voice and the disappointment in her expression made me feel irrationally guilty. Silly, but it did.

"I'm sorry, Nathalia."

She shook her head as though it didn't matter. "It's all right. The mirror showed the truth. I just saw what I wanted to see." Nathalia looked down at herself and plucked the pale fabric again. "I assumed. Like always."

Approaching her with the water glass in hand, I tried to think of something to say. Some sort of comforting words that would help her. Without warning or preamble, she raised the dress over her head and tossed it to the floor. With her hair shortened, no tresses to hide behind, every inch of her soft skin, still holding a subtle glimmer, was visible.

I forgot what words were as she turned to me, curves lit and shadowed by the inflow of moonbeams. *Fuck.*

A familiar ache, followed by a familiar throbbing, demanded I devour the banquet in front of me. To follow the honey scent in the air that was surely just a remnant of the temple candles.

No. Stop it.

The vicious beast in my head that shrieked at me to *take, claim, mark* growled in disapproval but fell back for the time being. My gaze flitted over her, intending to survey for any lingering wounds rather than to appreciate. I met her look and held out the glass to her. "How do you feel?"

Nathalia took it and gulped down the water. Wiping a thumb over her mouth, she cleared her throat and responded a little more clearly, "I'm fine, I suppose. A little off? It's hard to describe." She handed the glass back, and I went to refill it.

"I can't say I'm surprised. You've been through a lot." Coming back, I handed her another full glass, and she drank that down too.

"I'd say we both have." That haunted quality came back to her eyes, and I stepped forward to take her hand. She rubbed her thumb over my knuckles before releasing her grasp.

"In that hole your father kept me in, I had a lot of time to think, and I figured something out. Knowing the history you two had wouldn't have changed anything, not really. He would've gotten us eventually. Leraska, or K'sar, or whatever her name is, dropped the wards on Rowin. We weren't safe."

There was no way I'd just let her brush everything aside like my secrets hadn't indirectly killed her. I cupped her jaw in both hands so she'd look at me. I tried to keep my voice steady and firm, but instead it came out husky. "No. Don't do that. Be mad. Scream. Cry. Don't just push it away like it's *fine*."

Nathalia jerked out of my grip to skewer me with a glare. "I'm not, Ramiren! I'm being fucking *pragmatic*. It didn't matter if he was your father or a complete stranger. He would have grabbed us. His motives mean nothing. Knowing what he was, knowing your past, might've prepared me better, but the ending would have been the same."

"What did he do to you?"

She dropped her head forward, shaking it. "No. He's dead. There's no point."

My jaw clenched so hard it popped. "What did he d—"

Nathalia's eyes rose to meet mine. "I said *no*. Did you forget what that means?"

"Please, just tell me if he..."

In an instant, her frustrated expression softened, then shuttered as she realized what I was asking. "No. A small mercy, he never did that." She shook her head. "Gods above, you've changed. You never would've pushed a 'no' before, even for something like this."

"I know." I collapsed to the bed, pushing my glasses up and digging the heels of my palms into my eyes. "I've pushed a lot of things lately. I felt it. I felt you die. But that's for me to deal with, not you."

Her soft footfalls came closer. "What?"

I fixed my glasses and met her eyes. "My chest caved in. Not literally, of course, but—" With a huff, I continued, "That's no excuse. I'm sorry."

Nathalia placed the empty glass on the nightstand and eased onto the bed beside me. "I know what guilt and shame do, Ramiren. I'm not saying I forgive you. You still lied and kept things from me, but I do understand *why* you did it."

I muttered, "Even *that's* more than I deserve."

She replied, "That's the guilt and shame talking too."

Sometimes there are questions you have to ask, even if you don't truly want to know the answers. I had two such questions screaming in my head. I'd already asked one of them, and this was my second. "Do you regret me?"

"What?"

My throat bobbed. "Do you regret making your vow?"

She didn't talk for several seconds. Nathalia didn't speak without thinking, so I knew she was considering her answer, but those seconds dragged on like years.

Finally, she answered with a hushed tone. "No. I don't regret it. I still think you're a good man, Ramiren, but you do have your faults. You let your past determine your future instead of living in the present. You don't share secrets, even when you should. You put on pretty airs, but underneath those glasses is a man who would kill without remorse. I saw the look in your eyes in Gateway. I know a killer when I see one. You both revel in and hate the fact you're a broodling. You love the respect that comes from fear but fear the respect that comes from love."

That's not even a small portion of my faults, angel. "Entirely fair."

She stared into space with a far-off look, focused on nothing except her thoughts.

"What can I do for you, Nathalia?"

"Never lie to me again, to start. Never give in to your fear of telling the truth. I can handle just about anything, but not that."

I pulled her in close, tucking her safe and warm into my side. "I promise. If you need to talk about it, I'll listen. Whatever happened. The very least I can do is carry a piece of it."

Nathalia nodded and extracted herself from my embrace to stand. I stood with her, and she handed me the glass a second time with a sad smile that cut me in two. "Don't let your guilt ask for things, Ramiren." Her arms wrapped around her torso to hug herself. "Especially things you don't actually want to know."

The more I looked at her, the more painful it became. Helplessness was torture, and I couldn't shake the feeling that she was sinking somehow. "I *do* want to know, truly, but only if the telling will help you and not hurt you a second time. In the meantime, what can I do? Whatever you need, I'll do it."

"Anything?"

"Yes. Please. Anything. Just name it."

She took two steps toward me, so close we shared breath, and her hands lifted to rest on either side of my jaw. "Then make me forget for a little while."

I set the glass in my hand on the table beside the bed and tilted my head down to peer at her over the rims of my glasses. "You're sure?"

"I am. And Ramiren?"

"Yes?"

"Don't make it soft. That place couldn't break me, but slow and sweet with you might."

I'd been given a task, and I sure as fuck wouldn't fail. Tossing my gold-rimmed glasses to the table, where they tumbled and slid along the wooden surface, I smiled. "Understood."

Both of my hands went into her hair, gripping, as I crushed my lips to hers. Immediately, my tongue invaded her mouth. No longer asking for permission, I channeled my love for her and the lingering fear that I'd never see her again into the kiss. Her fingertips curled into my beard, nails biting into the skin beneath as she took what she needed. What I was more than happy to give.

Her arms wrapped around my neck as I bent down to lift her, and the kiss turned from deep to hungry. Knowing roughly where the bed was, I turned in that direction and strode forward. Her teeth sank into my lower lip, the sting going straight to my cock, and my knees nearly gave out.

When she tangled her hands in my hair, tugging and tilting my head the way she wanted, they did give out. Her back hit the soft coverlet, and I followed, lips, teeth, and tongues still entangled. The crushing vise of her legs wrapped around my waist, nestling my painfully swollen tip against her pussy.

Her guttural moan broke through the pleasant haze and scent of honey I'd been drowning in as I rolled her nipple between my fingers, and something within me, the thin thread of control I possessed, frayed a little more.

I pushed off her, her bright apricot cheeks and full, bitten lips taunting me. Daring me. To reward her for choosing life, I'd fuck her to within an inch of it. Reaching down to her legs, my fingers clutched her thighs in a bruising grip as I flipped her to her stomach. Air whooshed from her as she landed and bounced on the bed's mattress.

I snagged a pillow and stuffed it under her hips to raise them to just where I wanted them. Pressing my chest to her arched back, I could hear her breath sawing in and out as my mouth ghosted the rapid pulse in her neck. "Your word, Nathalia," I hissed. "What is it?"

"Hum-Hummingbird," she panted.

My canines nipped the sensitive shell of her ear. "Good girl." Another groan, and her ass lifted and pushed back into me. My open palm swatted her backside, just hard enough to give a warning. "I'll move you if I want you to move, angel."

Her forehead dropped to the blanket underneath her in total acceptance. I wanted to reward that too.

My lips and teeth blazed a trail down the curve and indentations of her spine, biting at the adorable twin dimples just above her ass. My seeking fingers ran along her sides as I moved down, down, until I pressed my face, nose to chin, into her drenched pussy.

I took a second for myself to inhale deeply, hands cupping the crease between her thighs and ass, before my forked tongue extended to its full length and lapped hard from one end to the other. Nathalia squeaked as her hips tried to rise along with my tongue, but my hands held them down to the bed.

My hips pushed into the side of the bed to relieve the pulsing ache in my cock, but that only made it worse.

Her whine cut off with a choke when my thumbs parted her and my lips joined in, first wrapping around her clit, then sucking with steady pressure. I grinned when her thighs began to quake and dipped my tongue into her pussy, delving as deep as it could go.

When I felt the first ripples around my tongue, I lowered my mouth again to her clit for a firm swirl around it.

"I— Fuck! *Fuck!* Ra—" The unhinged scream that tore out of her, combined with the pulsating clench of every muscle I could feel, nearly made me come in my trousers. I laved and licked until she collapsed into the mattress, then crawled back up to put my mouth near her ear again. My heavy breath stirred her hair as I whispered, "Mercy?"

She grinned. "Never."

A nip at the back of her neck made her hips twitch. I chuckled low. "Good." Straightening, I undid the laces and buttons of my trousers and groaned in no small relief when my cock was no longer confined.

Grasping her hips with hard fingers, I lined the tip to her entrance and murmured, "I'm only listening for one word, angel. And 'mercy' isn't it." I pulled her hips back as my hips snapped forward, sinking halfway in.

She shrieked as my veins flooded, overwhelmed by the bliss of her tight heat. "Fuck," I whispered, the word muffled and distorted by a wheeze. Her walls rippled around my cock, and I pulled back, only to get sucked back inside by the clenching fist of her pussy. There were still a few inches to go, and every slow inch I pushed in had her gripping harder around me.

Pinpricks of light burst in my eyes as another inch disappeared. I couldn't catch my breath. The feral beast in my head thrashed and clawed at its cage, seething and demanding I take everything. That creature, the ecstasy, my careful movements...it was almost too much for me to control.

But then she rotated her hips and whined, and that frayed, weak thread just...

Snapped.

I barked, "Spread. Now!" I pushed her knees apart with mine, and her thighs widened. I leaned forward, pressing my palms to her shoulders and forcing them down with my weight.

"Wish granted," I gritted. My hips thrust forward the rest of the way, and I bottomed out with another wheeze. Rolling my hips, my hands holding her shoulders down, I watched her nails gouge the blanket under her. I pulled back, only to slam into her again, and again, and again, each thrust faster than the last, her pussy drawing me in and pushing me out in a dizzying rhythm.

I was greedy. I wanted another scream. I wanted to hear her cry out, see her shudder, leave her unable to form words for at least a day. Maybe two.

But most of all, I wanted to mark and claim her for my own.

Before I realized what I was doing, I bent forward, canines grazing the back of her neck.

My eyes slammed shut, and I tried to ease the growing need by licking a small path where I really wanted to sink my canines in to pin her down.

It didn't work. At all. I clenched my jaw to get rid of the ache.

Permission. Need. Permission.

Nathalia's voice, clear as day, echoed in my head. **Do it!**

And I was done. My teeth sank in on a feral groan, and her body froze. Then her hips twitched once, twice, and her hands tore at the twisted blanket as she let out a harsh, sobbing scream.

The rush of scorching wetness around my cock as I ground out her pleasure tipped me over the edge. Without warning, the simmering ecstasy boiled over. Against her neck, still latched on, I bellowed as my body emptied itself into hers.

Taking a moment to catch my breath, I untangled myself from her, starting with my sore jaw to see what damage I'd done. Two perfect marks down the left side of her neck, red but somehow not bleeding, stared back at me. I brushed my fingers over them as I pulled my half-hard cock from her and tumbled to the bed beside her. My arms wrapped around her after I threw the soiled pillow off the bed.

"I suspect one of these doors is a bathroom," I murmured into her hair, brushing a few strands aside, my lips at her temple. "How do you feel about a bath?"

With a happy sigh, she replied, "I think I made it to Celestia."

My head jerked up, and I scowled down at her. "Not funny."

An impish grin accompanied her words. "It's a little funny."

I snorted, then kissed her hair. I swatted her ass again, then rose. "One of these days, I really *will* fuck the brat out of you."

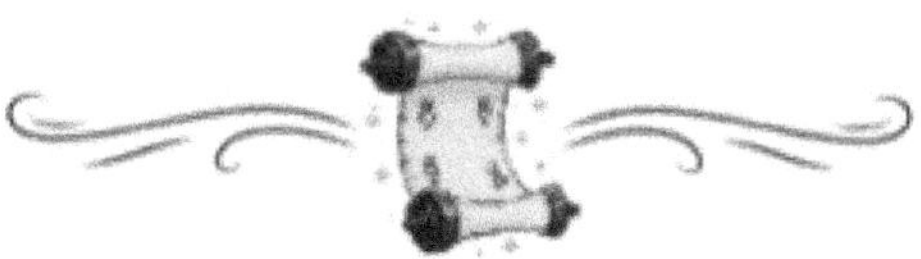

A sharp inhale brought me out of a pleasant dream. I glanced down at Nathalia tucked into my arms; her even breathing indicated she was still asleep.

Maybe I dreamed it?

The movement of a dark shape caught my eye. Lifting my head, I caught sight of red silk robes in the moonlight. Even without my glasses, I could clearly see the happy smile on Raewyn's face as she stared down at our entangled limbs.

She moved away with the soft pad of slippered feet, indicating she had no intention of waking us. The sound of the door opening, followed by a gasp, caused me to look. Raewyn stood at the open door looking at something, or someone, on the other side of the threshold, feylight from the hallway highlighting her alarmed eyes.

"I came to check on her," a deep, masculine voice murmured.

Fuck.

Raewyn whispered, "Oh, she's fine, Dad. Sleeping like a baby. Best not to wake her."

"Sure, thank you, Rae. I'll see her in the morning, then," Lord Maxlian replied.

Raewyn glanced back at us, then closed the door behind her with a soft click.

Chapter Twenty-Seven
Location, Location, Location

My eyes flew open at the loud banging on the bedroom door followed by a half-dressed Raewyn barging in. I squinted from the glare of the early morning sunlight, and I held my hand up to block the bright rays.

Raewyn ran to our bed, roughly shaking my shoulder as if to wake me up, even though I was obviously awake and glaring at her. "Up, up, up. Gotta go. Gotta go right now," she hissed, panicked.

Beside me, Nathalia, tucked in warm and comfortable, buried her face in the pillow we'd been sharing. She groaned, her voice heavy with sleep. "What?"

"Dad's here," Raewyn replied, her fingers slipping on the fabric buttons of her robes as she tried to close them. "And he just got a message from Rowin. Uldanna's dead."

It wasn't clear if it was the news of the elderly Queen of Camlynn's death or hearing that her father was just outside that made Nathalia jackknife, but all traces of sleepiness vanished. She shrieked, "What?"

"Exactly! *Now, get up*!" Raewyn yelled, even though we were three feet away. Stalking to the exit, she muttered, "Lazy people," then slammed the door closed.

Nathalia and I stared at each other for a silent beat, then scrambled out of bed. "Fuck! Pouch! Where's my pouch?" Hands in her hair, she spun in a circle, looking for any sign of it.

"Here," I called, tossing it to her from where I'd placed it the night before. She dug into it as I searched in mine. Piles of clean clothing, weapons, and armor were strewn about by the time we'd finished dressing. Stuffing what we didn't need back into our pouches, figuring we'd trade what wasn't ours later, we hustled out of the room and followed the sounds of several voices yelling.

Nathalia and I glanced at each other before the room's occupants came into view. Lord Maxlian and King Rofar, with Lady Resa appropriately dressed for battle holding her hands up between them, were attempting to stare each other down. We stalled in the parlor's doorway, just taking in the scene. The air smelled overwhelmingly of blood and something sickly sweet.

Wonderful. Dredon?

I heard nothing in response. His continued silence concerned me, having spent most of my adult life with his quips and sarcasm in my head. However, there was little to be done at the moment.

Lord Maxlian leaned over his wife's head to seethe at the fey monarch. "No right, Rofar. You had *no right*."

"I have somewhere to be and don't have time for this, Maxlian. Would you prefer your daughter remain *alone* while recovering? Is that what you're saying?" the king replied coolly.

"No! Of *course* not! But you interfe—"

"Natty!" Lady Resa cried happily upon spotting us. "You're awake!" She strode forward as the High General of Camlynn and the King of Tanta finally took notice of us and ceased bickering. "You look lovely, darling girl." Brushing her fingers over Nathalia's chopped hair, the Swordhand matriarch gave her daughter a tight smile and an even tighter hug.

"Thank you. Queen Uldanna is dead?" Nathalia leaned back, and her hands went to her mother's wrists to hold them. "What happened?"

"Oh. Well, we came last night when we heard you'd returned to us, but after we left Rowin, it seems Queen Uldanna was found dead. We don't know much more at this point. We received the message from the Assembly about a half hour ago." She looked back at her husband, whose reddened eyes had settled on me.

The high general's feathered wings ruffled as he stretched back his shoulders. "Good morning, Ramiren." He raised an eyebrow and asked pointedly, "Sleep well?"

His meaning could not be mistaken, and I'd had enough. *Fuck it. What's another broken nose?*

I smiled as brightly as I could and replied pointedly right back, "I *did*, thank you, though I suspect Nathalia slept even *better*."

Off to the side, standing next to a wide-eyed Tomin and hunch-shouldered Idora, Raewyn hid a grin behind her hand.

Lord Maxlian's face turned an interesting shade of dark pink. "Are you *suicidal*, broodling?"

My glare met his head on. "No, Lord Maxlian. I'm tired. *Exhausted*, really, and perhaps not for the reason you fear. I've spent the better part of a fortnight paying for my mistakes, but I will happily spend the rest of my life rectifying them. So with *that* out of the way, what do you say we put aside our differences for the moment and handle the current situation?"

The high general's jaw clenched as King Rofar spoke up. "He's right. You're wasting time. Now you mentioned the separated Twin Spheres. I don't need to know the specifics, but I assume that's why Uldanna was murdered. We need to confirm the second sphere is safe. Do you know where she kept it?" he asked Lady Resa.

She nodded with a wince. "We do, but it's possible she might've been...*persuaded* to disclose its location."

Nathalia stepped forward. "Then let's confirm and go from there." She looked at her father. "Did the Church of Horyn send its protectors to Rowin for the defense of the city?"

Lord Maxlian's lips thinned in annoyance. "They sent ten."

She frowned in confusion. "Ten what? Companies? Battalions?"

"Ten protectors. Total."

Her shoulders and jaw dropped. "That's *it*?"

At his resigned sigh, Nathalia blew out a harsh breath. "One thing at a time. We need to go. Do we have a mage for transport?"

"Oh. Yes. Here," Tomin said as he and Idora came forward. He looked at Lord Maxlian and asked, "Where to?"

"Castle Rowin's throne room, please," he muttered in reply.

"All right. Hands in."

Everyone except King Rofar moved into a circle.

Nathalia threw a smile to King Rofar, "Thank you, Your Majesty."

He bowed to her, "Good luck and gods bless, Lady Nathalia." He then turned to me. "You won our wager, Ramiren, so your favor is still intact. Please keep that in mind."

"Thank you. I will," I replied as Tomin began to count down.

Lord Maxlian looked his silver-haired daughter up and down with intense scrutiny. "Where is the shield I gave you?"

"Shredded and covered in an arch-devil's blood," she replied. "I'll have to use my old one."

"You don't need a shield. Shields are stupid," Lady Resa muttered.

Her father blinked, the corners of his mouth pulling down as he stared at his wife. "Barbaric."

Lady Resa smiled wolfishly at her husband.

A moment after the disheveled mage said "One," the parlor inside Castle Tanta disappeared.

We arrived in Queen Uldanna's throne room to find it in total chaos

The formerly immaculate throne room, polished floors speckled with reflective silver, was a wreck. The graceful painted statues had been toppled over. The green runner carpet leading to the throne dais showed more blackened scorch marks than fabric, and the simple throne itself lay in a haphazard pile of wooden chunks and ripped cushions.

I breathed through my mouth, both to settle the dizziness and to mitigate the nauseating but blessedly faint scents of terror mixed with happiness in the air. To my left, Lady Resa whispered, "Aw, fuck."

Lord Maxlian barked, "Glesen! Report!"

There were three individuals in the room, all bearing a four-pointed star on their battered shields. A burly man, an unruly beard obscuring half his face, approached and bowed to the high general. "Sir, the walls are holding, with about two thousand split between four rotations, as ordered. The three hundred battle mages still standing are beginning to show strain. Of Camlynn's forces, almost a hundred dead and twice that are injured. Unsure of Wistran's status, but all five siege towers have been destroyed. The Assembly is convening now to decide on the late queen's heir."

"So it's true?" the high general hedged. "Queen Uldanna is dead?"

With no emotion on his face, Glesen answered, "Yes, sir."

Lord Maxlian's eyes went to the destroyed throne before he approached it. Nathalia, Raewyn, and I followed, stopping beside him to see a deep round divot in the dais where Queen Uldanna's throne had previously sat. The hole was roughly the size of a grapefruit.

And it was empty.

"I'm guessing that's not a good sign," Raewyn muttered.

Facing Lady Resa, throwing a glance to her husband, I asked, "Resa, do you know exactly what K'sar has to do to activate the Twin Spheres?"

Staring wide-eyed at the debris, she pursed her lips. "A little? I know the relic takes a while to activate, at least." Her eyes met mine as though she abruptly realized something. "A cave. She needs a specific cave for it. We had to go there last time. The Quingo cave system in the Feylands. They're called the Torr Caves here."

At my and Nathalia's questioning looks, Lord Maxlian elaborated. "Torr is located between Rowin and Evraka, near a grove. Something about it being the heart of the continent."

Nathalia asked her mother, "What does 'takes a while' mean?"

"Hard to say, really. Last time, it'd been maybe, I don't know, half a day between when she got them and when we defeated her. Kesseth knew more about it than we did."

It didn't surprise me that Kesseth would be the one to ask, given he had been the one to find the relic's schematics in the first place.

Her husband turned to Glesen again. "How long ago was Queen Uldanna's body discovered?"

There was a pause before Glesen responded. "It was just before dawn, sir. Perhaps five hours?"

"So we transport ourselves to this cave system in the Feylands and beat her up? Again?" Raewyn asked.

Nathalia kneeled down to search in her pouch as Lord Maxlian let out a calming breath. "Yes. I think we have to try. Tomin, Idora, you aren't directly under my command, but I—"

"We're in, sir," Tomin interrupted.

Nathalia huffed, then grumbled, "Ramiren, I think you have my old shield."

I could feel Lord Maxlian's eyes burrowing into my skull as I crouched down beside her to look in my own pouch. "Here it is." After pulling the steel shield from the pouch and handing it to her, I took out my rapier as well and stood.

"Ramiren, you don't have to go."

"Save it." I grinned crookedly down at her, then belted on my sword. "You lost your sanity when you lost your life if you think I'm letting you run in without me. *Again.*"

Her cheeks colored as Raewyn chuckled and called out, "Everyone get over here and hold hands. No, I'm not holding yours, Tomin." The priestess moved to my other side as the tall mage came closer.

"Glesen, please inform Dorin he's to remain in command until I return," Lord Maxlian ordered.

Glesen replied, "Yes, sir." He and the two protectors with him saluted the high general, palms tapping over their hearts twice.

We gathered into a circle, as before, and put our hands into the center when we were ready to depart. Tomin's hand made careful movements in the air. "Three...two...one."

Like the high note on a plucked musical instrument, the tension and anticipation hung in the air as we waited for the mage to complete his transport.

And waited.

And waited.

It became too much for Raewyn as she mumbled in a singsong voice, "*Aaaany day now, Tomas.*"

Tomin gazed imploringly at Lord Maxlian. "I'm sorry, sir. I have no idea what's going on. It's like a door I can't get through."

Idora put a soft hand on his arm and whispered, "Let me try." We put our hands in again and listened to Idora's quiet countdown.

And just as with Tomin, we didn't budge. Idora licked her lips twice. "It felt like..." Her confusion disappeared as her face paled. "Wards. She's the one who put up Rowin's wards, right? She must've warded the cave in the Feylands too."

We all lowered our hands silently. "So what now?" Raewyn asked. "There's gotta be something we can do."

Tomin chewed on his lip then looked down at Idora. "Would several mages together be able to break through?"

Idora dropped her eyes. "I'm not sure. Possibly?"

Remembering the number of dead and injured reported earlier, I grimaced. "It's also possible K'sar thought of that already. If she learned from her defeat last time, she'd have taken precautions against people meddling in her plans."

The high general appeared to understand what I was getting at. He asked without turning his sight from where the second half of the relic had once rested. "Glesen, of those hundred dead, how many were mages?"

Glesen took a second before answering. "Perhaps half, sir."

Lord Maxlian grunted in acknowledgment as Tomin cursed loudly. "So," I began. "We need to somehow get through her wards and defeat her. Can we transport to just outside her wards and walk in?"

Idora and Tomin glanced warily at each other, as though afraid to answer. At Raewyn's prompting poke, Tomin finally did. "If she warded the cave in a similar manner as she did Rowin, but against everyone and not just devils, then no. The ward would repel us."

Gods-damn it.

Lady Resa sighed, looking up toward the ceiling. "Well, shit." It was a sentiment I echoed.

Lord Maxlian took his wife's hand. "Kesseth? He might be able to bypass her wards on his own."

She shook her head sadly. "No idea where he is."

Raewyn held up a finger. "Wait, we know a scryer in Elancia."

Lady Resa smiled thinly at her daughter. "Above all things, Kesseth likes his privacy. You can't scry someone who has the power and inclination to make sure he's not found."

"My favor from King Rofar?" I suggested. "I could call it in."

Lord Maxlian grunted. "He said he had an appointment outside the city and didn't tell me where."

Ignoring the deepening sense of dread that blanketed the room, I racked my brain, trying to think of a solution, as Raewyn sputtered, "Well, we have to think of *something*!"

To my right, Nathalia whispered, “Goodbye, Feylands house.” Confused by the odd statement, I furrowed my eyebrows. “What?” Nathalia blinked a few times and looked at each of her parents.

“This cave she has to go to, is there a section of it she needs? Like a specific chamber or something?”

Lord Maxlian squinted, trying to suss out her train of thought. “Yes. The cavern at the north end of the cave system has these crystals inset in the stone. That’s where we cornered her last time.”

A wide, devious grin stretched across Nathalia’s face. “I know how we can beat her, but we’ll need dwarven builders. A lot of them.”

Everyone stared at her, faces pinched and slack-jawed. Everyone except me. I grinned just as widely as she did.

Speaking to the group, Nathalia laid out her idea. “Sometimes the best solution to a problem is the easiest. Either we need to find an available group of rested and ready mages, or even druids, powerful enough to get past her wards and defeat her, or we beg the Tarindar for some kind of divine intervention, or...”

She bit into her bottom lip with glee. “We ask the Council of Dwarven Builders in Fomona to help with a crisis that threatens everything, including the home they’ve just settled into. We go to the Laethi side of the caves and have them build a structure that takes up the entire chamber where she needs to activate the relics, hopefully destroying the crystals in the process, or even collapsing the chamber entirely. What is built in Laeth appears in the Feylands, right? I doubt her wards would work against stone and wood. If the place she needs is demolished, she can’t do her ritual.”

“That’s...” Idora murmured.

“Brilliant,” I finished.

It was a stupid idea, with her father so close and armed, but I didn’t fucking care. I took Nathalia’s face in my hands and planted a searing and well-deserved kiss on her lips. A sputtered choke came from someone, and I reveled in it. “You’re a wonder with a sword, angel, but those hags took from you your greatest asset of all.”

Lord Maxlian growled, “Gods above, let’s just go, *please*.”

Chapter Twenty-Eight
Six Cuts

After going over the plan for each group, Idora frowned. "I've never transported more than five before."

Tomin kissed the top of her head, and her frown relaxed. "You'll do just fine." His words seemed to ease some of the tension in her shoulders, but her expression remained unconvinced.

Lady Resa smiled at her. "If it helps you, leave Max and me behind."

Lord Maxlian's nostrils flared, and he opened his mouth. Lady Resa put her fingers over his lips to quiet whatever he was about to say. "It's fine. We'll convince them, and you take as many as you can to the Torr Caves."

Idora gave a nod that was more like a short bow. "Yes, ma'am."

Nathalia strapped her shield to her arm as Lady Resa grimaced and muttered, "*Ma'am*."

Once ready, we moved to each side of the destroyed throne room, two circles of people with two different missions. Nathalia, Tomin, Raewyn, and I were to go to the caves, to ensure they were clear, while Lord Maxlian, Lady Resa, and Idora went to Fomona.

The three protectors saluted Lord Maxlian again as the throne room dropped away. A breath later, tall, wild greenery appeared, surrounding and partially covering the yawning-mouthed entrance of what I hoped was the Torr Caves. Something about the place felt vaguely familiar, but I couldn't quite put my finger on it until I walked a few paces to my left to see around the cave's opening.

A roughly ten-foot-deep natural rock shelter was hollowed out from the cliff wall of the entrance. I recognized it immediately as the shelter Nathalia and I had used after escaping her wedding. Five Wistran soldiers stood around the smaller opening.

K'sar sent soldiers here too. Nathalia was right.

My smile got wider when I spotted Prince Prick himself walking out of the rock shelter, relacing the front of his trousers.

I'm really going to enjoy this.

Rejoining the rest of my companions, I watched Jaylin and his five soldiers come around the side of the cave entrance and yell something to someone inside the opening, then walk in.

"Jaylin and at least five guards," Nathalia whispered, peeking between leafy branches toward the cave entrance below. "We won't be able to figure out how many more unless—"

Raewyn dropped the small branch she'd pushed to the side and shrugged as she finished her sister's sentence. "Unless we go down there."

Nathalia stared down at her sister. "*Or* we use our brains and create a distraction. Draw them out. Raewyn, you and Tomin can run around and start fires while Ramiren and I clear out those who remain behind. The foliage here is damp, so there'll be a lot of smoke. Double back if you get in trouble. Tomin, what's your specialty?"

"Illusions, Lady Nathalia." Tomin waved his hands like he'd done on the streets of Elancia, and a much larger cat than the one he'd conjured previously appeared mid-stretch.

"Good. Disorient and terrify them. Attack and drop back immediately. Over and over until they don't know the difference between their ass and the sky."

He nudged Raewyn with his elbow. "Want to go set some stuff on fire and be scary?"

Raewyn tilted her head back to look at him and actually smiled in his direction. "I like this plan."

Nathalia asked me, "Agreed?"

"Yes, it's a good idea." I smiled at her, impressed with the creative simplicity of her strategy. Recalling what I'd once told her, about her inspiration being a visitor, I said, "Your visitor arrived today, my dear."

Raewyn looked between Nathalia and me, her face twisted in confusion. "Visitor? Nat, is he talking about menstruation? Is he into blood play?"

Behind her, Tomin covered his snort with his hand. Nathalia's face turned a darker peach. "Raewyn..." She ran a hand down her face. "Go. Be safe, but go."

Raewyn saluted Nathalia in a pantomime of what the protectors had done for their father and snatched Tomin's arm, dragging him into the depths of the foliage.

Nathalia and I watched the cave entrance to see if any more soldiers came out. One appeared to speak to another, but that was all we noticed.

It only took a few minutes before a deep rumble shook the ground beneath our feet, then a flaring glow from the direction the two had disappeared. Above the treetops, a large fireball rose, and black smoke from the damp burning greenery filtered through the trees.

Alarmed shouts rose from the soldiers stationed at the cave's entrance, drawing my gaze. A few pointed at Raewyn and Tomin's distraction, calling for backup. Jaylin ran out to see what had happened, then yelled as a bolt of fire shot out from the trees, bursting against the side of the cave's entrance.

Three more soldiers, making a total of nine, joined their compatriots. Those nine sprang into action after a sharp order from their prince, rushing into the verdant overgrowth.

Beside me, Nathalia muttered, "Either he has a lot more guards than I thought, or he truly is a moron."

I brushed the back of her hand with my fingers, both to touch and prompt. "I suspect the latter, but let's go find out."

Rustling the thick brush and branches aside, we purposefully approached loudly enough for Jaylin to notice us. His eyes met ours and, with an exaggerated thigh slap, a shocked laugh burst from him. "Well, *holy shit*. She said you'd come here." He took a step back toward the cave, looking quite pleased with himself. "Are you going to try to talk me out of all this? Go ahead. I want to hear it."

Nathalia and I stopped about thirty feet away, drawing our weapons as we walked. "We weren't planning on it, eluva," I said, shaking my head.

When he recoiled, taking another two steps toward the entrance, I chuckled, flicking my fingers at him. "Run along. I haven't played Hide and Seek since I was a boy, but I'm sure I can manage. I'll even count."

Uncertainty crossed his face, then morphed into anger when I began. "One...two...three..."

He turned tail and bolted into the dark cave, and what sounded like two sets of footsteps rapidly faded. Beside me, Nathalia asked, "Eluva?"

I ignored the instinct to dodge the question. "Apparently, it means 'asshole' in Old Fey."

Her jaw muscle popped as she looked back at the cave, frowning. "I see."

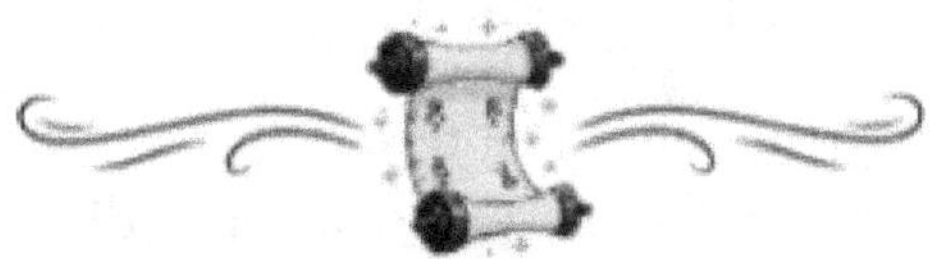

Nathalia tried to whisper, but the cave walls magnified the sound so much it was unnecessary. "Why my protector's oath couldn't have given me the ability to see in darkness like you, I'll never know."

Though my eyes easily made out details in the gloom of the tunnels, it didn't help much. This place was a maze. It seemed like we were going north, deeper into the cave, but I couldn't be sure. I had no real talent for tracking, but I did my best to follow the boot prints on the sandy floor while guiding my blind protector by the hand.

We came to a larger chamber. Burning hand torches stuck into the sand at our feet flickered light off the jagged rock around us. It smelled musty, and the dancing flames produced the only sound in the vast area.

Just as I caught sight of a punchable face and the soft glow of his ring's magical signature, our attention was stolen by a panicked, reverberating yell from behind us. Nathalia took a step backward. "That sounded like Raewyn."

I spoke low, the walls not close enough for my words to echo. "Perhaps. However, I promised no secrets. Jaylin is trying to sneak up behind us." Exhaling as I adjusted the grip on my rapier, I inclined my head toward the passage. "Go after your sister, angel."

"Jaylin?" My protector stood frozen, her head swiveling from me, into the darkness of the cave around us, then back to me. Her face stricken, she said, "I'm not leaving you alone."

Nathalia tried to pass me, only to be stopped by my raised hand. I chucked her under the chin. "I'll be fine. Trust me." With a soft smile, I leaned in to whisper next to her ear. "I know his capabilities. It'll be a piece of cake, and you know how much I love cake."

She turned her head slightly to narrow her eyes at me, an internal debate flickering in them.

Pressing my cheek to hers, I continued to whisper. "You have a good heart, angel, and you'd kill him too quickly. He needs to suffer. Please. Indulge me."

Eventually, she replied, "*All right.* Just remember, if *you* die, *I* follow." She rose to her tiptoes to press a too-brief kiss on my lips and snagged one of the torches. After giving me one last look, Nathalia took off, back through the tunnels.

I watched her leave, then heard a scornful, masculine voice behind me. "Well, you just did me a favor."

I turned toward the voice, trying to keep the giddy grin from my lips. Jaylin stepped into the light, and I thanked Jessina under my breath.

Dre? Can you see this?

Though there'd been no expectation of a reply from my pact vizier, considering his continued absence from my mind, I still wished he could witness what was about to happen.

"Did I hear right? You die, she dies?" He drew his thin blade, shifting his weight on the balls of his feet. When he moved to bring himself within reach, I didn't even twitch. "Two for one. Perfect, let's g—"

I held up a finger. "One moment, please."

My request caused him to abruptly halt and stumble back a step. His perplexed expression changed to one of incredulity when I sheathed my rapier and proceeded to remove my jacket. After tossing it to the side, careful of the torches, I rolled up my shirtsleeves and explained with a toothy smile, "I like that jacket, and cleaning it is an absolute *bear*. Believe me."

Redrawing my sword, I set myself into a basic fencer's stance. "You were saying?"

With a long-drawn-out sigh, he pulled his lips between his teeth. "Do you even know how to use that?"

"Certainly." I stretched my back with an exaggerated grimace. "I've received a few lessons."

"*Wonderful.* Allow me to give you another one. Free of charge."

Resisting the urge to roll my eyes, I studied Jaylin as he crouched low, bending at his knees while speaking. "This is called a lunge. You parry by turning your blade into it to push it aside, so the blade doesn't pierce you.

Like so." As promised, he performed a simple lunge, slowed down and overemphasized.

"Impressive," I deadpanned.

He settled into a fighting stance again, turning sideways, and shrugged. "I'm afraid that's all I have time for. If I showed you everything I knew, we'd be here for days."

"No doubt," I said, raising the tip of my rapier to a neutral position. My left hand, held out to the side, kept my balance. "Shall we?"

"Ye— AH!" Jaylin shrieked as the torch behind him flared, flames licking at his back, as I performed the same lunge he'd just shown me. My sword point flicked across his right bicep, blood welling in its path.

His free hand slapped over the wound while my feet adjusted to the side. He mirrored my steps in a shuffle, the perplexed expression on his face having returned as I said, "First cut, first reason, Your Highness. You nearly took her from me."

The smoky scent of fear rose as Jaylin blinked. "Wh—?"

Soft, childlike laughter originating from my left caused a wide-eyed Jaylin to startle and look. Doing my best to not enjoy this too much, I initiated a beat attack, batting his sword aside to draw a razor's edge of blood across his cheek. He stumbled back, his already bloody hand slapping to his face. "I d—"

"Second cut, second reason. You manipulated her."

Jaylin adjusted his grip on his sword, the tip quivering. "Stop it!" The prince cursed but didn't look this time when soft whispers came from the cavern's entrance.

New tactic, then.

I stepped diagonally in a feint, switching from his right shoulder to his left as Jaylin tried and failed to parry. My rapier slid along his blade, and the tip went into the joint with no resistance. The prick recoiled then thrust his sword out in front of him as more of a childish deterrent than a threat. "I said *stop*!"

"Third cut, third reason. You threatened her life." As I circled him, his sword tip followed my movements. I wheeled my rapier around, the tip weaving and bobbing in front of him to randomly tap his sword. *Tap. Tap. Tap.*

Jaylin quivered, hesitating. He disengaged, then lurched into a weak lunge. I turned my rapier point down to deflect and punched forward, the knuckle guard catching his cheekbone.

He cried out and hobbled away, just out of my reach. A bead of sweat dripped into his eye, drawing out a hiss as he dashed his hand across it. All it seemed to do was smear blood over his face.

Lowering my sword and straightening, I graced him with a smile. "I'll try my *best* to not enjoy this next part too much."

Jaylin sucked in air as every torch in the cavern went out. The smoky smell coming off him now was so intense it nearly made me sneeze. My nose wiggled as I quietly moved away from where he'd last seen me.

"*Fuck! Fuckfuckfuck*," Jaylin whisper-yelled. His heavy breaths rasped in and out of his lungs like he couldn't get enough air. Watching him spin around, back and forth, I stood perfectly still as his sword sliced around him with random swipes. "This isn't sporting, broodling!"

Dropping the tip of my rapier, I maneuvered behind him and arced it up, cutting a shallow groove across the back of his neck. He screeched and teetered forward, then spun and began swiping frantically again. But I had already moved to the side. Seeing him attack nothing but the air brought another smile to my face. "Fourth cut, fourth reason. You're helping your mother."

My feet pivoted back as Jaylin tried to pinpoint the origin of my voice. His sword continued its fruitless assault, the whoosh of his blade almost covering the sound of a whimper. The smell of smoke became pervasive. I knew I needed to end this soon, before my eyes began to water. *Ugh. Fine.*

I tapped his sword aside again, drawing a line across his other cheek, then another one across his upper chest. He wailed and almost fell backward onto his ass. *Gods, I wish I knew if those droplets were sweat or tears running down his face.*

"Fifth and sixth cuts. Fifth and sixth reasons. You insulted her, and you put her in danger." His sword snapped forward, and I batted it aside easily.

"I'm not perfect, of course." I parried his feeble attack again, stepping closer. He must've sensed where I was, because he gasped and nearly tripped backward once more. "I put her in danger too." Another parry, this time with a riposte, and I sunk my rapier into his stomach only to remove it immediately. "The difference is, I'll strive to make it up to her. Starting with you."

The weak, distant glow of a torch coming through the side passage illuminated the planes of Jaylin's face, highlighting his terrified expression. "Please stop t—"

"No," I replied as my rapier slipped past the thin leather armor covering his chest and into his heart. He gurgled, bowing forward, and I relished the thud as he finally toppled sideways. The torches began to relight as I leaned down to peer at his blood-covered face and whisper, "I honestly thought you'd be better."

I heard Nathalia behind me. "What in Horyn's name..."

The torches flared dramatically as I turned, grinning. "Hello, my dear. Find Raewyn?"

Nathalia stared down at Jaylin's corpse, blinking rapidly. "Yes. She and Tomin are..." She dropped the torch from her shield hand and stalked toward me, hissing. "Ramiren, *what the fuck*?"

My eyebrows went to my hairline. I glanced down at the dead prince, then back to her. "What? You insinuated I shouldn't die, and I complied. Really, Nathalia. Angry if I die, but angry that I didn't?"

She choked, throwing a hand toward Jaylin as if that explained everything.

It did, but I was having far too much fun.

After cleaning the blood off my rapier, I sheathed it. "Listen. Think about which one you'd prefer, then let me know. I'll be happy to oblige you."

After looking me up and down, she let out a deep growl as she threw her hands into the air. "I just... I mean, I *suspected* you were more capable than you let on, but—"

"Yes. Thank you for trusting me." I pressed a kiss to her temple. The sound of boots thumping heavily on sand got louder, and I redrew my sword as Nathalia's eyes widened. "That doesn't sound like Raewyn and Tomin."

"Footprints lead down here!" a voice called out.

She drew her sword as soldiers, some injured and some not, piled into the cavern. They spotted their dead prince lying on the sandy floor, and some of them spewed curses as they moved to face us.

Unfortunately, we were out of position to take on so many. Nathalia pressed her back to mine and asked over her shoulder, "Ever fought back to back?"

Adjusting my feet slightly to account for an ally behind me, I answered, "I have. Are you familiar with the Pelna Fos defense?"

Nathalia's voice held a tone of confusion. "What? No."

They advanced, surrounding us, and I parried an incoming jab, kicking at the floor and sending a spray of sand toward my attacker. "Tolik maneuver?"

I heard the clang of steel on steel and cursing brought about by frustration before Nathalia answered me. "Um. No."

Exhaling through my nose harshly, I parried another attack, riposting to stab another. "Nonda? Everyone knows Nonda."

Two dull thuds echoed behind me as Nathalia scoffed. "Ramiren, for fuck's sake, I wield a *longsword*. I went to Longsword School, not Rapier School."

"Right. Good point."

The next few minutes passed in a blur of yells, shrieks, and the metallic clamor of weapons. I wasn't used to fighting so many at once, so an occasional sword managed to slip in under my defenses, only to be repelled by the soft blue glow of a protective barrier from Nathalia. Her back was to me, so I had no idea how she was able to tell when or where it was needed.

I was preparing to land a finishing blow into the last soldier when a small bolt of fire from my right hit him in the back. The soldier gave a hoarse cry, arching against the searing strike before collapsing. A girlish giggle followed.

Nathalia straightened out of her fighting stance. "Raewyn! Where the *fuck* have you been?"

"Oh, well, after we sent you back to Ramiren, we got a little lost. This place didn't exactly come with signs saying 'Grumpy sister and pretty broodling this way.'" She pointedly ignored the look Nathalia gave her as she peered down at the soldiers lying in a disjointed pile at our feet. "Let's see. I got three of t—."

Tomin cut in as he stepped around her. "You got two. I took the first one out."

Raewyn scowled at him. "That is extremely untrue." Pausing in thought, she nodded. "Yeah. I'm pretty sure you're lying."

Tomin barked a short laugh. "Why would I lie? I have no need to lie."

Raewyn sniffed indignantly. "Then, perhaps you suffer from delusions and imagined it?"

Tomin shrugged casually. "Perhaps you have trouble counting?"

The tall mage pouted, rubbing his chest after Raewyn poked him hard with her index finger and said, "I am fully capable of counting!"

Lowering his hand, he conceded with an indulgent grin. "I have my doubts, but if it makes you happy, then you got three."

I grimaced as the overwhelming scent of honey, from *both* of them, caused my eyes to water.

Appearing mollified, Raewyn looked back down at the dead fey. "Hm. Guess Ramiren got three also." Pointing at Nathalia's pile, she chirped, "And...Nathalia got four. She won."

Tomin glanced around the cavern, then pointed at Jaylin. "Who killed that guy?"

Nathalia muttered, "Ramiren did."

Raewyn gasped happily, clapping her hands. "Oh, then Ramiren won. Jaylin's worth at least two, right?"

Despite knowing exactly what saying the words would do, I couldn't resist. "I think Tomin is correct. You *do* have trouble counting."

Chapter Twenty-Nine
Maker's Mark

An hour later, as we waited outside the northern chamber Lady Resa had specified, a crackle in my head startled me.

Ren? Ren, can you hear me?

My sharp inhale caused three sets of concerned eyes to stare at me.

Nathalia came closer and placed a hand on my arm. "What's wrong?"

"Nothing, my dear." I rubbed my thumb over the back of her fingers to reassure her. "It's a bit of a long story, though."

Yes. I'm here. Are you all right?

Define all right.

Nathalia studied me with a tilted head. "We might be waiting a while for the mage and builders to arrive. I'll listen if you want to tell me."

"I do, but I need a minute."

With a small, understanding smile on her lips, she nodded and moved away to give me privacy.

Are you injured?

Oh. No. Did you know the Citadel has dungeons? I mean* dungeony *dungeons. As in barred doors, a jingling ring of keys, and a leaky bucket to piss in.

No, I most certainly did not. They imprisoned *you?*

Oh, yes. Maester Vondo apparently didn't appreciate what I was trying to do. So is she up and about? Breathing? Did she use her first breath after experiencing the miracle of resurrection to yell at you?

After pinching the bridge of my nose, I pushed my glasses back up. *Yes, to all of the ab—*

Wonderful.

Though he hadn't witnessed her return, he should've been able to see her now.

Wait. You can't see her? Or my surroundings?

No, and unfortunately I only have a few more minutes.

Pinpricks of awareness turned into waves of goose bumps crawling over my skin. *A few minutes until what, Dre?*

Oh, nothing too bad, though the burly brute in charge of the dungeons might just be grumpier than you. And bald. And smelly. Frankly, I'm rather concerned at the perfect accuracy of dungeon warden stereotypes.

Though I wasn't exactly pacing, my restlessness at the dual situations, here and at the Citadel, did make me start walking slowly around the cavern.

Dre. What's going on?

So I was only given a few minutes to inform you that you're being summoned to the Citadel for questioning. They wanted to send an actual **letter,** ***but I argued this was more efficient.***

Part of me had expected this to happen, though perhaps not so soon. *Questioning?*

Yes, the maesters have their panties in a twist at you not dissolving the pact room immediately upon Nathalia's death.

That makes sense.

And the fact that you didn't immediately let Nathalia's soul move on to Celestia when you saw it in the room.

I see.

And that you somehow acquired a soulstone.

Understood.

Also, your attempt to bring her back, thereby reminding them of their not-so-shiny past. Truth be told, I'm having a hard time determining which they're more angry at: your flagrant disregard of protocol, your insubordination, your not-entirely-worthless trinket, or the fact it worked. The King of Tanta was just here too. He told them everything.

Dre.

Yes?

I'll be there as soon as I can. It might take a day or two, but I'll get you out of there. I promise.

Take your time. Dungeon Warden and I are going to go play poker. Thankfully, not a dirty euphemism. Take care, Ren.

Pausing my walk, I closed my eyes and exhaled a calming breath. My concern was not for my power or position. As far as I was concerned, they could take both with my thanks and be done with it.

It was Dredon's circumstances that had guilt punching me in the chest. Though he'd acted without my prompting him to, he'd still harassed and threatened a maester of the Citadel on my behalf. And without the knowledge he'd given me, Nathalia might still be dead. Or worse, a confused soul wandering aimlessly for eternity.

Something brushed my cheek, and I opened my eyes to see Nathalia staring back at me with a faint half-smile on her lips. Though she didn't say a word, her obvious worry was a balm.

Tonguing the inside of my cheek, I thought of how to tell her without making her fret. "Do you remember my pact vizier at the Citadel? Dredon?"

She made a face. "Yes, I remember. He kept watching me like I was going to put cow dung in his boots."

Despite the multiple different issues happening, my lips twitched. "That's the one. He provided some information to me that was very valuable. It seems his methods of intelligence gathering have ruffled some feathers at the Citadel. His voice has been absent since your return, until just now."

She scrutinized me as she assessed what I said. And apparently what I didn't say, because she replied, "This information he gave you... Was it about me?"

"It was." I rubbed my lips together, trying to decide on the right words. "We haven't had time to discuss what happened that allowed you to come back, but he was instrumental. However, that's about to bring consequences down on both our heads. I've been asked to report to the Citadel as soon as possible."

Nathalia gave a single nod. "When do we leave?"

She'd done no poking or prodding about what was happening. Just simple support. My weak smile bloomed into a full one as I took her face in my hands and kissed her forehead. Running my nose along on her soft skin, inhaling her scent, I answered, "Thank you, angel, but I need to go alone."

"I can't protect you if you keep going off alone, Ramiren."

"I know, and I promise this will be our last parting. You were welcomed as a guest before, as a personal favor to me from Dean Miscala. Usually only students, maesters, and pactmakers are allowed at the Citadel unless expressly invited. I'll be safe and come back as soon as I can."

She began to lean into me when Raewyn said, quite loudly, "Wonderful! It looks like they're here!" The priestess looked my way, a warning in her eyes.

I smiled and promptly ignored that warning, as did Nathalia, figuring my current proximity to her walked the line between receiving a glare and a disembowelment from her temperamental father.

Pulling her closer, I knew it would be worth it.

Nathalia laid her cheek on the top of my shoulder just as Lord Maxlian, Lady Resa, a strained Idora, and...

Blinking, I watched over a dozen dwarven builders, fully kitted out in cross-breasted robes and elaborate beard styles, stride into view.

A cheerful Lady Resa approached Raewyn and hugged her. "Rae. How was it?"

"Oh!" Raewyn snickered. "Fun. Chaos aplenty. Ramiren killed Jaylin with paper cuts."

Nathalia snorted as I smirked at Raewyn. "Rapier cuts, Raewyn. I'm not sure you can perish from paper cuts."

"Well," Raewyn drawled. "If there was anyone that should've volunteered for the research, it was Jaylin."

Lord Maxlian looked like he was chewing glass as he stared at us. "Nathalia."

"Hm?" she hummed, not lifting her head.

"The builders are here. Would you like to go over your plan with them?"

"Sure." She kissed my cheek, perhaps longer and louder than she needed to, then sauntered over. "Hello, everyone. Thank you for coming. I'm Nathalia."

One came forward and placed his thick palms on opposite shoulders, crossing his arms over his chest, to bow in greeting. "I am Dahvii, Fourth Builder of the Council. Lord Maxlian and Lady Resa Swordhand made an odd request but a very good argument for it. Said you needed some help raising a building in a *cave*?"

"Yes. That's correct. The druid named K'sar, though Ramiren, Raewyn, and I"—she indicated everyone in turn—"knew her by other names, intends to activate two relics, which will have catastrophic consequences for both Laeth and the Feylands. I'm sure my parents told you why your assistance is needed?"

"They did, yes. We've never raised a building in a cave before, however. Usually our sites don't have..." He grimaced. "Walls and ceilings." His grimace turned into a displeased frown. "Or people, for that matter."

"Understood, and I hope you know we wouldn't ask if it wasn't urgent *and* necessary."

"Sure. There are certainly some *ethical* concerns, Miss Nathalia, but I agree. Your parents wouldn't have asked on a whim." Dahvii looked around, surveying the area. "Here? Is this the cavern?"

"No. It's just down that passage." Nathalia pointed to a broad tunnel to our right. "If you'll follow me?" She called out to a few builders who'd begun to pick up the sputtering light sources scattered about. "You won't need to bring torches."

Dahvii waved his fellows on as he walked after Nathalia. We rounded a dark corner, ambient light from up ahead confirming the torches weren't needed. After twenty feet, the tunnel opened into an enormous open chamber, unremarkable except for its size and the thousands of small, luminescent blue crystals that dotted the sides and ceiling like stars.

There had been no curiosity in me to see this place. I knew we'd come here eventually, so I hadn't ventured down the tunnel while we were waiting. Now that I was seeing it, though, I understood.

Peering at the crystals through my glasses, I could see that every single one of them glowed with a magical signature.

Dahvii bellowed over his shoulder. "Don't touch the crystals!"

A few curious dwarves who'd begun to creep closer to inspect the odd blue minerals jutting roughly an inch from the stone grumbled but backed away.

"So." Dahvii clapped his hands and rubbed his palms together. "Build a structure large enough to fill up this place and disrupt her ritual. Is that right, Miss Nathalia?"

She replied, "Yes. How long does it take for you and your builders to raise a structure?"

"Of this size?" Dahvii squinted as he glanced around. "It'd take one of us probably about one work-hour. I have fourteen dwarves with me, two of whom will need to stabilize the cave so that it doesn't collapse, so..." His head bobbed back and forth as he did the math.

"Five minutes," Nathalia and Dahvii said simultaneously.

Dahvii grinned at her, showing two top teeth made of gold. "Yes, Miss Nathalia. Five minutes. Shall we get started?" At her nod, the builder tossed his head toward the entrance. "You will all want to stay back. Don't cross the threshold."

As we began to leave, Dahvii started to shout assignments. "Rafe, Gorn, channel your song into the walls and ceiling for stability. Everyone else, take your places."

Nathalia leaned against the wall outside the chamber, facing in, and I mirrored her pose just behind her. I leaned in and whispered to her, "I've never actually witnessed the raising of a structure before. Have you?"

Nathalia shook her head, keeping her eyes on the cavern.

We all watched silently as the builders took their places throughout the chamber in a strange pattern I didn't entirely understand. They pressed their palms to the cave floor below them and, in a united chorus made of soprano, alto, tenor, baritone, and bass voices, began to sing.

Like the pattern they'd set themselves in, I didn't understand the words they sang. The unfamiliar melody sounded both haunting and comforting.

Soon enough, the rumble of moving sand and stone joined in to somehow harmonize with the builders' singing, adding to the song instead of eclipsing it. The more thunderous the rumbles and cracks from the earth became, the louder the dwarves' voices grew.

The tiny hairs on the back of my neck lifted as the sand beneath their feet started to glow faintly. As one, the builders all stood and backed toward us, still singing their melodious, strange song.

Once they passed the chamber entrance, the roaring rumble became deafening, finally drowning out the builders. I squinted in the blinding light coming from the ground, tilting my head down to see over the rims of my glasses.

Simultaneously, the builders raised their hands, palms facing each other shoulder-width apart, and slammed them together in a single, booming clap.

An entire building made of stone and wood erupted from the ground, already fully constructed, and shot toward the chamber's ceiling. Nathalia gasped and backed into me. Arms around her shoulders, I steadied her, my eyes unable to tear themselves away from the building that kept rising and widening until it finally stopped abruptly.

A closed wooden door stood proudly in front of us, now the only way to enter the chamber beyond.

"Well. Here's hoping there was no one else in there with her," Dahvii muttered as he stepped forward, murmured something under his breath, and pressed his hand to the door jamb. When he withdrew it, a burning sigil marked the frame and then disappeared, even when I looked through my glasses.

Silence reigned, until Raewyn peeked from around her mother. "So. Done?"

Dahvii inclined his head. "Done, miss."

I looked at Tomin and Idora, the latter still pale and exhausted. "Someone will need to check if it was successful."

Tomin smiled at his partner. "I'll go. You're worn out." She gave a muffled thanks, her face brightening a tad in gratitude.

"It might be best if I have someone come with me, though. Just in case."

"I'll go," Lord Maxlian stepped to the mage's side and placed his hand on Tomin's arm. The tall mage began his arcane movements and started his countdown.

I held my breath, hoping he'd disappear, which would mean the wards were down and K'sar was likely incapacitated. Or at least disrupted.

Tomin reached the count of one...

...and disappeared with Lord Maxlian.

Raewyn squealed. "Oh, good sign!"

A few torturous minutes later, Tomin and Lord Maxlian returned. The high general held two glowing golden orbs in his hands as a green-faced Tomin proceeded to fall to his knees and vomit.

Raewyn gagged and covered her mouth, looking away.

My stomach rolled, and saliva filled my mouth reflexively at the sound and smell, but I managed to swallow it down with a grimace. "I'm guessing it worked?"

Tomin stood on shaky legs and kicked sand over his regurgitated lunch. "Um. Yes. Water, anyone?"

One of the dwarves, a smaller woman with twin braids wrapped around her head, handed the mage the waterskin from her belt. Lady Resa looked from Tomin to her husband. "K'sar?"

Lord Maxlian made a face but said nothing.

"Ooh, yes. That." Tomin took several large gulps of water and coughed. "She is definitely no more."

Nathalia's jaw dropped. "Leraska, err, K'sar is dead? You found her?"

"Mostly?" Tomin took another drink then handed the waterskin back to the builder. At Nathalia's questioning look, he elaborated. "Yes. And before you ask how we're sure, let me put it this way. You could probably spread her on toast."

No one made a sound until a slow chuckle began to bubble out of Raewyn. It got louder until she snorted, holding her stomach with both hands. "Oh, that's good. Could probably spread her on toast. I am *definitely* stealing that."

Chapter Thirty
The Steps You Take

A day later, the King of Wistran unconditionally surrendered.

Castle Rowin's throne room had been cleared of debris, and one large, ornate table with chairs on each side had been placed in the center. The defeated king's dazed eyes stared down at the scrawled list of reasonable reparation demands the Assembly and Lord Siron Tremsley, Camlynn's new heir-apparent, had drawn up.

Though the poison that had muddled the fey king's mind had left his system, with K'sar no longer feeding it to him, the Valisetan priests tending him indicated the effects would likely follow him for the rest of his life. A sad conclusion to a baffling series of events.

It wasn't known if K'sar had always been Queen Milanda Loranaskan or if the real queen was murdered and K'sar took her place. It wasn't even known if Jaylin was her son by birth or stolen from his true mother.

Those answers would likely never come to light.

The one thing that *did* come to light was the ring Jaylin wore, identified as a Master Ring. Like the Twin Spheres, it too had a mate, called a Slave Ring. Made from Incubi's Breath, it gave the Master Ring's bearer complete control over the unfortunate being wearing the Slave Ring. The only caveat was the Slave Ring had to be put on willingly.

It didn't take much to guess what ring Jaylin was going to give Nathalia at their wedding, presumably to make her find and retrieve the Twin Sphere in Rowin.

Nathalia and I stood beside her parents, along with Tomin, Idora, and Dahvii, as Lord Tremsley explained in a surprisingly gentle and sympathetic manner what it would take to repair the damaged relationship between Wistran and Camlynn.

I barely paid attention, my thoughts consumed with fear for Dredon and the shocking ambivalence I felt toward the Citadel's possible consequences for me.

I shifted my weight from one foot to the other as I breathed through my mouth. Old Me would have breathed it all in, taken in every hidden emotion and secret I could glean from this momentous occasion. I would have studied the words used, the body language that conveyed more information than rehearsed rhetoric ever could, and kept that knowledge to myself to be used at some point in the future.

However, New Me simply didn't give a fuck, and a muffled chuckle escaped me at the hilariousness of it all. Beside me, Nathalia met my eyes, and I cleared my throat to cover it.

I'm sorry, angel. I'm merely anxious to leave.

Nathalia's voice in my mind came in loud and clear. **Nothing is stopping you, darling.**

My eyebrow raised, and I chanced another glance her way. *Darling?*

You have an endearment for me. Gods above, let me have one too.

And you settled on "darling"?

Simple, yet effective. You're free to protest, but then I'll ask for Raewyn's help to come up with something else.

Darling is perfectly fine. I did my best to hide my happy grin, not wanting to draw more attention to myself. *You sound much clearer than when we talked in...that place.*

As it turns out, practice makes perfect. And also, apparently, dying.

Not funny.

It's a little funny.

A low, unhappy rumble reverberated through my chest involuntarily. I tried to cover the sound with a chest thump and a cough. "Apologies. Scratchy throat."

A few members of Camlynn's Assembly peered my way curiously, but I noticed a distinct lack of scowls and disapproving stares, likely due to our service to the realm.

It took another hour, boredom mitigated only by my and Nathalia's occasional mental banter, before the introductory negotiations concluded for the day. At the first opportunity, I pulled Nathalia to an empty alcove. Without a word, my arms wrapped around her shoulders to pull her close for a kiss. She made a throaty sound when I nipped her bottom lip with one of my canines.

"Going now?" she asked, her hands settling on my lower back.

With a nod, I replied, "I am, but as I said, I'll come back as soon as possible."

"If you need help, let me know." The corner of her mouth rose. "I'll come rescue you."

My left eyebrow went up. "You can't get there if you're not a pactmaker or with one."

Giving a slow and exaggerated shrug, she said coquettishly, "Well then, I suppose I'll have to *convince* one to take me there, won't I?"

Pressing a kiss to the tip of her nose, I smiled down at her. "I'll see you soon, angel. Question for you, though." I gently tugged on her choppy, silver stands. "Do you like your hair as it is now?"

She scrunched her face, though I was unsure if it was due to the random question or because the answer was obvious. "Ah. No. Not particularly."

"Mm, I suspected as much."

"Good luck, and I love you."

Not being able to help myself, I kissed her again, inhaling the unique trio of scents that only came with her affection. "I love you too." I stepped out of her warm embrace. A chill ran down my spine as I snapped the fingers of both hands twice. This was going to be both the easiest and hardest decision I'd ever made.

Glancing around at the broken ruins surrounding me, I strode up to the half-shattered statue of a robed elven woman holding a simple quill aloft in her right hand and a tucked book in her left. This far east of Pidantar on Kirgan Island, the air blew cold and harsh, and that chill from earlier returned.

With a sigh and a grimace, I prepared myself before touching the quill and book simultaneously.

My eyes closed against the sudden but expected gust of freezing wind that stopped as soon as it started. A violent shudder locked up my muscles as I opened my eyes to see a familiar open courtyard with a thick green lawn stretching into the distance, sporadically interrupted by fountains and flagstone seating areas for either studying or enjoying the perpetually warm weather.

A few students and maesters walked past me without paying me any mind. I barely noticed them as I looked at each of the six different-colored spires encircling the courtyard. Dredon hadn't told me where to go when I got here, but he hadn't needed to.

I stepped off the platform and headed to the tallest spire, a plain, gray-stoned monstrosity that no student wanted to be summoned to.

The route to my final destination had been memorized within my first year here.

Stepping through the open archway and turning left, I went up a short flight of stairs. A right turn later, I stood in front of Dean Miscala's office. The carved door was currently closed, so I knocked twice and entered when the voice inside commanded.

The dean's office was, in a phrase, an organized disaster. Neat stacks of parchment and books sat on every available surface, though her desk was conspicuously clear, except for a single sheet of pale vellum face-down on the surface.

Twin windows behind her were half hidden by potted plants, either sitting on the sills or hanging from the ceiling. An enormous book with small, neat calligraphy sat open on a stand in one corner, a black quill nestled in the book's gutter.

Dean Miscala, an umber brown–skinned willowy elf with sharp amber eyes and a black braid that reached to the back of her knees, smiled sadly as I entered and stood up from her chair to extend a hand. "Ramiren. You've had a busy couple of days."

Bowing low, I took her hand with a firm grip. "A busy couple of weeks, really. Dredon told me I'd been summoned?"

"Oh. Good. He did tell you. Based on his expression when he had those few minutes to inform you, I wasn't sure if he was instructing you to come here or telling terrible jokes." She motioned to a chair facing her desk.

Sitting, I smiled ruefully. "There were a few jokes, but he told me, yes."

She leaned her hip against her desk and crossed her arms, sighing. "I'm sorry to have to bring you here, but Vondo insisted. Unfortunately, based upon what Dredon told us, he was right to."

"Understood, ma'am. I hope you don't hold Dredon accountable. He was acting on my behalf."

Dean Miscala raised a black eyebrow. "You told him to do that? Threaten Vondo?"

My instincts pushed me to lie, but I couldn't. "No."

She narrowed her eyes. "Is that so?"

This truth, however, came easily. "Dredon is many things, but he is also intensely loyal. He'd have done anything I asked, but I didn't tell him to threaten Vondo."

"Be that as it may, you did break several protocols. Care to explain those?"

I grinned wide. "Not particularly."

She didn't look amused. "This isn't a joke, Ramiren. If you don't provide a plausible explanation for refusing to dissolve a pact room *and* calling back the soul that had been housed within, you may be stricken from the Registrar of Pactmakers."

"Then do it. I just request that you give Dredon back his freedom. Maybe give him a menial job for a few years if you feel the need to punish him. He'll be bored to tears, but he's an elf. A few years is nothing."

"Ramiren." She licked her lips. "You don't care?"

"I do care. Honestly, I think I'd prefer it if you *did* remove me. I grow tired of the secrecy. It's done nothing except hurt those I care for."

Her shoulders fell, along with her jaw. "You're not even going to fight for it? All you'd need to do is hand over the soulstone in your possession, write that ridiculous remediation letter, and then you can move on. Why?"

It struck me as amusing that one of the simplest questions in existence almost always came with the most complicated answers. I sat for a moment, thinking, putting emotion and logic together for the exact right words. When I had them, I graced Dean Miscala with my brightest smile.

"What if I find another soulstone someday? I don't want to have that power. I don't want the temptation to keep souls imprisoned, even for good intentions. I benefited once. I don't regret it in the slightest. But what happens if the next one benefits me too? Then the next? That road is not a swift descent on a slide but a series of incremental steps going downward. Bit by bit, with compromises, self-delusion, and half-truths, until everyone is something to be used, much like our less-than-illustrious forebears, Dean. It's a monumental power that no one should have. History will not repeat itself with me."

Dean Miscala peered at me with a mix of sympathy and finality. "That's your final decision?"

"It is, Dean. With every ounce of respect I have for you, I am done."

"Very well." She straightened, then sat down at her desk. She picked up a sheet of vellum, and I could see the dark silhouette of writing on the other side in the light from the windows behind her. "Your privileges will be stripped from you. All current pacts that are able to be dissolved will be. All pact rooms will be deconstructed. Your pact ledger shall be recorded for posterity. Your pact vizier will be reassigned. Do you have any questions?"

I expected a hint of panic, or even a stab of sadness, but there was nothing of the sort. All I felt was intense relief. "No, Dean Miscala. No questions."

"However, it seems you have very influential friends." She held the vellum up. "King Rofar of Tanta and a Paquan priest named Wohlin came here to give their accounts of events, then presented a letter with several well-written endorsements on your behalf." She put the vellum back down and smiled at me.

"Wohlin also said that from trials and failure comes wisdom, which I agree with. And with what you just said, I think I'm exactly right to offer you this. I want you to teach here at the Citadel. Specifically, ethics. I want you to instruct future pactmakers to constantly question themselves and their motives. Our occupation, especially with our history, requires a conscience, or, as you said, history repeats itself. I just ask that you keep quiet about what transpired."

What?

I heard Nathalia reply. **Ramiren? What's wrong?**

Oh. Sorry. Nothing's wrong. I'm fine. I'll tell you when I see you.

My eyes wouldn't stop blinking. "I'm... What?"

She exhaled a breath that was almost a chuckle. "Ramiren. Citadel. Teach. Ethics."

Despite myself, a laugh escaped me. "You're sure? What about Vondo? And Dredon?"

"Oh, it'll upset Vondo quite a bit, but then again, what doesn't? As for Dredon, I have just the job for him. I think five years reading those remediation letters I mentioned and passing judgment on disgraced pactmakers begging to get their privileges back would suit him just fine."

I closed my eyes and made a face at Dredon's proposed consequences, which forced a laugh from the dean.

She came back around the desk and offered her hand again. "So do you accept my offer, Ramiren?"

This decision affects more than just me.

"I'll need to think about it and discuss the opportunity with another."

"Oh yes. Dredon mentioned you had a protector now." She laced her fingers together when I didn't take her hand. "I'd allow her to reside here as well. You'd no longer be a pactmaker, so that rule wouldn't apply to you."

"Thank you, Dean. That's very generous. I'll talk to her and let you know." With a deep inhale, followed by a slow exhale, I was ready. "And thank you for giving me a moment. You can take it now."

"Before I do, one last question. Where is the soulstone?"

Again, the instinct to lie was there. I quashed that, too, even if I knew she'd take something from me that I now held sacred. Truths weren't supposed to be easy or convenient things. They were meant to build. "I still have it," I said as I pulled the necklace from my pocket.

"I'm sorry, Ramiren, but you will need to hand that over for destruction."

"I know," I replied quietly. My thumb caressed the polished surface as I peered down at it. It pained me to let it go, but I didn't want to count on it falling into the wrong hands. I took the pendant off the broken chain and placed it in her outstretched palm without another word. "If the stone could be removed and the rest returned, I'd consider it a personal favor to be repaid. It holds more value to me than just a soulstone."

"*Just* a soulstone," Dean Miscala murmured, amused. "It's entirely possible. I'll see what I can do." With that, she walked over to the open book in the corner and picked up the black quill.

"Ramiren Orasti," she said, clear as day. The book flipped on its own to earlier pages, and I watched as the names of hundreds of pactmakers went by, those who'd graduated after me and taken up their profession.

Eventually, the pages settled. Dean Miscala lowered her black quill to the parchment and crossed out my name.

Chapter Thirty-One
Never Again

I had no idea what to expect, but when Dean Miscala and I walked down the well-lit stone steps under the Maester's Spire, led by a smiling human man with a full head of hair, irritation mixed with reluctant amusement as I realized Dredon Nodaska was a gods-damned dirty liar.

The clean stairway led to a clean hallway, lined on either side by four wooden doors. The human man, who had told me his name was Argus, took out a single silver key from his pocket and went to the far door on the left to open it.

Dean Miscala looked at me and tilted her head. "What is it? You look like you don't know whether to laugh or cry."

"Quite frankly, Dean Miscala, I'm not sure either."

The door opened, and Argus stepped aside. "Dean Miscala, Pactma— Erm, I mean. Si— Uh..."

Holding up a hand, I chuckled. "Ramiren is fine."

"Ramiren!" yelled a very familiar voice from beyond the door. Shaking my head, I huffed and stepped past a patiently waiting Argus into the "dungeon."

Except it most certainly wasn't the dungeon that had been described to me. I stood in a small but comfortable sitting room, several books and even a deck of cards sitting on the low table between the two overstuffed chairs. To my left was a bathroom complete with fey plumbing, and straight ahead a bedroom with a large bed. No bucket. No mean dungeon warden. No rats.

My eyes swiveled back to the overstuffed chairs, or rather the eluva who was sitting in one.

"Hello, Dre. My, you didn't exaggerate at all. Your accommodations are terrible. Really, Dean Miscala," I said, looking over my shoulder at the elven woman. "This is utter outrage. There's not a single thing Dre here could have done to warrant such *foul* and *cruel* treatment."

"All right, all right! I get it. I'm an ass," Dredon said, standing to his full seven-foot height to roll down the sleeves of his maroon shirt. Cool blue eyes stared back at me. "I guess sarcasm doesn't translate well through a mindlink."

"Oh, trust me. It translates just fine, old friend. And when you told me you were basically five minutes from dying from either starvation, rat bites, or the flux, I noticed something very interesting."

Dre puffed a breath upward to move the dark brown hair that had flopped into his eyes. "That you actually cared and worried about me?"

"No. I was curious about who won the game of poker between you and Argus here."

Behind me, Argus choked. "Please believe me, Dean Miscala, I would *never*—"

Dean Miscala interrupted him, amusement in her voice. "It's fine, Argus. It's just Dredon being Dredon. I think we'll let these two talk. He's free to go, so you can leave the door open."

Their footsteps quickly faded, and I continued to stare at Dredon. Dredon continued to stare back.

Our staring contest ended when Dredon's watery eyes blinked. "Fuck. How do you do that, you unnatural abomination?"

I grinned and pulled him into a firm hug. "You're just too pretty, and I can't look away."

He was so tall, it felt like I was being embraced by a giant. "Ah, so you brought freedom *and* flattery. Wonderful. Have a seat."

When we'd settled into our chairs, I started. "So I have good news, bad news, and worst news. Which do you want to hear first?"

Dredon reclined. "Uh, let's hear the good news first."

"I'm asking Nathalia to marry me."

Dredon's eyes went wide as saucers. "Oh, shit! Tha— Wait. Wait, wait, wait. Pactmakers don't marry, Ren." Those wide eyes suddenly narrowed. "What's the bad news? Wait, what's the *worst* news?"

"Choose wisely, Dre."

"Ah, fuck!" He dropped his head to the back of the chair and stared at the ceiling. "Worst news. No! Wait. Bad news."

My grin couldn't be contained. This was far too much fun. "You're sure?"

He didn't look at all sure when he answered, "Yes. Bad news first."

With no idea what to expect in reaction from him, I just spit it out. "I'm no longer a pactmaker. My name was crossed out. But Dean Miscala offered me a position as a maester."

And he went back to being bug-eyed. "Oh. Oh, that's... That's great. Right? I mean, what would you be teaching?"

"Ethics." I stretched out in the chair, crossing my ankles to get comfortable, as I expected we'd be here for a while. "I haven't decided yet if I'm going to, honestly. I have to talk to Nathalia first."

His teasing grin made me want to punch him. Not too hard, but somewhere sensitive. "I mean, can't you do your weird mind-talk that you do with her?"

"I want to discuss it with her in person."

"That's silly." At my look, his smile dropped. "I mean, that's smart. Very smart. She'll like that, and I'm glad I'll continue to see you around here if you accept." He winced as he looked down. "And if I still have a job here after all this."

Cheerfully, I reassured him. "Oh, you do."

Dredon sat up instantly. "I do? You pulled that o—" He slumped into the chair. "That's the worst news, isn't it?"

Even more cheerfully, I said, "It absolutely is."

His face went stony as he asked with surety, "I'm doing remediation requests, aren't I?"

"You are."

Pulling a pillow out from behind him, he stuffed his face into it and let out a muffled scream.

The next morning, I crept into Nathalia's bedroom, closing the door behind me with a soft *click*. She stirred at the barely audible noise but didn't awaken fully. Padding over as quietly as possible, I sat on the bed beside her and leaned over her sleeping form to run the tip of my nose along the pulse in her neck. Moving higher, I let my lips brush the shell of her ear as I whispered, "Wake up, angel. I have a surprise for you."

Nathalia stirred again, then groaned as she brought one hand to my chest and another to rub briskly at her pale face. Her hair stuck up at odd angles, and the dark circles under her puffy eyes told me exactly how well my beautiful protector had slept. "Mm. Morning," she murmured groggily, covering her yawn. She blinked half-lidded eyes and looked up at me. "You're back."

"Yes, I'm back." I shifted to let her sit up. "And as I said, I have a surprise for you, but you'll need to do something for me."

The pillow crease across her cheek shortened when she smiled. "I like surprises. What do you need?"

"I need you to go downstairs and bathe and wash your hair. I'd help you, but your father might try to drown me, and that would disrupt my plans."

She snorted and climbed out of bed. I pressed a kiss to her forehead before heading for the door. "Come to my room when you're ready, and don't bother getting dressed." I said over my shoulder and went to prepare for the most important question I'd ever ask.

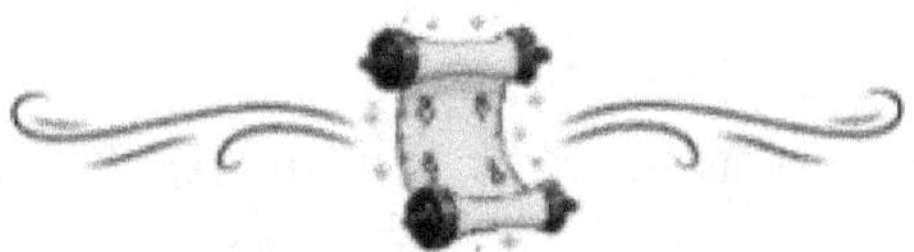

After rolling up the area rug and placing the simple chair on the hardwood floor, figuring it'd be easier to clean everything up afterward, I called out at the gentle knock on my door, "Come in."

A fresh-faced Nathalia stepped in and closed the door behind her. Her uneven wet hair had been combed back, and I saw she'd followed my directions by wearing only a green linen robe. Nathalia started toward me, then slowed her steps as she looked over what I'd set up. She appeared more curious than confused. "Combs and scissors?"

I picked up the silk cloth and pins I'd laid on the bed. "Yes. If it's all right with you, I'd like to cut your hair."

She came up to the chair, grinning slightly. "So that's why you asked me about it yesterday." Nathalia sat down. "I didn't realize you knew how to do this."

I placed the silk around her shoulders, pinning it close to her neck. "I've done it a few times. I have several strange skills borne out of either boredom or necessity."

When she turned her head, probably to ask about said strange skills, I moved her head back to facing forward. "Keep your head still," I chided, teasing. "You wouldn't want me to lop off too much, now, would you?"

She grunted, but stayed still as she asked, "What strange skills?"

I picked up the thin scissors and comb from the side table and began to section her hair. "Well," I drawled as I concentrated on evening out her chopped layers. "You know I'm adept with cosmetics."

"Right."

"I'm a decent poker player, though not to your sister's skill."

Nathalia muttered as I tilted her head forward. "I still can't believe she gambles."

I grinned, setting a rhythm of combing her hair, pinching the strands between my fingers, and snipping. "I'm a decent writer. I can juggle three balls very well, but four balls very poorly. I'm adept at identifying birds and have a book of interesting feathers I've found pressed between the pages." Moving in front of her, I bent down to check how even the sides were. "Though, to be honest, my only true skill was learning and keeping secrets."

She met my eyes warily. "But no more?"

Shaking my head slowly and emphatically, I replied, "Never again." Circling her to resume my task, I continued. "So with that said, I have a few more secrets to share."

Her back tensed and straightened. "Like what?" she murmured, then inhaled but didn't exhale.

She couldn't see my face, so I felt free to grin as widely as I wanted, though I tried to keep my voice stern as I leaned in to whisper in her ear. "Like you are the shiver in my spine." When she visibly shivered, my grin widened even more. "And the warmth of sunshine on my face. To me, you are the goose bumps that erupt on my skin from a cooling breeze. You are the pause between heartbeats and the deep breath of anticipation."

My eyes focused on the two circular marks on her neck, faint and barely visible, but one could see them if they knew where to look. "I've already given you my greatest secret, angel. My second greatest, however, is that you have absolutely ruined me."

I stood up, continuing to cut her hair like nothing had happened. The breath she'd been holding escaped in a wheeze, and I bit my bottom lip, my grin becoming giddy. I knew her reaction to what I said next would involve a jerking movement, so I held the sharp scissors away from her.

Though there was no real need to look at her face for this, because I already knew what her expression would be, I still tilted to the side to watch. "So as compensation for utterly destroying any wish I might have had for another, I'm asking you to marry me."

As expected, her head snapped to the side toward me. She shrieked, "What?"

Placing my hand on her shoulder to settle and calm her, I clicked my tongue in disapproval. "Don't move, angel, or your hair will be even worse off."

Nathalia faced forward again, practically vibrating in the chair as she clutched the armrests. "Why?" she choked out.

We really need to work on improving her self-esteem.

Yet I answered her nonsensical question all the same, because she needed to hear it. "You have something no one else ever can or will—every part of me. The good parts that love and adore you. The parts that want to give you the world and earn your forgiveness. And the bad parts too. The ones that want to burrow under your skin so you can't ever be rid of me, not even when you beg for mercy, because that mercy will never come."

She turned in her chair to look straight at me with soft eyes. "I love both sides of you, but what I mean is, why are you asking me when you told me pactmakers don't marry?"

Oh.

Oh, shit. I think I fucked this up.

Clearing my throat and brushing a few silver hairs off my trousers, I murmured, "So, about that." *Oh, just come out with it.* "I'm not a pactmaker anymore."

She shrieked even louder. "*WHAT?*"

Wincing, I tried to grin, but it probably looked more like a grimace. "I really didn't want losing my occupation to be part of my proposal."

"Ramiren." Her eyes took on blue flecks as her lower lip trembled. "I'm so sorry."

"Oh, don't be. Truly." I kissed the top of her head and stepped behind her again. "Once I learned the truth, it was inevitable, but due to King Rofar, his priest, and the way I worded my resignation, they're offering me a maester position teaching ethics. I wanted to discuss it with you before accepting or declining."

She stayed silent as my scissors snipped a few more errant hairs. *Nearly done.* "So is that a yes?"

There was more silence, then she spoke hesitantly, "There's one problem."

My heart leaped and fell in a single breath. I stalked around to stand in front of her with a raised eyebrow. "What's the problem? If it's your father, I'll deal with him." I scowled. "Why are you smiling? Is there something else?"

A mischievous light came into her eyes as her smile turned into a smirk. "You didn't get down on one knee to ask me."

Twice. How have I managed to fuck up the same proposal twice*?*

In response, I placed the comb and scissors on her lap and dropped to both knees. "Apologies, my dear. You are correct. Now..." I looked at her expectantly.

She mused, "I'm going to miss that pact room."

"Yes, yes. I will, too, *but...?*" I prompted, waiting. The anticipation was making me lightheaded.

She furrowed her eyebrows, thinking. "You'd be a good maester, I think. I mean, we both *know* you're good at giving instructions."

She's going to be the death of me.

I groaned, my chin dropping to my chest as my eyes closed. "Nathalia..."

A stifled chuckle confirmed my suspicion that she was doing this on purpose. "Hm?"

I muttered, tortured, "You're killing me."

Her fingertips lifted my chin, and I felt her forehead rest on mine. When her soft lips brushed mine, I shivered.

"Yes. I'll marry you."

Happiness, warm as sunlight, perfumed the air with oranges and lit up my insides as my grin grew so wide my cheeks hurt. I leaned over to pull her in tight when she placed a halting hand on my chest. "On one condition," she said.

"Name it. Anything."

"I don't want you to marry me because you believe it's what *I* want. I urge you to ask me because it's what *you* want."

Though I'd been mistaken about her reason for asking 'why' earlier, this was a true indication of how little she thought of herself.

"My love, first, you know I wouldn't ask you unless I wanted to."

"Sure—"

"Second, if I had a wish that could be granted, it wouldn't actually be a pony. Or even to self-determine when I stay or go. It'd be for you to see yourself the way I do. Please, no more doubts, no more questions, and no more thinking of yourself as a burden. You are not a burden; you, my dear, are a *blessing*."

The blue flecks in her golden irises returned as her eyes became watery. "I can come with you? To the Citadel, if you accept?"

"By personal invitation of Dean Miscala. I wouldn't even consider it if you couldn't."

When she nodded, I pulled her into my lap, hearing the metallic clank of the scissors hitting the floor. Her arms wrapped around my neck, and I inhaled the lovely three scents that emanated from her. "My cordani," I whispered.

She leaned back to look at my face. "Your what?"

Oh. Right.

Nibbling on my lowered lip, I winced. "So you remember that voice in the pact room? Cordani?" At her uneasy nod, I continued. "About that..."

Chapter Thirty-Two
The Mirror of Souls

That evening, I sat down in Lord Maxlian's study with the intention of informing him he was going to become my father-in-law and having a nice, civil discussion about the future.

That didn't happen.

"No! Absolutely not!" Lord Maxlian roared from across his desk. "I forbid it!"

Like the eye of a storm, I leaned back in my chair and said calmly, "There is no forbidding *or* allowing, sir. I asked, and she agreed. Your opinion doesn't matter. I'm telling you as a courtesy to you and because *my future wife* wants peace."

"You didn't even ask for my blessing," he growled. His white wings rustled as he stood from his backless bench, pressing his palms to the top of his desk to glare at me. "You didn't ask me *first*!"

How's the talk going?

Could be better.

"Is she your *property*? Are you wanting to draw up a bill of sale?" I tilted my head and narrowed my eyes. "I'd urge you to not push her away with a temper tantrum. You know as well as I do that when she wants something, she's single-minded about getting it, and you becoming an immature caricature of yourself will only alienate her."

He pushed off his desk and rounded it to come closer. Something about his demeanor put me on alert and made me stand. He raised his index finger to within a hair's breadth of my face and bared his teeth, seething. "*She'll do as I say.*"

The vicious, greedy creature in my head, usually only active with Nathalia moaning under me, reared up and clawed at his cage. He was just as done with this juvenile display as I was.

I made sure to bare my elongated canines when I gave him a blank stare. "I broke my moral code for your daughter, *Max*. What the fuck do you think I'll do if you try to take her away?"

He bellowed, nearly cracking my eardrums. "*Is that a threat, broodling?*"

With his proximity, I wiped the spittle from my face without looking away from him. "Threat. Promise. Same thing. I know you don't trust me or my motives, and I don't blame you. My reticence has caused heartache for many, your daughter especially. She has agreed to let me make amends as best I can, for which I'm eternally grateful. Accept reality. It *will* happen, whether *you* want it to or not."

When he pulled back his fist, I understood his anger. Lord Maxlian adored Nathalia and hated what I'd done to her. He'd say anything to make me go away, even if that meant acting like a brooding chicken. However, he'd already gotten a free shot, even broken my nose. He would not get another.

I jerked back to avoid his punch, toppling my chair backward with my legs. His strike whooshed past my face, unbalancing him.

If calm diplomacy wouldn't work, perhaps goading him into exhaustion, until he was forced to sit and listen to me, would. "You already got me once. Don't be greedy."

He yelled, and his other hand swung in an arc toward my temple.

I dodged that blow too.

On and on, around the study and over furniture, Lord Maxlian lunged and jabbed as I ducked and evaded, throwing out the occasional taunt to rile him up and tire him out sooner.

Toward the end, when even I was becoming fatigued, he managed to slam his fist into my stomach. I danced away, holding my middle as I watched him collapse against the wall and slide down, out of breath, half the feathers in his wings sticking out at odd angles.

As I had been hoping, the dim light of resignation shone in his golden eyes, so like his daughter's, as he stared at me. "Fine. Ramiren, I—"

The door slammed open as Nathalia burst in, flushed with rage. She stalked toward me, even as her gaze narrowed on her father. She spat out, "What the *fuck* did you do to him now?"

"*Him?* He's the one who..." He scowled. "Wait, how did you know I did *anything* to him?"

She gave me a once-over, then turned back to her father. "Because I can feel when he's injured, of course."

Keeping your own secrets now, angel?

Not intentionally. It just never came up.

That explains how you knew to ask about my dislocated shoulder.

"Wait. Hold on," he muttered, standing shakily to his feet. "Of course? What do you mean you can *feel* when he's injured?"

Nathalia shrugged as though confused by his question. "Remember? I'm his protector. He's my charge. I don't recall it ever being brought up at the Horyn Academy, but—"

Lord Maxlian's narrowed eyes landed on me like a ton of bricks. "That's not a protector boon, Nathalia."

"Oh." Nathalia hooked a hand around my elbow and looked at me. "Maybe it has something to do with this cordani business?"

Lord Maxlian froze, still as a stone statue. "What did you just say?"

"What? Cordani business?"

Lord Maxlian teetered on his feet, but I wasn't sure if it was from our fight. "How do you know that word?" He looked at each of our faces, back and forth, as dawning horror spread across his features. "How?"

I patted Nathalia's hand and smiled at her. "Shall we tell him?"

When she gave her consent, I turned to Lord Maxlian. "We'll need a strong beverage to get through this story. Trust me."

Several minutes later, three snifters of brandy drained dry, Lord Maxlian Swordhand, High General of Camlynn and Lord Protector of Horyn, stared at the floor, his head supported only by his shaking hands. He sniffled. "So that's why the Dark Drop rejected you. Their mirror created your soul; there'd be no reason to devour you." He finally lifted his red-rimmed eyes to me. "Your soul would've begun to deteriorate again without her, wasting their effort."

I sighed slowly. "That's what Nathalia's soul indicated, that the Lorindar pantheon is, above all, not wasteful."

Lord Maxlian's head lowered again as he digested what we'd told him. Long seconds ticked by with no words spoken, until Nathalia broke the silence. "Father, I understand why you fought against him, against us. I do, truly. But it won't work. Certainly not anymore."

"I know," he whispered.

"I love him," she said firmly. "And he loves me."

"I know," he whispered again. "I'm sorry."

Nathalia leaned forward, placing her hand on his knee. "Then you also know that you won't be able to stop anything, and I'm fairly certain Mother would murder you if you actually tried."

"She would, yes," Lord Maxlian muttered after a beat.

"Though you might be dead soon anyway. That ugly ceramic vase Jenny gave her a few years ago is in pieces in the corner."

Lord Maxlian's head snapped up. "Oh, fuck!"

One Year Later...

Where is my wife?

I took a seat on the lip of a fountain, one of three in Lady Resa's expansive gardens, to look around the lively gathering. Conjured feylights danced above to provide soft but plentiful illumination, just as we'd wanted. It was a subtle but lovely reminder of the carnival that had been our beginning.

After unbuttoning my black-velvet waistcoat, I rested my elbows on my thighs and watched the celebration from a distance with good wine in hand and a content, satisfied smile on my face.

My eyes flitted from one group to the next, people who had naturally congregated in small circles. Many of them were unknown to me, but most I recognized.

King Rofar, Princess Sornya, and their entourage sat beside a few local nobles. Based upon the look in the king's eyes, he was bored to tears, but he kept his expression neutral. The princess had been the surprise of the evening, generously providing music for the ceremony earlier. Her father had not exaggerated her skills. Retrieving her voice had certainly been a good deed.

Dredon was giggle-drunk and trying to persuade a bow-tied M.A.L.C.O.L.M. into saying as many unhinged things as possible, as Georgina, Tomin, and Idora looked on warily.

Lord Maxlian and Lady Resa meandered about like excellent hosts. I'd never seen Lady Resa blush so hard until everyone had started gushing about her green thumb. Their entire brood was spread throughout the paths and flower beds. The twins, Bryl and Bryn, entertained people with the simple, harmless magic they'd learned at the Sorcera Academy, because their father had drawn the line at "purple fireballs."

Tilla orchestrated a knife-throwing competition. She won, of course.

Kaleb assisted in the catering, and I made sure to request his apple turnovers.

The only person missing was my mother, but there was no doubt in my mind she watched my wedding day from Celestia with the same contented smile I wore.

Ravik didn't get an invitation. Nathalia had long forgiven him, but I had not. Not because of what he did, or why, but because of whom he did it do.

My eyes finally found where Nathalia was holding court, Raewyn beside her. I watched as Nathalia was offered a glass of wine. When she refused with a smile and a few words, Raewyn's eyes bugged out. The priestess jumped to her feet, excitedly twittering at her older sister, and ran toward her parents.

Curious, I stood and walked over to my breathtaking bride, accepting pats on the shoulder and several congratulations along the way. When I reached her, she grinned tiredly at me and pulled me down to the bench beside her. Making sure that I didn't sit on the pale embroidered gown she wore, the same one she'd been dressed in for her resurrection, I wrapped an arm around her shoulders to pull her in for a kiss. "What was that about?"

Nathalia sighed deeply. "Raewyn thinks I'm pregnant because I refused my sixth glass of wine. I didn't have the heart to correct her. Or the opportunity, for that matter. Frankly, if I have any more alcohol, I'm going to look like Dredon."

Following her line of sight, I saw Dre, wide-eyed and panicked, stumbling away from a red-eyed M.A.L.C.O.L.M. I gave a breathy laugh. "Are you going to tell her?"

Nathalia smirked as she watched Raewyn zip from one group to the next, chattering like an excited chipmunk. "Nah, this is more fun."

"She's going to be very disappointed. And probably embarrassed."

She covered her wide yawn with a hand. "Oh, probably. But those are also the least dangerous consequences of assuming, wouldn't you say?"

"She might not ever speak to you again."

"Unlikely. She's incapable of holding a grudge." She pointed her chin at Raewyn happily spinning a befuddled Georgina around. "Case in point."

"Do you want to go?"

Nathalia rolled her head on my shoulder and nuzzled into the crook of my neck. "No." After she yawned again, longer this time, she muttered, "Yes."

"Shall we say goodbye to everyone, then?"

She cracked her neck and stared up at me with bleary eyes. "No. Let's go home."

"As you wish, my love." Making sure her arms were around me for the journey, I snapped the fingers of both hands twice.

Epilogue
Five Years Later - Present Day

• • • •

Ramiren closes the thin book sitting on his podium and turns a smile toward the tiered seating where his students sit. "As this is our last session for this quarter, I wanted to say I hope this class was enlightening. Helpful, even. It was meant to give you a foundation to build your code, the set of rules by which you govern yourself and your dealings. May this code not be looked on as a restraint, but a map of your own integrity. By Jessina's grace and that code of honor, I hope you are able to practice this trade as long as you wish."

Ramiren steps around his podium, taking his glasses off his nose to clean smudges from the lenses with a handkerchief. "And now, before you leave, I have one last assignment for you."

The collective groans never fail to make Ramiren smile, even though the assignment in question is no essay or questionnaire. At least the kind of questionnaire they're anticipating. "Begin to develop your code. Consider what you can live with and what you cannot live without. Define your boundaries, and understand that you will need to defend them with every weapon in your arsenal, as many out there would happily trounce on them. Guard your integrity as though your life depends on it, because it very well might."

He places his gold-framed glasses back on his nose and slides them into place. "Now, does anyone have any parting questions?"

One student, Luca, a young fey woman with a gentle spirit and sharp mind, nervously raises her hand. "Do...do you regret it, Maester? Giving it up?"

Ramiren slowly smiles, then turns to look into the left corner of the room to see Nathalia standing at attention, a casual hand on her sword. Ready to defend as ever. Seeing the minuscule curl of her mouth, he knows she's hearing every word.

"I see you all want another lecture from me?"

A wave of soft chuckles fills the classroom but quickly quiets when Ramiren begins to speak again.

"People often don't regret things, or decisions, or outcomes. They regret situations. That the thing had to happen at all. If I had to say it, I regret it had to happen that way. Remember, your history is as unique as your fingerprint. Your life experiences, good and bad, have shaped you into who you are now, and that's because failure is a teacher. Shame and fear are teachers, just as love, joy, and pleasure are. Just as I am. But if you're asking if I regret giving up my *abilities*?"

Ramiren's eyes flit back over to Nathalia, who meets his gaze for a long beat before turning back to the class.

"No. It was the easiest deal I ever made."

The crackle from the gray-stone fireplace and the turning of parchment pages are the only sounds in the comfortable room. Nathalia sits curled up on one side of the sofa, a red leather-bound book in her hands. Her eyes stay riveted on the last page, even as a sniffle escapes her.

On the other end of the sofa, Ramiren leans against the arm rest, a blue leather-bound book in his lap. He, too, is reading the last page. A tumbler of liquor in one hand, he takes a sip and sets the glass down before closing the back cover. He places the book next to his drink and smiles.

"Almost finished," Nathalia whispers.

Ramiren reaches over, taking her left foot in hand and pulling it to his lap to rub her cold toes with his warm fingers. "Take your time. I don't have any classes to teach tomorrow." He murmurs, as though not wanting to disturb her reading.

She sniffles again, sighs, and closes the back cover of her book as well before wiping her face with the back of her hand.

"So who goes first?" she asks.

"Mm, I can." He kneads his fingers into the sole of her foot, thinking. "The beginning was a bit slow, but it picked up quickly." Leaning his head back to rest against the sofa's cushions, he throws her a feral grin. "And you *slightly* exaggerated some of our lessons, angel."

Nathalia shrugs, conceding nothing. "I don't know what you're talking about, darling. My account of our lessons was entirely accurate."

"Overall, though, it was a good story. Engaging and fun." Ramiren chews on the inside of his cheek. "I noticed you made a lot of improvements and added more detail since your first draft."

Nathalia groans, sinking further into the sofa. "I made so many adjustments, and it feels like it still wasn't enough."

Ramiren smiles at her, then leans down to kiss her instep. "Well done, my dear. I'm proud of you."

Nathalia grins, wiggling her toes. "My turn?"

At his nod, she starts, "So, first off, it's better than mine."

"It's not a competition, angel."

"Oh, I know, but it's still the truth. There were some parts I had to stop reading, honestly, but I loved the ending. I loved the whole thing, really. And..." She frowns.

"What is it?"

"Nothing. It's just...my soul was a bit of an asshole to you." "It didn't have your heart and mind, and it'd been imprisoned

without its consent. We know what that's like, don't we?" He reaches for her other foot to rub that one too. "I did have a question about yours. You didn't write down what you said that time when you started babbling in Celestial during one of our lessons."

Nathalia raises an eyebrow. "Correct, I did not."

He pauses rubbing her foot and waits. And waits. Then he shoots her a droll expression when he realizes she won't say it without prompting. "So what did you say?"

She gives a bratty grin, her upper teeth biting firmly into her bottom lip. "Hummingbird."

With an exaggerated scowl, he mutters, "All right. That's it." She squeals as he lunges for her.

The End

Ramiren, Nathalia, Kaleb, Bryn, Bryl, Raewyn, Idora, Ravik, Dredon, Tilla, and Tomin will return.

ACKNOWLEDGEMENTS

To my father, who instilled a love of literature and fantasy in me. You're not allowed to read this either.

To my mother, who taught me to always go out and get what I want.

To Cyndi, my editor. I think this is the start of a beautiful friendship.

To Cassie, my beta reader. Sorrynotsorry for making you cry.

To Jenna. You know.

To my ARC readers. You are very much appreciated.

To those who picked up this duology and decided to give it a shot. Thank you!

To Cyndi Brown from TikTok, who gave me the name Dahvii. It's a great name.

And finally, I must acknowledge the generous nature of my TBR. You are an icon. Nearly everyone knows of you and accepts your place in this world. Despite your fame (or infamy, as the case may be), you are always there for me. Just when I think you are drained away to nothing, you replenish yourself to keep your place at my side.

Watching. Waiting.

Like a dark stalker in a black motorcycle helmet. I can't see what is no doubt a cruel smile, even when he lifts the visor with a tattooed hand. His wicked eyes lock me into place, like trapped prey...

Fuck.

add to cart

www.ingramcontent.com/pod-product-compliance
Lightning Source LLC
LaVergne TN
LVHW010640110826
845149LV00014B/2895

* 9 7 9 8 9 9 9 8 5 3 2 6 4 *